I0710555

SHELL SHOCKED

A GEN X LOVE STORY

STELLA MONTROSE

Copyright © 2025 by Stella Montrose

All rights reserved. This book or parts thereof may not be reproduced in any form, stored in any retrieval system, or transmitted in any form by any means – electronic, mechanical, photocopy, recording, or otherwise – without prior written permission of the publisher.

Cover design: Mickey Chan

Cover Illustration: Heather Noethe

Photographer: Hyler Media

Model: Alexander Mariani

This is a work of fiction. Names, characters, places, and incidents either are the product of the author's imagination or are used fictitiously, and any resemblance to actual persons, living or dead, business establishments, events, or locales is entirely coincidental.

stellamontrose.com

Ebook ISBN: 979-8-9906331-1-7

Print ISBN: 979-8-9906331-0-0

This book is dedicated to the unsung heroes of the service industry, past and present—specifically, those in service in restaurants as well as salons and spas (lunch break? I don't know her.) The family found and friendships forged in those trenches are priceless treasures.

CONTENT WARNING

- Religious Trauma
- Retelling of the sudden death of a teenage sibling
- Reaction to recalled controlling/narcissistic behavior/abuse
- Adult sexual content
- Reaction to recalled SA/ intimate partner violence
- Retelling of the groping and outing of a trans character
- Unplanned pregnancy
- Ruptured Ectopic Pregnancy

PROLOGUE

SHELBY

July 1991

THE CACOPHONY OF CHAOS HIT ME AS SOON AS I WALKED INTO THE kitchen. The clattering of plates, the hiss of something fat laden hitting hot cast iron, the loud, low hum of the dishwasher. The laughter of the servers intermixed with the cursing of the cooks. A night and day difference in atmosphere from the quiet din of the dining room at Angie's Bistro. It was my first day as a server, and my trainer, Naomi was giving me the tour.

I'd decided I needed a better serving job than my casual breakfast and lunch gig at the Sunshine Cafe if I wanted to move out of my parents' house and be less dependent on student loans. It was the summer before my sophomore year at UW Milwaukee where I was chasing an English Lit degree.

Angie's had seemed upscale enough to make decent money, but not too stuffy. I didn't love the idea of having to

1

figure out parking downtown, but at least it was close to school.

Naomi pointed to the dish pit. "That's Andy over there. And Miguel. We all do our best to scrape our plates and get rid of trash to make their job easier. They have us trained well." She winked at Andy, and as he smiled and blushed, I was willing to bet he liked her for more than just her courtesy. She turned my attention to the prep tables. "That's Steph, and our pastry chef, Gina." Swinging back around to the line I caught sight of a head towering above the pass-through expo shelves. A figure well over six feet tall, topped with waves of dark hair and a black bandana used as a headband.

Naomi pointed to a large, bearded ginger and his thinner counterpart. "That's Chef Grant, and his sous chef, Juan." Finally, she pointed to the tall, dark haired line cook, "And last but not least, Ari."

When she said his name, Ari turned his head, gave me a quick glance, then turned his attention back to his pan. Suddenly he spun toward me again—a full-on double take. I had not been expecting the full lips and a jawline as sharp as the knives on the wall. My mouth went dry. Naomi gestured to me, "This is Shelby."

I waved awkwardly at everyone and we headed off for the next part of the tour.

"Ari?" I tried to come off as casually curious about his name while at the same time hoping Naomi would tell me every single thing she knew about him.

"I know. Cute right? His name is Aristotle. Something about his mom being obsessed with Greek philosophy. I don't know why he works here, though, His dad is David Ristow.

"David Ristow, as in 'it's your money, honey' David Ristow?" The owner of the largest investment firm in the

Milwaukee area, his face was plastered on billboards and on TV, both in commercials and as frequent fixture front and center at most home Bucks' and Brewers' games. It was weird that his son was working as a line cook.

"He must still get some money from Daddy, though. He has a *really* nice car and a huge apartment on Lake Drive. He has parties all the time, so you'll probably get to see it.

"Cool." I said, as I was trying desperately to appear as such.

About a week later it was just one of those shifts. Awful, cranky, demanding guests, a bad case of the dropsies, and I couldn't engage the server's multi-tasking function in my brain for the life of me.

"Hey!" I shouted in a full panic in the general direction of the kitchen line. "Can you put a rush on table fourteen? I completely forgot to put in their order!"

Ari turned around and bent down to peer at me through the pass. "It's always best to address one of us by name and wait for 'heard.'"

His tone was condescending, and I bristled at being corrected.

"Now, what's the magic word?" Ari asked, his eyes boring into me. I never noticed how vividly green they were, offset by thick, dark lashes. My stomach flipped.

"What? Oh, sorry. Please."

The edges of his mouth turned upwards into a subtle, mischievous grin. He put his hand to his ear. "What was that?"

"Please."

"One more time?"

I sighed exasperatedly. "Please, Ari!"

He grabbed the ticket giving me a full closeup view of his fully tattooed, sinewy forearms. He stared me dead in the eyes and cooed, "Damn, baby. I love it when you beg." No one else had heard him—it wasn't a joke for the masses. It was meant just for me.

I froze. I had no idea how to respond to that. He'd barely ever said two words to me before and now what? Teasing? Flirting? Just being plain creepy? In any case, my rattled server brain would certainly not be recovering that night, and I felt sorry for my poor tables.

"I'll put a rush on this for you, Shelby. Don't worry." He winked, and my knees nearly buckled at the sound of my name from his mouth.

That night we both finished up around the same time. He had a healthy head start out to his car, a black, sporty BMW he'd parked all the way toward the back of the lot. I caught him turning back to look at me twice, once even making a complete three-sixty as he was walking. He got into his car and sat still. I was parked close enough to see that he was staring at me, watching me get into my car. It wasn't until I started it and began to pull out of the space that he finally started his engine.

Every day after that, I started to get butterflies on the way to work. Or, as my friend Kendra and I would call them, "butter flutters." This was the way we'd describe the way thinking about kissing a boy made our stomachs feel. We'd been best friends since fourth grade, and having been immersed in Christian education, we were sheltered and awkwardly naive for most of our adolescence. We'd have made Sweet Valley High look tawdry.

I would go out of my way to ask favors of Ari as sweetly and politely as I could, every chance I got. "Ari, may I please have an extra au jus?" Heavy emphasis on the 'please.'

He would deliver what I'd ask for with a wicked smile and whisper, "That's my good girl."

And I'd roll my eyes at him, but only because I needed to deflect how unhinged it made me when he'd said that. Like that.

There were other nights I'd see his car in the parking lot on my way out. Even when I was sure his shift had ended hours before. Even if I hadn't seen him in the kitchen at all. And always, when I would get in my car and start it, as soon as I'd pull out of the parking lot, I'd see his headlights come on in my rearview mirror.

Weeks later, Naomi and I were headed to Ari's house for a party. He would be seeing me out of uniform for the first time and I desperately wanted to make an impression. I decided to wear a yellow and black hippie sundress with spaghetti straps and my Doc Marten combat boots.

Ari's duplex was indeed on Lake Drive complete with a view of Lake Michigan from his front porch. This was most definitely not something he'd be able to swing on a line cook salary.

As we walked in, I was surprised at the casualness of the event—there were only about eight people in the living room milling about with EMF's "Unbelievable" playing at a perfectly reasonable decibel level in the background. Ari walked into the room, saw me, and stopped dead in his tracks. His eyes were dialed into me, onto my face, and then raked up and down my body. I might as well have been naked– exposed and vulnerable, yet wielding a strange and unfamiliar power at the same time.

BESIDES HOURS LONG MAKE OUT SESSIONS WITH PLENTY OF GROPING and a bit of dry humping, I'd had sex exactly once. My high school boyfriend and I decided to take the plunge one day in our senior year when his parents were out of town. We were both so nervous, but when we started kissing on his bed, things just progressed organically, like they always had. We just didn't have to stop this time. Or be afraid of someone walking in.

He was bending over backwards being so gentle and precious with me, but I didn't want that. I was more than ready, and I wanted him to just pour himself into me without restraint. We didn't have that pesky hymen to deal with after all—my cherry had already been popped during an unfortunate encounter with a set of monkey bars when I was in third grade.

It ended up being clumsy "insert Tab A into Slot B", lasting approximately thirty seconds, but I was enthralled with how he'd lost all sense of himself while inside me. It made me feel strong and powerful. I didn't get near the friction I needed, and I didn't orgasm, but I wasn't too worried. I held out hope that the next time would be better. I could show him what I liked.

But I never got the chance. The next day he was acting strangely distant.

It turned out he'd had an attack of conscience, specifically the kind baked in by religion. He'd felt what we had done was a sin of the highest degree, and we must never do it again. In my mind, it was only a minor transgression, already made by most of our friends on a regular basis, and easily forgiven. No need to be expecting the fire and brimstone.

I felt spurned. Rejected. I'd desperately wanted him to want me, to crave me, his desire overriding his conscience at every turn. For weeks I would try and seduce him, to win over his indoctrinated righteousness, but it was no use. We broke up shortly after, and I found myself questioning my faith and pulling away from the church as a result of my bruised ego. By the time I started college, I was well on my way to being a full-fledged free thinker.

THE WAY ARI WAS LOOKING AT ME THEN, THERE WAS NO DOUBT HE'D be up for sin. Of any kind, at any time. And I doubted it would take much to tempt him.

He smiled and shook his head, willing himself back to reality.

"Hey, you made it!" he said, completely ignoring Naomi. Unfazed, she went to the kitchen to help herself. "Can I get you something to drink? I've got beer, tequila, vodka, gin, mixers." His lips curled into a lopsided grin, green eyes twinkling. "What's your poison?"

Your mouth.

I looked at the Rolling Rock in his hand and pointed to it. "Beer's fine." I hadn't experimented much in high school and didn't have much experience with drinking, but Naomi was driving, and I needed a little liquid courage if I wanted to talk to Ari.

"I really like your place." It was the lower flat, and not at all your typical twenty something guy apartment. No leather sectional, giant TV, or video game consoles in sight. He had a nice fabric matching sofa and loveseat, tasteful lamps, throw pillows, rugs, even a console table near the front door. I thought maybe Daddy owned the whole duplex.

"Thanks. My mom likes decorating our places. It makes her happy and I really don't care either way, so I let her do her thing."

I took a sip of my beer, and I could feel Ari's eyes on my

mouth. Being alone with him was so much more intense than I could have imagined.

"Would you like a tour?"

My mind conjured a scene where we'd be alone in his bedroom. He'd close the door. Look at me with those fiery emerald eyes. Pace and stalk me like an animal with his prey. The things that would happen next were things I'd begun to imagine when I was alone at night in my bed. I was grateful to have my beer at that moment; my mouth suddenly bone dry. It seemed every drop of moisture in my body got the message to migrate south, converging in the valley between my legs. Being an only child had blessed me with a spectacularly vivid imagination.

I followed him to a spare room with a leather couch, a giant flat screen TV, and at least three video game consoles. *Ah, there it is.*

"Yeah, I'd have a nicer place if I went back to school. My dad tried to cut me off when I dropped out but thank God my mom fought for me. He compromised and let me keep half my monthly allowance."

"What were you going to school for?" It was the most he'd ever spoken to me that wasn't laced with flirtation, but the blatant entitlement woven through everything he was saying was turning me off a little.

"I was going to Marquette majoring in finance. My dad wants me to get into the family business. Take it over someday. But I want to be a chef and open my own restaurant. It's all I've ever wanted, and I'm going to do whatever it takes to make it happen."

"Wow. That's cool. But your parents aren't supportive, I take it."

"Not at all. My older brother, Dave, got into medicine. Became a surgeon. Obviously, my dad loved that, couldn't find fault with that, and he knew he had two other kids to groom into good little soldiers for the Ristow Investment Group. My older sister Andrea works for him, but he's always thinking maybe she'd get married, have babies and leave. Like he wouldn't be able to count on her. She keeps saying she doesn't want a family, but I'm not sure he believes her. And my mom is hoping it's not true either, having grandkids is all she ever talks about. Dave and his wife Rebecca, who is also a surgeon, aren't having kids."

"Are you thinking you want to go to culinary school?"

"Yeah. I'm saving up, but I want to study in Europe or even Asia. I want to bring something unique to the table."

"Literally. To the table." I quipped. Ari's face lit up with a wide, luminous smile of appreciation. I could tell he liked having someone on his side.

"It would be nice to have my parents' help to open a restaurant too. At least some connections for investors; I mean my dad knows everyone. But he doesn't believe in what I'm doing. I'm out here on my own."

"But this way it will mean so much more when you make it, don't you think? When you have a successful restaurant that you built on your own, not only will that show them, but think of how proud you'll feel."

"Hmm, I guess." Ari smiled and lowered his eyes. When he raised them again to look at me, the fire was back, and I stiffened a little. He pointed a thumb toward the living room. "I...I should mingle. Help yourself to food or whatever."

I watched him walk away feeling a little disappointed that our time alone was over. I sighed and went to go find Naomi.

A little while later she asked if I wanted to join her outside for a smoke. Ari and two others, Didi and Josh, were in the already in the backyard sitting around a defunct fire pit passing a blunt.

"Smells of the devil's lettuce out here," snarked Naomi. "Oh, by the way, Ari, Larry and Cindy are fooling around in your bedroom."

"Jesus Christ. Guess I'll be burning the sheets." He turned to me holding out the joint. "Do you smoke?"

"Sometimes." Kendra and I had gotten high a few times recently with her new boyfriend, Craig. I'd jumped at any chance I could get to see her since she'd been so wrapped up in him in the weeks since they'd started dating.

I took the joint and took a cautious hit. The last thing I'd wanted was to start coughing uncontrollably and make a fool of myself in front of Ari. Especially since his eyes were on my every move.

It was a hot and unbearably sticky July Sunday with more and more clouds gathering as the afternoon went on. While we were outside the sky had turned a dark gray, and I could smell and feel the heaviness of an impending storm. I looked up and felt a fat raindrop land on my face.

"Oh shit. It's raining." Naomi and Didi started walking back towards the house. Josh shrugged and followed them leaving me once again alone with Ari.

"Are you going to head in, too?" I asked him.

"Nah, I like the rain."

"Me too." I took a hit of the joint I had forgotten was in my hand. "Can I ask you a question?"

Ari held out his hand and curled his fingers twice, silently asking me to pass it back. "Shoot."

"How come I always see your car in the parking lot? Like, long after your shift is done, or even on your days off?"

He sat still. A raindrop hit the joint and extinguished it. Ari tore off the wet part, twisted what remained of the end and re-lit it. "Well, some nights I was waiting for Larry or Juan 'cause we had plans to go out after they got done."

His explanation was thin, clearly not the whole story. I pressed, "And the other nights?"

He paused. "The other nights... the other nights." It was as if he was reciting a poem. He looked down at his feet. "The other nights I want to make sure you get to your car safely." He looked up at me from his chair and shrugged as if to play it off as a casual thing. "Sometimes I hear the guys in the dish pit or the bartenders talking about you. I just want to make sure you're okay."

"Oh." I didn't know what else to say. I grabbed my left thumb tightly with my right hand. It was a self-soothing mechanism I'd had since I was little, I'd often spend an entire dental visit or a whole parental lecture white knuckled. "Can I ask you another question?"

He tilted his head down and looked up at me through his long lashes. "Yes."

Why was that the sexiest sound I'd ever heard? It was more than a simple yes. It was an invitation. Or a dare.

"Have you ever dated anyone at work?"

Ari put the joint to his lips and took a couple of deep, short burst draws. With his inhale held he croaked, "Dated?" He exhaled the plume of smoke and locked his eyes onto mine. "Or fucked?"

Even with my sheltered upbringing I'd heard the word hundreds of times. But it had never before sounded so loaded. And this was not only loaded but cocked and aimed directly at me. It was as if tendrils of ether, midnight black and laced with sin, had followed the word out of Ari's mouth. Invading my ears and winding their way down, twisting around my insides and tying them into knots before diving deeper and deeper until they finally reached their intended, forbidden target.

More fat raindrops were falling now. "Either," I said, the word barely audible.

"Actually neither. You've heard the expression 'Don't shit where you eat?' Well, I keep it plain and simple. Don't fuck where you work." His eyebrows pinched. "Everyone is so fucking gossipy all the time. I just wouldn't want to deal with all that."

I bowed my head a little trying to hide my disappointment. He was telling me there wasn't a chance, when I'd been so sure something was starting.

Just then, the heavens opened.

Ari and I looked at each other with a shocked amusement as sheets of rain soaked us in seconds. The mood and our expressions immediately shifted as we watched each other's clothes cling scandalously to our bodies leaving nothing at all to the imagination. His white T-shirt molding to his muscular chest and abdomen, the thin fabric on my sundress affirming I wasn't wearing a bra. Electricity that had nothing to do with the storm crackled wildly between us.

We stood for what seemed like a lifetime of devouring each other with our eyes. The rain felt warm and had a heady summer smell that added to the intoxication of the moment. I took a deep breath of resignation, since he had told me in no uncertain terms that nothing was going to happen, and I began to walk past Ari toward the house.

As I brushed past him, he grabbed my wrist. He spun me around and I crashed into him, our bodies pressed together, impossibly close.

He put his large hands on my face and brushed the wet hair out of my eyes with his long fingers. His eyes locked and loaded, fiery and frantic.

Holding my face firmly, his commanding mouth laid claim to mine. Lapping the rain off my lips before breaching them with his tongue. Pulling my bottom lip in between his teeth. I was convinced if he'd pulled away from my mouth and let the rain in, I would just let myself drown. I'd never been kissed like that before, like he was trying to consume me, and I was instantly all in. I silently proclaimed myself his new religion, my body the altar on which he would worship. I grabbed and pulled at his shirt, clawed at his shoulders trying to draw him closer. He was so impossibly tall, like a tree begging to be climbed.

He pulled away and smiled, taking my hand and leading me back toward the house. We had just walked under the covered deck where it was dry when, in two steps, he had me pressed up against the back side of the house. Kissing me again, moving my wet dress up and down my body, cupping my breasts. I could feel his erection through his thin wet khaki shorts pressing up against my belly, and I felt like I might spontaneously combust at any second. He pulled away from me and smiled again, tenderly brushing another piece of hair from my cheek. My eyes bounced from one raindrop to another on his epically beautiful face.

"First you beg. Now look at you. So fucking wet for me," he said, his voice thick and dripping with wicked innuendo.

He chuckled at his own joke. I looked down nervously and giggled too. Was the Devil asking me to dance? I was terrified and enthralled at the same time. Before I knew it his expression transformed. His smile disappeared and his eyes burned with an intensity that made me shiver. In seconds he was pressed against me again, his fingers tangled in my hair, his mouth at my ear whispering his lusty inquisition. "Well, are you? Are you so fucking wet for me, Shelby?"

Oh my God. Was I ever. It was all breath and heat and magic.

Sex and sin.

I nodded against his shoulder.

"Show me." He licked the rain off my neck, and I felt his

hands make their way south. I spread my legs. I'd never needed anything more than I needed him to touch me just then, but I also needed to know. I screwed up my courage and asked, "What about don't fuck where you work?"

He moaned as he pushed aside my panties and his middle finger slowly began to infiltrate. "I'll quit."

CHAPTER
ONE

SHELBY

May 2012

I GIGGLED WITH DELIGHT AT MY REFLECTION IN THE MIRROR—ANY AND all attempts at a scowl were made in vain since the Botox had taken full effect. Kendra had convinced me that since I was about to be on television, I should just bite the bullet and try it.

"It's no big deal," she'd said. And she was right. Tiny poke, poke, poke and it was done. The RN had instructed me to make my "frowny face" on and off for the next hour so the neurotoxin would get where it needed to go, do what it needed to do. Kendra had come along and got her poke, poke, poke too, and we'd decided to go bargain hunting at TJ Maxx after the appointment. As Kendra stood across from me looking at clothes, I burst out laughing. Dutifully making her frowny face over and over, she appeared to be absolutely repulsed by every single top she was thumbing through on the rack.

Now, two weeks later, I couldn't stop staring at the smooth

space between my eyebrows and testing to see what muscles I could still control.

"*Mira*, Shelby! Stop making faces in the mirror so we can finish your makeup!" Lyric scolded. Lyric Vasquez was one of the receptionists and the makeup artist at Aspire, the salon and spa where I'd spent the last ten years working as a massage therapist and esthetician. She flipped her long straight black hair behind her back and stomped her thigh high boot clad foot on the floor.

"Sorry." I said, still giggling.

I let her finish her work as I playfully dangled my legs on the high makeup chair trying to shake out some nervous energy. Clients would often need a step stool to get into Lyric's chair. She was over six feet tall and refused to compromise her ergonomics.

Lyric came into Aspire five years before as a newly transitioning girl of eighteen desperate for a job in the beauty industry. Her parents had kicked her out and she seemed to be in search of a new family as well. The owners, no strangers to the power of being given a chance when one is needed the most, hired her on the spot. Not only did we help her learn makeup and the ins and outs of running a salon, but we also helped her move through her transition as best as we could.

I had the privilege of giving Lyric her first ever eyebrow wax. The expression on her face when she saw herself in the mirror for the first time—witnessing a rebirth, someone in that magical moment they are finally able to see themselves as their most authentic self, was an honor and an experience I could never have imagined.

Since then, she has proven to be a genius with makeup, not spending much time behind the front desk anymore with all the client requests and referrals she gets. Every so often someone in her chair or some client walking through the salon will give her *that look*. I cannot imagine just going through life, simply trying to exist, meanwhile people are trying to figure you out, like you are a puzzle to be solved. I don't understand how someone's gender expression has to be anyone else's business—it would make no difference if they were the barista at your favorite coffee shop or a high-powered attorney. You'd still get your coffee just the way you like it, and they'd still likely be screwing you on billable hours.

"Bert and Ernie are not gay. Simple as that," said Dimitri playfully from the hair station across from where Lyric was working her magic with my face. He sectioned off a piece of hair on his client and aggressively painted it with lightener on top of a piece of foil. "First of all, their apartment is boring. Second, they wear the same clothes every day. And do not get me started on Bert's eyebrows!"

Talia laughed from her chair in front of Dimitri. "They most definitely are gay. And Bert is the top." Talia was Dimitri's best friend, the Grace to his Will.

"Um, Ernie most definitely tops from the bottom," offered Lyric.

Dimitri cackled. He'd arranged to do Talia's hair off the books that morning while the salon was closed for the shooting of a reality TV show episode. As if on cue, Randall, the co-owner of the salon, walked around the corner. Randall was a tall, thin, bald, bearded Black man with delicate, refined features and always impeccably dressed. That day he was wearing slim fit black wool pants and a dark gray cashmere turtleneck sweater.

"Dimitri, you said you'd be done by the time they got here," Randall said as he looked at his watch, "which is in less than thirty minutes. You haven't even got half her foils in because you fools are too busy talking about muppet sex."

"I didn't think it was a big deal since they'll be in the spa," said Dimitri.

"They will start at the front desk. Do you think Darius would let this happen if he wasn't going to get to be on TV? Maybe they can film that part at the end, and you will be done by then. In any case, you need to start behaving."

Randall started to walk back up to the front desk, then gracefully turned on his toes to face Dimitri and Talia. This poised, impossibly elegant man, opened his mouth and with a straight face said, "And it's obvious that Bert is the Dom and Ernie is a little masochistic brat since he is always trying to piss Bert off with his mischief in order to get punished." With that he walked away, and we all nearly choked with laughter. Randall's fiftieth birthday was coming up and I was struck with divine inspiration. I would commission an artist and gift him a beautifully framed portrait of the leather clad duo in a provocative position with Bert using his own nose as the ball gag in Ernie's mouth. I was thrilled with the prospect of getting to watch Randall Mercer-Watts absolutely lose his shit.

"What's this TV thing again? asked Talia.

"Have you heard of that show *Dare Me to Do it*? The one where the guy goes around and does weird jobs with people?" Dimitri asked her.

"I've heard of it, never watched it though."

"Shelby made a video audition thing to have him come and do waxing with her. I guess the show has kind of become a little more serious though. He likes to talk about equity and sustainability and stuff like that now. Right, Shelby?"

"Yeah." I nodded. "And really getting into the people more than the job itself. They decided that since my job isn't usually done by men, they could do a show like that. I had to kind of come up with answers to the question of why more men aren't estheticians."

"Because I don't want a man waxing my hoo-hah," said Talia.

"Exactly. But *why not?*" I challenged.

"Uh, I don't know. Just… no."

I laughed. "Well, I had to come up with a better explanation than that."

"Show her the video!" Lyric told Dimitri.

Six months before it began as a joke. Which turned into a dare (fitting for a show called "*Dare Me to Do It.*") Darius and I were talking about the show, and he suggested I make a pitch. I laughed it off at first, but the idea kept poking at me. I was comfortable in front of the camera by then, since the year before Darius had encouraged me to work my signature pinup style and make YouTube video tutorials for hair and makeup. I'd done them under the alias Cherrie Bombshell, not really wanting to get attention from people I knew. It can get weird with male clients, not to mention some family members, but my salon family had seen them all. Including this one.

"Holy shit!" Talia shouted as she watched my audition video on Dimitri's phone. "No wonder they are coming here! This is hot as hell."

"Right?!" said Dimitri. "And Shelby has a huge thing for the host, so it was like she was doing it just for him." He would stop working and look at Talia in the mirror every time he talked to her. No wonder they were taking so long.

"Eww. He's so…old." Lyric scrunched up her face.

"He's forty-seven. That's not old to me." I countered. I'd just turned forty in January. Dimitri was right—I did have a crush on the host.

In fact, I'd had a crush on him since I was thirteen years old.

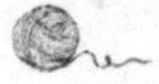

BACK IN THE EIGHTIES, JAKE FORD WAS ON A SOAP OPERA CALLED *Sault Ste. Marie*. To this day I'm surprised it stayed on the air for ten years when people had such a hard time pronouncing the name—*soo saint marie*. Jake played Foster McBride, the son of wealthy shipping magnates in the northern Michigan town who wanted to bartend and own a bar instead of getting into the family business. He'd spend his days rebelling against his birthright in tight T-shirts and bedding practically every woman in town.

I bought all the teen magazines that featured his pictures and papered my bedroom walls with his face. He had a hint of an ethnic ambiguity, which in hindsight I thought maybe they'd been actively trying to minimize to increase his "marketability." They did that a lot back then, and I'd even wondered if Jake Ford was his real name. These days on his show he often slipped into easy and fluent Spanish while warmly interacting with employees he'd encounter on the job. In any case, to me, he was so much more mysterious and alluring than the blond or sandy haired, freckle-faced, milquetoast boys that filled the other pages of the magazines. Dark hair, deep, dark chocolate eyes, strong angular features, and a bottom lip so full it had a crease in the middle.

My crush had waned over the years since he'd stepped away from the spotlight, only occasionally making a guest appearance on a drama or crime show. When my son Brody stumbled onto his show on the Encounter channel a few years ago, however, I couldn't deny that Jake Ford could still get my attention. I liked him with miles on his face, and his eyes held the promise of so many stories. He'd matured, especially since the show had shifted in the last couple of years to be less silly and more substantial. He liked to feature the people far more than the job and get to the heart of why people do what they do. Way sexier to me now than a softly filtered bartender on daytime TV.

"WHAT LIP COLOR?" LYRIC ASKED ME. "I KNOW YOU'RE PICKY."

"Vixen." It was a fun, bold, bright red that looked surprisingly good with my dark red hair done up in victory rolls and wrapped in a black bandana.

Randall came around the corner again, this time with an urgency in his long strides. Laser focused on Lyric and me, he said, "I need you two to come up front right now and help me talk Darius down from the shelves again."

Darius was also a beautiful, bald and bearded Black man who, when he smiled his big, bright, cherubic smile, you could see exactly how he had looked when he was a little boy. He was much shorter and stockier than Randall, and some of the stylists had recently taken to calling them "Key and Peele" as the resemblance was comically accurate.

Darius was a self-proclaimed hyper-focused perfectionist when it came to his clients which made him an incomparable and brilliant stylist. He'd made his way through the LA celebrity hair scene for years until he met Randall. Randall loved Darius, but he could not abide by his volatile and chaotic lifestyle and soon became intolerant of the clubs and the drugs. He gave Darius an ultimatum—move to Milwaukee, Randall's hometown, and settle down, or lose him. In 1992 they opened Aspire just outside of Milwaukee in the adorable suburb of Tosa Falls. In 2002, they started a cosmetology and barbering school in Milwaukee's inner city which provides grants and tuition assistance for underprivileged young people who want to get into the trade.

Yes, Darius was a hyper-focused perfectionist when it came to hair, but even more so with the aesthetic of the salon.

The front desk had a coffee bar with an apothecary vibe. On the back counter was a beautiful espresso machine that looked like an Italian sports car. The shelves above held cups, saucers, beautiful lidded glass and ceramic containers housing a large variety of teas, mortars and pestles just for fun, and little plants nestled in among everything. Often, you'd see Darius standing there, hands on his hips carefully considering the shelves, and, usually, within minutes, he'd be taking everything down to rearrange it. Making little micro-adjustments for hours.

He was standing in front of the shelves that way when we walked up to the front.

"Darius. Honey, we don't have time. They'll be here in less than ten minutes." I gently told him.

"I know, but I just know that when I watch the show, I'll find the one thing that seems out of place, and I'll wish I'd fixed it."

I rubbed his back. "Lyric will make you a latte. While she does that, you can move a few things—on one condition." I held up a finger to his face. "You can't pick anything up. Only slide things side to side or forward and back."

He nodded and stepped forward to begin his ritual. Randall smiled at me and mouthed, "Thank you."

I was suddenly becoming increasingly nervous and somewhat nauseated at the realization that my teen crush would be there any minute. I'd appreciated having been distracted by Dimitri and Talia, and I'd somehow been soothed by the fact that Lyric hadn't seemed that impressed, or even bothered at all, that a TV crew was coming to our salon.

Darius had adjusted a few things on the shelves and was halfway through his latte. He was feeling better. I, however, was becoming more unhinged by the second and began to pace in front of the door.

"Hey... I wanted to tell you something," Darius said to me.

"Don't do it," Randall cautioned, shaking his head.

"I've got to tell her. I feel like I need to tell her," Darius pleaded, his hands making an exaggerated in and out gesture against his chest.

"Tell me what?" I asked. They were making me nervous.

"I met him. Jake. Back in the day," he explained. "I styled him for a couple of magazine photo shoots."

"Oh my God! Maybe I had your work on my wall. How cool is that?"

"Yes. Maybe. But Jake was... well, he was kind of a dick."

I laughed at his drama. That didn't surprise me one bit. I would think a twenty-something soap star slash teen idol would rarely have been a kind or overly polite person. "And? I mean, was he like a homophobe? Was he mean to you?"

"No, nothing like that. He was just arrogant and opinionated. Thought his shit didn't stink."

"Hmm," said Randall. "Sounds just like someone else I knew back then...except I told him all the time how much his shit stinks." He winked at me. "How did the two of them not get along?"

I laughed. None of it bothered me in the slightest. In fact, if he were still a dick, it would help alleviate my crush and I could more easily navigate the shoot. Be less flustered. Less fangirl. I sincerely doubted, however, that he was the same person Darius knew. Obviously, he could pretend to be whoever he wanted to be on the show—he was an actor after all—but in my gut I felt like the show shifted because of his genuine interest in people and their stories.

I stood at the window of the salon, both wishing they would hurry up and get there and hoping they would be late. Maybe even hoping they wouldn't show up at all. I was getting my "nervous tummy" which wasn't anywhere near as cute as it sounds. Instead of little butterflies I just felt like I had to take a very large poop.

"Shelby, get away from that window before you put your little nose print on it," scolded Darius.

I was just about to back up when two large, black SUVs drove past. My stomach dropped as they made Y turns and pulled up in front of the salon. "Holy shit, they're here." My palms were sweating. My palms never sweat.

I walked quickly to stand behind Darius and Randall. I did not want to be the first person they saw or talked to when they walked in.

Out of the first SUV came three men, two of whom I recognized from the show. They would often cut to the crew if they tripped over something or there was a particularly bad smell someone was reacting to. Dan, the assistant director who's often used as a guinea pig for comic relief on the show, popped out of the second SUV followed by a woman. I assumed it was Rita, the producer and the only person I'd had contact with.

The passenger door opened, and I finally saw him.

Jake Ford.

He was taking a painstakingly long beat in the SUV. He had sunglasses on, and it looked like he was on his phone.

When he finally did get out, he made a few three-sixty turns and looked up the height of the building and down onto the street. He was getting a lay of the land. I'd imagined it was part of his process and it would all be included as part of the "story."

He began walking toward the salon doors. Toward me. With what seemed to be a series of expertly choreographed movements, he ended his call, put his phone in his back pocket and swiped the sunglasses off his face.

As he reached out his arm to pull the glass door open, I couldn't help but think how surreal this moment was. I had been watching Jake Ford through glass screens for twenty-seven years, and now he was about to breach the last one that stood between us.

CHAPTER
TWO
JAKE

As I walked into that unassuming little salon, my eyes immediately found her. She was peeking out from behind a group of people at first, but then when she noticed I recognized her, she smiled and came out to greet me.

It had been an ordinary Monday when the forwarded email landed in my inbox with the subject line: **Check this out ASAP.** Rita Agbayani, my co-executive producer, was the first to field all the emails and video audition submissions for the show. Typically, it would be a video from someone's phone uploaded in an email, but this was a YouTube link. Usually that meant a well edited, semi-professional looking submission and I always looked forward to them. The videos always ended with someone saying "I dare you" as part of the deal.

This video, however, I could have never been prepared for.

It began with a familiar song, The Heavy's "How You Like Me Now," the camera focused on a blank wall. Into the frame came a woman with magenta hair put up in a 1940's style, luminous porcelain skin, winged eyeliner and pouty red lips. I remember immediately sitting up in my chair, at attention, and leaning in closer to get a better look.

She never spoke. While the song was playing, she motioned for the camera to pan down to capture the hapless subject on her table, a man lying face down exposing one of the hairiest backs I'd ever seen. Seriously, he looked like the missing link. When the camera panned back up to her she dipped a stick into what looked like a pot of honey, letting the wax run off back into the pot. At one point she mimicked a lick. *Jesus Christ.* I wasn't even sure what the hell the job was yet, but I knew I wanted to go there to do it.

She began to "apply" the wax, but just out of the camera view. Then she showed us the clean strip she was about to use and again, did something out of view. An exaggerated motion of ripping and then showing the camera a strip covered with hair.

I smiled, knowing enough about editing to be able to appreciate the hell out of this. It was fast becoming my favorite submission of all time.

As the song skipped to its instrumental crescendo, the lighting switched to a frenzied strobe. While dancing along to the music she was pulling strip after strip, almost maniacally, making plenty of eye contact with the camera.

When the song was nearing the end, the video faded to black. The next scene was a closeup of a pair of red lips whispering in her model's ear. Another fade to black, then a second later the lights were on, and her model was sitting up.

He had his back to the camera, and she was peeking out

from behind his shoulder. Waxed, or, I'm guessing, artfully shaved as part of the *greatest edit ever,* into the hair on his back were the words I DARE YOU.

I sat back in my chair and couldn't wipe the dumb smile off my face. The show had been changing quite a bit and I wondered how I'd be able to backtrack and go learn how to wax and be silly with this woman. I knew I needed to figure it out. I pressed replay. Maybe more than once.

It was when I finally minimized the submission video that I saw them. Off to the right-hand side of the YouTube homepage were several other videos set against a bright aqua background. Same magenta hair, porcelain skin, and red lip all under the name Cherrie Bombshell. Just as I thought; she was no amateur after all. I was more than a little curious and I clicked on the first one.

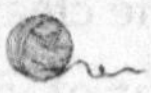

I TRULY HAD NOT EXPECTED HER TO LOOK IN PERSON LIKE SHE HAD IN the videos. I thought maybe the pinup thing was just for drama or part of her YouTube persona. But nope. Here she was looking like a sexy cartoon. Like if Jessica Rabbit had a day job.

Over the years, I have learned to control (or at least to identify while working to control) the aspects of my testosterone driven maleness that could potentially get me into trouble.

First, there is Cave Man. Cave Man notices (or whatever the least subtle form of notice is) the things primitive man cared about. *TITS! HIPS! ASS! This one would make good babies!* These enter my brain as marginally useful information and I immediately file them away as inappropriate for this moment in time.

I've come a long way since puberty. Or at least since my frontal lobe had fully developed.

Next is Mad Man. I named him this as I picture John Hamm in his iconic role as a womanizing ad man in the late 1950's. What he notices are more nuanced, but only slightly less misogynistic. Mostly things that make women innately femi-nine-- lipstick, high heels, long mascaraed lashes, a diminutive stature. *She's so pretty and fragile. I could protect her.*

The default I strive for I call Evolved Man.

Cave Man noticed the way the letters curved on Shelby's black Aspire T-shirt and how she filled out her fitted black pants. Son of a bitch made an hourglass gesture with his hands in my head.

Mad Man noticed her hair, her makeup, her petiteness, and the way she tried to hide wiping her hand on her pants before shaking mine. *She's nervous. Fuck, she's cute.* He wondered if she wore matching lingerie. *She might even be the stockings and garter type.*

Evolved Man noticed the sparkle in her eyes and the warmth in her smile. And a little tingle of electricity when our hands touched.

"Shelby? Hi, I'm Jake."

"Hi, Jake, nice to meet you." Still smiling. But still nervous. She gestured to the man standing next to her, "This is–"

"Well, I'll be damned. Darius! It's good to see you, man! It's been a long time." I enthusiastically extended my hand for a high five handshake and pulled him in for a hug. He was older, a little heavier, balder and more bearded than I remem-bered, but I'd recognize that infectious smile anywhere.

"Great to see you too, Jake. I wasn't sure you'd remember me."

"Of course I remember. We did, what? Five, six shoots together? I remember 'cause you always had the good Hollywood gossip. I couldn't wait to sit in your chair and hear all about all the straight actors who hit on you."

He laughed, "Yeah, back then I thought everyone was in the closet and into me."

"I always wondered if you'd tell the next client that I hit on you, too."

"Uh, I'm pretty sure you did hit on me," he joked.

"You might be right—you're a damn handsome man." I laughed. "This is your place?"

"It is." He introduced me to his husband and then to a statuesque femme fatale named Lyric. Clearly the lost love child of Cher and Antonio Banderas.

I turned back to Shelby. "While the guys are unloading the equipment, why don't you show me around?"

"Ok! Do you want to see the whole place or just where we'll be..." She made ripping gestures with her hands—it seemed she was finding words to be somewhat elusive. Still nervous. I wanted so badly to put her at ease somehow. *It isn't just been just being on TV, right?* I mean she was so comfortable in front of the camera in her videos. And then the thought occurred to me. *Was she nervous because of me?*

I'd guessed she was in her late thirties which meant she was a teenage girl when I was on the soap. And in the magazines. It usually made me cringe a little internally to interact with a fan from those days, mostly because I didn't like who I was then. But this was different. I suddenly felt like I *wanted* her to have been a fan. I immediately pushed the thought away. Evolved Man reminded me not to get too caught up in myself—this was work, and I had to remember the tone of the episode we were doing.

"I'd love to see the whole place." I told her. "I know we're focusing on why men don't typically do your job, but it always gives me a good perspective to see the space and how everyone interacts with one another."

"Oh! We closed the salon for the morning. For the filming. Should we not have done that?"

"Oh no, it's fine! We always worry about intruding anyway. It's all good."

She seemed to be starting to calm down a bit, and we began our tour. What struck me right away was how cozy and comfortable the salon felt. I was so used to very minimalist or industrial decor in salons where the spaces felt cold and intimidating. This was just the opposite, teetering on the edge of maximalist but done in a very tasteful and purposeful way. Exposed Cream City brick (the only other time I'd been in Milwaukee was to film a show about reclaiming Cream City brick from old buildings before they were demolished. I had no idea Milwaukee was nicknamed Cream City because of the brick made from native clay and not Wisconsin being a dairy state. Always learning new things with this job.) Natural light spilling into the space from the large windows. Afrocentric art on the walls and live plants everywhere. There wasn't a hint of an intimidating vibe anywhere to be found.

We walked through the bank of hair stations. Twelve altogether, warm brown leather chairs and large round mirrors. All meticulously clean and free of clutter. Except one.

Shelby read the slight confusion on my face. "This is Dimitri and his friend Talia. Sometimes people come in on their off days to do friends and family."

I turned to the twosome. "Hey, how's it going? I'm Jake."

"Yeah, we know who you are." Dimitri's lips curled into a devilish smile aimed right at Shelby. She shot him a look full of daggers and shook her head.

"How'd you like Shelby's video, Jake?" he asked.

I swear I saw Shelby's cheeks flush. "That's the reason I'm

here." I smiled at her and the crimson deepened a little. "Hey about that...," I motioned for her to walk with me out of earshot of the stylist and his friend—I didn't want to give him any more ammunition to embarrass her. "You know how we always show at least a little bit of the audition video before the segment? Well, we won't be able to show yours. I tried, but we weren't sure it would be appropriate for the tone of the episode. And...it's a...well, it's a family show, after all." I grinned.

What I'd told her was only partially true. The truth is hers would have been the only video in the episode and it would have felt unbalanced. I'd spent weeks racking my brain trying to figure out how to spin an episode around waxing with the show's new tone. Since we'd done an episode last year about women doing jobs mostly done by men, I got the idea to do one about jobs rarely done by men and the reasons why. Shelby's segment would be first and I was grateful she'd agreed to the more serious subject matter surrounding the job itself. With the other two jobs, a daycare worker and a labor and delivery nurse, we had approached them. That was something we'd never done before, and of course, there would be no audition video.

"Yeah. I thought about that after I'd sent it. I guess I just really wanted to get your attention."

Oh, you did. No doubt about that. I nodded.

She walked me around the whole salon before taking me through the door into the spa area where the crew were unloading cameras and equipment outside of one of the rooms.

"Oh good, you found it," said Shelby.

An attractive brunette peeked her head out of the room. "Hi!" She stepped out into the hall to get Shelby's approval of her booty shorts. "This okay?"

Shelby nodded and turned to me. "This is our model, Amber. She's one of the other estheticians, so she's used to newbies."

"Hi Amber. Thanks for helping us out today," I said. We all stepped into the room.

"So, I am all set up for us in here, but I can adjust anything if you need more room or whatever." Shelby offered. "Oh! Your uniform!" She hurried out of the room.

I had forgotten that part of the pre-filming communication was Rita asking if there is something they prefer for me to wear. Most of the time it's my own clothes, safety equipment or coveralls. Shelby came back smiling and bearing...of course —a black bedazzled Aspire T-shirt.

I smiled and started to unbutton my shirt, trying not to look at Shelby. I didn't want to know if she'd be watching me, I knew it would have been way too distracting. I handed my shirt to Dan, but before I tried on my new uniform, I couldn't help myself. I looked toward where Shelby was standing just in time to catch her eyes trailing over my chest and then lifting to lock with mine for a few loaded seconds. I couldn't let myself get all caught up in this moment, however, I had a job to do. I pulled the T-shirt over my head and outstretched my arms, turning side to side to show off for the room. "How do I look?" I kind of regretted not doing that on camera, but I thought it would ultimately be more tongue in cheek if we'd just start the show with me in the shirt.

Shelby grinned and gave me a thumbs-up.

Back to business. I said, "Okay, so we'll start filming, but keep it loose so we can see how it's going. We never know how the acoustics will be, and sometimes we'll have to tweak lighting and things as we go. The most important thing to remember is, this is not live. We can shoot, stop, mess up, go again... it doesn't matter. That's the magic of editing. There will be times that maybe you say something and part of it doesn't get caught, but we will like it, and want you to say it again. The best you can remember it, that is. It might sound a little daunting, but don't worry. You'll do great.

"This is kind of your show," I explained further. "Yes, I want you to show me how to wax, but primarily I want to delve into the *why* this is mostly a job done by women. You do get that it's not my intention to demean this job in any way, right? It's more that I want to get into what has happened up until now between men and women to make a woman hesitant to ever get a bikini wax from a man." I had been a little worried that she thought I wanted to make fun of her. "Amber will be on this table, right?"

"Yes, but...I need to tell you she doesn't want her bikini done. She's perfectly happy with a leg wax, but at the end of the day, she wasn't comfortable with everyone seeing her grown out pubes," Shelby explained. Amber looked mortified.

I stifled a laugh. "Oh no, that's fine. The network was having issues with that anyway. We can still talk about bikini waxing though, right? And if everyone is comfortable, maybe we can even discuss this conversation."

I introduced Shelby to the boys as they finished setting up. Jeff, our main camera guy, was 6'4" and lanky as hell. He could pretzel himself into positions a contortionist would envy to get the shot he wanted. He's loved the more serious tone the show has taken, seeing things through more of a photojournalist's eye. We called Mohammad and Ben the Wonder Twins. They had been documentary filmmakers and could both float between camera, sound, lighting and all things tech. Absolutely brilliant on the fly. I must have done something right in a past life to have had these geniuses on my team since the beginning.

"Later I'll do an intro spot outside the salon and then a

quick little thing with you and Darius at the front of the salon. I always like to promote the business a little when I can, and I'm so happy to be able to do that for Dar. I still can't believe it's his place." I ran my hand through my hair, caught in a wave of nostalgia. "By this point you and I will have met, and I'll have introduced you already. So, we'll just be able to start. You okay?"

Shelby nodded. Rita and Dan stood just outside the open door. They would be catching the things that I wasn't, interjecting if they felt like we needed another take. Boom and cameras in position, I nodded to Jeff we were ready to begin, and he counted us down.

"Okay, Shelby. I guess you're about to teach me how to wax."

"That's right. And this is our brave model, Amber."

"I am sorry in advance for any pain I may cause you, Amber," I said. She smiled and nodded.

Shelby grinned at me. "Don't worry, I'm a very good teacher. I won't let you hurt her. Too much." She winked.

I got a little flash of some kinky thought I had no business thinking and immediately pushed it away. "Why don't you show me your setup here."

Shelby turned to the cart between us and explained all the things we'd need, gloves, sticks, strips. She talked about "double dipping" and that we can only use a stick once before throwing it away. We'd go through a lot of sticks. She handed me my gloves and gave the wax a stir. Then she put some solution on a cotton pad and wiped down Amber's leg. I jumped slightly at a loud snap. She broke one of the wooden applicators in half.

"We go through so many of these. It helps save waste." She heaved a sigh of determination as she got ready to train me. "Okay. The most important thing to remember is that you want a thin, even application in the direction of hair growth." She demonstrated with ease. The honey-colored wax had a great deal of dripping potential– as she had so seductively demonstrated in the video. I had to work hard to keep myself from getting too distracted thinking about that. She expertly scraped off one side of the stick on the wax pot and held her hand underneath it as she brought it to Amber's shin. In one fluid motion she spread it from just underneath the knee all the way down to the ankle. Then she threw the stick half away and went back to repeat the whole process.

"Some people might pull out the strips at this point and start removing, but I find that applying the wax to this whole quadrant of the leg gets this done much faster."

Once she had all the wax applied, she grabbed a strip, placed it on one side of Amber's ankle, pressed it with her hand several times, held the skin below it and ripped. The paper on the table made a crinkle noise as Amber lurched.

"Oops! Sorry. I forgot to tell you I'm a jumper." Amber said.

"That's okay. I think we all jumped with you." I laughed.

"Do you want to try?" Shelby asked me.

"Not yet. I'd rather watch you do this whole part, then I can start with the wax on the other side?"

"Okay." Shelby continued her task. This was one of my favorite parts of the gig. When I watched people who were so very good at their jobs, when movement becomes a well-choreographed dance—it's hypnotizing.

Efficiency porn.

There was something else I noticed about Shelby.

When I was in college, I had a history class with a teacher I nicknamed Professor Mush Mouth. He glossed over his consonants like he was perpetually practicing a ventriloquist act, his lips barely ever touching. It drove me crazy, and I'd almost dropped the class because of it. Since then, I've come to greatly appreciate people who have a sharp edge to their consonant pronunciation. Shelby not only had a soft melodious quality to her voice and an endearing hint of a midwestern accent, but her diction was giving me goosebumps in my brain. Her c's cracked like the ice in my scotch glass. Her p's popped like bubble wrap. Her t's were a tiny spoon tapping the side of a teacup. Watching *and* listening were pure pleasure.

"So now let's get down to it. You're called an esthetician, right? A skin care specialist." I asked.

"That's right."

"Do you know any male estheticians?"

"There was one guy in my class when I went to school, but he never actually worked in a spa though. He got right into makeup. Last I'd heard he was representing and educating for a popular makeup brand, doing very well. When we were in class, the teachers had to ask our client models if they minded working with a male student. We all had to have a certain number of each service completed before we could graduate, and I think he barely made his quota. Mostly because we let him work on us."

"The other students?'

"Yeah."

"So, if someone called and tried to schedule a bikini wax, they'd ask if they'd be okay with a guy, and most of the time they'd say no?" I asked.

"Exactly. At the time a lot of us were pretty naive. We knew him, knew he was harmless. We didn't really understand the problem. But we also knew he was gay, so that helped."

"And they wouldn't tell the client that, because that would have been weird and awkward, not to mention a violation of his privacy, right?"

"He'd even offered for the instructors to tell the clients on the phone, he didn't mind. But they wouldn't do it. They would try to alleviate their worries by telling the client that they would be observing the whole time. Sometimes that was enough," Shelby said.

She finished the outside of Amber's shin. She'd been able to maintain the conversation effortlessly while doing her job. I wasn't sure I'd be able to say the same.

"Okay, Jake. Your turn."

THREE

SHELBY

Yes, Jake Ford could *definitely* still get my attention.

Living, breathing Jake Ford. Older, yes. Even a little gray in the temples. He was less muscularly cut than in his soap days, but still fit. He was shorter than I pictured him to be, and that wound around my brain in an unusual way. Jake was around 5'10" and I was 5'3." I'd been used to much taller men, and I found myself imagining all the ways in which Jake and I might better...fit.

For a man who didn't mind getting dirty, it seemed he also took great pride in being clean. Perfect scruff on his face. His dark, wavy hair was cut in a way that looked perfectly tousled without much product. *Touchable.*

His style seemed effortless, but I could sense the care with which he chose his clothes, more than likely having every-thing altered to fit perfectly. Before he'd changed into his "uniform" he wore a black button-down shirt, the front tucked in, sleeves rolled halfway up his forearms. Dark gray denim pants cuffed just so, and... black brogue boots. Specifi-cally, Frye James Lug wingtip boots. I had recently fallen in love with the quirky style enough to give a pair as a gift months before. A gift that had gone unappreciated. I was happy to finally be seeing them on a man and I found it bonkers that that man was Jake Ford.

I was surprised and delighted to know that he may have been a secret sartorialist this whole time.

And he smelled *amazing*. It wasn't all leather, cedar, tobacco... the usual manly odors. It was citrusy, spicy, pleasantly musky, and undeniably sexy. But the individual notes I could not place—the combination of whatever it was had created something entirely new.

And he had *taken his shirt off*.

I told myself I wasn't going to look. I was already fangirling so hard I didn't think I'd be able to keep it together if I saw his bare chest. But *of course* I looked. And no, not quite as ripped and sculpted as he had once been, but still trim, toned abs, and beautiful pecs and shoulders that indicated regular gym visits.

And for the one second our eyes met before he put the T-shirt on, I feared I might burst into flames.

As I was showing Jake how to apply the wax, I decided it would be easier for him to learn with a full applicator stick, not one broken in half where he'd likely get more wax on his fingers than on Amber's leg. He dipped it in the pot of wax, slid off the access, and held his other hand under the stick as he brought it over to the table.

"Good. Now you're going to want to angle the applicator stick about forty-five degrees so it's a nice even application." Without thinking I put my hand over his to guide him like I've done with the other estheticians I've trained over the years. He flinched ever so slightly at my touch, and the full weight of what I was doing hit me like lightning. I didn't want to snatch my hand away and ruin the take, so I continued as if there wasn't a storm raging in my nervous system.

"What is it about being waxed by men that makes women uncomfortable? In your opinion." Jake asked.

"I don't know that it's necessarily waxing in general. Eyebrows, legs, other parts might be okay." I paused. "But now that I've said that I'm not even sure that it would be ok."

"What do you mean?"

"Well, in order to get waxed, you have to grow out your hair. Look at Amber's legs. There is a fair amount of hair, right?"

"I'd say so. Sure."

"Do you have any reaction or opinion about that?" I asked him. He was taking a long time to get the wax on the section of Amber's leg he was working on, so we had to pivot. "Why don't we go ahead and start using the strips now before the wax cures too much." I handed him a muslin strip for him to put on. "Put the strip on firmly, leaving a little lip for you to pull. And then press it onto the wax in the same direction the hair grows." He did as he was told. "Good. Now hold her ankle here like this and pull fast toward her head along the length of her leg, not straight up in the air."

I'd trained enough people—correction: women—over the years to get the point across well. Not only was this going to make this much more comfortable for Amber, but Jake would immediately look like he knew what he was doing. Even if I'd intended for this to be fun and funny when I submitted my video, I now knew that the smoother this went, the more the topic would hit home. No need for comic relief.

He pressed. He geared himself up. He pulled. He had the reaction everyone has the first time they successfully wax a body part; staring at the hair-filled strip in his hand, feeling a thrilling little shock followed by deep satisfaction looking at the smooth, hair free line he'd made. He ran his fingers softly over Amber's shin, and I was surprised at a tiny ping of jealousy.

"Hey! I did it!" He giggled. "I hope that didn't hurt too much." Amber shook her head, and I took note that she really tried hard not to jump that time. I smiled at her gratefully.

"Okay. Before all of that you were saying?" Jake asked.

I was impressed at his ability to multitask and smoothly get back on topic. He was clearly a pro.

"I asked you if you had an opinion about Amber's hairy legs. Not 'oh, she has hair because we were going to be waxing her,' but a reactionary opinion when you first looked at her." He had been concentrating on smoothing another coat of wax and he paused to look at me. Carefully considering his answer.

"Wow. That's a good question." He took another beat. "I will be completely honest. It was a thought I blew right past because I knew what we were doing here, but yes. When I first looked at her legs, I had a reaction that was probably not too favorable. You know, if I'd grown up in South America or Europe, it would be a non-issue."

"And you probably wouldn't be circumcised either."

My hand flew to my mouth as if I were trying to scoop the words out of the air and shove them back in. The shock on Jake's face was blatantly apparent. "Oh my God! I don't know why I just said that."

The silence broke in seconds with everyone erupting in laughter, including Jake, the director, and the producer. It immediately made me feel better.

"And this is why we have editing!" Dan choked. He took a deep breath. "Once everyone contains themselves, Shelby, I'd love for you to respond to Jake. Maybe this time without talking about his penis."

I looked at Jake still laughing, my face hot and likely beet red.

"Also, Jake, I'm gonna need you to take at least one step away from Shelby. You're not on a date, dude." Dan added.

Now Jake was blushing. I'd seen the show enough to know how much these two like giving each other shit, but this was on another level. And it certainly wouldn't make it onto the show.

I took several deep breaths and tried to gather myself. "That's just one of many reasons that women wouldn't want to be waxed by men. They would feel self-conscious about growing out their hair, even though it's what you are supposed to do. It's as if we want men to think we just are effortlessly hairless all the time."

"Or are women conditioned to want men to think that?" he responded.

"And you have eluded that men, at least American men, have been conditioned to want or even expect women to be hairless."

"Touché."

"But, probably, yes. Conditioned by the media, societal expectations, our mothers, etcetera." This was good stuff, and I was really impressed at his tone. He wanted to explore this so thoughtfully, saying the things I was implying so that they really came across well. At the same time, highlighting the problems with all of it. "I told you before we started that Amber did not want her bikini area waxed today, not only because she'd be on TV, but because that would mean we'd have to acknowledge that she had pubic hair in the first place."

Jake nodded without smiling, which I'm sure might have been difficult for some men. "Okay. Elephant in the room. Apart from the hair itself being an issue, what do you think is the biggest reason women wouldn't want men to wax them?" he asked.

By this time, Jake had become quite proficient at waxing straight areas, now it was time for the knee. I had Amber bend hers and I began to show him how to navigate curves. Then I moved back on topic. "Women don't just feel uncomfortable being waxed by men—and let's just jump right to bikini waxing—I would think some of them downright frightened at the thought. A woman in a vulnerable position. Undressed. Laying down. Completely exposed. And then he is going to be working on not to mention inflicting pain in this most sensitive and sexually concentrated area. He could be the kindest, most personable, most professional male esthetician ever and it still would be a hard no for the majority of women. The only man that gets a pass to have access to this area has a white lab coat and degrees on his wall proclaiming him an OB/GYN."

Jake's mouth dropped open slightly and he stared at me as if I'd just demystified the Big Bang. He shook his head and continued. "Exactly. It just wouldn't happen. Because all the thoughts would be there, right? The women would wonder about how he thought they looked, feel awkward about having any hair at all, and then go deeper and darker into why a man might want to be doing this in the first place. Like there has got to be an ulterior motive, etcetera."

"Not to mention the power play. The man is standing and fully clothed. The woman is lying on a table and mostly naked. He is controlling every aspect of the situation."

"Let me ask you a question, Shelby. Have you done Brazilian wax for men?"

I took a pause, much longer of a pause than was comfortable and I was grateful once again for editing. I began cutting more strips from the roll of muslin. This is what every esthetician does to breathe and buy time when something isn't going quite right. "Yes." I finally answered. "But I don't do them anymore. And not for the reason you're probably thinking."

"Before you tell me the reason, I'd like to know how you feel the dynamic is different from women waxing men to men waxing women."

"Well, first let me say, I've had some good experiences waxing men and some not so good experiences. Two of my regulars could not have been better to work with. One was a paramedic whose wife said she'd wax hers if he'd wax his and we talked about his daughters and normal things. He also was very good at holding his stuff."

"Wait. Holding what stuff?" Jake looked amused.

"Well, when you are waxing the scrotum, the skin is loose. You get better results, and it doesn't hurt as much if they stretch the skin while we are working."

"Oh." He smiled. "I'm picturing that, now, thanks. Go on."

I giggled a little. It was never pretty, that's for sure. And I remember being so surprised at how hard they could yank on their flaccid penis like so much skin taffy without it seeming painful at all.

"My other decent client was a nudist, and he would come in before he and his wife went to camp. He was like seventy. But then there were countless others. Like the guy who read the Playboy article that promised it wouldn't hurt and it would make his junk look bigger. Or the ones who just think it's a clever way to get a woman to touch them. Ironically, it is much easier to wax a man while they are aroused, and everything is... tighter, but obviously that comes with a host of other problems. Expectations. I will say that it was always a little sadistically satisfying to know that as excited as they may have started out, it was going to go south for them *real* fast. Once the pain hits, things...deflate." I wondered how much of this was going to make it onto the show.

"Hmm, I bet. You always felt in control of the situation?"

"Yes, and although there were the borderline creeps from time to time, I was the one standing and clothed, and they were the ones lying and naked. Also, I had a pot of hot wax I could have dumped on them at any time."

"Fair point." Jake pointed his index finger at me and grinned. "You said you don't do them anymore. How come?"

"It's a little embarrassing. It has to do with me and my skill level. I'm good at everything I do in my job, but I couldn't get good at that. Not as good as I wanted to be anyway. There was always more bleeding than I wanted, and the...topography is just so complicated. Just when you'd think you were done, boom—there's another patch of hair you missed around this corner, or under that thing."

Jake smiled, his eyes twinkling with amusement.

With the end of Amber's wax came the end of the conversation. Jake gushed and thanked me and Amber profusely as he closed out the segment. When Dan announced the cut, he looked at me and said, "That was great. You did great!"

I smiled gratefully.

Once the cameras were off, I was immediately rocked with all that my nervous system put on hold during the shoot. I had prepared, I knew the things I wanted to say, but I hadn't expected it to come out so effortlessly. I think Jake must have been a tremendously talented interviewer because it felt so comfortable, so natural, and I was able to do my job at the same time. All while trying to ignore that not only was my teenage crush standing right next to me, but also that he was respectfully considering everything I had to say. The latter was something I was not accustomed to at all.

While Jake was out in the hall talking to Rita, I found myself standing around awkwardly not knowing what was supposed to happen next. The next thing I knew, Darius was coming down the hall announcing that lunch had arrived.

While we were filming, he, Randall, and Lyric had set up a buffet table out in the reception area and had sushi and teppanyaki delivered from the Japanese place down the street. Leave it to Darius to pull the smoothest move ever and earn my eternal gratitude for the fact that my time with Jake Ford was not yet over.

The team left all their equipment to be dealt with later and sprinted toward the food. Jake seemed excited and impressed at the gesture and at the spread, especially since Darius also had a bin with ice and Japanese beer. Darius never missed an opportunity to show off his entertaining skills and we often held events at the salon—holiday parties, brand promotions, and fund-raisers for the cosmetology school. The serving equipment was always onsite (and of course, all meticulously organized.) I immediately realized how hungry I was, but I wanted everyone else to get themselves sorted first. Jake filled a plate, grabbed a beer and stationed himself standing at the front desk. I served myself a few things and made my way over to him.

"So, I used to watch you on *Sault Ste. Marie*. I was a big fan."

Jake smiled. "I'm glad you waited until after we were done to tell me that. I might have felt self-conscious otherwise."

"Why? I'm sure you have people saying that to you all the time." I was actively trying not to seem too flirtatious but failing miserably.

"Sometimes, sure. And while it's always flattering, I'm trying very hard to prove I've grown up a lot since then. Is that why you started watching this show?" The way his eyes considered me just then made my stomach do a back flip.

"Actually, it wasn't even on my radar until my son stumbled on it a few years ago. Now I feel like I've seen most of the episodes during the marathons the Encounter channel does."

"How old is your son?"

"He's nineteen. His name is Brody."

"You do *not* look old enough to have a nineteen-year-old son. And I'm sure *you* get that all the time," Jake said.

"I had him when I was twenty." I used to say I was nineteen when I got pregnant. But while the getting pregnant part was unplanned and terrifying, the day Broderick James Ristow was born was the best day of my life.

"You're married."

It was a statement, not a question. I thought I caught a nearly imperceptible hint of disappointment, but I decided it was in my head. "Yes." I reflexively touched the third finger of my left hand. "I don't wear my ring to work since I'd have to take it off so much. I...well, anyway," I trailed off. I desperately needed to change the subject. "I do find it funny that sometimes the magazines still write articles about you like you're still a teen heart throb."

"Hmm. Like what?"

"Just last month there was one of those fluffy 'twenty-five fun facts about Jake Ford' at the back of some gossip magazine," I said.

"Oh? I must have missed that one. What did it say?"

"You know, the usual. Pets, hobbies, favorite movies, music taste. Speaking of which, I wanted to ask you about that. You say most of your favorite bands are prog rock—Rush, Pink Floyd, King Crimson. Then you go way off type and say Depeche Mode is your favorite band of all time." I pause for effect. "It's because of a girl, isn't it?"

Jake had been taking a drink of his Sapporo just then and nearly did a spit take. A reflexive smile sprang to his face before he had a chance to decide how he was going to respond.

It was absolutely because of a girl.

I found myself having to fight the urge to lick the drop of beer off that full bottom lip of his, and I was grateful he beat me to it.

He touched his finger to his nose and tapped twice. "You got me there. Her name was Chloe. She was the makeup artist on *Sault Ste. Marie*. She was a couple of years older than me, and I was utterly enchanted by her whole goth style. All black all the time. Fishnets, Doc Martens. We dated for almost a year."

Thirteen-year-old me would have killed to have been this girl. And even in that moment, the way he spoke about her with such fondness, it stung a bit.

"She got me into the darker, edgier side of new wave, Depeche Mode being my favorite. And they are still making such great music. I also tend to listen to Nine Inch Nails in some of my darker moments. Another significant departure from prog rock."

It struck me that Jake's darker moments were likely spent in solitude. I pictured romantic melancholy, all somber and poetic. Much different than the kind of darker moments I was used to.

"How about you, Shelby? What kind of music do you like? I don't want to assume it's only rockabilly and electro swing."

Wait. What? "You don't strike me as someone who'd know about electro swing."

He visibly squirmed and cleared his throat. Running a crooked finger back and forth under his bottom lip, he looked down and stammered, "I... I looked it up after I watched some of your makeup tutorials."

Holy fuck. He watched my videos. It quickly dawned on me that of course the link for the submission video would take him to YouTube where it would have so helpfully shown him all the other videos featuring me along the right-hand side of the screen. I liked to play music in the background while talking through the pinup hair and makeup looks.

"But back to music." Jake diverted.

"No, it's not just rockabilly and electro swing—that's mostly to fit the vibe of my videos. I like all kinds of music. Funk, fifties and sixties Soul. Blues. I like new wave and Depeche Mode, too. Some rock, some pop. Definitely *not* prog rock."

"No?" He smiled and shrugged. "Eh, I know it's not for everyone. But like, what's your favorite band?"

"I don't know. I have music for moods, just like you do. I can't think of a band right now that I would consider my absolute favorite."

"Do you have a favorite song?'

I didn't skip a beat. "'I Can't Go for That/No Can Do' by Hall and Oates."

Jake threw his head back and laughed.

CHAPTER
FOUR

JAKE

Her answer was so *immediate*, it completely caught me off guard.

Although, if I'm being honest, pretty much everything about Shelby Ristow caught me off guard. Even before we met. It had taken every ounce of discipline and professionalism to stay in the game today, and not just get all caught up in the wonder of her.

"What?" I asked, still laughing.

"Yes," she said with a stone straight face. "Don't judge. I have a deep, abiding, and unapologetic love for that song, and I don't tend to trust people who don't appreciate its genius."

"It's a good song, I'll give you that. But it's certainly not on any of my playlists. What is it about that song that you connect with so much?" I was genuinely curious.

"It's the rhythm. It takes me back to playing on my grandmother's organ she had in her living room. You could press a button and choose a samba or bossa nova beat to be in the background as you played, and then you immediately sounded like you knew what you were doing. I loved spending time at their house. I think that's why I love the song so much."

"I totally get that." While she was explaining, a memory triggered for me too. The song was still on heavy radio rotation throughout the early eighties and in May of 1984, I remember my mother singing along to it as we drove to my little brother's last baseball game of the season. Actually, his last game, period.

I don't let myself think about that day much at all.

After lunch all the equipment was brought up to the front for us to shoot our "intro" spots outside and at the front desk. When we finished, Darius and company kept asking if we needed any help packing or loading or if we'd like coffees for the road. I couldn't help thinking that this had been one of the best days of shooting we'd had in long time, everyone was so accommodating, so likable. And they'd fed us. I knew we'd all be talking about it on the ride to Chicago, along with them giving me plenty of shit for my inappropriate proximity to Shelby.

Once the gear was all loaded into the SUVs, Rita began the goodbyes. "Shelby, do you want me to take a picture of you and Jake? Do you have your phone on you?"

Shelby looked visibly rattled. "What? Oh, I..."

Darius came out from behind the front desk where he had been making an Americano for me, phone in hand. "Here. Use mine. Shelby's camera is crap."

Shelby looked up at him and smiled gratefully, an inside thing between the two of them that I couldn't decipher. Rita took Darius's phone, and I went to stand next to Shelby. I gingerly put my arm around her shoulder. She paused, then her arm was around my waist. She was trembling a little and my heart tugged slightly out of concern for her. Rita got a shot of

Darius and me, then gathered everyone for a few group shots. I regretted not giving her my phone for another picture of Shelby and me, but how would I have explained why I'd wanted it?

"Well, I guess we're off. This has been amazing. Honestly, this has been one of the best experiences I've—" I gestured to my team, "we've ever had." I turned to Shelby. "You should be so proud of yourself."

I don't know what made me say that, and I sincerely hoped I didn't sound condescending. "You spoke so thoughtfully, so articulately. It was a serious subject, but you still managed to wrap it in something lighter, even managing to have a little fun. That's a hard balance to strike. All in all, perfect TV. If you ever need a job, let me know." I laughed a little to take the heaviness out. She looked like she was getting a little emotional.

"Thank you for saying that. It means...it means a lot." This woman who had been so confident in her videos and during the shoot was now having a hard time accepting compliments and it was making me upset. Like no amount of convincing on my part would make her believe that she had done something so amazing. At the same time, I was completely drawn to to her complexity. The juxtaposition of self-assuredness and self-doubt.

I felt compelled to open a door. "Would you want us to reach out and let you know when the episode will air? We have your email—"

"Oh! That would be great. I'll have everyone over for a watch party." She was smiling again.

The truth was, we never did this. And the look that Rita gave me was proof. She knew I'd be the one reaching out and not her, which went against the "one point of contact" rule that we had. I had no idea what I was doing anyway—she was married. I was in a relationship. I felt the need, however, to maintain this connection with her for as long as I could.

In that moment she was smiling at me with those bright eyes of hers, containing nearly every shade of blue imaginable, like swirling galaxies full of secrets I would never learn. I decided to be brave knowing this would earn me another dirty look from Rita.

"May I have a hug?"

Shelby paused and grabbed onto her left thumb with her right hand fisted, knuckles turning white. I immediately regretted the ask until she stepped forward reaching her arms around my neck. I wrapped my arms around her and splayed my fingers to cover as much surface area as possible. I tried to be as subtle as I could while I inhaled the scent of her. Then she stepped in once more, until we were fully breasts to chest, pelvis to pelvis. I had to have an emergency meeting with Cave Man—no other body part was invited to this party. I let her be the first to break contact; even then, it seemed longer than a typical friendly hug.

I extended my hand to Darius. He took it and pulled me in for a hug as well. "I'm so glad I got to see you again, Jake. We both did a lot of growing up in these years, didn't we?"

"We sure did. God, I love how small the world is sometimes. Seeing you brought back a lot of memories." I looked down at the floor. "Some regrets too."

"That's how it usually goes. But we don't need to spend too much time on those regrets. Especially when we've learned from our mistakes. They've helped make us who we are." He turned and looked at Randall with such love and admiration. I was so happy for him finding this quiet, beautiful life outside of Hollywood.

As I walked out, I turned toward the salon one last time.

Shelby was standing by the front desk but facing the door. Looking at me.

I put my hand up. One more goodbye.

We began the ride to O'Hare. The rest of the team were flying out in a few hours back to San Francisco, but I was spending the night in Chicago. The woman I had been seeing for the last seven months was hosting a fundraiser downtown and the timing with a shoot in a city so close worked out perfectly for me to be able to go.

Holly worked for Built To Sustain Inc., a large green architecture firm with offices in San Francisco and Chicago. They held fundraisers several times a year to make it possible for non-profits, low-income families, and housing projects to get extra funding for green construction. We'd met when I'd had a shoot at a company that recycles glass for high efficiency windows the same day she was there trying to finalize a new contract.

I was going to have time to check in to my hotel, shower and make sure my suit was presentable with no major wrinkling before meeting her at the event. I was staying at Swissotel which was always my choice when in Chicago. It was not too big, but modern and a little bit quirky. A great location, too. I liked to walk around in cities and explore, finding used bookshops, little art galleries, cafes and dive bars no-one but the locals know about. I wouldn't have time to do this on this trip, Holly and I were heading back to San Francisco the next day early in the afternoon, but I'd have time to go to my favorite cafe in the morning, at least.

I finally got myself settled in my room and decided I had time for a disco nap. I figured I'd be up late and the last thing I'd want to happen would be to crash and burn when Holly needed me the most. I set a timer on my phone, pulled the duvet cover down, and took off my clothes.

No sooner had my head hit the pillow when a picture of a cartoon face with creamy skin, red lipstick and bright blue eyes floated in front and center. The rest of her body came into view, and she turned to walk away from me, beckoning me to follow her. We walked into the room in the salon where we filmed, and she sat on the table. She grabbed my hand, "Jake. I want you," she said. I held her face firmly in my hands and kissed her. She clawed at my back and pulled me to her. Just as things were getting more interesting, my timer went off. I woke up rock hard and bound out of bed to take care of the little problem in the shower. Picturing Shelby the whole time.

I made myself presentable and drove to The School House, an event space about fifteen minutes away. Traffic was on my side, and it was only five o'clock when I walked in. Guest arrival wasn't to begin until five thirty, and I anticipated Holly would be getting stressed with last minute details. I was more than happy to provide a friendly face and moral support.

My mouth dropped when I walked in the room. It was like a wonderland—a starry night theme, everything glowing purple and twinkle lights everywhere. Lavender, black, white, and gray flower arrangements as big as I was, elegant place settings, calligraphy name cards. Anything and everything that people with all the money love to see at these things. Holly was originally from a wealthy Chicago suburb, and she was able to enlist her parents' social connections to pad the guest list.

I spotted her across the room. She gave me a bright, beaming smile and that's when I first noticed the shift.

By then I'd come to know how she was at go time, flitting around like a madwoman, a million last minute list items to be double and triple checked. Nervously smoothing her dress or second guessing her wardrobe choice altogether, finding a mirror every few minutes to check for lipstick on her teeth or a hair out of place.

But this. This was an entirely different Holly. She was breezy and relaxed. Smiles that came easy and naturally as she looked through the menus on each of the place settings while speaking to the head cater waiter. One of her assistants came rushing up to her and whispered something in her ear. I thought *this is it. This is where it all falls apart.* She merely spoke two sentences of instruction. The assistant satisfied, rushed off.

"Hi! You made it."

"Hi! Wow, Hol. This looks phenomenal." I kissed her on the cheek. "I got here early to see if I could help, but it looks like you have everything under control. And you look absolutely stunning." She was wearing a metallic pewter silk dress with a halter top slit down to the waist. Holly and I were the same height barefoot, she now in five-inch heels towered over me, but I didn't mind one bit. Her honey blond hair was pinned up on one side with soft waves down her back.

"It really came together well. I think having a few of these under my belt now is finally paying off. It doesn't make sense to sweat the details that guests wouldn't notice anyway."

WHEN WE HAD LITERALLY BUMPED INTO EACH OTHER THAT FIRST DAY at the glass recycling company, she had her portfolio in her arms with paperwork spilling out onto the floor. Her outfit was rumpled, and she was more than a little flustered. Her meeting had not gone well, and she looked as though she was about to cry.

She didn't know me from my soap days, but she recognized me from *Dare Me to Do It,* her dad's favorite show. She was a beautiful mess, and I couldn't help but think of all the ways I wanted to try and help her. I asked her on the spot if she'd like to have dinner with me, and she stared at me for nearly a full minute as if I were speaking a different language.

What I would learn over the next few weeks was that she was thirty-five and the youngest of four daughters, her older sisters far ahead of her in all things career and family. Things that came easily to them throughout their lives had been elusive to her, but that didn't stop the unceasing pressure from her parents. She'd spent her whole life trying to play catch up and measure up and it never seemed to be enough.

But I loved taking care of her.

We took classes together in things that sparked her interest, and she learned she could excel at things if she was passionate enough.

I was enamored with the way she looked and with her body, encouraging her to feel the same way. Over the next few months, I could see her beginning to feel better in her skin. This new-found confidence in herself began to spill over into her career, too. She was more assertive with vendors and contractors, more communicative with clients, and her bosses began to take notice. She got a promotion and was given the responsibility of organizing the fundraisers.

THAT NIGHT, ALL OF IT CULMINATED IN A POISED, BEAUTIFULLY radiant, successful woman running a high-profile event like it was a Saturday afternoon errand.

I used to have to rescue the conversation if she felt awkward, but I clearly didn't need to stand by her side this time. Once guests started arriving, I wandered around with my cocktail in hand. I was still representing her, so I put on an affable grin as if I was just content as all get out to be there. It usually wouldn't take long for someone to recognize me and strike up a conversation. I never wanted it to be all about me all the time, so I'd redirect and let people tell me about themselves. For the most part, these people were all pretty much the same, more than happy to talk about their high profile, high earning jobs, their kids at Ivy League schools, or their lavish trips to Europe.

But every now and then, I'd get a snapshot into an interesting life—an innovative start up business, or someone giving up soul sucking corporate law to pursue human rights pro bono work. It was like spending hours at the beach with a metal detector and finally finding treasure.

The evening was a smashing success. I always loved the spectacle of the live auction, where they manufacture so much drama. 'We have to beat what we raised last year so let's up the ante here, people!' Last minute "unbelievable" opportunities, whipping everyone into a wild, money flinging frenzy.

Holly was responsible for speaking at the beginning and the end of the auction and she was articulate, funny, and effortlessly charming. I would love to be able to say I was entranced, but I was coming up short.

She didn't need me anymore and it was taking the wind out of my sails.

When most of the guests had gone, Holly made sure everything would be taken care of in her absence and we headed out to the car. I was in my head, and I hoped I wouldn't kill her post event high with my newfound melancholy. I knew she was expecting me to fuck the living daylights out of her in celebration of a successful night. She'd let herself have a few drinks after her speaking responsibilities were over, and she was getting handsy with me. I wanted to make her night complete, I wanted to give her that, but I felt so very distracted and disjointed. My day had been an absolute whirlwind, and I was exhausted.

I thought maybe once we got to the hotel, and I settled into the familiarity of her I would be okay.

I started the car, making my way out of the parking structure to head back to the hotel. The SUV's radio was tuned to some contemporary hit station and an overplayed Train song came on. I watched out of the corner of my eye as Holly, registering that she didn't like the song, reached toward the radio to change it but didn't know quite how it worked in the unfamiliar car. The hey-ey's rang out followed by lyrics bemoaning lipstick stains on left side brains.

Thoughts of Shelby flooded my mind. Her face. Her eyes. I tried to push them away. I had to focus on Holly. *Just get through tonight.*

She finally managed to change the station. A familiar rhythmic thumping. A samba/bossa nova beat and Darryl Hall's voice filled the car.

Fuck. Me.

I can't go for that either, Darryl.

I'd never been a person who believed in fate or what the "universe was trying to tell me," but, until now, I'd never liked the message quite as much.

CHAPTER
FIVE
SHELBY

I stood in the lobby staring out the door until I saw both SUVs pull away. Frozen in some kind of trance asking myself over and over if that really had just happened. Had I just spent several hours with Jake Ford where for much of the time I was channeling some confident woman well versed on feminist issues surrounding beauty? Was I charming? Was I *flirting?* From somewhere inside, my adolescent-self had poked at me to make the most of this opportunity and so I did. I was grateful too, no regrets. Well, maybe one. But that would be something to worry about another day months from now, and between now and then I was sure I could figure out what to do about it.

I helped Darius and Randall clean up lunch, then went about getting the treatment room cleaned up after the shoot. I threw away the paper from the table, put the strips, gloves and other supplies back into the cabinets, and sanitized my tweezers. I was taking my time, lingering on implements that all now contained other memories besides ones with clients. I knew it would be a while before I wouldn't immediately be reminded of Jake Ford during every leg waxing appointment.

I never worked on Fridays, and I was grateful that I didn't have to switch gears and try to be professional. But despite having the day off, I wasn't in a hurry to go home. I rarely was since Brody had gone to college. He used to be the reason I'd rush home, but now I often felt more at home when I was at work.

WHEN I GOT PREGNANT WITH BRODY, I FINISHED MY SECOND semester of college, morning sickness and all, but since he was due in July, it didn't make sense to register for my junior year. I never went back.

It was decided it was better for me to be a stay-at-home mom. But both grandmothers adored Brody and either hovered over him at our place or played tug of war to have him at theirs.

When he was around eight and I'd been spending his school days wandering around the house not sure what to do with myself, I got it in my head that I wanted to go back to school. I knew it wouldn't be a hard sell with the grandparents, they would be more than happy to watch Brody whenever I'd need.

The hard part would be convincing Ari. He worked so much that he liked the idea of having me home to "man the fort." I thought going back for my English degree would be a stretch, so I decided to follow in my Aunt Connie's footsteps and learn massage therapy. I'd always looked up to her, especially since she was the comically polar opposite to her sister, my mother. She was a modern-day hippie, a living, breathing flight of fancy. When she'd first gotten into massage, she'd brought over one of her books to show us. It was published in the early seventies and in the illustrations demonstrating the techniques everyone was naked—both the therapist and the client. I'd giggled at how red my mother's face had gotten.

Ari bristled at the idea at first, but once I started school and he became my practice guinea pig, he softened a little. Aspire was the first place I'd applied, and Ari liked the idea that I'd be working for gay men and with a bunch of women. Darius desperately needed another esthetician, so within my first year, he encouraged me to go through the training and get dual licensed.

"Hey, Shel. Why don't you head home and relax. We've got this." Darius pulled me out of my trance, standing and staring at nothing at the front desk. The afternoon clients were beginning to file in.

"Oh, yeah. I've got to go home and make sure the kitchen is all set for Ari. He's making my favorite seafood chowder tonight to celebrate."

"Is that right?" Darius seemed surprised, but then smiled. "That's sweet. How much are you going to tell him about how today went?"

"I haven't decided yet." I blushed. As far as Ari knew, it was just one of Brody's favorite shows and Darius had coerced me into doing this whole thing. He had certainly not seen the audition video or knew about Jake Ford's face on my bedroom wall.

He had given me some pointers for being on TV since he was a bit of a local celebrity. All the local news outlets loved him for their 'must do' spots or cooking demos. He oozed charm and he was still so very easy on the eyes. When it was a woman interviewing him, she'd often be visibly flustered.

"Don't say absolutely all the time," he'd told me. "Look at the camera here and there to engage the audience, but don't talk directly into it. Try not to fidget or say 'um.'"

He had no idea how much camera experience I already had. But my videos were all about talking directly into the camera. And it wasn't being on TV that I was worried about. It was more about keeping my cool with the host of the show.

I decided to stop at the store on the way home to buy some fresh flowers. While passing through the bakery section, I spotted a beautiful loaf of fresh sourdough. Sourdough was part of the deal with Ari's seafood chowder, so I thought *I should buy it.*

But if I bring it home and Ari had already bought it, he'd wonder why I bothered. Why I wouldn't I have trusted that he would have gotten it? He knew full well how much it was an important part of the meal.

But if I didn't get it, and he'd forgotten it, he'd be upset with himself. Maybe even to the point that the whole thing would be ruined. And find a way to blame me for it all.

I stood in the bakery section having a familiar internal debate. It certainly wasn't always about bread, but so often I'd spend time trying to see things from every angle, trying to find the best solution. Unfortunately, I'd been terrible at geometry.

I looked down and realized I was cutting off the circulation in my left thumb. I decided to buy the bread and put it in the pantry. *This way if Ari brought his own loaf home, I could use this one another time. And if he'd forgotten it, I could just "coincidentally" have had this loaf I'd bought for sandwiches.*

I walked into the house and put the bread in the pantry. I grabbed a vase and set the flowers on the kitchen counter. I sighed as I looked around. I rarely called it *my* house. It felt more like somewhere I was staying rather than a home to me, even after more than seventeen years.

ARI'S PARENTS HAD HELPED US BUY A HOUSE ONE SUBDIVISION OVER from theirs in an affluent suburb about thirty minutes west of Milwaukee. His mother Marion had overseen a remodel and took it upon herself to decorate as well. Ari never had much of an opinion himself, although he was very particular about how the kitchen would be set up after he'd finished his culinary training.

And it was determined by everyone that I was too young to know what I liked.

I'm convinced that if hell exists it wouldn't be fire sprays and molten pools. It would be a square box painted beige, furnished in beachy pastels, and decorated with framed calligraphy cursive instructions for life.

Although, sure, maybe in hell they'd say "Suffer. Cry. Beg." instead of "Live. Laugh. Love."

I learned quickly that anything new I brought into the house was a personal affront to Marion and she'd make her hurt feelings known to anyone and everyone who would listen. After a while, it just wasn't worth it.

The two things I had been successful at bringing into the house without much fuss were plants and books. I'd created cozy little garden library vignettes all over the house—places where I felt comfortable and safe. I'd also found a beautiful vintage vanity at a flea market. I'd lied and said I'd inherited it from my Great Aunt Marjorie (who had not died nor had she, in fact, existed at all). Marion looked down her nose at it, suggesting a "coat of paint, at least." But in the end I won, and there she sat in her original, albeit slightly scuffed, glory in my bedroom.

And in the bottom right-hand drawer under some silk scarves lived a small laptop, a DSLR camera, a tripod and a ring light. The secret world of Cherrie Bombshell.

It was nearly 2:30 p.m. and I decided to text Ari. I figured he'd probably gone into work for a while on his day off too, considering I was busy all morning. He was very involved with everything to do with his restaurant, not just back of the house. He oversaw all the hiring of the staff, the wine and spirit list, and the schedule. The only thing he left solely to his managers were the books.

He'd leaned into his name from the very beginning, deciding to do his culinary training in Athens at the Chef D' Oeurve to learn from the best while at the same time learning all he could about Mediterranean food. He left to spend two full years there right after our wedding, his little son only a year old. He didn't want to upset his immersive experience and after the first few months, he refused to come home for visits, wanting me to go there instead. The first time was magical, like a movie honeymoon. He was so excited to show me everything, so enthusiastic, so alive and bursting with passion. He took me to Santorini and the sunset made me cry.

When I'd gone the second time, he'd become so bonded with his fellow students, so deeply immersed in the program, the culture and in "his process," he'd leave me at his little apartment or to wander around on my own for hours and hours every day. I never went back.

> Hi! The shoot went great today. I'm home already. What time do you think you'd be here?

I DECIDED TO POUR MYSELF A GLASS OF WINE AND CALL KENDRA. She'd been texting me all day, and I kept pushing her off, wanting to wait until I had time and space to give her the full rundown. She was the only person with whom I could share every delicious detail.

"Soooooo?"

"Oh my God, Ken. It was amazing. I don't even know where to start."

"Start at the beginning. How did he look?"

I took a deep breath and let out a moan.

"That good, huh?"

I spilled the entire contents of the morning in as much detail as I could remember, finding myself shaking with excitement all over again at the retelling.

"Jake Ford watched your videos? Like, all of them?"

"He didn't say specifically, but definitely videos, plural."

"Holy shit, Shel. It sounds like he is into you."

"What? No. That's crazy."

"Why is that crazy? You are super hot, and those videos are awesome. Plus, it sounds like you held your own during the interview. It definitely seems like your little crush has a crush."

I could feel myself blushing. Kendra was right about half of it; I had a full-on married woman crush. I would never act on it, and I knew the feeling would pass. But for the time being it was odd, like a puzzle piece whose edges have been altered—I was having a little bit of a hard time fitting into my life.

I heard the back door open. "Hey, I think Ari's home. I gotta go."

"Okay, you saucy harlot. Love you."

I smiled. "Love you, too."

I walked into the kitchen and my heart swelled at seeing my beautiful baby boy. "Hey! What are you doing home?" I asked. Brody told me he most likely wouldn't be coming home during finals, even though he was only thirty minutes away at Marquette.

"I wanted to come and hug you. I know today was a big deal."

My heart exploded. I don't know what I did in a previous life to deserve a son as sweet as this, and I tried never to take it for granted. "Aww, thanks baby. That means a lot."

He wrapped me up in his arms and it was always so surreal to have him envelope me. He wasn't quite as tall as his father, but still towered above me.

"How did it go?"

"It was great! I can't wait for you to see it."

"Do you know when it will be on?" Brody asked.

"They said they'd let me know." I didn't tell him Jake said *he'd* let me know.

"Do you mind if I do a little laundry? I have a date this weekend and I want to wash my sheets."

"No problem." Over the course of Brody's life, we'd had open communication about sex. At least on my end. It was important for me to share everything I wish I had known growing up, bypassing all the shame I'd had to deal with. He was always pretty tight lipped about who he was sleeping with, however, and I never felt it necessary to pry.

My phone dinged.

I've got a chance to meet with that investor
tonight. Last minute thing. I'll be home late.

I felt a pang of disappointment. Nothing about the TV thing or the chowder. But the lack of an apology was not surprising, I know he'd been trying to get this meeting for months. Ari's father David had put up the money for Ari's original restaurant and then twice for second locations that he wanted to open. The first one was a pretty risky concept based on Greek Mythology, dancing on the edge of kitsch. It lasted less than eighteen months. With the second, he thought, 'if it ain't broke...' and just recreated his original restaurant further west in the suburbs. It lasted a year. David refused to fund any more experiments and just suggested expanding his current place instead. Ari didn't do well with the word no, so he'd been looking for investors on his own.

Brody wandered back into the kitchen. "Dad won't be home. He's got a last-minute meeting," I told him.

He rolled his eyes and sighed. "I'm sorry, Mom." He rubbed my back. I hated that he'd felt the need to apologize for his father. And that he'd been doing it often and from a young age.

"It's okay. I'm just so happy you're here. Are you hungry?" I asked him.

"Always."

I pulled out the sourdough bread from the pantry and went to grab the rest of the ingredients intending to make Caprese paninis with mozzarella, tomato, basil and a little balsamic vinegar. Brody snuck past me to rifle through the fridge. "Do we have roast beef and provolone? I think I just want a straight up sandwich."

I pulled out some deli turkey. "This okay?"

"Yeah. Where's the mayo?"

"You mean *may-o-naise*?"

Brody smiled and stood back. He hunched up his shoulders and squinted his eyes shut. "I got nowhere else to go!" Heaving dramatic breaths. "I got nowhere else to go!" Perfectly imitating Richard Gere's character Zack Mayo in *Officer and a Gentleman* having a meltdown in the rain. I laughed.

For years I'd been into rewatching all the tearjerker movies from the eighties and nineties like *Terms of Endearment*, *Steel Magnolias*, and *Beaches*. I appreciated the opportunity to cry without abandon. Without anyone asking why. Often, Brody would snuggle up next to me and watch too. It had since become our thing, quoting lines to each other whenever possible. Ari would roll his eyes at us or miss the joke completely and get annoyed, so it was always more fun when it was just the two of us.

Hours later I was settled on the couch watching a cozy British baking show on TV. I thought it was funny that I now knew what it might have been like behind the scenes of a show like that. I wondered what our spot would end up looking like after the editing.

I heard the back door. Ari had arrived, along with a familiar mix of excitement and dread. If the meeting had not gone well, the high that I'd been on most of the day would surely be over. I steeled myself and walked into the kitchen.

"Hey," I said. I wanted to be supportive, excited for Ari. But at the same time, I needed him to know how disappointed I was that he hadn't considered or even remembered the events of my day and what it had meant to me.

"Hey!" He was smiling and holding a bottle of champagne. The meeting had gone well. "Alan is going to talk to his partners, but he's very interested. If it all goes well, we could have the money by mid-summer." He walked over to me and gave me a closed mouth kiss with an exaggerated sound, "Mmmuah."

"That's great." I was trying, but I could tell my tone fell flat.

Ari could tell, too. "What's up? I thought you'd be thrilled."

And I thought you were making me seafood chowder because I filmed a fucking TV show today. "I'm just tired, I guess. I am happy for you."

Brody walked through the kitchen on his way to flip the laundry. "Hey Dad."

"Hey, Brods. How's it going?' Ari tousled his son's hair, but Brody shrugged him off.

"Did you forget that Mom had her TV thing today? She said it went great and she's really excited about it."

"Oh, shit, Shel. Yeah, I forgot." Ari had a split second of managing to arrange his face in an expression of remorse, but it quickly, reflexively turned to a smirk when he said, "Oh, I bet you were nervous. Were you so nervous, baby?" He reached out to pet my hair, but the look I gave him made him reconsider and he withdrew his arm. "Oh. You're mad at me, huh?"

"She should be." Brody interjected. "Acknowledging it at all would be the least you could have done today." I looked at him with tight lips and shook my head; our unspoken *don't poke the bear*. He glared at his father one last time and came over to me to kiss me on the cheek. "I'm going to bed. I'll probably be gone before you wake up, so I'll say goodbye now. I love you, Mom. I'm so proud of you."

"I love you too, baby." And with that, Brody went upstairs.

"Do you still love me too?" Ari walked over to me, he put his hands on my shoulders and kissed my neck. A jolt of electricity shot through my spine. The attempt at smoothing things over was about to begin. I sat on a stool at the island while I watched him pull two champagne flutes out of the cabinet.

"Yes." I was still glaring, but my tone was softening.

"Good." He popped the bottle with a loud flourish and poured us each a glass. Picking his up, he said, "A toast! To me finally getting my funding, and to you for...doing a cool TV thing."

I picked up my glass too. I guessed that was as good as I was going to get. "To us."

Ari took a sip and put down his glass. "Aww, baby. I can tell you're still upset." He walked over behind me and moved my hair away from my neck. He pressed his lips on the sensitive spot where my neck met my shoulder and trailed a row of kisses up my neck and behind my ear. My heart rate increased, the beat itself intensifying. His fingertips grazed along the front of my chest, teasing over my breasts, my nipples. I closed my eyes and leaned my head back into Ari's chest.

His hand made its way down my stomach, inching ever further south.

There was no hesitation, spreading my legs for him had become as automatic as breathing.

Ari moaned his approval.

That voice. The heat and the familiar smell of him. The way he knew every centimeter of my body and exactly what it needed and when, all combined to elicit this response that was almost completely out of my control. My mind could be annoyed, irritated, or even enraged with him. My heart could feel betrayed and abandoned. My soul crushed. My spirit broken. But my body? That traitorous bitch would always, always surrender.

He moved his hand from between my legs and grabbed me tighter, one arm across my chest, the other splayed across my neck and throat, his mouth at my ear. "You're so ready for me, baby. I am going to fuck you right here in the kitchen."

"But Brody..."

"If he comes downstairs, it's on him."

"Just hang on one second." Ari let me go and I grabbed my phone to text Brody saying we were arguing. That it was best not to come downstairs.

Ari lifted me up off the stool, his long fingers quickly unbuttoning and unzipping my pants. He lifted my shirt off, his hungry mouth on the tops of my breasts exposed above my bra. He pulled off my pants and underwear and lifted me onto the island. He knelt, his face diving in between my legs tongue first. I arched my back and stifled a scream.

While his head was lowered and his face out of my direct line of sight, I took note of the dark wavy hair and indulged in a moment of picturing Jake Ford in Ari's place. I began to grind into his mouth and had to bite my lip to keep quiet as the first wave of orgasm crested. I convulsed so violently I thought I might bruise my tailbone on the marble countertop.

Ari stood and I was immediately yanked out of my fantasy. "Am I forgiven yet?" He kissed me sloppily, serving me a taste of his version of an apology.

"We're getting there." I began to unfasten his pants.

"Oh, we're getting there are we? I know you." He aggressively fisted my hair with one hand while he cupped between my legs with the other, the pressure of both becoming increasingly rough and possessive. "I know you've got at least one more in the chamber don't you, baby? This next one won't come so easily."

For a minute, he'd allowed me to believe I was in control. And that he was making amends. But the tables had turned, and Ari's favorite game had begun.

In no time at all, I would be reciting my mantra for mercy, "Please. Ari... please."

He still loved to hear me beg.

CHAPTER
SIX
JAKE

July 2012

Six weeks after spending the morning at Aspire, filming had wrapped for the season, and I was sitting in the editing bay in our offices in San Francisco with Rita and our head editor, Jay. We never used to involve ourselves much with post-production unless we had to, leaving it solely up to Jay and his team, but ever since we shifted the tone of the show to be something a little deeper than just getting dirty, it became important for us to make sure nothing gets lost or misinterpreted. Luckily Jay has never taken it personally—we were just consulting after all, not telling him how to do his job. It did mean that the show had become pretty much a year-round gig for me. As soon as post was done, I'd start combing submission emails and videos and vetting the people and locations for next season, starting the whole process all over again.

Changing the show was something Rita and I went to bat

for two years ago. She was one of the assistant producers at the time, but she and I had a lot in common. We were both children of immigrants and we would often have these deep conversations about life in this country as first- generation Americans.

Sometimes we'd film these moments of magic when someone would talk about the difficult "family" part of a family business, or the effects of burnout during long shifts to the point of tears, only to have them edited out. The executive producer at the time thought they were too heavy. That America didn't want too much real in their reality shows.

Rita and I went to the network with the new pitch and to show them that we were serious, I had to be ready to walk. I don't think they liked the idea as much as they liked me, but at least they were willing to give it a try. We'd all been a little nervous about losing sponsorship and were right to be—a good number of the companies selling things like pickup trucks and workwear to more conservative consumers bailed immediately. They argued that no one wanted "bullshit human interest stories" or systemic societal problems "shoved in people's faces as part of a political agenda." But other, more inclusive companies were more than happy to take their place. After a few months and a scary little dip in viewership as our audience changed, we found our groove. The show resonated, and for the first time we were getting positive reviews from critics as well. The network was thrilled.

With work being so consuming, I didn't have to think too much about my personal life. Or lack thereof. I'd ended things with Holly a few days after the fundraiser in Chicago. It didn't have as much to do with my little crush on a certain pretty pinup as it was Holly herself no longer needing me as much. She'd been hurt and confused, but not nearly as much as she would have been a few months before. Before I helped her turn her light on. I'd been able to convince her that she'd outgrown me. That there would be someone else out there more deserving of her love, and that she deserved to have someone who could give her more time and attention than I could. This was my standard breakup conversation—framing it in such a way that for them to argue against it would be to argue against how amazing they were.

TODAY WE WERE WORKING ON THE EPISODE WHERE I EXPLORED JOBS men don't often do. The episode with Shelby. I had been both looking forward to this round of edits and dreading it at the same time. I'd gone on a bit of a Cherrie Bombshell video bender for a while after I'd met her, but I ultimately decided it was best just to let it all go and try to move past my crush. She was married, and I was pretty sure I'd imagined any interest or flirtation on her part.

"We'll start with the waxing spot." Jay said, and Rita agreed that we should start with the segment that would start the show and move on from there. The interview with Shelby was certainly on the serious side, but the other two segments we filmed as part of the same episode were much heavier, the last one being the most emotional piece I'd ever done. We needed to set the tone and take the viewers on this journey.

I thought I had prepared myself for seeing Shelby again, but when he started rolling the film and there she was, I felt a tingle of electricity along my spine. Especially at seeing myself right next to her.

"And you probably wouldn't be circumcised either." Jay nearly spat out his coffee when Shelby blurted her line on the screen.

"Oh, man. I wish we could leave that in. Fucking gold," he said.

I shook my head at him even though I was laughing a little. I half thought about asking him to make a gag reel. Just for me.

"Jesus Christ, Jake," Jay said, "How long are you blushing after this? Even if we edit this line and the laughing, you still look flustered. The viewers will sense something happened that they missed."

Dan's warning for me to step back from Shelby because "we weren't on a date" came right on the heels of the circumcision comment, and I knew it was probably going to be a while before I'd be looking normal on the screen.

Watching the footage, I saw how much I had been glancing at Shelby throughout the whole thing. Staring at her more than watching what she was doing, even as she was trying to teach me. A knot was forming in my stomach as I worried maybe I'd ruined the whole segment with my puppy dog eyes. We pressed on.

Rita sighed and rubbed her forehead "We are just going to have to roll with the chemistry. Clearly, it's going to be unavoidable, I just hope it won't taint the piece too much. Agh, Jake! I wish we'd had you play devil's advocate a little more. She'd have sparred with you, and that would have made it even better. Probably would have diffused a lot of the tension, too."

"Tension?" I sat forward in my chair. "What do you mean?"

"The sexual tension?" she challenged. "I mean, I was there, and I saw it in person, but I didn't think it would translate this much on film. God, I hope we can pull this off."

"Let me watch through the whole thing a couple of times," offered Jay. Why don't you guys go to lunch, and I'll try to figure this out."

I raked my hands through my hair. I'd had moments of unprofessionalism before when someone would start making casually sexist or racist comments to me during filming. Because I was a man and because I could pass for white, they assumed I thought like they did. Even though the comments would be edited out, I could still see myself seething under the surface throughout the rest of the piece. Once, we had to scrap the entire thing and do a montage throwback episode to fill the gap.

I had chemistry with people too. Really delightful people who were pure joy to be around. Once, while reviewing the footage of a spunky and sweet eighty-year-old woman who planted surprise gardens in lower income neighborhoods in the middle of the night while wearing a headlamp, I'd watched myself light up like a Christmas tree on screen.

But never had the chemistry led to unprofessionalism. I felt awful.

"I blame myself too," Rita said at lunch." I should have been paying closer attention. I should have taken you aside and told you what I was noticing during filming."

Rita and I had gotten close over the years, and I decided it was best to just be honest. "I don't know that it would have made a difference. I can't remember a time when someone got under my skin like Shelby had. I just had a day of being human, I guess."

"Well, hopefully Jay can make it work. I'd hate to have to cut the whole thing, but we could probably make it a two-segment episode if we absolutely had to."

The thought of that made me feel sick. Not just because I wanted to bring these issues to light, but also how could I possibly tell Shelby that her segment wouldn't air because I couldn't control myself around her?

We got back to the editing bay and Jay was smiling. "I

think I did it. Thank God you filmed with two cameras. I just edited for close ups and focused a little more on Shelby. Now it just plays like she's got the crush."

"What?" I furrowed my brow and stared at him.

"Yeah. Here, watch."

He started rolling the edited footage and that's when I noticed Shelby had been sneaking glances at me too. Angling her body to face mine, smiling discreet little smiles that seemed to be just for herself. Wiping her hands on her pants. Balling up her fists. Fidgeting. Blushing.

After I recovered from the shock of this revelation, I said, "No. Absolutely not. She's married with a kid for Christ's sake. And even if you're not seeing it as attraction toward me, it reads as nervous and undermines everything she says. I'd rather scrap the whole thing than embarrass her like this."

"I'll play around with it some more and see what I can do. I don't think we need to give up on it just yet. But for now, let's move on," Jay said.

The rest of the episode proved much easier to navigate. I found my eyes getting teary all over again when we got to the end of the last segment, just like I had when we were filming. I sensed that this was going to prove to be our best episode yet, and although Rita and I never said it out loud, I think we both thought that for the first time we might have had an Emmy contender.

I'd have been gutted if that happened without Darius and Shelby.

Thankfully, Jay was an editing genius. He managed to make the piece sing, despite my moon eyes and Shelby's fidgeting; the chemistry between us lending itself to the subject matter in a way I hadn't expected.

At 7:30 p.m., I dragged myself out of the offices. I thought about stopping off at my favorite market and buying things to make myself dinner. I liked to cook. It was usually very meditative for me, but cooking for one that night would likely have had me sliding into a loneliness funk. Instead, I stopped at my favorite Thai restaurant and ordered takeout, grabbing a beer at the bar while I waited.

When I walked in my house, I was greeted by a giant ball of fluff named Lunchbox, his wagging tail reminding me I'd agreed to dog sit for my upstairs tenants for the weekend. He was essentially the house dog, coming downstairs to visit me even when they were home. I squatted to give him some love, burying my face in his fur. That night I was very grateful to have the company.

Even though I hadn't cooked, I set a place at the dining room table. I like ritual and I'd been trying to eat mindfully lately, not just shovel food in my mouth as I watch something on TV or look at my phone. Eating this meal mindfully, however, just meant my mind was full of Shelby Ristow.

I cleaned up after my dinner, pouring the last of a bottle of wine into my glass as I sat down in front of my laptop. All evening I'd been flashing back to the footage that Jay had edited to highlight Shelby's fidgeting and nervousness. I thought about the little hitches in her demeanor while we were eating lunch, too. I managed to convince myself—the wine helping significantly—that she was feeling the same things that I was, and what I was about to do was well worth the risk.

Along with edits, we had been arranging the season's episode air dates with the network so I had a rough idea of when Shelby's episode would air. I had promised her I would let her know, after all. I pulled up her submission video email that Rita had forwarded me and copied her address: cherriebombshell@yahoo.com.

. . .

Hɪ Sʜᴇʟʙʏ,

We just finished the first round of edits for our episode and it's shaping up really well. Rita and I agree it will probably be one of our best and I'm so excited for you to see it. It looks like it will air on December 12th, but if that changes, I will let you know.

I want to say something here, and I may be way off base, but I felt like there may have been something going on between us that day. Watching the footage made me wonder too. I know you're married, and the last thing I'd want to do is overstep, but I also don't want to miss out on something either. You said you were a fan of mine once upon a time—well, I've become a fan of yours. You are a spectacular woman, and I haven't been able to get you out of my mind since we met.

If there's anything here, let's talk. Otherwise, I'd completely understand if you tell me to fuck off, or don't respond at all.

Waiting in the wings,

Jake

Iɴ ᴍʏ ᴅᴇꜰᴇɴsᴇ, ɪᴛ ᴡᴀsɴ'ᴛ ʟɪᴋᴇ I ᴡᴀs ᴘᴜᴛᴛɪɴɢ ᴀ ᴡᴏʀᴋɪɴɢ relationship or even a friendship in jeopardy. In fact, it was likely I'd never see her again. I drained my glass and hit send.

A few days later when I checked my inbox, I saw a new email from k.a.cooper@gmail.com. The subject line read: Regarding Shelby

Hɪ Jᴀᴋᴇ,

My name is Kendra and I'm a friend of Shelby's. I am helping her out with catching up on some emails and I saw yours. I will relay the first part of your message to her about the show, thank you.

As for the second part, well… that's complicated. I'll tell her about it at some point, but for now I will have to delete your email. Two weeks ago, Shelby's husband was killed in a car accident.

Regards,

Kendra

CHAPTER
SEVEN

SHELBY

December 2012

THE LOW, CONSTANT BUZZ OF THE TATTOO GUN WAS BEGINNING TO PUT me in a trance. Heather was three quarters of the way through my latest body art piece, and I was on the cusp of tattoo fatigue—that place where you feel somehow equal parts light-headed and murderous.

"Do you need a break, Shelby?"

Part of me wanted to power through and just get it over with, but I figured ten minutes wouldn't hurt. I could get up and move around, try to find my Zen, and reward myself with my favorite tattoo survival item, an ice-cold Orange Crush. I didn't drink soda much, and if I did, it was usually diet. But something about the sugar and nostalgia made everything right with the world when I'd be near my breaking point.

And speaking of breaking point...

Six months before, to the day, at 11:46 p.m. a doctor from Froedtert Hospital called to tell me that Ari had been in a car accident and had been brought in by Flight for Life. That I needed to come to the hospital as soon as possible. That I needed to call family. I called Ari's sister Andrea and asked if she'd be able to pick up Brody since she lived downtown near his school. I didn't want him driving knowing he'd be worried (likely more so about me and my mental state than the state of his father). I called Ari's parents and asked them to meet me at the hospital. Thinking back, I should have asked David to pick me up, but I needed some time alone to begin to process what was happening. I was on autopilot, driving in a haze. If you'd ask me to describe how I got to the hospital that night, I wouldn't be able to tell you.

Once I got to the emergency room, I was intercepted by a deputy sheriff. He told me the best they could determine from witnesses was that Ari was passing a car on the left of a two-lane highway too close to a hill. He didn't see the oncoming car until it was too late to cross back over to his lane. He veered off the road on the left side to avoid the head on collision, lost control and flipped the car several times.

None of this came as a surprise to me. Ari had always been a reckless driver. The floor mat beneath the passenger seat in his car had been worn where I would try to slam on an imaginary brake. The handle on the door practically had grooves where my fingers would dig in during high-speed turns.

Once Brody, Andrea, Ari's parents, and his brother Dave arrived at the hospital, the doctor called us into a private room. He explained that they'd managed to revive Ari twice in the helicopter, but they hadn't been able to get any vitals on him since he'd been admitted. He was on life support, and it wasn't looking good. We all went into the room to see him, hooked up to a myriad of machines, beeping and breathing, tubes and cords attached to every visible body part. A gash bifurcating his left eyebrow was held together with three small butterfly bandages, and a large swath of mottled purple bloomed from his hairline to his cheek. He looked so helpless and weak. And so much smaller somehow. It shocked me to my core to see him so contradictory to how he normally was. Marion threw herself on top of her youngest son in the hospital bed and wailed while David stoically rubbed her back.

Brody held my hand as we stood back from the bed just watching. I was numb, idly searching for the feelings I thought I should be having. *Should I be wailing with Marion? Should I be chasing down a doctor and grabbing at his lapels begging him to do more?* The tears weren't coming, but I dabbed at my eyes with a tissue anyway.

The only thing that felt right for me in the moment, and for many moments after that was to put my arms around my precious son and breathe.

I continued breathing through the business and busyness of death. Ari never made a will expressing what he'd have wanted under these circumstances as invincibility was such a large part of his personality. It was all left up to our best guess. We chose to have him cremated and hold a memorial service at a funeral home with a celebration of life event at the restaurant afterwards. With Ari's local notoriety as well as David's very public persona, there were hundreds and hundreds of people paying their respects. I played my part at the funeral home in the receiving line, but Marion was the shining star. There were times throughout the day I considered her, utterly bewildered as she seemed to be reveling in the attention far more than she was grieving the loss of her son.

I didn't have one tenth of her energy to try and deal with the throngs, so I stayed quiet. That's the thing about death and grief, everyone processes it so differently, no one batted an eye that I barely spoke to anyone. I stayed in my little bubble with Brody, Kendra, Darius, and Randall. Brody did make the rounds for the sake of his grandparents, knowing people were very eager to shower him with their condolences and affection. Andrea would come check on me from time to time. She had been a huge help with making all the arrangements and serving as a go between with her mother and I, knowing I could only handle Marion in small doses.

I put the urn filled with what remained of my husband up on the fireplace mantle under the large framed black and white photograph of us on our wedding day, then crawled into the bed in the guest room where I stayed for the next two weeks.

During that time, I was vaguely aware of people in a constant state of hover. Between Andrea, Kendra and her husband Gary, Darius and Randall, and occasionally my parents, there was almost always someone at the house taking care of Brody and I. Making food for Brody and keeping him company. Coaxing me to eat a few bites and drink water. Helping me up and into the shower from time to time. Sitting in bed with me watching sappy movies, and if I could keep my eyes open for the whole two hours, they'd consider that improvement. I remember someone asking about my laptop and passwords to check on emails and automatic payments, making sure I wouldn't get too far behind. I remember reminding someone about my YouTube email account that no one knew about.

Once my fog lifted enough, I got up and got outside. The summer sun and breeze were much needed balm for my weary soul, replenishing me enough to be able to make some decisions and get back to work.

David brought up the subject of Ari's restaurant, wondering if I'd wanted any say in its future. He was still so financially wrapped up in the place, but Ari's sous chef, Jason, was interested in buying him out over time. His plan was to keep the concept as it was for one year, complete with a picture of Ari near the host stand out of respect, then do a total rebrand.

I told David in no uncertain terms that I wanted nothing to do with it. I explained to him that it would be too hard, that there were too many memories attached to it.

But the truth was that the restaurant had been the source of most of Ari's stress. Stress that he would bring home, and stress that I found myself having to deal with in a myriad of ways.

It caused me stress directly too, when he would come home smelling more like perfume than Mediterranean food. The first time I called him out on it, he told me I was being paranoid, bemoaning the fact that I didn't trust him. It was a simple explanation, he'd said. One of his wine reps had come in, she happened to wear a lot of perfume and she was a hugger. I believed him.

Until I found the condoms. I had an IUD.

Apparently "Don't fuck where you work" had gone out the fucking window.

I gave up confronting him. Fighting Ari was always an exercise in frustration, and the aftermath...well, that's a story for another day.

David dropped the subject, and I was glad to never have to think about it again.

I'd gone back to work within the month, happy to have the day to day in my happy place. I just had to get through the story of my widowhood with every single client and be inundated with their well-intended, yet emotionally exhausting condolences.

After a while, Darius encouraged me to explore going public with Cherrie Bombshell and he helped me set up an Instagram account. Within a month, I was getting DMs for low profile modeling opportunities and public appearances at local classic car shows and VFW events. I was even part of a motorcycle company's calendar where I posed as Miss July with a sparkler in one hand and a Bomb Pop in the other suggestively headed toward my open mouth.

Every once in a while, during the photo shoots or events, dark thoughts would creep in. A man's voice in my head.

"What do you think you are doing?"

"Aren't you a little old for this?"

"You should be ashamed of yourself, you fucking whore."

I'd get rattled, sometimes having to employ the grounding and calming techniques that my new therapist taught me. Most of the time I'd be able to get myself together and move on.

THAT NIGHT AFTER MY TATTOO APPOINTMENT, KENDRA, GARY, DARIUS and Randall would be coming over to watch *Dare Me to Do It*. It seemed like a lifetime ago that I'd spent the morning with Jake Ford and so much had happened since. When I'd gotten up out of my bed after Ari died, Kendra casually told me that the show had emailed me with an air date for our episode. I thought about asking her if the email had come from Jake, but that seemed unlikely, and I had let it go.

I stood in the mirror at the tattoo shop admiring Heather's handiwork. It was a piece I had wanted for so long, and it meant so much more at that moment than I ever could have imagined. On the outside of my right hip and thigh was a beautiful pinup mermaid done in Heather's signature anime-esc style like the two other pinup tattoos she'd done for me. This beauty had raven hair, ruby red lips, bare breasts and a tail comprised of breathtaking iridescent scales in greens and blues. Her ocean scene was set with swirls of blue, sea stars, seahorses, and an octopus. The quote surrounding her was my favorite of Anais Nin—*I must be a mermaid for I have no fear of depths and a great fear of shallow living.* Tears filled my eyes as I took it all in.

"You don't like it." Heather lamented.

"No! That's not it... I just..." I stammered, my emotion getting the best of me. "Heather, I love it so much. I can't begin to tell you how much I love it." I turned and opened my arms to hug her.

I was so grateful my friends were bringing the food because I was running late. I made it home just in time to beat Gary and Kendra into my driveway. Darius and Randall were only five minutes behind.

"Oh, Shelby! I just love your Christmas decorations!" Darius exclaimed sarcastically. I had exactly one Christmas themed flower arrangement on the kitchen island, an impulse purchase from Sendiks to try and be "festive." I'd told my in-laws that I didn't have the energy, that the decorations we put up every year were too difficult to deal with, what with this being the first Christmas without Ari and all.

But Darius knew the truth. I hated all our decorations because, of course, Marion had picked them out. And with the help of my therapist, I was beginning to make my way beyond my incessant people pleasing patterns.

I pulled a bottle of champagne out of the fridge and five flutes out of the cabinet.

"Veuve Grand Dame? Limited edition?" asked Gary. "You being on TV is definitely something to celebrate, but wow."

Gary was in beverage sales so he knew his stuff. I thought this might have impressed him.

"Actually, I have another reason I want to celebrate. I've come to a pretty big decision." Everyone stared, hanging on my every word. Once the champagne was poured, I held up my glass and said, "I've decided to sell the house."

"Oh, Shelby. That's amazing!" Kendra came over and wrapped me in her arms. She grabbed her glass and held it high with an arm still around my shoulders. "To new beginnings!" Everyone clinked glasses and repeated the phrase. Kendra smiled at me, "So do I have to ask if I get the job?"

"You get the job." My best friend had been a realtor for over fifteen years—of course I would trust her to sell the house and find me my perfect home. "I've got to talk to David first. I think technically they still own it." I had it in my head that I would talk to David alone and not involve Marion until it was absolutely necessary. I had a feeling she wouldn't understand, and that it would be a whole dramatic play I'd need to rehearse for.

I had been feeling an almost unbearably strong pull to begin to form my own identity. Trying to find the whole of who I was without Ari. And without his parents.

I'd moved my vanity into the guest room, and I bravely bought a few decor items of my very own since Marion was not likely to see them. I was comfortable in that room, but for the most part I hated wandering around the bleak, bland McMansion that has never felt like home. It was time to find a place that did.

I ate and talked with my beloved friends, mostly about the kind of house I had in mind. And Darius and Randall were thrilled when I said I wanted to move to Tosa Falls and closer to the salon. Not just for convenience. The quaint little village had charmed its way into my heart.

"We'll be neighbors!" Randall beamed.

"T minus five minutes!" Gary reminded us, although we'd all had a watchful eye on the clock. We grabbed our wine glasses now filled with a tasty pinot that Gary had brought and made our way to the living room.

I grabbed a blanket thinking if my embarrassment got the best of me, I could always throw it over my head. I always felt a cringe when I would first hear myself talk while editing my videos even after I'd been doing it for so long. And if my Midwestern accent was going to be so obvious next to Jake's smooth toned voice and perfectly ambiguous TV dialect, I thought I might have to leave the room.

The *Dare Me to Do It* theme song came on and I got my first glimpse of Jake in almost seven months. It felt surreal seeing him once again on the screen after standing next to him in person. I could almost feel his warmth and smell his unique and distinctive fragrance.

The show began with Jake standing out in front of Aspire. I barely remember this part, but I bet if I looked hard enough, I might see myself looking out of the window. He introduced the show.

"Last season we did a show featuring women who did jobs most typically done by men. For this episode we wanted to explore jobs *not* often done by men, and the reasons behind it. My first stop is here," Jake gestures to the sign behind him, "Aspire Salon and Spa in Tosa Falls, Wisconsin where I will talk to an esthetician, or skin care expert, and find out why men typically don't perform waxing hair removal."

The camera follows Jake entering the salon our "meeting for the first time" even though it had been filmed after we had shot the whole scene with Amber in the treatment room. I looked over at Darius and smiled. He was such a proud papa with his salon baby on TV. His efforts to make everything perfect seemed to be paying off.

As the segment went on, I looked around the room and four pairs of eyes were on me almost as much as they were on the television screen. I wasn't sure if they were surprised and impressed that I'd held my own during the interview or if, like me, they were floored at how palpable the chemistry was between me and Jake. I had stolen glances at him throughout the shoot, I couldn't help it. What I hadn't noticed was that he had been doing the same thing. Even in the beginning, when he should have been paying attention to what I was showing him.

They'd edited out my long pause before I'd admitted I'd waxed men. A pause I had taken because Ari never knew and could never know that I saw and touched other men in such an intimate way. Imagining his reaction to this revelation, my heart began to thrum in my chest, my hands trembled, and my eyes filled with tears. That day in May, I had no idea that Ari wouldn't be around to see this. *How could I have possibly been able to keep this from him?* Someone from work, or his parents, or his friends...someone would have asked him about his wife being on television and he would have tracked it down. I was so naive and cavalier. *What had I been thinking, taking a risk like that?*

Without me saying a word, Kendra came over and sat beside me. "Gary, pause it."

She gently grabbed my arm to sit me up straight and clasped both of my hands in hers. "Look at me, Shelby. He's not here. You don't have to be afraid. Do you hear me? You don't ever have to be afraid again."

I looked at her and nodded. Everyone in the room looked at

me with such caring concern in their eyes. They all knew how difficult Ari had been, maybe not in as great of detail as Kendra, but I'd confided in each of them quite a bit over the years. Their support had been everything.

I was grateful at that moment that Brody was at school studying for finals, having promised he'd watch the recording. I wasn't nervous for him to see it even though he'd see his mom borderline flirting with another man. I knew Brody wouldn't judge me for that. I was grateful, however, that he wasn't watching me have this reaction at the thought of his father seeing the show. There was so much he didn't know.

"I need you to keep watching this and watch yourself and how fucking amazing you are. I'm so fucking proud of you, Shelby." Kendra's wine intake to F bomb export ratio was rapidly increasing. Her eyes were teary, but she took a deep breath. "Okay?"

"Okay." I nodded.

We looked at Gary and he pressed play.

I had to admit to myself that I was pretty fucking amazing after all. I had been so nervous, but very little of that made it to camera. I knew in theory I had all my answers on deck, and these were things I'd thought a lot about over the course of my ten-year career. But I never dreamed I'd be able to articulate it so well and in front of my adolescent crush no less. There was one little scene where I remembered we had just started again after Dan had told Jake to take a step back from me because we "weren't on a date." Jake had gotten so flustered. Remembering that and our flirtatious conversation after shooting. Remembering the hug. My heart started to pound again. But this time it wasn't the edges of panic.

"Ken?" I said sheepishly as I held my blanket up covering half my face. "I think I have butter flutters."

She looked at me and a huge smile spread across her face. "There is something happening there, no doubt about it."

Darius and Randall nodded in agreement.

The rest of the show was amazing. I understood why they aired my segment first.

The second part was about why men aren't often daycare workers. Jake and the woman he had been interviewing, Jocelyn, talked about how young men are now more commonly becoming nannies, but primarily because they are studying early childhood development for an education or psychology degree. She explained that the job interview involved the obvious question of 'Why do you want to work here?' And for women, the answer could be "Because I love children." When a man said the same answer, it was different. She said she couldn't help but be skeptical that there might be a deeper and much darker "why."

This was all interspersed with Jake wiping little mouths and sitting cross legged on the floor playing with toy trucks and puzzles while nonchalantly wearing a plastic tiara. Toward the end, a tiny little cherub-faced, curly haired girl, not more than two years old, stood at his feet, reaching up her arms and opening and closing her fists. The universal sign for "pick me up." Jake immediately, instinctively scooped her up into his arms. She promptly put her thumb in her mouth and laid her little head on his shoulder and I think both Kendra and I felt our ovaries lurch.

The last segment was Jake taking a turn as a labor and delivery nurse. The woman giving birth was so generous, volunteering to be filmed and allowing Jake to be just as involved as all the other nurses. Her husband was just as accommodating. Jake was kind, attentive, eager to learn and to help.

After a commercial, they'd indicated he'd been allowed to

observe while they'd checked her cervix. The mom-to-be had even offered to have Jake do it, but he explained that the hospital lawyers and the show's liability consultant had given that a big thumbs down. When it came time for her to push, Jake took his place up near her head, cheerleading opposite her husband. When the baby crowned, the obstetrician encouraged Jake to come down to get a better look, the camera going back and forth between faces—Jake's and the soon to be parents. With wide, unblinking eyes, Jake held his hand to his mouth in rapt attention. The healthy baby girl soon fully entered the world, and they placed her on mom's belly. Jake looked at the camera, completely at a loss for words, laughing with tears streaming down his face.

At the end of the segment came the end of the show. Jake was emotional and raw. He talked about how while the women he'd featured last year did nothing to warrant the inequality and mistreatment they'd experienced in those jobs, in these cases, men had. He apologized profusely on behalf of his gender, and somberly explained that because of the way they've historically behaved, trust had been broken time and time again. And now they—he'd included himself the whole time and used the word "we"—were missing out on some of the most incredible experiences in the world.

By the end of the show, as I looked at all my friends, I knew without a doubt that every single person in the room now had a big old fat crush on Jake Ford just like me.

CHAPTER
EIGHT
SHELBY

January 2013

"Pack your bags, bitch. We're going to Vegas!" Kendra announced as she walked into my house on a bitterly cold Friday in late January.

"What? When?"

"We need to be at the airport in two hours. Darius got coverage for your clients through Tuesday, and Brody and your parents have our flight and hotel info. No excuses. Let's get you packed!"

"I'm not sure why you think I'd be fighting you on this—a vacation that I didn't have to plan, pay for, or stress about? Somewhere warmish and snow free? Yeah, this seems pretty fucking ideal to me." I hugged my spontaneous, thoughtful, and generous friend and kissed her cheek.

"I was hoping you'd see it that way. Now, let's get a move on." She let me go, but not before giving me a playful slap on the ass.

After an uneventful day of travel, we rolled up to the Hard Rock Hotel in the late afternoon. I'd been nervous about packing so quickly—typically I am a fastidious list maker, but Kendra was helpful, giving me just enough hints about what she had planned for me to feel prepared. I did ask her to stop at CVS on the way to the airport, telling her I needed a few more travel size items, and that I could just quickly run in by myself. While she'd been helping me pack, she encouraged me to add at least one lingerie set, stockings and a garter, and I got to thinking about another item that might come in handy.

I'd been to Vegas twice with Ari, write off trips for "research and development" to check out how some of the famous chefs were doing multiple concepts. We'd go to Thomas Keller's or Daniel Bouloud's restaurants and while I'd thoroughly enjoy my experiences, he'd find a way to find fault with nearly everything. We'd gone to shows, which I loved, and we'd gambled, which I hated. Mostly because of how stressful it would be if Ari lost money.

I was beyond happy to be there with Kendra.

She planned dinner for us at Mon Ami Gabi, but she said we didn't need to dress up too much—that would be the following night. We ate dinner, drinking and laughing until we ached. I couldn't remember a time when I had felt so relaxed, so carefree. We spent the entire evening at the Paris, having cocktails at the bar, playing slots and giggling our fool heads off.

We were good and spent when we made our way back to the Hard Rock and up to our room. We got into our pajamas, and I looked at Kendra and our single king-sized bed. My eyes filled with tears.

"Shel! What's wrong?"

I could hardly begin to articulate how hard it was hitting me that the thing my soul was needing more than anything was a sleepover with my best friend (my grief bed notwithstanding). And she was giving me that. "We...we haven't done this in..." I stammered.

Kendra smiled. She knew where my head and my heart were. "Years. Years and years."

"It's my fault. All the times you wanted us to go away together, and I couldn't make it work."

"Not your fault. Never your fault, you know that. It was always him."

Kendra could never abide by Ari's name in her mouth. She always referred to "him," or "your husband," or even, when she was feeling particularly feisty, "the asshole."

Kendra had planned a girls' trip to Napa for her thirtieth birthday, but Ari had been in the midst of damage control for soon to be failed restaurant concept number one, and he had guilted me into staying home to support him.

Kendra and I climbed into the bed with just the nightlights on and lay facing each other. "I'm glad you didn't get double beds. I like being close to you," I told her.

"Me too."

"Ken, I promise I am going to make it up to you. From now on, I'm going to be the friend I should have been all along."

The truth was, I'd been horribly jealous of Kendra for years.

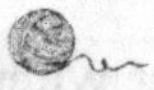

CRAIG, THE BOYFRIEND THAT SHE'D HAD WHEN I MET ARI, WAS NOT all that different from the dominating force that had swept me up in his riptide. We both were caught up with these magnetic men, consuming us, consuming most of our time, and keeping us from seeing each other very often. We never blamed one another, both deeply understanding our roles as the objects of these obsessions. When we would get together, it would be to fawn over and compare notes about how smitten we were with these men who seemed so ready and willing to burn the world for us.

When Ari and I got married a year after Brody was born, Craig proposed to Kendra in the middle of our reception. He hadn't had a ring. We both agreed years later that he'd just hated the thought of being outdone, so he'd performed the grand gesture spontaneously. And very publicly.

We didn't do much together as a foursome. Ari and Craig, while similar in a lot of ways, were cut from different cloths. Craig resented Ari's "silver spoon" upbringing, and Ari thought blue collar Craig crass and uncultured, especially after he'd gotten back from Greece.

While I was having my challenges with Ari, Kendra was beginning to see cracks in her own fairy tale. We stopped comparing notes, instead finding ourselves constantly making excuses. We canceled dinner with them at the last minute because Ari had an emergency at the restaurant. Kendra couldn't come to the concert with me because Craig had hurt his back on the job that morning.

And then Kendra became uncharacteristically clumsy.

A slip on the ice blessing her with a black eye and cut across the bridge of her nose.

A fall down the stairs and a fractured wrist.

A broken rib she blamed on a bad cough.

I tried to intervene, to help, but she wouldn't confide in me. Both her pride and her shame in equal measure had kept her closed off, and she assumed I had my hands full with Ari and my little son.

A few years later, my brave friend had had enough. She left Craig, got a restraining order, and began to move on. Luckily,

Craig quickly found a new object for his obsession and left Kendra alone.

Once she was free, she came for me. Her eyes were wide open, and she saw how similar Ari was to Craig. I would insist over and over that Ari never hit me. That my situation was different. That we were happy. But she seethed for Ari. He couldn't stand her either and he resented the rift she was trying to put between us. There came a point when Kendra and I didn't speak for over a year.

She met Gary around the same time I started at Aspire. He'd convinced her to reach out to me and we began to repair our relationship, and slowly, over time, we managed to get back to the friendship we'd had. She let things go with Ari, for the most part, but always made sure to remind me that she'd be there for me no matter what. Anything I needed. Any decisions I was ready to make.

I was jealous of Kendra for being able to wake up from her nightmare and get out. And then I'd become even more jealous because she'd found Gary. Gary was the opposite of Craig. The opposite of Ari. He was cute, sweet, and one of the funniest people I'd ever met. He might not burn the world for her, but without question or hesitation he would wrap her in his arms and shield her from any and all fiery chaos surrounding her. I tried so hard to be happy for her, but it was a constant reminder of what I didn't have.

SHE LOOKED AT ME FROM ACROSS THE BED. "YOU ARE A PERFECT friend. It's not about a fifty-fifty balance for us. I haven't needed you in these last ten years like you've needed me. And that's okay. Maybe now we'll be boring? Can you imagine?"

I laughed. "Maybe there will be less drama, but girl, it's never gonna be boring."

"True." Kendra's smile was wide and warm. "And tonight is proof. I haven't seen you this happy and relaxed in, I can't tell you how long. And oh my God, how long it's been since I've heard you laugh this much."

"I'm getting there. It's not good all the time, but it's much more good than bad. Kelly is giving me some good coping strategies."

"How is therapy going?"

"Really well. She helped me to realize that the reason I was so exhausted after Ari died wasn't necessarily grief. It was my nervous system getting the message that it was finally able to relax. That I didn't have to be on such high alert all the time. Living with Ari wasn't as much walking on eggshells as it was navigating an active minefield. I was absolutely fried."

"Oh God, Shel. I'm sorry. He was absolutely exhausting. Not to make this about me, but when I realized that to be in your life, I'd have to play nice, it was so fucking ridiculous trying to deal with him. You never knew if he was going to take the simplest thing, twist it the wrong way, and make it a whole dramatic scene. And I was just someone on the outside. I can't imagine what it was like living with him."

"It took me a long time, but at some point, I realized that Ari was never going to change. He was the constant, and I had to learn how to manipulate the equation around him," I admitted.

The next day after breakfast in our room, we made our way to Fremont Street, ducking in and out of casinos and shops. Kendra surprised me with spa appointments in the afternoon and it was such a treat for me to be pampered for a change. Most of the time I am way too analytical while having services done on myself—I always feel as though I'm conducting a practical interview for a new hire, and it's hard for me to tune out. That afternoon during my massage, however, I fell asleep.

Walking back to our rooms in our blissed-out massage haze, Kendra asked, "How long does it take you to get ready? Like *ready* ready?"

"Full pinup, photoshoot ready? Maybe an hour and a half, give or take?"

"Perfect. We have seven o'clock reservations downstairs. You shower first."

I styled my hair half up half down with a few victory rolls, and a red rose off to the side that matched my lipstick. I put on a black lace thong, my stockings and garter, and an off the shoulder body contouring dress in a bright blue that complimented the color of my hair while bringing out a more vibrant blue in my eyes. Kendra wore a dress with a vintage vibe and let me pin a flower in her shoulder length blonde hair she'd styled in loose waves. I was touched that she was game for this style solidarity a little outside of her comfort zone.

"I'm so jealous you don't have to wear a bra. I should just do it. Get my boobs done," Kendra said looking at my chest while cupping her own.

"Just let me know if you decide to do it. Dr. Sonders is amazing."

I'd gotten my augmentation a few years after Brody was born. I was self-conscious about how my breasts had changed after pregnancy and nursing, especially since Ari didn't seem as nearly obsessed with them as he had once been. Watching him pay more attention than ever to other, more perky chested women, I began to worry. As soon as I'd floated the idea of surgery to him, he was thrilled, and afterwards it was like an X-rated Christmas morning every day, with Ari enjoying the hell out of his new toys.

Before we left our room, I stared at the cashmere wrap I held in my hand. I'd packed it knowing I might need it since January nights in Vegas can still be chilly. But I used to have to have it on hand for another reason. When I would go out with Ari completely dressed up, in the beginning of the evening he would want me uncovered. He'd want to parade me around in a dress, sometimes clingy, sometimes a high thigh slit or showing abundant cleavage, with him so proud of his trophy. And then, as attention toward us would increase, whether real or imaginary, I would keep close watch until his pride turned to something else. His jaw would set, his eyes would dart around the room, almost throwing out a challenge to anyone who might dare try to take a stab at his prize. That would be my cue to put on my wrap and defuse the situation as best as I could.

I would not need it tonight. The realization made me smile and stand up straighter, augmented chest held high.

Kendra decided we had time for one drink at one of the casino bars downstairs before we went to dinner. "Hey, hang out here for a minute. I just want to run over to the restaurant to make sure they're running on time," she said.

"Sounds good." I sat on a stool, put my clutch on the bar and swiveled around a bit to people watch. When I swung back around to face the bar, a pair of hazel eyes stared at me under a retro-style fade haircut, with a perfectly groomed auburn beard framing a full set of lips.

"Good evening. I'm Bryce. What can I get for you?"

I tilted my head and smiled, "Hi there, Bryce. What do you recommend?

"Well, it would need to be a drink as lovely as you are. How about a lavender martini?"

"Ooh, cheesy line, Bryce. Be careful." I grinned at him.

"Hey, I'm a bartender in Vegas. Several chapters of the

employee handbook are dedicated to cheesy lines. There was even a quiz." He winked.

I smiled. "Which you passed with flying colors, I'm sure. Fair enough. And yes, that martini sounds perfect."

Not two seconds after Bryce put my lovely, light purple drink in front of me, I heard a gravelly voice in my right ear. I jumped at the sudden invasion of my personal space.

"Well, well. Look at you."

I slid as far to the left as I could on my small barstool and turned to see the source of the intrusion. I jumped again.

He was a huge hulk of a man, shiny, shaved head with a jet-black beard. Comically black, the color of shoe polish. Obscenely orange-y tan. He was wearing a tight mock turtle-neck showcasing every bulging muscle in his shoulders, chest and arms. Likely having spent hours every day coaxing them to full bulk and they then becoming the whole of his personality. He had a tiny waist and his poor, neglected legs seemed to wither beneath his massive upper body. I'd wondered how he just didn't topple over from being so top heavy. I had the image of a cartoon circus strong man come to life and I had to stifle a giggle.

"Can I buy you a drink?"

"Just got one. I'm all set, thanks." I was trying not to encourage him in any way.

"Mind if I just join you then?" He sat down without an invitation. "I hate the thought of someone so beautiful sitting here by her lonesome."

"Just because I'm alone, doesn't mean I'm lonely. I'm just fine by myself."

The Strongman was clearly not getting the hint.

"So tell me, Beautiful, which would you prefer? The two of us at a jumping nightclub at a private VIP table with bottle service, or a quiet dinner in my penthouse suite?"

"Neither. Which do you prefer? Bench pressing Barnum, or bicep curls with Bailey? Because clearly, squat thrusts are not part of your repertoire."

A loud chuckle came from behind the bar, and I turned to see Bryce polishing glassware just a foot away, trying to make it seem like he wasn't paying attention.

"I don't know what that means, but I like you. You're spunky." Strongman said, showing no signs of backing off.

"I just want to sit here and enjoy my drink, so I think you better go," I told him. "Besides, I'd hate for you to be late for your next show at Circus Circus. Wouldn't want to disappoint the kids." That earned me another laugh of approval from Bryce. I liked that he was getting my references to this guy's comical appearance.

The Strongman looked at me more perplexed than ever. Seconds later I watched his eyebrows furrow and his lips become tight as my rejection was finally getting through his bald, orange skull. "Okay, wow. A bitch hidden in a pretty wrapper. What a surprise."

"Listen," Bryce said as he came to my rescue, "I let this go on long enough. The lady clearly wants you to leave. If you don't, I'll call security. And maybe the ringmaster, too."

I started to giggle uncontrollably even while the Strongman was still standing next to me. I didn't care about being polite. Everything about him was hilarious to me by that point. Bryce laughed along with me, and the Strongman finally stormed off in a huff, no doubt in search of another poor woman to annoy. Or unintentionally amuse.

"Oh my God. That was awesome!" Bryce said, wiping a tear from his eye. "He was ridiculous!" Once he composed himself, he stood in square front of me. Considering me. He put his tattooed forearms on the bar and leaned closer, eyes trained on mine, "And you? You are magnificent."

My stomach did a somersault. It was the perfect mix of cockiness and reverence. He wasn't overbearing or making me nervous in any way. Well maybe in a very good way. And he was *really* cute. "How old are you?" I asked him as I tilted my head.

"Twenty-eight."

"Oh Lord." I rolled my eyes. He was a baby.

"Why do you say that? You can't be much older than me."

"I'm thirteen years older than you. That's like 'I could have been your babysitter' years older than you."

"Are you offering? Because I could really be into that," Bryce said, his mouth mischievously turning up at the corners.

I laughed. It felt so good for someone to be flirting with me, and for once I wasn't worried about any consequences. My mind started to wander. Maybe that impulse condom purchase hadn't been so silly after all.

"What's your name?"

"Shelby."

"Beautiful. What are your plans for the evening, Shelby?"

I loved hearing my name come out of his mouth. I thought about how it might sound even better later, all breathless and sexy, when we'd be all sweaty and tangled up with each other.

"My friend and I have dinner reservations at 35 Steaks at seven, but after that I don't know."

"Ooh, carnivores, I love it. Why don't you come back here after dinner? I get done at eleven."

Kendra strode up quickly to the bar next to me and immediately began assessing the situation. She didn't seem as pleased as I would have thought. "Hey. What's going on?"

"Well, this is Bryce and he's made me a delightful martini. Here try."

She took the glass from my hand and slammed my drink in two gulps. My eyes got wide as I stared at her for doing something so out of character. She seemed squirrelly, like she was up to something.

"What the hell?" I asked.

"Mmm, that *was* a good drink. Now we have to go." Kendra grabbed my hand and dragged me off the stool.

I apologized awkwardly to the cute bartender as I threw some cash on the bar. I hoped I'd be able to convince Kendra to come back after dinner. I did not want to be done with Bryce.

We walked over to the restaurant and made our way to the hostess stand. I glanced over at the crowded bar and my heart skidded to a stop. I blinked several times to make sure I wasn't imagining what I was seeing.

There, on the third bar stool from the left, was Jake Ford.

I turned to Kendra and grabbed her arm. "Oh my God! Oh my God! Jake Ford is here! He is actually here!" I tried to whisper but I doubt I'd been successful.

She looked behind me toward the bar and smiled. Her expression was all wrong. I fully expected her to revert to thirteen-years-old with me and be freaking the fuck out like I was.

Instead, she had this warm, benevolent expression in her eyes as they came back to meet mine.

She put her hands on my face and said, "I know, my love. He's here for you."

CHAPTER
NINE

JAKE

I stood behind Shelby as Kendra was explaining how I came to be here, patiently waiting for my turn to greet her. I took the opportunity to admire her luscious curves in the body-hugging blue dress she wore, and I allowed Cave Man a moment since her back was turned. *Are you sure we need steak? Cuz man, I could just gnaw on that ass for a good long while.*

With her red platform heels and the retro seams running up the back of her stockings, Mad Man wondered once again about the real possibility of a garter, nearly salivating at the thought.

Evolved Man was enchanted by the fact that she was dressed to the nines for what she'd thought to be just a night out with her best friend.

Although it did make me wonder if she was looking to meet someone for a fun fling. Testing the waters to see if she was ready to get her legs out from under her, so to speak. The thought of this made me think maybe I didn't need to be so precious with her, though I would still let her take the lead.

With her hands still in Kendra's, she turned to look at me,

and I finally got a glimpse of the face that so often had a starring role in my dreams. I nearly stumbled backwards. *God, how could I have forgotten how fucking gorgeous she was?*

LAST JULY, WHEN I'D GOTTEN KENDRA'S EMAIL TELLING ME ABOUT Shelby's husband, I sat frozen in shock for long minutes trying to absorb what she'd told me. I was immensely grateful that she had intercepted my message, and Shelby had not had to deal with my pathetic attempt at hitting on her, especially considering what had happened. I thought carefully about how to respond, and I hoped I wouldn't sound too cheesy or trite.

HI KENDRA,

I am so very sorry to hear this news. I know first-hand how difficult a sudden loss like this can be.

I know it may sound strange considering I don't know Shelby well, but honestly, if there's anything I can do, please don't hesitate to let me know.

Also, I'd like to offer my sincere apologies for the inappropriate nature of the second part of my last email…although…if I'm being honest, I'm not sorry. Shelby is an extremely compelling woman, and I felt I needed to take the chance—no matter how slight it may have been.

If you feel it's appropriate, please extend my condolences.

Jake

IT DIDN'T SURPRISE ME WHEN I DIDN'T GET AN IMMEDIATE REPLY. I'D crossed the line again, and I was sure they were all going about the business of moving on. I figured that's just what needed to do and as usual, I threw myself into work.

Months later, in mid-December, I did get a reply.

Jake,

I won't lie to you. I bristled at the little "chance" you tried to take with my best friend, particularly surrounding the circumstances (which of course you couldn't possibly had known.) I am fiercely protective of Shelby—we have been best friends since we were nine years old.

But because we've been friends that long, I had a front row seat to her adolescent obsession with you. The posters covering her bedroom walls and how everything we did all summer always revolved around when "Salte St. Marie" was on. I was right there when she was bursting with excitement when she found out you'd be coming to film with her. And I was right there yesterday when we watched the show.

To watch her light up like that onscreen. Watch her be so confident, eloquent, and funny… let's just say it had been a while since I'd seen that side of her. And you'd brought that out. The chemistry between the two of you was undeniable, and I had no doubt the little crush she'd had all those years ago resurfaced.

I know how extraordinary my best friend is and obviously you realized it, too.

I would love to do something special for Shelby, and if your offer still stands, I would like your help. Any chance you'd be up for meeting us in Las Vegas in the next month or so?

Kendra

Once again, Kendra had left me reeling.

My brain was compartmentalizing pieces of the email,

knowing I would be scouring my calendar any minute for a break to make the trip to Vegas work. First, however, I had to try and wrap my head around Kendra's revelations about Shelby's fan crush. I had my suspicions when I was there with her that day, but to have confirmation like this was mind blowing. To think we'd each gone into the day, her excited to meet her favorite soap star, and me excited to meet my favorite video vixen.

Kendra and I emailed back and forth over the following few days. She told me she'd be happy to work around my schedule, that they could most likely be far more flexible. We exchanged numbers and texted details as the trip got closer. I decided to book a room in the same hotel for sheer convenience, hoping I didn't seem presumptuous. I could only stay the night, I had to head out the next afternoon and meet up with the crew in Utah.

Kendra finally led her shocked best friend over to me, and I could see Shelby's eyes were a little glassy and the tip of her nose ever so slightly pink. She was clearly emotional at the lengths Kendra had gone to make this night happen. It warmed my heart to know that Shelby had someone like that in her life. Everyone should be so lucky.

"Take good care of my girl, Jake," Kendra said.

"Of course I will." I smiled and resisted the urge to hug her. She'd done me an enormous favor too, after all. "Thanks for this."

Kendra looked a little taken aback, then smiled. I think it made her feel good that I wanted to be here just as much, if not more, than Shelby.

Shelby turned her attention back and forth between Kendra and me several times. I could imagine her wheels furiously turning, wondering how much communication had gone on between us and curious to know the details of how this had all transpired. Kendra turned to Shelby, "I've got a poker game starting in fifteen minutes, but if you need anything, don't hesitate to text." She put her arms around Shelby and gave her a squeeze.

"I think I'll be fine," Shelby said. They let go of one another, and Shelby turned to me and smiled. I became acutely aware of my heart's frenetic rhythm. She may have been reeling a bit at this surprise, but having known about it in advance was doing little to quell my nerves. I offered her my arm and she took it immediately, gliding her hand around my bicep and sending a shiver through my spine.

The Maitre'd led us to a corner booth like I'd requested; I wanted to be able to sit next to her rather than across from her at a regular table. The steakhouse was 50's style Rat Pack themed, and my stunning pinup date fit right in. I noticed the attention we were getting as we crossed the room, and I didn't assume any of it was for me.

After we'd settled into our booth, I wanted to get the awkward part out of the way. I put my hand on hers, "I just need to tell you how very sorry I am for your loss."

"Thank you," she said, as she offered a shy smile. This was a people pleasing gesture I knew well. It can be unnerving talking about death so even the bereaved sometimes feel compelled to make their well-wishers feel more comfortable.

I looked down at my lap and cleared my throat. "I know how devastating a sudden death can be. My brother passed suddenly of an undiagnosed heart condition when he was sixteen."

"Oh, Jake. I'm so sorry. How old were you?"

"Nineteen. My mom and I were at his baseball game, and he collapsed while running the bases. One second, he was there, the unstoppable superstar athlete he was, and the next, he was just gone."

"How awful." Shelby put her hand on top of mine on top of hers. "What was his name?"

I felt myself stiffen reflexively. "Trevor." I hadn't spoken his name in years. Shelby and I shared a somber smile while I stayed quiet, gently ending the subject of my brother. I also wanted to give her space to talk about her husband if she wanted to. Out of the corner of my eye I saw the waiter approaching and Shelby withdrew her hands.

He greeted us, gave us his spiel, took our drink order, and with that, the page was turned on the whole conversation. I realized how much I missed the warmth of Shelby's hands.

She smiled, let out a little breathy laugh through her nostrils, and shook her head. "I still can't believe you're here. That this is actually happening."

"I'm having a little bit of a hard time with it myself. I really never thought I'd see you again." The waiter came back with our drinks, and I was grateful for something to do with my hands. My nerves were still threatening to get the better of me.

I ran my finger around the rim of my glass of scotch before picking it up and taking a healthy swig. "What did you think of the show?"

"It was amazing. I won't lie, though, the other two segments were way better than mine."

"Not better, just different." I gently corrected her. "All of the things you talked about were valid and important. And just because we were waxing, and things got silly here and there didn't mean it still didn't land. I mean, I was having a serious conversation with a crown on my head at the daycare." I smiled.

"A tiara, actually."

"What's the difference?" I asked her.

"I think it has to do with it not being a full circle? In any case, it was definitely way too dainty to have been a crown."

She laughed. I was relieved we were both beginning to relax. "And when the baby was born? Holy cats. I was bawling."

"That was probably one of the best moments of my professional career." I took another drink. "Hell, probably one of my best moments, period. To be there to witness a couple become a family, this brand new little being coming into the world...," I held out my hands as if it'd been me who'd caught her. "If not for the show, I never would have experienced that. Kids just weren't in the cards for me."

"Well, you seemed to be a natural with them at the daycare. Especially that little girl."

"Shit." I sighed and drew my eyes upward. "She had me wrapped all the way around her tiny finger and she knew it." I smiled as I thought of little Maddie and her dimples.

"You know, I wouldn't be surprised if the episode is nominated for something."

"Shhhh! You're not supposed to say it! You'll jinx it." I jokingly admonished her. We were starting to hear rumblings from the network, but we didn't want to get our hopes up.

"Darius made a bunch of 'as seen on TV' social media posts. He's been loving the attention."

"I'll bet! I still can't believe I ran into him like that. I love how small the world can be sometimes."

The waiter came back to take our order. We hadn't even opened our menus, but we snatched them up off the table in an attempt to make a last-minute decision. I'm easy, give me a mid-rare ribeye smothered in bleu cheese and a baked potato and I'm a happy man. I wanted to draw out this dinner as much as I could, so I ordered a couple of appetizers for us to share, too.

As Shelby was looking at the menu, I caught the waiter looking down at her cleavage as if he was getting ready to dive in head-first. I smiled and shook my head. I couldn't blame him, but the dude needed to teach his Cave Man some manners. Another woman's date, or likely the woman herself, might not be as understanding and he'd wind up with a fist to the jaw.

After he'd gone, Shelby put her elbow on the table and turned to face me squarely. "Is Jake Ford your real name?"

"No."

"What is it then?"

"Jacob Ford."

She tilted her head back and giggled. I laughed too. I knew where she was going with this. Not only is it a fake sounding "Hollywood name," but evidence of my Latino heritage is obvious enough for those who choose to pay attention.

"My father, Geoffrey Ford, is Australian, but he went to medical school in Venezuela where he met my mom, Daniela. He got a fellowship at the Oregon Science and Heath University in Portland, so they got married and emigrated. My brother and I were born here in the US."

"So, when you said that if you'd grown up in Europe or South America you wouldn't think body hair on women would be a big deal...both of your parents are from cultures like that. And they are also cultures that don't..." she trailed off, slightly embarrassed.

I smiled remembering how this conversation had gone, and how it had so tragically ended up on the cutting room floor. I raised an eyebrow at her. "Shelby, are you about to ask me if I'm circumcised?"

She giggled and blushed. "Maybe."

"Well, because I was born here, and it was becoming the norm by the mid 60s, it's likely my mother's OB cautioned my parents against having their son look different than the other boys in the locker room. Does that answer your question?" I shifted in my seat. Someone knew I was talking about him, in front of Shelby no less, and I needed him to calm down.

She pinched her eyebrows as if she thought I was upset about my parents' decision. "It does." She cleared her throat and changed the subject. "Do your parents still live in Portland?"

"My mom does. My dad was the cliché doctor who had an affair with a nurse and got her pregnant. He left us when I was five and Trev was two. Just picked himself up and plugged himself into a whole new family. He moved to New York after his baby was born, but he lives in Hawaii now, retired." I felt my spine stiffen. I hadn't picked at that old scab in quite some time, and it was a little surprising how sore it still was.

"Ugh, I'm sorry. That sucks." Shelby's eyes were filled with empathy and deeply fixed on me. Once again, she reached out and put her hand on mine.

This time, I turned my hand right side up and interlaced my fingers with hers. The energy shift was palpable. I took a slow, deep inhale in a feeble attempt to replace the air that Shelby kept knocking out of my lungs. We were locked in a stare, each searching for something undefinable in the other's eyes with a desperate kind of curiosity.

She broke first, smiling and looking down at the table. But she didn't let go of my hand.

I wanted more of these little moments of magic, so I continued the conversation. "How about you? What's your family like?"

"I'm an only child. My parents are very religious, so I grew up going to church, Sunday school, bible camp, and Christian school all the way through twelfth grade," she said.

I couldn't help but smirk as I looked her up and down, realizing that the image she's cultivated for herself, her vivacious self-expression, video persona included, is proof of her rebelling against her upbringing. It was beyond obvious, and it was captivating me even more. "So, suffice to say, you've broken away from the church?"

"Starting in high school, I started to question it. My parents never encouraged me to go to college thinking I would just become a good Christian wife and stay at home mom. When I told them I wanted to go to college they threw a bunch of brochures at me for Christian universities, but that didn't interest me at all. In my first English class at UW Milwaukee, I had to write a paper on the exploitation of women's sexuality in advertising, and that was when I pretty much shut my Bible for good," she explained.

"What's your relationship like with them now?" I was also curious about her husband and having had her son so young, but I thought those subjects may have been too sensitive to broach.

"It depends. When they don't make passive aggressive comments to me about getting back to church or quoting scripture during everyday conversation, it's okay. But we've never been particularly close. They weren't touchy-feely parents, and they are both fairly socially awkward. When I would have problems, even when I was little, they wouldn't console me in the way that most parents would. They would just encourage me to pray about it or 'give it to God.'"

I shook my head. "That's a shame. I mean, we don't need to get into a whole thing about religion, but some of the worst people I've ever met have proclaimed to be Christian. They espouse their faith and virtue in one breath and then spew the most vile, judgmental, racist, sexist, or homophobic garbage you've ever heard in the next." I gave her a gentle smile. "No offense to your parents."

"You're right. And my parents have their moments, believe me. Good old Bob and Eileen Baker. Judging people from dawn til dusk and heaven bent on a mission to save the world one soul at a time."

I couldn't help but laugh at the elevator pitch she had for her parents, even though I could only imagine her struggles reconciling all of that through the years. I was grateful my experience with religion hadn't been nearly as traumatic. "My mom grew up a devout Catholic. My brother and I were baptized, and she took us to mass every Sunday, but when my father left, so did her faith. Then, after Trevor died, she found her way back. Now, her faith gives her peace, and her church gives her community. It's beautiful, really. But she doesn't feel like it's her job to save everyone or to judge anyone. It's so interesting how religion can mean different things to different people," I said.

Shelby sat up straighter, her gestures becoming more animated, her energy positively effervescent. "My parents, especially my dad, believe that their existence as white, Christian, Americans is the baseline. Everyone who doesn't look like them is "other" and everyone who doesn't agree with their beliefs is wrong and destined for hell. I know so many people who grew up like this. And are *still* like this. Never actively meeting and engaging with people who are different from them, never traveling outside the country... hell, never even opening a book after high school. Other than the Bible that is. And they mostly use that to quantify sin and justify their bigotry."

I'd only had one drink, but damn if this woman didn't already have me spinning. I wished that I could just wander around inside her beautiful brain for a few days.

I became painfully aware when our two-and-a-half-hour dinner was coming to an end, and I was not at all ready to let Shelby go. I thought about what we might be able to do after this. The casino floor or a loud club was not the answer, and me suggesting taking the evening to one of our respective rooms was too presumptuous. Or, at the very least, premature.

I thought there must be a place, maybe a cocktail bar where we could hole up in a quiet corner. Where I could sit close to her and hold her hand. Tuck a stray strand of hair behind her ear, and feign the inability to hear her when she spoke, so she'd have to lean closely into mine.

I tried to ignore Mad Man and Cave Man chiming in.

Put our hand on her knee gliding up slowly to find the garter clasp.

Those full, red lips tightly wrapped around our c—

Fellas, calm the fuck down, Evolved Man interjected. *She's a widow.*

But Cave Man made his point with an image included and I had to slightly, hopefully subtly, readjust my pants. *She's a widow. She's a widow. She's a widow.*

I decided to sneak off to the front desk and ask the concierge for some suggestions. I pulled out my phone and glanced at it. "Hey, I'm so sorry to do this," I told Shelby. "I need to make a call real quick. It's a work thing. I'll be right back, I promise." I leaned over and gently kissed her on the cheek. I hadn't thought about whether I should or shouldn't have. It felt instinctual, and like the most natural thing in the world.

She blushed. "Of course. I'll be right here."

I walked as quickly as I could through the casino to the front desk.

CHAPTER
TEN
SHELBY

I sat and watched as Jake walked away from the table. He looked mouthwateringly handsome in his slim cut black suit with a crisp white button down, the top two buttons casually undone. Jake wasn't the tie type, opting instead for a funky little pocket square. His presence still felt so warm and solid, just like I remembered. And he still smelled so completely intoxicating.

I was tilted completely off my axis—finding this whole thing so surreal. Kendra covertly conspiring with Jake to make this happen was blowing my mind. She had tried explaining to me how this had come to be after she'd told me what Jake was doing there, but my brain was only able to process fragments of what she'd said. Something about an email she'd intercepted, and how she felt about watching us together on the show. I promised myself I'd press her for all the details later.

The thought occurred to me that maybe Kendra hadn't just planned for me to have dinner with Jake. Had she thought maybe I was ready for something else? She'd casually been asking me about "getting back out there" in the last few months. At first, I thought it a little fast, but knowing how Kendra felt about Ari, especially in these last few years, I was sure she just wanted to see me happy.

I had been revving my engine a little with Bryce out on the casino floor, after all, so why not shift gears and do the same with Jake? I reached into my clutch to grab my lipstick and my compact. My fingers found the end of a foil packet and I pulled it out. A condom. And underneath it, one more. The ones that I had packed were tucked away in the outside zippered pocket. And were a different brand.

Kendra.

I smiled and warmed with affection for my brazen friend.

It was then that I made my decision. My body had been vibrating since the first moment I saw Jake. For the first half hour or so it was because of my nerves, but then for a different reason altogether. The chemistry we'd had on that day last May was noticeable to me, but this...this was different. We still had our banter and I loved talking with him, but this time we were able to add the physicality, and it was unraveling me in the best possible way.

It was obvious Jake was feeling this way, too.

I decided I was going to give my teenage self what she'd always wanted, even if in her innocence she couldn't possibly have known all that would entail. Forty-one-year-old me knew well enough for both of us, and my imagination switched on in high definition.

The object of my sexual awakening was to be mine.

When I would make my videos, I would often channel sirens and femme fatales that inspired me. It gave me confidence and helped me get out of my head. Cherrie Bombshell was not only flirtatious, but she also oozed sexuality. I closed my eyes and called upon my muses. Marilyn. Betty Page. Dita Von Teese. Sabina Kelley.

I began to reapply my lipstick and as I did, I caught a man staring at me from the next table. My first instinct was to recoil and hope and pray that no one else had noticed. But I quickly remembered that "no one" was no longer a concern. If I was serious about slipping into my alter ego, I thought I might as well practice before Jake got back.

I tilted my head down and peeked back up at the man through my lashes. I smiled. The blush and sudden fidget in his seat told me everything I needed to know. He quickly overcorrected to keep his female dining companion from noticing what was going on and tried focusing all his attention back onto her. But he couldn't keep himself from glancing back at me. This was a fun game.

By the time Jake returned, I was ready.

He slid into the booth. "Sorry about that. So, there's this little speakeasy up the strip. I thought that would be a nice place to go for another drink?"

I angled my body to face him and put my hand on his. "I have a better idea. You have a room here, right?" He nodded as I bit my lip and paused for effect. "I think we should go there instead." I slid closer to him, positioned my head in the crook of his neck, inhaled and kissed him in the soft, warm place behind his ear. I slid back a bit to wait for his reply.

He looked down at the table and a grin spread wide across his face. He looked up at me, put on a more serious expression and began searching my eyes. I nodded without having been asked the question.

Jake paused for a few seconds, his index finger rubbing back and forth across his chin. "Shelby, I want nothing more than to take you to my room. And...and you seem to have this fire in your eyes. I just need you to know that the reins are in your hands here. Anything you want or don't want, it's all up to you. I am at your service." He trained his deep brown eyes on mine and ran his tongue over his bottom lip. He reached out and held my chin gently between his thumb and crooked index finger. "And at your mercy."

I came close to breaking my resolve, nearly melting into a puddle, but I was able to stay steady. The only puddle I had to contend with was the one suddenly blooming between my legs. I arched my back, rolled my pelvis forward, and pressed the epicenter of my ache into the booth as hard as I could trying to eke out some fraction of the friction I was desperately craving. The smooth leather was giving me nothing.

We made our way to the elevator and as we stood inside Jake grabbed my hand. He leaned up against the back wall and brought my hand to his mouth gently turning it right side up. While maintaining his intense eye contact, pupils fixed and dilated, his lips crushed dry and soft against the sensitive skin on the inside of my wrist. I felt the tiny flicker of his tongue, swift and hot, and I felt as though the elevator cables had snapped. It was all I could do to keep my legs steady underneath me, trying to maintain my cool seductress facade. I managed to quickly recombobulate myself, allowing a grin to curl the corners of my mouth letting him know the gesture was appreciated.

We stepped off the elevator and walked to his room with Jake stepping slightly ahead of me to unlock the door. He turned to look back at me once more before he opened it all the way. Another silent question, and once again, I nodded my yes.

We crossed the threshold, and he turned to face me. He stood still, inviting me to come to him—it was clear he meant it when he'd said everything was up to me. I moved slowly toward him, our eye contact never wavering. I reached out and touched his cheek as I moved the whole of my body in against his. I raked my hand through his hair to the back of his head and pulled his mouth toward mine.

Our lips locked in an instant. That perfect amount of suction that indicates a kiss is wanted. Needed.

Within seconds of the connection, however, he pulled back, angling his face away from mine as I found myself lunging after his lips. I felt a pang of rejection, thinking maybe he was having second thoughts.

He reached a hand up to my face, framing my ear with his fingers and his thumb caressing my cheek. With his other hand, he traced his fingers over my forehead followed by a thumb over my bottom lip. His unblinking eyes following every trail of his touch. His fingertips grazed softly down my neck and back up again. He was considering me. *Studying me.* A sharp pinch of self- consciousness caught me, as if he were able to read my thoughts and somehow know all the secrets of my soul.

Jake's chocolate eyes were hot and intense as he licked his lips, and when he pulled them into a half smile, my stomach hit the floor.

I was thrust back in time. It was as if he'd pressed rewind on this whole scene and on my whole life and I was standing at the door with the sudden awareness that the boy I'd been on a date with was going to kiss me goodnight.

It wasn't butter flutter butterflies gently batting against my insides. Instead, forty or fifty caged pterodactyls thrashed and threatened to violently burst their way out.

He inched his face closer to mine and I closed my eyes. It was all I could do to keep from shuddering when his soft lips first brushed against mine. It was the perfect escalation of intensity, starting languidly tentative, the most delicious tease. It continued then with the curious exploration of lips and of tongue tips, pulling away to readjust facial angles, then coming back together, each time laced with a little more greed until we were fully consumed in one another.

Jake's kiss was both commanding and yielding in equal measure. A completely unfamiliar concept.

Ari's dominating kisses had been a means to an end, intense and cursory, not unlike wide open mouth tongue wrestling in porn. I'd always find myself coveting characters in movies who seemed to kiss in order to convey everything they weren't able to say.

And now it's me in the movie.

Cherrie was faltering, swooning. Contemplating just giving in. Trying to convince me to just allow ourselves to be washed away and drown in this moment. In Jake.

But I couldn't lose myself. Control was something I had grabbed onto with all my might, and I was afraid it was the only thing allowing me to participate in this adventure. I couldn't just be along for the ride. No, I needed to write and direct the whole thing—it was the only way I could possibly know how it would end.

I shook Cherrie by the shoulders and told the bitch I needed her to get it together and stick to the script.

I pulled away, smiled, and started walking toward the window. I glanced around in a quick reconnaissance to see what I could have at my disposal, spying a square ottoman opposite the sofa. I knew exactly how I was going to play this.

From halfway across the room, I kept my back toward Jake as I pulled my hair to one side. I unzipped the back of my dress, slowly pulling it down my arms. Once gravity got hold of it, I let it fall to the floor. I could feel Jake's volcanic stare as I was sure he was noticing my stockings, garter, and thong. Also, likely, my lack of bra. I liked this tease. I would stay still until he came to me.

Which was in a nanosecond.

He was pressed up against my back. Kissing up the side of my neck. His hands moving across my stomach and over my breasts. "My God. You are so fucking beautiful," he said between mouthfuls of my skin. Skin which had erupted in goosebumps so intense, I was convinced I'd sprouted quills.

I reached up behind me and tangled my hands in his hair. I could feel his erection pressed against my back and I began to move my body up and down a little, offering him some well-deserved friction. A low growl signaled his appreciation.

I turned my body around and our mouths found one another again. This time, just as I could feel him completely consumed by the moment, I was also pleasantly surprised at being able to notice the more subtle cues of a man's desire. I pulled away from the kiss bringing my hands to his chest to feel the rapid fire beating of his heart. The heaving as he struggled for breath. The dilation of his pupils as his eyes burned into mine. It was deeply intense, but without any hint of darkness. I began to unbutton his shirt.

His hands moved over my body. I began silently pleading for them to land where my need was the greatest, me aching in a way I hadn't for so long. It was tortuous. I spread my legs a little, hoping he'd take my cue.

With his palm flat against my stomach, he slid his way down. Making his way between my thighs, he cupped me at first, and then pressed more firmly with his middle finger, gliding back and forth over the slippery surface with just the whisper of lace between us. I whimpered and dug my fingers into his shoulders, bending my knees trying to connect more firmly with his hand.

"Damn." His breathy whisper made me shiver. He inhaled sharply, licked his lips and bowed his head. I didn't need psychic abilities to know he was imagining what it would feel like to be inside me. What I might taste like. Another wobble in my resolve I had to quickly brush off.

I unbuckled his belt teasingly slowly and began to unzip his pants. He held up one finger to me and reached into his back pocket, producing a condom. "This is not me being presumptuous. This is me being prepared." He smiled a mischievous smile, "And extremely hopeful."

He slid his pants down and took off his socks. He watched with fascination as I unfastened my garter clasps and slid off my stockings. He then closed what little distance remained between us and with gentle fingertips, he traced around my waist and the edges of my thong.

He got down on his knees and planted angel soft kisses on my stomach and hips. I couldn't tell if he was trying to tease me or to draw out the moment for his own sake, but he choreographed the removal of my last remaining item of clothing off to be slow and deliberate. Millimeter by painstaking millimeter. He drew his tongue along my sensitive bikini line and looked up at me as my thong finally breached my hips and slid down my legs. As he shifted his gaze downward, his lips parted, and I could feel his breath heavy and ragged as he beheld me. On his knees, with his hands on my hips, staring straight ahead at the place that may very well prove to be his undoing, he whispered, "Shelby." It was a benediction.

Cherrie nearly fainted.

I brushed off the momentary loss of control and regrouped once again.

I led Jake by the hand toward the ottoman, hooked my fingers in the waistband of his boxer briefs and carefully unveiled his erection. My mouth reflexively dropped open as my eyes captured an image far better in reality than any I'd conjured in fantasy. If each person who appreciated a dick were able to design the perfect one to suit them, this would be mine to a T. It was fucking *beautiful*.

I pushed his chest gently, encouraging him to sit on the ottoman. I knelt in front of him, his eyes widening in wonder. I wrapped my hand around his length and stroked him, while maintaining my eye contact. Saliva filled my mouth, and I was tempted to taste him, but I resisted.

My stomach somersaulted as the realization hit as to who this was and what I was doing. A huge smile spread across my face. *Oh, goodness. Innocent, adolescent Shelby wouldn't know what to make of any of this— sweet, summer child that she was.*

I took the condom out of his hand, opened it and unrolled it over him. He watched my every move, riveted.

I stood, held his shoulders and swung a leg over to straddle him. It was my turn then to draw out the moment. As desperate as I was, I managed to grasp him and stroke his tip gently back and forth across my threshold. My muses were encouraging of Cherrie's tease.

Jake used this proximity to cup my breasts and tease my nipples with his tongue. *There needs to be much more of this in round two*, I thought to myself. I knew I desperately needed to take my edge off, however, otherwise I could so easily have lost control again.

I lowered myself slowly down the length of him. Jake's mouth opened as he tilted his head back, a baritone moan escaping from deep inside him. "God, Shelby. Fuck, you feel so good," he hissed.

I loved my name in his mouth.

I loved the reason.

Every centimeter I let him stretch and fill me, little fires were being extinguished along the way, easing some of my ache. Filling my desperate hollowness. Once I sank fully, I began to move back and forth on his lap, grinding and finding as much friction as possible. He grabbed my ass cheeks, pulling and pushing along with my rhythm, but not taking control of it. Not changing it.

I could feel my climax fast approaching. Everything was so deliciously slippery, and I was hitting my friction just right. My heart was pounding as the gates opened and that exquisite first wave of dopamine released, like the moment the roller coaster crests the top of the hill. This was where I wished I could exist forever. As the wave crashed and dazzling sparks of light flashed behind my eyes, I threw back my head and screamed. I rode all the way through my orgasm, blissfully full and long. I was vaguely aware that even as my muscles clenched around him, Jake hadn't joined me just yet.

As I came down from my high, I decided I would take a beat, and then continue my rhythm for him to finish.

The beat I immediately regretted.

In that split second, a wave of a different sort overtook me. A megaton wrecking ball of realization hit as to where I was and what I was doing. And not in a good way like before.

Cherrie Bombshell and the muses had left the building.

I had been so busy pretending to be someone else, pretending to be ready, I hadn't stopped to consider that maybe I wasn't. At all.

I tightly shut my eyes trying to push away the onslaught of intrusive thoughts.

I began to tremble uncontrollably. Blood rushed in my temples and a high-pitched ringing filled my ears. I couldn't catch my breath.

There were two choices here, and I had to decide fast. I could either fall apart and be reduced to a pile of naked rubble on the floor, or I could react...differently.

I chose the latter.

I cocked back my arm and slapped Jake across the face as hard as I could.

CHAPTER
ELEVEN

JAKE

What. The. Fuck.

It took me several seconds to process what had just happened.

Cave Man and Mad Man were ecstatic. I could tell by the way my cock lurched inside Shelby as the hot sting of the slap fully registered. *Fuck yeah! This kitten's got claws!*

Truth be told, I was no stranger to pain during sex, but that had been a very long time ago.

My curiosity of all the things that could happen on a night like this immediately expanded from the typical *Will she spend the night?* and *Does she like to cuddle?* to *Will we need Bactine?* and *Will there be a broken lamp on my hotel bill?*

I caught Shelby's shocked expression at what she had done; a flash of a recoil as if she expected me to react violently. Almost immediately, however, she moved into recovery mode. She kissed my face softly, several times, where it was most likely beet red. Where it might even have borne her handprint. She kissed her way down my neck and resumed her rhythmic grinding as if nothing had happened.

Meanwhile, I could feel her stilted breath as she tried desperately to stifle her crying. My shoulder became wet with her tears.

Evolved man needed to get involved.

"Hey, hey. Stop." I whispered as I gently grabbed her hands from my shoulders. "Just hold on a second." I peeled her body away from mine until she was facing me. Her face was streaked with tears, her nose runny and red. She looked down, ashamed.

As much as I've appreciated Shelby's beauty up until now, nothing could hold a candle to this. Broken wide open, exposing her softest insides, I was spellbound.

She choked and sputtered as she tried to inhale, trying to get enough air in to speak. She put her hands over her face.

"Oh my God. I don't know what happened. I didn't mean..." she whispered, nearly too embarrassed to speak at all.

"Hey. I know." I pulled her hands away from her face as I encouraged her to look at me. "I know." I raised my hand to wipe another tear just as it crested her lower eyelid.

"I'm so sorry."

"It's okay...You just had an emotional response. It happens." I gently lifted her off me and guided her to the bed to sit down. "Hang on. I'll be right back," I told her.

I grabbed a bottle of water from the fridge and the two white bathrobes from the closet. Yes, I would be giving a robe to Shelby to preserve her dignity as we moved past this moment, but there was a reason I needed one for myself. I didn't want her having to concern herself with my erection that wasn't going anywhere anytime soon. You see, Evolved Man liked another kind of pain.

Not physical pain. And not the affliction of it.

No, he had a thing for emotional pain and the irresistible allure of being able to fix it.

My name is Jake Ford and I have a savior complex. Hero or "white knight" complex. Whatever you'd prefer to call it.

Evolved man often conspired with Mad Man to rescue the "damsel in distress." And this exquisite damsel was in more distress than I'd come across in quite some time.

To be fair, I didn't get off on the pain itself. It was the vulnerability and the emotional intimacy. And for me, this was a hundred times more intimate than my having been inside her just minutes before.

I helped Shelby on with her robe and then pulled her into me. Holding her head against my chest, I tried to temper my breathing in order to calm her.

WHEN I WAS NINETEEN AND HOME FROM THE UNIVERSITY OF ARIZONA for the summer, my mother and I were watching my little brother Trevor play his last home baseball game of his junior year. It was a big deal, scouts had come to see him, and he was looking down the barrel of a full scholarship. He had everything going for him, all of it in the palm of his hand.

After hitting a monster line drive straight down first, as he was rounding second base, his legs gave out from under him. We all thought he tripped.

But he didn't get up. He lay there motionless. My mother and I stood immediately, her with a vise grip on my arm. I started to move to guide her down the bleachers toward the field, but she stayed frozen in place. I had no choice but to stay frozen with her and watch it all play out like a bad dream.

Coaches and staff ran out from both teams. All the players stood in a broad circle on the field around him, paralyzed with fear and helplessness.

He's got to be okay. Just move a little, Trev.

His coach scanned the stands until his eyes found ours, all color drained from his face. He shook his head.

One of the coaches had begun CPR. The paramedics arrived and began their efforts.

All of it had been in vain, however. Trevor was gone before he hit the ground.

The explanation we got for my brother's SCD, or "sudden cardiac death" was an undiagnosed hypertrophic cardiomy-opathy, the thickening of the heart muscle making it hard for it to pump blood effectively. It's common for it to go undetected, and it's spectacularly unfair how quickly it can take a young life without warning.

My mother was in shock. Her body moving, breathing and talking only because it remembered how. My aunts, uncles, and cousins poured in from Venezuela to help. I was so grateful to be taken in by their warm and enveloping compassion as they took care of absolutely everything. I was just a kid, and I didn't know anything about planning a funeral, much less how to process my own grief.

After my brother was buried, after all the relatives had gone, my mother collapsed into a pile on the bathroom floor.

Her grief had sent her gastrointestinal system into chaos, and she couldn't keep anything inside her. I put pillows and blankets on the bathroom floor, and every few hours I'd bring her soup, crackers, fruit, and water, trying to get her to eat and drink for me. After a few days, she seemed to be able to hold things in a little better, so I gently coaxed her into her bedroom. There she stayed for weeks.

I'd read to her, and we'd watch movies, but mostly she slept. I made the decision I wouldn't be going back to school that fall. My mother needed me too much.

After consistently meeting her where she was and not pushing too hard, by mid-summer, she was ready to start venturing outside. Short trips at first, since she still tired so easily. We would conveniently bump into her friends while we were out and about—I'd arranged for this in advance since she was adamant about not having the energy to see anyone on purpose. Every little encounter seemed to add a little more to her life meter. By late fall, she was beginning to seem like herself again.

At Christmas, a few of the relatives made the trip back to Portland since it would be the first one without Trevor. The firsts are the hardest, so everyone was respectfully somber. But my Uncle Mauricio, who was notoriously crude and inappropriate, said something off the cuff and made my mother laugh. A full, wonderful, exuberant belly laugh where tears streamed down her face. At that moment something clicked inside me.

It struck me that I had been the catalyst for her emergence from the deep, dark depths of her grief. That, if not for me, she may have stayed in that bathroom. I proclaimed myself her savior and the realization felt exhilarating.

My immature, underdeveloped brain locked this information in, and over time, it became infused and intertwined with my personality.

I didn't go back to Arizona, but I did take a few classes at the local community college. I saw an ad for auditions for a community theater play so I gave it a shot. I got the part, and the rest, as they say, is history. I'd found my passion.

I'd also found a seemingly endless supply of wounded, lost and broken people I could fix. Especially once I headed to LA.

I made friends with a few guys who needed a nudge, but mostly it was the women that I was drawn to. I could become anything they needed. A strong, solid, grounding force. A gentle, kind, soothing presence. A "tough love" disciplinarian, filling in for Daddy's inadequacies. It wasn't always romantic, but when it was, the physical part of the addiction was a high beyond any drug. I felt powerful, like I was healing them with my sex.

My acting fed my addiction, and my addiction fed my acting. I was completely full of myself most of the time. For a long time.

Chloe, the goth dream girl makeup artist, had been such a beautiful disaster, but she nearly took me down with her. She had not only introduced me to industrial music and the edgier side of new wave, but she'd also showed me an edgier side of sex. Riding crops, floggers, candle wax, nipple clamps, and the like. I responded especially favorably to being bitten, even more so if it left marks. Once, when she was stroking me while simultaneously biting the flesh just above my knee, she broke the skin with her sharply pointed canine teeth. She licked the wound and the second she showed me my blood on her tongue, I came so hard I broke a blood vessel in my eye.

Our dynamic had started out experimental and fun. Over time however, it became clear that she had some demons from her past that she was trying to exorcise through me somehow, and even though I still liked it, it was edging further and further into dangerous territory. I was locked in, however, bound and determined to help her any way that I could.

We became a codependent mess.

Somehow, I managed to break myself free from her grasp just as she was falling further down, ultimately losing herself to a heroin addiction for a while. Last I'd heard she'd been clean for a long time, gotten married and had kids. No thanks to me.

The dangerous dance with Chloe had scared me enough to

seek therapy. I wanted to develop healthier relationships, but I was inconsistent, and I could never seem to get to the heart of where my issues lived. And the problem with a savior complex is that your ego becomes this uncontrollable monster that convinces you what you are doing is good and necessary. You are helping people. You can't see past that to the damage you are doing— to other people and to yourself.

Holly had been the closest thing I'd had to a normal relationship, but when I ended things because there was nothing more I could do for her, I knew enough was enough. I found myself a new therapist, and it had been going well. Until.

Until I got Kendra's email about Shelby's husband.

Shelby, whom I was struck by in an instant in her audition video. Whom I'd watched as she played Cherrie Bombshell instructing her viewers on the perfect pinup pout or dry hair roller set. Whose beauty and magnetism in person tripped me up more than I'd ever thought possible.

And now she was a grieving widow?

This was more temptation than I could bear, and it seemed to be well worth a backslide. I didn't tell any of this to my therapist. I was fully aware of the slippery slope leading to nothing but trouble both for myself and for Shelby, but there was no way in hell I could resist.

WHEN I'D RETURNED TO THE TABLE THAT EVENING AND NOTICED HER switch flipped on, that look of fiery determination in her electric blue eyes, I was delighted beyond words.

Somehow, I sensed it was vital to let her have the wheel with me eagerly along for the ride.

But I could *not* let her hijack our first kiss.

I pulled away from her lip lock to take my time.

To memorize every centimeter, every curve and angle of her face. Tease out and savor the exquisite anticipation. Indulge in the deliberate manipulation of time that is so rare an opportunity.

Of course I was desperate to touch and taste every inch of her impossibly creamy skin and I ached to fuck her senseless.

But since the day we met, I had been *dying* to kiss her, and I'd be damned if I let it be just a pit stop on the way to our final destination.

I wanted…I needed it to *mean* something.

In my soap days, women would be so afraid to be nervous around me. They wanted to appear so cool, so together, they thought it would make them more appealing, so they'd put on an act. Become someone else. Little did they know, I'd likely have been much more entranced by the opposite.

While I'd stepped away in the restaurant, Shelby had put on this persona as a defense mechanism, a coat of armor to hide her nervousness and give her courage. It amused me to no end that I recognized it immediately. She was channeling her YouTube persona; Cherrie Bombshell had come out to play. Between that and the bravery a few glasses of wine can provide, she'd proclaimed herself ready, willing and able.

But as soon as I pressed pause on our kiss, I saw it. The tiny cracks in her armor. When I pulled away from her to dive deeply into her eyes and trace the contours of her beautiful face, I watched and felt as the pulse in her neck quickened to a machine gun pace. Her jaw slacked, parting her pillowy lips. Her chest began heaving in waves and I could practically feel the vibration of her pounding heart. I was affecting her as much as she was affecting me, and I relished this momentary glimpse of her vulnerability.

Then, as I initiated the kiss the way that I wanted, as our lips met, as I teased and tasted, exploring her warm, delicious mouth, when our tongues danced together in a perfect steamy tango, I felt her melt. Her legs threatening to buckle beneath her, her body becoming heavier in my arms. She was on the cusp of surrender.

She broke our kiss to regain her composure and become the steely temptress once again, but I knew it would only be a matter of time before her armor failed completely.

AND NOW HERE SHE WAS, FALLING APART IN MY ARMS.

I let her go momentarily to grab the duvet and pull it down. I sat at the head of the bed propped up on pillows. "Come up here with me," I said as I patted the spot and outstretched my arms.

She smiled weakly and crawled up next to me. She fit herself perfectly in the nook I'd made and laid her head on my chest. I would let her take the lead—this moment would only be what she needed it to be. If she started to kiss me and we continued where we'd left off, if she wanted to talk, if she fell asleep, if we just continued to lay here with no words—just me stroking her hair, caressing her back, any or all of it would be perfect. I was just grateful to have her in my arms, bearing witness to her most personal pain.

"I'm so embarrassed. I have no idea why I would have done that. I've never hit anyone in my life. I've never even spanked my son." She was trying hard not to cry again.

"Sometimes our emotions get the better of us, especially if we've experienced tragic loss or trauma. My mother went through all of it. She'd be in the middle of something mundane and start to cry. Or laugh. Or scream. Waves of grief come crashing down at the most inopportune moments. Believe me,

I really do understand. And you didn't hit me all that hard." I lied. My cheek still throbbed, and I wished I could put ice on it without making her feel worse.

"Still. I'm so sorry." She managed to look up at me, her blue eyes swimming and makeup streaked across her face like abstract art. My heart lunged and I was reminded of my body's aching need. I wrapped my arms tighter around her.

I was hoping she'd say more, talk through more, let me in more. But she continued to remain alone in her own head, every now and then snuggling in a little closer.

Another hour went by, and Shelby got up to use the bathroom. She began to gather her clothes. "I think I'd better go. I'm sorry tonight turned out like this," she said.

"Turned out like what? Honestly, I had such a wonderful time at dinner, and it has been an absolute honor to spend this quiet time with you. Really."

She looked at me bewildered. As if it were impossible that a man could enjoy an evening that didn't end with him having an orgasm.

"Plus, getting to see you naked," I made an elaborate chef's kiss. She smiled gratefully and headed back to the bathroom. When she came out, she'd smoothed her hair and scrubbed the makeup off her face. Looking so fresh and innocent and still so vulnerable, I knew I desperately needed to see her again. This couldn't be the end. "I'm in Chicago for a few days in March for work and I'd have a chance to tack on a few extra days...I was wondering if you'd be interested in coming down and meeting me?"

She looked at me and glanced down. "Maybe? Can I have a few days to think about it? I'm house hunting and I'm about to put my current house up for sale. There's a lot to do. Plus getting the time off..."

"Okay, no pressure. Why don't I give you my number so you can let me know. It'd be somewhere around the fifteenth."

She took her phone out to put in my contact information. "Like I said, I just have a lot going on right now. We'll have to see." She moved toward the door.

It was hard to be optimistic, she seemed like she was going to find any excuse not to meet me, and this would be the last time I saw her. Again, I found myself with nothing to lose. I crossed the space between us and put my hands on either side of her face, gently demanding her full attention. "Shelby, you are an amazing woman. I really, really want to see you again."

She closed her eyes and tilted her head, reaching a hand up to press mine more firmly against her cheek, just for a second. I kissed her softly on the lips, then she took my hands and removed them from her face.

"Goodbye, Jake." And she was gone.

There was nothing left to do, so I poured my body into the bed.

THE NEXT MORNING, I WENT TO THE HOTEL GYM AND TRIED TO WORK out some of the erratic emotions swirling through me. It helped a little, but then I immediately undid all my hard work when I subsequently had four cups of coffee. Being over caffeinated at the airport is rarely a good idea, especially when undercut with angst and uncertainty. I was unreasonably irritated with everyone and everything. It sucks being a minor celebrity while simultaneously having real human emotions. God forbid Jake Ford gets short with someone. It's assumed from then on that I am a just another Hollywood asshole.

When it was my turn at the TSA checkpoint, I reached into my front backpack pocket for my passport. As my hand sunk deeper, the back of my fingers brushed against something soft. Something lacy. In hindsight, I probably should have waited to inspect it until after I was through security, but my curiosity got the best of me, and I pulled it out. There, dangling from my fingers right in front of the burly TSA agent, was Shelby's black thong. I quickly shoved it back in the pocket, but the agent's cheeky smile and the shake of his head told me I hadn't been quite fast enough.

Once past security, I found a bench and reached into the pocket again. Along with the underwear, there was a note written on the hotel stationary.

> *Jake,*
> *Thank you for everything tonight. I am still so very*
> *sorry for the way things ended, but I'd love to be able*
> *to make it up to you sometime. I owe you (at least) one.*
> *Shelby*

SHE INCLUDED HER PHONE NUMBER. THE BEST I COULD FIGURE WAS she'd made her covert moves on her way out of the bathroom. Right before the conversation about Chicago. She knew full well we'd be seeing each other again.

Stealthy little minx.

I entered her number in my phone and took a picture my hand holding Shelby's underwear.

I'm guessing you're responsible for this? Probably worse things I could have pulled out of my bag at TSA.

;)

So... Chicago?

Yes, Chicago. We'll talk details soon.

I WAS NO LONGER UNREASONABLY IRRITATED. INSTEAD, I WANDERED around the Las Vegas airport with a big, dumb smile plastered on my face, much preferring to look like a Hollywood idiot rather than a Hollywood asshole.

CHAPTER
TWELVE
SHELBY

March 2013

Things moved quickly once Kendra and I got back from Vegas. I was highly motivated to get my new life in order, so within the week I went to meet with David about putting the house on the market. As I'd expected, Marion got wind of the reason for my visit and was up in arms about it. "How could you possibly sell Brody's childhood home?"

"He's a sophomore in college, Marion. He's barely home now as it is, and he wants to get an apartment downtown for the summer when he starts his internship with David."

She pursed her lips tightly and shook her head. "You know, I spent a lot of time, and we spent a lot of money making that house a beautiful home for the three of you. And to think that you can just leave that easily? What about Aristotle? What about the memories?"

That was my in. "That's exactly why. The memories. It's much too painful to be in that house, everything reminds me of him. I just can't do it anymore." None of it was a lie, it just wasn't painful in quite the way she was thinking.

Marion finally agreed, but the whole conversation upset her so much that she took a pill and went to bed. David opened a bottle of wine and invited me into his office to continue the conversation. He pulled a folder out of his file cabinet and glanced at its contents.

"Ari's life insurance paid out in August, right?"

I nodded.

"And you'll have ten years to withdraw his retirement funds as beneficiary, so we don't have to worry about that right now."

David had set everything up, life insurance and IRAs, as well as living trusts for us before Brody was born. It made dealing with money after Ari's death virtually seamless. Money handling and planning for our future were never Ari's strong suit, preferring instead to live in the present, like Peter Pan in a perpetual Neverland where things are just magically handled. In the real world, David dealt with all the big life financial things, and I was responsible for all the household bills and expenses. I was grateful that I didn't have to go digging much through Ari's personal financials, though. God knows what I might have discovered.

He sat at the desk and opened his laptop. "Let's look at the comps and see what the house is going to be worth. Then you'll know between that and the life insurance money, what you're looking at as a budget for the new house." Leave it to David to completely leave emotion out of it and get right down to business. I appreciated that.

"Actually, I don't want any money from the sale of the house," I said.

He looked up at me, confused.

"I know you and Marion bought the house, and I know

how much money you've spent over the years. I want you to keep the money."

David pinched his eyebrows and looked down at the desk. "I hope you don't have the impression that you are beholden to us. That was never our intention. We were in a position to help you out, so we did. And we were happy to do it."

"I know. And I don't feel beholden. It's just time for me to do it on my own. And I can. I don't need a big place since it's just me. My car is paid off and I have a good job. I will be just fine."

David nodded his head and smiled. "I know you will be, Shelby. And I understand how you might appreciate this opportunity to start fresh. You were so young when you started your family." He closed his laptop and folded his hands in front of him. "I will insist, however, that you let me continue to support Brody's education."

"Deal." I warmed with gratitude and affection for this magnanimous man.

The house sold in less than a week. We had agreed to a quick closing, so I took some time off to focus on packing and arranging an estate sale for the contents of the house I wouldn't be taking with me. Which was nearly all of it. While Marion was busy arguing my getting rid of "perfectly lovely things," David insisted that I should keep the proceeds of the sale. I decided the proceeds would be well served as donations to the Mercer-Watts Foundation and the Aspire Cosmetology and Barbering Academy.

The only things I'd be moving besides my clothes and personal things would be my books, my plants, and my beloved vanity.

What I was dreading the most was unearthing memories contained in photos. I pulled out our wedding album without looking inside and put it in a large tote. Every picture of Ari, or of Ari and me went inside. Intent on keeping Brody's baby and childhood albums, I took out any pictures that included Ari putting them in the box, planning to explain the reason why to him when he was older. I'd asked Kendra to store the tote for me at her place since I wanted to save these things for Brody, but I could not stand the thought of them in my new house.

Soon I was inhaling and exhaling deeply in my very own three bedroom, one and a half bath bungalow in Tosa Falls. The difference in the energy of the space compared to the other house was staggering, and I wished I'd had the courage to move months earlier.

It was only a few blocks from Aspire, but the proximity to work hadn't been the main selling point for me. It was the enclosed sun porch that spread the entire width of the front of the house. The southern exposure wouldn't have the sun blasting me in the morning or late afternoon, only bless me with plenty of wonderful natural light. I decided I just needed to find a lovely vintage inspired sofa and it would make a perfect spot for reading. My new house was comically empty on move in day as Kendra, Gary and I accomplished everything in a few trips. I had perfectly timed the arrival of my new bed frame and mattress, so I'd at least have that for the first night.

The following night, I would be driving to Chicago to meet up with Jake.

We'd texted often and had spoken on the phone a few times a week. It was a pleasant distraction from the chaos of the move. It had also been effective at getting me past my embarrassment over what had happened in Vegas.

With my new start, even as sparse as it was, I was feeling much more settled. I may not have been ready that night in the Hard Rock Hotel, but I felt quite confident that I would be this time.

I'd often let myself delve into memory and fantasy

regarding everything that happened up until my breakdown. All the little intimate moments leading up to going to his room. And once we were there; how his hands had felt. How his lips tasted. The sounds he made. The way he said my name.

Every so often I'd get a flash of two figures in white hotel robes tangled up together on the bed, one holding the other in his arms while gently stroking her hair. I could not seem to reconcile that one of those people had been me. I feel like I left my body during that time, unable to comprehend how someone who hardly knew me could possibly be so tender and compassionate. How a man could so easily move beyond his need in the moment to tend to mine. It was completely foreign and incomprehensible. It was much easier to spool up that memory into a ball and tuck it away in a corner.

Jake said he'd be working until around seven that Friday and I really didn't want to deal with Chicago rush hour. I decided I'd leave my house around seven thirty to make it there a little after nine. I was fine to not make any plans for that night assuming there was only one thing we'd be doing anyway. He'd asked me to pack a nice dress for the next night and I got the impression he really appreciated me in full pinup regalia.

Halfway to Chicago it started to rain. I never loved driving at night, much less in a semi unfamiliar city, and the addition of the rain was adding to my stress. I decided to try and relax myself by indulging in a little fantasizing about Jake. "Sweet Nothing" by Calvin Harris and Florence Welch came on my shuffled playlist and my brain flashed with strobe images of Jake and me in his hotel room in time with the music.

That magical movie kiss, my hands in his hair. His hands around my waist and splaying across my back. Him coming up behind me, hot breath on my skin as his tongue traced up my neck. How his eyes flashed so hungry and wild as I straddled him.

The next verse, I began to imagine what it would be like when I got to his room that night. How he might open the door and grab me by the wrist to drag me inside. No words would be spoken, our mouths too eager to do other things. How he might push me up against the wall grabbing my arms to hold them above my head with one hand as he tore open my shirt with the other. His greedy mouth licking and nibbling, greeting every new bare inch of my skin the second it was exposed.

Him deftly taking off his belt with one hand, pulling it out of the last loop with a snap...

The realization of my heart pounding and my chest heaving thrust me into the present moment. My knuckles turned white on the steering wheel as my train of thought thankfully came to an end just before Jake's face became someone else's. Memory and fantasy were converging. Past and future. I pushed it all aside and concentrated instead on my upcoming exit.

I decided there was a special place in hell for the person who thought it a good idea to design an Upper and a Lower Wacker Avenue. Navigating them always seemed like driving in an MC Escher drawing. I finally made it to the hotel, grateful for the valet parking and finally being relieved of my car.

I made my way through the lobby and found the restroom. Locking the door of the stall, I opened my overnight bag and pulled out the cleansing wipes I'd brought. The swampy state of my nethers after that harrowing drive would simply not do at all. I took off my clothes, cleaned myself up as thoroughly as I could, and put my trench coat back on. Trench coat and heels and nothing else. Yes, I know— it's a move so very cliché, like cinema seduction 101, but honestly, what man wouldn't appreciate it?

I surprised myself by keeping steady as I rode the elevator up, and only needing a few deep breaths as I walked down the hall toward room 312.

I knocked on the door, trying to keep myself from devolving into tremors as I heard footsteps coming toward me. The door opened and the second Jake and I saw each other we started laughing. There he was in nothing but a robe, and me in nothing but a trench coat, my sexy caper much less subtle than his. We both looked each other up and down acknowledging the very little material standing between us and nakedness.

He stood aside as he let me into the room.

"How was the drive? The weather looks pretty nasty out there."

"Jake?"

"Hmm?"

"I don't want to talk about the weather." I started to undo the belt on my coat, and he came toward me in a rush of movement. I was still on edge from my drive and at the thought of seeing him, I was happy to have him take the wheel.

He parted my coat as his hands made their way to my bare waist and drew me to him. His eyes met mine with a fiery intensity and he tilted his head down to kiss me. He smelled so clean and fresh, the signature "Jake" scent nowhere to be found. But I liked this too.

His hands caressed my skin as he slowly slid my coat off my shoulders. He was very much in command of his desire, and it was throwing me. Did he think I was so fragile after what happened in Vegas? His fingers tangled into my hair, and he grabbed a handful to tilt my head to the side so he could devour my neck. It wasn't aggressive or painful, just enough of a claiming to reassure me he didn't think me too precious or breakable. After my mini freakout in the car, I was grateful for his restraint, though too. I nearly giggled at my horny Goldilocks list of demands. *Not too soft. Not too hard. Sex me up juuust right.*

Jake pulled his face away to consider me. "What?"

I realized I was smiling. "Nothing. Just happy to be here."

"I'm happy you're here, too. Very happy." He opened his robe.

I smiled wider. "Yes, I can see that."

I mimicked having my hands bound together. "I almost brought silk scarves for you to tie me up with."

"Is that right?" He tilted his head with curiosity and smiled.

"You know, a little insurance policy so I won't slap you again."

"But you're not going to slap me again, are you?" His grin turning mischievous.

I shook my head.

"That's my good g—"

Without thinking, my hand flew to cover his mouth before the word escaped. "Don't call me that," I spat. "Never call me that."

His eyes wide with shock, he gently removed my hand from his mouth. "Okay. Noted."

I recoiled with shame at my outburst. "I'm sorry. I didn't mean to sound so harsh. I just don't like being called that at all." It didn't sound like something Jake said regularly, maybe he just got caught up in the little game he thought we were playing.

I liked games once upon a time.

I didn't anymore.

When you don't know the rules or are even asked if you want to play at all, it's no fun.

"I understand." He ran his thumb tenderly over my cheek. "Anything else I should know?"

I was getting frustrated with where this was going. It was becoming less a sexy rendezvous and more of a therapy session. I just wanted to get carried away and feel beautiful and feel pleasure, and instead he was trying to get into my head. I get that he was trying to be respectful, but it was pulling me out of the moment.

I knew how to pull us both back in.

I wrapped my fingers around his erection and licked my lips. I planted kisses down his neck, and across his collarbone. Licked my way down his chest and stomach, and as gracefully as I could, I got down on my knees. Grasping him fully in my fist, I looked up at his face which had become filled with wonder. The conversation was officially over.

I swirled my tongue around his tip. Jake hissed and gently fingered a lock of hair on the side of my face. I wrapped my lips around him and took him greedily into my mouth. He stroked my cheek as he exhaled my name, "Shelby."

"That's it, baby. Take it all."

"God, I love fucking that pretty mouth of yours."

I shuddered at the dark, intrusive voice in my head. I hoped I'd be able to move past it if I just concentrated harder on what I was doing.

"That's right, suck my cock, you filthy, fucking whore."

"Mmm, yeah. Swallow every last drop. You're such a little slut for my cum, aren't you?"

Tears pricked at the back of my eyes and my heart started to hammer violently. I didn't want to bow to my first instinct and bolt. I didn't want to collapse into a mess again.

Jake put his hands in my hair, and I froze. *At any second he will grip the back of my head. Firmly, with fingers splayed. Or he'd grab a handful of hair at the scalp and hold fast. And I'd have no choice but to take it. Gag on it. Choke on it. Like a good girl and a filthy whore.*

A memory flashed of little Brody crying because he didn't understand why Mommy got to eat popsicles all day sometimes when he could only have one. But when my throat was bruised, raw and swollen, and every swallow was razor blades, it was the only thing that helped.

I desperately needed to feel into the present moment. To what was actually happening and not what I was conflating with what had happened in the past.

Okay. Deep Breath.

Five things I could see. A small stain in the shape of Florida on the grey hotel carpet. My trench coat in a heap on the floor a few feet away. The loops of soft white terrycloth on the edge of Jake's robe. The abstract swirl pattern of hair on his thigh. The rippling muscles in his stomach tensing and relaxing.

Four things I could touch. The plushy friction of the carpet against my knees. The soft skin on the back of Jake's knee. The smooth, satiny heat of him in my hand. My poor, needy kitty, who, with an ebb of warm, liquid silk and a stab of deep ache, let me know how jealous she was of my mouth.

Three things I could hear. The hotel room's obnoxious HVAC unit. The sound of footsteps in the hall. Jake's intense but measured breathing.

Two things I could smell. Jake's hotel soap clean scent and the hint of a pheromone laced sweet muskiness that was replacing it as he began to sweat.

One thing I could taste. Well.

My breathing was becoming calmer as I became more present.

I was able to pay much closer attention.

Jake's hands threaded tenderly through my hair, combing

ever so gently, then twirling a strand around his index finger. His hips stayed steady.

I was in control.

I looked up at his face. One moment he was looking up at the ceiling, lost in sensation. The next he was looking down at me. His jaw tense, his eyes burning, his expression full of lust and white-hot desire, but there was not one hint of darkness.

Only reverence. Adoration. Appreciation. Awe.

I tilted my head to meet his hand as it came toward my cheek. I felt safe enough to continue my oral assignment with new-found fervor. I felt so cared for. Cherished. This tenderness was all I'd ever wanted from Ari. Any hint of it at all amongst the frenzy would have sustained me, but it never came. I could feel the tears forming again, and I was powerless to stop them.

Jake stroked down my face toward my jaw and put slight pressure under my chin with his finger—a gentle beckoning to draw me away from what I was doing. He sank down on the floor with me and kissed my tears as they fell.

"Shelby," he whispered. "What can I do? Tell me what you need."

The tears were flowing freely then. Another gesture I'd always craved, but never got. *Tell me what you need.* I was on the verge of breaking apart again.

I could just tell him. I wouldn't have to beg.

But I couldn't speak. Instead, I held the lapels of Jake's robe and kissed him hard. He mirrored my intensity, drawing us both up onto our knees, bodies pressed tightly together.

He broke the kiss to stand, holding onto my hands to help me up. I gasped in delighted shock as he scooped me up in his arms and carried me toward the bed, placing me gently down with my head on the pillows. Jake took off his robe and crawled to kneel above me, taking in every inch of my body with his eyes. Here was this voraciously hungry man, but somehow, even with his plate now in front of him, he was able to take his time and appreciate and admire the presentation.

He traced my skin with fingertips so gentle, I prickled with goosebumps and began to tremble. His fingers moved in lines and swirls, and I realized he was tracing the edges of my tattoos.

"So beautiful," he whispered.

I melted into the bed. Into his touch. He lowered his head onto me and made his way down my body. Taking his time, taking pieces of me into his mouth at regular intervals. I gasped and arched into him as he found erogenous zones I never knew I had. His fingers pressing into my flesh, his teeth gently scraping across the skin between my ribs. He was devouring me, but in an achingly tender way.

I soon became impatient and began writhing my body under his, signaling my need for him to go lower.

With my arousal acting as a homing beacon, he finally reached his destination between my thighs. He teased me, lapping with his tongue a few times, he then zeroed in on my clit and latched on. His mouth sucking and pulsing gently at first, then, as he slowly increased his speed and intensity, I increased the intensity with which my hands fisted the sheets. I raised my ass higher and instinctively he put a hand under me to hold me at this preferred angle.

I had a flash of familiar fear that it would all be taken away any second, just as I'd be ready to come. I put my hand on the back of Jake's head. *I could tell him what I needed.*

"Don't stop, Jake. Please don't stop."

And he didn't. Overloaded with need and greed, I silently pleaded for him to introduce his fingers into the mix. Then, as if I were able to transmit my thoughts directly through my clit, he did just that. As he expertly curled them into a "come hither" that would no doubt make me come harder, I braced my hands against the headboard to push my body harder into the deliciously filthy fray.

This man didn't just eat pussy—he worshiped it.

Just as the sounds of gospel choirs and visions of angels weeping nearly overtook me, I looked down and met Jake's wolfish eyes. The intensity of the intimacy jolted through us both, and he managed a moan, even with his mouth full. The salacious sound combined with subtle vibration sent a tremor through my whole body and toppled me over the edge into ecstasy.

I screwed my eyes shut and my head tilted back unnaturally far as if on a hinge. My mouth dropped open and I emitted a series of nearly inhuman squeaks, some of which were a frequency I'd imagined only audible to animals.

A breathy chuckle came out of Jake's mouth against my overly sensitive nerves and I spasmed and wriggled up toward the head of the bed.

As I came down from my peak, he propped himself up on one arm. Looking me straight in the eye, he wiped his mouth with the inside of his hand, then ran his tongue across his fingers before putting two in his mouth to suck them clean. I stared in wonder at the sexiest thing I'd ever seen, and my stomach lurched with the realization the object of my teenage obsession had just licked my arousal off his fingers.

Jake deftly rolled on his condom and positioned himself above me with the familiar pause I'd come to know as he subtly checked in. I nodded. The time of tears was long over.

He guided himself inside me swiftly and fully. The poor man had waited so long for his turn, and I wanted him to have it. I arched up to meet his every thrust, letting him know he didn't have to hold back for me. We clawed and scraped, digging our fingers into each other in a desperate attempt to get closer. I traced my tongue across his shoulder to taste the saltiness of his skin. The flesh felt so good in my mouth I dared to squeeze my teeth together. I felt his fingers press deeper into me and a rumbling moan escaped his mouth.

Something told me to push a little further. I found the sensitive place where his shoulder met his neck and sank my teeth in. Firmly, but not nearly hard enough to break the skin. He flinched and shuddered, but then sank into the sensation with another moan.

I raised my legs higher to invite him in deeper and I caught up to his rhythm with my hips. He pushed his shoulder closer to my mouth and growled softly, "Harder, Shelby. Bite me harder."

I increased the pressure of my jaw.

Sucking saliva through his teeth, the pace of his thrusts became frenetic. "God, Shelby. Fuck!" Jake tensed, shook, and shuddered his earthquake release. Once his convulsions had stopped, he surrendered his weight onto me and panted heavily into my neck.

He likes to be bitten. I smiled as I filed away that bit of information, wondering what other interesting things he liked.

CHAPTER
THIRTEEN
JAKE

In those seconds before full cognition every morning, in the space between asleep and awake, I was often in a geographical fog. More often than not, I'd be in some mid-grade hotel where I had to reorient myself to the city and the job. Usually not my favorite, much preferring to wake up in the familiarity of my house. But this morning, in this hotel, as I turned my body over and came face to face with the most beautiful pair of bright blue eyes, I was grateful for my nomadic life bringing me to this point.

I smiled and stretched my arms over my head. "Good morning." I reached over and pulled Shelby into me for a kiss. "How did you sleep?"

"Really well. I had a dream about having sex with Jake Ford." She giggled.

I considered how I felt about hearing my full name come out of her mouth. I had been hearing it in a different way than most people hear their name for almost thirty years. Being introduced as a guest on a teen spotlight show where it was usually followed by screaming. Fans using it to address me before gushing and asking for an autograph or picture. It had been better lately, as I was proud of the thing my name was associated with these days.

I know she was just being silly, but to Shelby I just wanted to be Jake.

I cupped her face and stroked her cheek with my thumb. She looked down and a hint of a blush bloomed on her cheeks. She was thinking about last night. I wondered if it was embarrassment at her tears or the happy butterflies like I was experiencing when I played back the night in my mind. Likely a mix of both.

I'd never been with a woman who showed me so much in such a short time. She didn't tell me a thing, and maybe she never would, but she ran nearly the full gamut of human emotion last night. The sudden burst of anger—I'd had a fleeting thought that the "good girl" thing was to do with something dark and sinister from her childhood and I'd hoped against all hope that I was wrong. Remorse. Tension. Anxiety. Calming. Melting. Tears, surrender and ecstasy. She was a kaleidoscope and I'd been positively transfixed.

I had fallen to the floor completely consumed by her exquisite tragedy. I could never have imagined a woman so undeniably compelling, her tears like magnets drawing me deeper and deeper. Whatever she had wanted, whatever she had needed, I would have given it to her. I'm not a religious man, but since I was already on my knees, I vehemently thanked the heavens in that moment for her wanting and needing me.

I was able to make her come so easily even though she had broken wide open, so raw and exposed. Most people might delve into paralyzing self-consciousness, their insecurities hijacking any hope of orgasm. Not Shelby. In those moments she chose to trust that I could give her what she needed, and she gave herself over to me completely. It was the greatest high I'd ever experienced, and I knew that's what I'd be chasing from now on. I could hear my therapist in my head cautioning me, and at some point, I'd consider being more careful. But later. Much later.

I pride myself on being able to take cues and read people well—body language, micro expressions and the things they don't say, but it delighted me to my core to find Shelby was excellent at taking cues as well. The pleasure of my cock buried in her perfect pussy married with the pain of my flesh caught between her teeth, God. She rocked my fucking world.

Shelby ran her hands over my body, and began to wiggle her hips, inching closer to me.

"What's going on here?" I put my hand on her ass and moved her a little more.

"You're not the only one with morning wood." She laughed, then grasped my erection and began to stroke.

I put my hand between her milky thighs and felt her deliciously slick. "Mmm. Guess not."

She reached over for a condom on the nightstand, opened the package and rolled it onto me. She turned away onto her side and shimmied her ass, backing into me in wordless instruction. Eagerly I turned on my side to meet her and slid deep into her from behind as she tangled her top leg with mine.

We fucked in glorious slow motion. Her hips pressed back to meet my every stroke, our bodies rocking together in rhythms that felt practiced and familiar—like we'd been dance partners in another lifetime.

It felt luxurious and decadent. Like something I shouldn't be allowed to have. Something that was bad for me. And truth be told, it probably was, but I didn't give a fuck.

I wanted to indulge in her completely. Inhale the essence of her hair and the remnants of last night's perfume behind her ear. Memorize how her soft skin felt beneath my fingers and tasted on my lips. Record every moan, every whimper. I wanted to etch all of this into every fiber of my being because I knew that in a week, in a day—hell, in an hour, just how badly I'd be craving her.

I reached around to give some love to her clit and was delighted to find her fingers already there. I put my hand on top of hers, moving in slippery circles right along with her. In no time we were spiraling together in rare synchronous orgasm.

When we were done languishing in bliss and I'd finished my turn in the bathroom, I came out to find her wandering around the room. "Why am I blind? Where's the coffee maker?"

"You passed it on your way out of the bathroom."

"Ah, gotcha." She went over and busied herself with starting the coffee and I just smiled as I watched her. Naked as the day she was born, and not a second thought about it. I'd even put a pair of boxer briefs on. I loved how comfortable she was without clothes. I was used to women who race to cover up or dart through the shadows like naked ninjas.

"What do you want to do today?" she asked, looking at me over her shoulder.

I tore my eyes away from her perfect, heart shaped ass, slid up behind her and wrapped my arms around her waist. "I thought we'd go have breakfast and take a walk along the river. We could go shopping or go to the art museum? You've probably been here a lot, is there anything you like to do?"

"Honestly, I usually hang out in neighborhoods like Logan Square or Andersonville, not usually downtown. Breakfast and a river walk sounds great. It looks like a decent day outside."

"Listen," I said as I traced along her neck with my nose, "if we have any hope at all of leaving this room, you are going to have to put clothes on immediately."

I'd wondered how long it would take her to get ready to head out, not knowing what her daytime routine might be. Turned out a quick shower, a little mascara and lipstick, and hair up in a simple ponytail with a faded black bandana took less time than I needed for myself. She wore a fitted black and white checked button down darted perfectly to highlight her body shape, a black cardigan, cuffed dark wash skinny jeans and bright red Chuck Taylor high tops. My favorite cartoon in casual perfection.

I also loved that she wore the perfume she had on the day we met. Sweet honeysuckle with a hint of tea rose. Vintage and classic, but not old fashioned, it thrust me right back to that day and I couldn't stop smiling. I also appreciated that she had a "nighttime" perfume too. In Vegas and last night, she wore something much more sensual, a sultry jasmine and oud combination that conjured an image of the dark and sexy underbelly of the Orient in the mid-century.

I'D FILMED A SHOW WITH A SCENT SPECIALIST IN THE FIRST SEASON. IT was meant to be funny, synthesizing fake urine spray for camouflaging hunters, the smell of human excrement recreated for pranks and the like. But Gerald was very passionate about his craft and had a nose like I never knew a human could. We talked about scent in length, well beyond filming, and still have a relationship to this day. He offered to help me create my own signature scent, and we worked together over the course of several weeks to be able to give my sense of smell space to rest and develop, and to acclimate to the intensity of the project. The final product became top notes of bergamot, mandarin and lavender, spices in the center-- anise, caraway and pink peppercorn, and a base of amber, vanilla, musk and oak moss.

Shelby's perfumes were exquisite, and I thought that maybe when our time together was over, I might be tempted to work with Gerald to try and recreate them.

AFTER BREAKFAST, WE WANDERED AROUND DOWNTOWN CHICAGO. It was a blissfully mild spring day, sunshine and low 60s. Every little while, she'd point out a restaurant whose name she'd recognized. Each time, I'd ask if she'd been there, and she'd say no.

"So, how is it you know about all these places, but you've not been?" I thought maybe she had a restaurant bucket list she had yet to tackle.

"Well, I used to hear a lot about restaurants. Particularly Chicago restaurants. My husband...my late husband, Ari, was a chef."

This was the first time she'd mentioned him. I knew I would have to watch myself here. I was so curious about him, but I didn't want her to shut down if the conversation got too intense.

"He had a restaurant downtown Milwaukee called The Scorpion and the Frog. It's a Mediterranean fusion place."

"Ari. That's short for..."

"Aristotle. His mother was really into Greek philosophy and loved the name. He played right into it, though. He went to culinary school in Greece when our son was a baby, then his dad helped him open the restaurant shortly after he got back. I suggested he call it "Aesop's Tables.""

"That's clever."

"He loved it, but when we looked it up there were already three other restaurants in the country with that name. I tried to convince him that if he was the only one in Wisconsin it would be fine, but he couldn't stand the thought of not being original. So, he settled on the name of one of Aesop's fables."

"Except it's not. The Scorpion and the Frog was a loose adaptation of one of Aesop's fables, but not actually his." There was a time during my late teen years when I was a little obsessed with Greek philosophy myself. "It's a commentary on narcissism."

Shelby stopped walking and studied my face, blinking several times like a computer processing information. She looked out over the river, she shook her head subtly, and in her profile, I saw a hint of a smile. It didn't seem to be fondness or wistfulness or nostalgia. I would have guessed that she was feeling smug.

The late husband portion of the conversation had ended as organically as it began, and I was grateful. No fanfare and no tears meant that the subject could very well come up again.

I was beginning to realize that Shelby's complicated emotional state may have had less to do with her husband's death and more to do with the man himself.

We made our way back to the hotel to rest and get ready for dinner. I'd made reservations and I wanted to give us plenty of time. Shelby was not to be rushed, especially with the plans I had.

"How long will you need to get ready for dinner?" I asked.

"Hmm, a little over an hour. Are we okay on time?"

"Perfectly fine. Hey, I uh..." I stammered. I wasn't sure if this was going to come out right—I didn't know how to ask without sounding creepy. "Do you mind if I watch you get ready?"

She looked at me inquisitively, her eyebrows pinched slightly. She tilted her head and her face softened. "Not at all. Let me jump in the shower and then I'll set up my stuff."

When she'd finished in the shower, she grabbed her toiletry bag and brought it to the desk. Looking out the window seemingly surveying the amount of natural light she had, she then went into her suitcase and pulled out a lighted mirror. I was impressed.

She carefully laid out her things. Brushes, eyeshadow palettes, false eyelashes, curling iron, hairbrush and accessories. The desk was filled with all things girly and Mad Man was beside himself.

She grabbed her phone and a portable speaker. After a quick scroll, a swing beat started with a woman's voice singing about how she was "too damn hot."

She was going about this almost as if I wasn't there. I wondered if this was kind of meditative for her—something she really loved, like getting your mise en place ready before beginning to cook. She went back to her suitcase and pulled out something red, then took off her robe and slowly slid a red, lacy thong up her thighs. She picked up a matching red bustier and put that on while facing away from me so I could watch while she fastened each of its many hooks. She grabbed a small, zippered pouch and from that pulled out a garter and stockings. She put the garter on and slid the stockings on one by one, fastening each at the top effortlessly. During all of this she'd steal a few glances at me to make sure I was watching.

I was.

I wasn't even blinking. I didn't want to miss a second of this show. I was awestruck that she seemed to know exactly how I'd wanted this to go.

She made her way over to the desk and I sat on the edge of the bed. At some point I would need to shower and get dressed too, but for now, it was all about her. She began with her hair. Sitting up straight, straighter than was probably comfortable and arching her back, she began to curl her hair and twist it into a few victory rolls at the top, carefully securing them with bobby pins she'd opened with her teeth. She was leaving the back down and long, so she made sure to curl those into loose ringlets before carefully brushing them out to make soft waves. She pinned a red rose off to the side. A red rose that matched her lingerie and it made me giddy that I'd be the only one who knew.

Every now and again, she'd meet my eyes in the mirror. She'd smile a little smile and continue doing what she was doing. She'd bop along or sing a little with the music just like she did in the Cherrie Bombshell videos.

By this point, I was crawling out of my skin with need. I rubbed my hands up and down my thighs to try and distract myself. I knew this was going to be something, but catching this live show was way more exciting than I could have imagined. Particularly because instead of hundreds or even thousands of people getting to see her, this time it was just for me. And she seemed to know how it was affecting me.

But the capper, the *pièce de résistance*, was her putting on her lipstick. We were coming to the end of the show, and this was the finale. Tracing the outline of her perfect pout before filing it in flawlessly with the fire engine red color. And now I'd tasted those lips. Those magical lips that felt like velvet wrapped around my cock. I raked my hands through my hair as I began to sweat.

She looked at me in the mirror. "Are you okay over there? You're awful fidgety." She smiled.

"Yup. Just fine." Lies. Far from fine. Ready to explode, in fact.

"You don't look fine," she mischievously accused as she held the lipstick tube away from her mouth. "You look like you have a secret."

"Is that right?"

"Yes. I think you really like this. I think this is turning you on." She turned to face me instead of continuing to look at me through the mirror. "In fact, I think you'd really like to touch yourself right now."

I swallowed hard. "Hmm." This could be amazing or spectacularly embarrassing. I was so hot I was willing to bet I'd jerk it three or four times and that would be that. That's not sexy. "Maybe."

"Give me one second to fix this part of my hair."

"And then what?"

"And then it's my turn to watch you."

God. Damn.

This was happening. *My fucking fantasy come to life.*

She finished her hair and spun around. She swung her legs over the arm of the chair and stared at me, heat burning in her perfectly made-up eyes. "Your turn."

It was all I could do to not undo my pants as fast and as furiously as I wanted to. I wanted to turn her on too, and masturbating like I had just clumsily stumbled into puberty was not going to do that. At least I didn't think so. I unleashed myself and slowly started stroking.

She placed the fingernail of her index finger gently between her teeth. Watching as her eyes would go between meeting mine and down to what I was doing was spurring me on even harder. This was not going to take long.

She looked like she was readjusting herself in her chair, but she slowly got up and made her way over to the bed. She put her hand on my chest and knelt next to me. She tilted her head toward mine and brought her lips to my ear. After grazing her tongue along my earlobe, she asked, "Do you touch yourself when you watch my videos, Jake?"

I nodded feverishly.

"Did you touch yourself while watching me even before we met?"

I nodded again, unable to control my panting.

"Hmmm." She trailed several kisses along my neck. "Well, then that's something we have in common."

That was it.

I came like cannon fire.

Shelby took no time at all with her own orgasm. I certainly hadn't wanted to mess up her hair and makeup, so I helpfully suggested she perch herself on my face.

For all the sins I've committed, being anointed by this woman's pussy was an absolution I didn't deserve. But until my true nature was discovered, until the day it would all implode, I would feast on and bathe in her sacrament every chance I got.

After the waiter took our order, I turned to Shelby and smiled. I scrubbed my hands over my face, a little nervous to ask my question.

"So...you know my secret. How much I liked your videos, and how I watched you even before we met. It's all out there. You said we had that in common." I grinned and put my elbows on the table, my face in my hands in an expression of pure fascination. "I want to know more about that."

She let out a giggle, and then a large sigh, like she was psyching herself up for the confession. "Well. To put it bluntly, you were my sexual awakening."

"I beg your pardon?" That I had not expected.

She nodded. "My mom watched all the daytime soaps and once when I stayed home sick from school in seventh grade *Salte Ste. Marie* came on. I'd never watched soaps with her before and she felt the need to explain to me when people landed in bed together how much of a sin that was, blah, blah,

blah. Then you came on the screen. Tight black T-shirt, earrings, bad boy grumpy hotness. It piqued my interest for sure."

"So, wait. You had your sexual awakening watching soaps with your mom?"

She laughed. "No, that came later. It was the beginning of that summer when I started watching in my bedroom. It was at the peak of the whole 'will they/won't they' with Foster and Nikki? Remember?"

"Oh yeah, that was kind of fun." The storyline had dragged on for months, and it got a lot of attention. I got a lot of attention after that, too.

"Anyway, the argument in the alley, in the rain, how you grabbed her and kissed her. And then when you took her into the stockroom at the bar, pressed her up against the wall with her arms up over her head...well. I started to feel things in places."

I stared at her trying to picture her at twelve or thirteen lusting after Foster McBride. God, he was such an ass, but I'll admit, fun to play. I never really understood the whole "bad boy" appeal, but man, after those episodes, things ratcheted up for me in a big way. At the time I thought it was a big deal, the fact that I couldn't throw a stick without hitting a woman who'd eagerly spread for me. Looking back, though, I have many more regrets than fond memories.

She continued. "I stumbled upon my mom's romance books around then, too. You know, like the bodice rippers with the shirtless guy on the front? I remember wanting to read them because I thought they'd be nice love stories and then, boom, the sex would start. I remember being so shocked that my perfect Christian mother would have these books, but then I really got sucked in. Instead of the guy on the cover of the book, though, I would picture you."

"So, you'd be reading one handed then?" I arched an eyebrow at her.

She giggled, "Sometimes, yes. I was brought up to believe that sex and masturbation were these shameful, forbidden things, so I struggled with my sexuality throughout my teens. Like, to be having these thoughts and feelings that felt so good and so natural to do something about. How could it be a sin? I wasn't hurting anyone."

"Yeah, that's fucked up. I can't imagine growing up like that."

She shrugged. "How about you? Did you have a sexual awakening?"

"For boys, a sexual awakening can happen if the breeze changes," I laughed. "But no, I guess I did have a significant moment. And I'm pretty sure I am in the company of thousands of other boys who came of age in the 70s, especially those of us with single mothers." I inhaled deeply for dramatic effect. "I fondly remember the day I discovered the intimates section of the Sears Catalog."

Shelby laughed a loud, hearty laugh I hadn't heard before. It was melodious and infectious, and I wanted to make her laugh like that all the time. When I wasn't making her scream, that is.

"Are you serious?" she squeaked.

"Hell yeah! One day you're innocently flipping through the toy section and then you accidentally stumble upon ladies in bras and underwear, nightgowns, lacy teddies. Something clicks. I had to hide it under my bed after I'd stuck a few of the pages together." I chuckled. "Later on, I had all the obligatory posters on my bedroom walls like Farrah Fawcett and Cheryl Tiegs. Oh, and Maeve St. Vincent."

"Maeve St. Vincent, as in who played Nikki's stepmother Cassie on the show?" Her eyes got wide.

"Yup. I got cast having no clue she was on it. Walked in on day one and came face to face with my fantasy. That was surreal to say the least."

She was staring at me with a strange expression I couldn't figure out until she cocked her head to the side and smirked. "Sounds familiar."

Holy shit.

"Did you and she ever...?" she asked.

"Oh hell no. She was older, married and never even gave me the time of day unless we were in a scene together. I'd kind of gotten over her by then, too." I took a breath. "Had you gotten over me by the time we met? I know that seems like a strange question to ask since, well, everything that's happened. But I'm curious. How were you feeling about filming the show?"

"It was weird. My teens and adult years went along and yeah, you were fading into the background. Sometimes I'd see a picture or movie poster and smile a little out of nostalgia. Then my son Brody was flipping through the cable channels a few years ago and we stumbled on *Dare Me to Do it*. A lot of those memories came back, and something else. I decided I liked you with a little more age, your face was much more interesting to me. Like you've lived a couple of lifetimes in the years in between and you seemed to have so many stories."

She put her hand on my face. My heart began to race at the tender gesture and at what she was saying. I had rarely in my life felt as seen as I did just then.

"And the show. We liked it when it first started, how silly it could get. But when you started asking people to share deeper insights, asking them about their lives and their feelings, and being so genuinely interested in their stories, well. My crush came back."

She smiled and her sparkling eyes told me she was telling the truth.

I am rarely at a loss for words, but I had nothing.

Shelby put up a finger as the waiter passed. When he approached the table, she said, "Can we get two shots of Malort, please?"

I looked at her bemused.

"Have you had it?" she asked.

"I've heard of it. And not good things."

She laughed. "It's a rite of passage I need to share with you as a Chicago adjacent resident. It's like the liquor equivalent of 'smell this and tell me if you think it's bad.'"

The waiter brought the small cordial glasses and placed them in front of us. Shelby picked up her glass and held it up. I did the same.

"I guess an appropriate thing for me to say at this point is, I dare you."

I laughed as our glasses clinked. I inhaled as I brought to my mouth. It didn't smell too bad at first, saffron and fruit I couldn't place, but when the notes of burning oil and chemical sludge hit, I winced. I bravely took a sip.

Jäegermeister is fucking delicious compared to Chicago's prank liquor.

Shelby made a face after taking a sip of her own. "I'm going to tell you how I describe this to people, and you tell me if you think it's accurate." She put her glass down and crossed her arms on the table. "Rubber bands soaked in grapefruit juice."

Damn if that wasn't right on.

CHAPTER
FOURTEEN
SHELBY

April 2013

"I'M REALLY FEELING THE TENSION IN MY LOWER ABDOMEN," THE client on my table said. I adjusted my movements to just below his navel. "Mmm, a little lower than that." He smiled and put his hands behind his head.

"This area is the boundary for the scope of my practice. For anything further toward the pelvic region, I'd recommend seeing a physical therapist," I said.

I looked around the room to make sure everyone was paying attention. Dimitri still had his hands behind his head just killing it playing his role as the creepy client.

"I don't know, it sounds so weird and clinical," Jess argued.

"That's kind of the point," I said. "If you try to say things in a casual or nice way, they can more easily counter your point and catch you off guard. It's all part of their game. If you shut them down with clinical or legal language, it usually works better."

This was the second ethics and safety class I'd given for the spa employees at Aspire. We were role playing real life scenarios so they could practice how they'd respond, feeling less awkward and more empowered. Darius and Randall were sitting in to get a better frame of reference on how to help protect their employees. Lyric, still being the operations manager for the front desk, also wanted to be there to get an idea of how to vet clients even with the first phone call. We were covering it all.

"Where you'd go from here all depends on how you're feeling. For me, I would end the session at this point. He's clearly a creep and I'm uncomfortable."

"I just don't get why these guys don't just go to the rub and tug places. They are easy enough to find." Darius said. He seemed so unsettled at the thought of his employees having to navigate these situations.

I sighed. "Because it's not necessarily the "happy ending" they're after. It's seeing how much they can get away with. The more legitimate the establishment, and the younger, more inexperienced the therapist, the more fun the game is for them." Ten years in the business as a woman had unfortunately given me plenty of experience with these predators.

I sent everyone out of the room while I instructed Dimitri what he was to do for the next scenario. They all filed back in minutes later to find him face down on the table.

"Candace, why don't you take this one. Undrape him and start some effleurage on his back, then concentrate on the lumbar area." She did as she was told.

She was working for a few minutes waiting for something to happen. I could see her puzzled expression as she raised her hands off of Dimitri's body.

"What are you noticing?" I asked her.

"Well, it seems like his low back hurts. Or he's ticklish."

"What makes you say that?"

Candace looked at his muscles while she tried to continue her massage. "Because he keeps tensing. It's kind of frustrating."

"He's doing that on purpose," I told her.

"What? Why?"

"He's moving his penis," I said with a straight face.

Dimitri stifled a giggle.

"He's doing what now?" Randall interrupted.

"Yes, he's contracting his muscles, like a man Kegel. He's trying to stimulate himself," I said.

"For the record, I am not." Dimitri lifted his head from the face cradle. "I'm just doing what Shelby told me to do and it feels so freaking weird."

"God, why are men so gross?" Lyric scowled.

"How would you deal with this one?" Jess asked. "I would feel super awkward about calling this out."

"You don't have to admit you know what he's doing. You could say something like, 'I'm noticing you are tensing a lot in your low back. If it's painful, I can adjust my pressure, but it's counterproductive for me to work on this area if you can't relax.' I bet just letting them know you are aware of something going on might make them stop."

When the class was over Darius, Randall, Lyric and I all continued to talk.

"In my day, you just took it in stride. All the flirting, the jokes, even people touching you. It was 'all part of the job', and you just had to get through it and get that cash." Darius looked forlorn.

"I mean, there is a difference between being out on a salon floor and having someone creepy in your chair, versus being in a room alone with a naked man." I was trying not to get too defensive; I knew where he was headed, and his heart was in the right place. "But yes, you're right. No one should have to put up with any of it. What do you think about having a class with the stylists where we brainstorm and role play solutions for them too?"

"Good idea."

I'd made plenty of mistakes with clients throughout my career. I'd been a people pleaser and an optimist, always trying to see the best in humanity, forever giving the benefit of the doubt. I would brush off a graze of fingertips on my thigh while giving a massage, even though it lingered a bit too long to be accidental. I would write off their splayed legs as hip issues instead of an attempt to call my attention to or grant me better access to their man parts. I would tell myself that I was the one clothed and in control, and the second I felt unsafe, I could easily leave while the client on my table could not. Did I? Not once.

I would politely answer personal questions because I didn't want to be rude. I could feel myself getting caught up in their grooming game, and still, did nothing to put a stop to it. The way I'd been conditioned within the confines of my personal life did nothing to empower me in my professional one. If anything, it made me more subservient, and far more susceptible to this predatory behavior. I told myself it had never gone so far as to have been considered assault, but I'd often felt disgusted and violated, nonetheless. It was unaccept-able and it needed to stop.

After Ari died, I took every ethics class I could find, arming myself with knowledge, and I became determined to pass along everything I'd learned. I wanted to protect our employees so that no one would have to go through the things that I had.

Later in the day when I had my first client, a facial, my mind began to wander from the muck of the morning's subject matter to much more pleasant thoughts. I'd wandered with these particular thoughts a lot lately, getting my butter flutters every time.

Jake.

It was easy to think of him in this room where we first flirted, but now our experiences together had expanded to things I never could have imagined in my wildest fantasies. Most of the time I still had a hard time believing it was real.

I finished up at work, these days I was always eager to get home to my cozy new house. I walked through the door at around 8:30 p.m. and immediately began my nighttime rituals. I changed out of my Aspire clothes and put on soft silky pajama bottoms and a camisole. I washed my face and took my time with my skincare routine which, like for most estheticians, was extensive and indulgent. I moved my body through a slow-flow yoga routine and made myself a cup of hibiscus tea.

I made my way to the sun porch to read for a while. One of the first things I did when I moved in was insulate the walls and replace all the windows with high efficiency, well-sealed ones. It was important for me to be able to use this room comfortably all year and Wisconsin winters can be brutal and unforgiving.

I came to the end of a chapter around 10:30 p.m. and started to gather my things to go up to bed. I grabbed my phone just as a call was coming in. It was Jake.

My pulse quickened and I smiled as I answered. "Hi there." No need for the inquisitive hello.

"Hey. I know it's late, but I am driving and I'm having a little bit of a hard time staying focused. I thought I'd try talking to someone. And I liked the thought of that someone being you."

"Aww, I like that too. Where are you?"

"I'm driving through Nebraska...wait, maybe Kansas? Seriously all these states blur together after a while. I'm on my way to a job."

"Alone? Huh. I would have thought everyone traveled together."

"Everyone else does, but not me. I like to drive by myself whenever I can. It's a good way for me to clear my head and think about how I might frame an interview depending on the job. Once in a while, if I have time, I'll drive over a thousand miles by myself instead of flying."

"Not all at once, right?" I suddenly worried about his safety.

He laughed. "Not usually, no. I can easily do stretches of eight or nine hours and then my assistant Brenda will find me a hotel along the way and set up a reservation. I like driving across the country like this. Meeting people in gas stations, motels, restaurants. It keeps me connected and gives me inspiration for the show."

His admission made him exponentially more attractive to me. He could so easily fly in and out of places, do his job, and be off to the next thing, but no. He likes to exist in the heart of things. Finding wonder and purpose in people and small moments.

"How was your day?" Jake asked.

I told him about the class I had given thinking he might find it interesting.

"God, I hate that you've got to work so hard to diffuse these creeps. I could tell that there were more issues than what we talked about when we filmed the show, but shit. That sucks."

"We role play so they feel less awkward about putting a stop to it in real life situations." I took a pause. "I'd let things go too much in the past. Let these guys get away with more than I should have."

"Did anyone ever cross the line?"

"The line is whatever you make it as a massage therapist. Someone telling you you're pretty can be a line," I said.

"I meant—"

"I know, and no. I was never assaulted. But my line now is miles from where it was when I first started. Now I take absolutely no shit." I felt a little surge of pride at my newfound agency when I heard the words come out of my mouth.

"Good for you. What changed?"

I knew what changed, but I couldn't explain it to Jake without getting into things I couldn't discuss with him.

My pause must have been long enough that he felt the need to redirect.

"I'm sorry, I'm prying. My interviewer comes out all the time, even when I don't mean it to."

"I can see that," my tone was soft. "It does make you a sparkling conversationalist."

"Shelby, everything about you sparkles."

I smiled and tilted my cheek against the phone. A rush of tingles wound through my belly.

"Speaking of interviewing, I think I hurt my therapist's feelings yesterday," Jake said.

"What?" I began to process the fact that Jake was in therapy, and as curious as I was about that, I'd never, ever ask. I would expect the same courtesy of him, after all.

"Yeah, we were talking, and she said, 'I want us to unpick that.' I was like 'What the heck does that mean-unpick' and she tried to explain 'You know, get to the heart of things, dissect things' and I was like 'You mean unpack?' She's Scottish. I guess they say unpick."

"Unpick. Is that even a word?" I laughed. "It makes me

think of picking a scab. Well, I guess that could be applicable to therapy. Like 'don't unpick that too soon, it will bleed.'"

Jake laughed. "Yeah, and I've always wondered about unpack too. Like you're supposed to be picturing the trauma box or unearthing something underneath. But unpacking? Unpacking what? Groceries? A weekend bag? A steamer trunk? A moving van?"

I think you're getting punchy," I chided. "I hope you're getting to your hotel soon."

"No, I'm okay. Do you know what I'm saying, though? If you're trying to hold on to the analogy of unpack then the task of unpacking will be dependent on the thing you've buried and the amount and complexity of the shit you've piled on top of it."

His words began to resonate in a way that surprised me. I sat up and gave myself space to consider him, wondering in which ways he might be broken. Considering all that we might have in common. Certainly, our trauma would be coming from very different places—I wasn't sure if his was all to do with his brother's death—but we were both wading through and working through our respective emotional baggage just the same.

"I prefer the analogy of unraveling," I said. "Like the pieces of ourselves we hide or memories or things we don't want to face are balls of yarn we have wound up tight and tucked away. So then in therapy it's time to deal with them. Unravel."

"Hmmm," Jake mused. "What would be an example of the pieces of ourselves we hide? You don't have to get personal. I am just curious."

"I don't know...parts of our personality we don't want to show. Or that someone else doesn't like. Things we want to say but know we can't. We hide them because it makes it easier."

"It makes what easier?" Jake asked.

"Everything." I didn't want to have to explain in more detail, and I hoped he wouldn't ask. It was strange how much I appreciated this, though. It was comforting to talk to him about these things, even if it was only around the margins. "And then when you pull out the ball of yarn to unravel it, often it needs to be untangled as well."

"I like your analogies much more. I will tell my therapist we are using them from now on and I won't be in danger of being rude and laughing in her face."

I sat with my head tilted against the back of the couch. I liked these conversations. Jake was truly a natural interviewer and I liked delving deeper—as long as it didn't get too personal. *I must be a mermaid. I have no fear of depths and a great fear of shallow living.*

"Hey, I'm coming up to my exit. I'm going to have to let you go in a minute."

"Okay. If you need to do this again, I'm here."

"Thanks, I appreciate that. I really like talking to you." He hesitated. "So, uh, I'm planning a trip to Portland in a few weeks to see my mom. I was wondering if you'd want to meet me there?'

I was taken aback. "Ummm..."

"Not to meet her or anything. No, my time with her would be separate. I'd just like to share my hometown with you. It's a really cool city."

"I would like that. Text me the dates and I'll see what I can do," I said.

"I want to arrange your flights so can I put you in touch with Brenda? I have more miles than I know what to do with, and I don't want to inconvenience you."

"Sure, that would be nice."

"I can't wait to see you." Jake said.

"Me too."

"Goodnight, Shelby."

"Goodnight, Jake."

I sank into the couch and sighed knowing the next day, after hot yoga, my therapist and I were going to pull out and unravel another ball of yarn. I was going to have to press pause on my happy, distracting thoughts of Jake, and once again swim in memories that were no fun at all.

CHAPTER
FIFTEEN
JAKE

Late April 2013

"So, this woman you've started seeing. Tell me more about her." Dr. McCallum said.

I'd admitted to my therapist that Shelby existed and was someone I was spending time with, but I was still holding most of her story close to the vest. "She's pretty great." I wanted to seem casual, but I was finding it hard to keep my enthusiasm for her in check. "She lives in Wisconsin. She's a massage therapist and an esthetician—I guess you'd call her a beauty therapist in the UK. She's smart, funny and vivacious. I really like her." I shrugged as if I didn't know what else to say.

"You smile when you talk about her. Things must be going well. Between your work schedule and her living so far away, how often are you seeing each other?"

"It's been averaging about every six or seven weeks. We talk on the phone and text quite a bit. She's meeting me in Portland on Friday."

"Is she going to meet your mother?" she asked.

"No. We aren't anywhere near there."

"Where do you think you are then?" she asked with an arch of her eyebrow. She could sense I was holding back.

I fidgeted a little in my chair. "Oh, you know, we're just taking it day by day. She has her life and I have mine. And when we get together, we have a really great time."

"Jake..."

"What?"

"You know what," she said. "I'm having my doubts as to whether you'd have the capacity for the casual fling you are painting a picture of here. I want to know what it was about her that attracted you in the first place. Is she divorced? A single mother? In recovery?"

Lorna McCallum was tough, and after nearly a year together, she'd started routinely calling me out on my bullshit. "None of that, I swear. She is a single mother, but her son is in college. And she's not struggling financially or lacking in self-confidence or suffering from anxiety or depression. She's really in a great place."

"I want to believe you, Jake. I am just trying to help you to avoid the pitfalls that you usually find yourself falling into. With your history, you are particularly skilled at finding those people who have significant emotional issues, even if you don't know what they are at first. I want to make sure you're being careful, especially if you want to try and make something serious out of this relationship."

"No, I get that, and I appreciate it. Shelby is just... she's different. She got under my skin. She's as fun as bubble gum, but as nuanced and complex as a gourmet meal. I'm just enjoying the hell out of getting to know her." It felt good to tell this bit of truth.

"I see. But if and when you do get to know her, and there

are things that come up...complexity doesn't always come from light places, you know. Just be careful not to get all wrapped up in the secrets she may reveal over time."

I appreciated Dr. McCallum looking out for my wellbeing, even if I wasn't ready to be honest with her just yet. I was in no hurry to work through the stuff with Shelby. I wanted more time to uncover her pain, to coax out the darkness and fill her with my light. I was fully aware that it probably would not end well for either of us, but I couldn't help myself. I wanted more moments of her breaking open and falling apart in my arms.

Dr. McCallum was trying to help me avoid pitfalls, but she didn't know that I knowingly and willingly dove into this canyon so deep I had yet to touch bottom.

FRIDAY MORNING, I DROVE TO PDX TO PICK UP SHELBY. WHEN I SAW her emerge out of the airport doors, I smiled to myself at how impossible she was to miss.

She spotted me and walked up to the SUV, her bright eyes beaming.

I got out to help her with her suitcase and open the door for her. Before I could get to the other side of the car, she put up her hand. "I got it," she said. "Get back in the car." She opened the back door and set her carry-on on the seat, then she climbed into the seat next to me. "Good airport etiquette." She crinkled her nose at Getty Lee's voice coming through the speakers, before heaving a sigh as she smiled at me. "Hi."

I had a big, dumb smile on my face too, that didn't have anything to do with her adorable show of distaste for Rush. "Hi."

I'd expected this bit of awkwardness when we'd first see

each other, the infrequency of our visits not allowing for immediate comfortable familiarity. I didn't mind it, though. Just another layer adding to the excitement I felt.

Her expression shifted as her pupils dilated and her eyes lowered to my mouth. She licked her bottom lip and pulled it between her teeth.

My electrons instantly became aware of her proximity, all traces of awkwardness vaporizing as the magnetism kicked in full force. I unbuckled my seatbelt and lunged at her, muscle and sense memory overtaking me. I snaked a hand around the back of her neck and kissed her more aggressively than I'd intended. She met my intensity head on and tangled her hands in my hair, angling her body toward mine as much as she could. Everything else faded from my reality. There was only her.

It wasn't until the impatient driver in the car behind us laid on his horn that we were thrust back to reality. So much for good airport etiquette.

"Are you hungry?" I asked.

Shelby nodded, her cheeks flushed and mouth kissed pink.

I took her to my favorite breakfast place where Shelby gave me a lesson in her home state's Bloody Marys, often containing enough accouterments to provide breakfast on their own, and a customary beer chaser on the side. Leave it to Wisconsinites to enhance their alcohol with more alcohol.

After breakfast I knew exactly where we'd go next. We wouldn't be able to check into the hotel for another couple of hours and while both of us were itching to get out of our clothes and have a proper hello, we needed to kill some time.

"Oh, my goodness!" Shelby put her hands over her mouth in shock as she absorbed Vintage Blush, a well-stocked and well styled vintage furniture store just kitty corner from the restaurant. She looked like Augustus Gloop walking into Willy Wonka's chocolate factory, her eyes the size of planets.

"This place is *amazing!* We don't have anything like this in Milwaukee. If we did, furnishing my house would have been so much easier."

I watched her wander around looking at everything. She'd run her hand along a piece in reverent admiration just before something else caught her eye and she was off again.

And I watched the women at the counter watching her. She fit in here so perfectly with her faded cropped overalls, an oversized black cardigan sweater that looked as though it may have belonged to her grandfather, and well-worn Doc Martens. She wore her hair in twin braids with her signature casual style black bandana worn like a kerchief this time instead of a headband.

"Do they deliver? To Wisconsin? No, don't tell me. I would buy the whole store."

I laughed. There was a large wood vase that she kept going back to. It was a little more 70's than I might have thought she'd like, but she was obviously enchanted. I could see her wheels turning as if wondering how it might fit in her suitcase. When she wandered away again, I went and looked at the price. It was $24. Definitely a "fit" thing, not a money thing.

We headed toward the hotel and had them hold our bags while we wandered around the downtown neighborhood. I wanted to show her Powells, willing to bet she liked the smell of old books as much as I did. Watching her saunter up and down the aisles, cocking her head to the side to read the spines, positioning herself up on tip toes or down in a squat so as not to miss anything on the upper or lower shelves, I couldn't take my eyes off the sexy bibliophile. At that moment I cursed the store for being so big. I didn't want to rush her, but I was getting dangerously close to achieving cliché bookstore pervert status, peeking around the shelves at her with my looming hard-on.

Later that afternoon, lying next to her naked and sweaty body, I gently serpentined my finger down her spine. "Remember in Chicago when you told me you saw Dita Von Teese at the House of Blues?"

"Mmhmm." She was still in her post sex haze.

"Would you be interested in going to a burlesque place tonight?"

She lifted her head, her interest piqued. "Ooh, that would be very cool! I'd love that."

"I feel like I need to tell you that it's burlesque, yes, but also an alternative exotic dance club," I said.

"Like strippers?"

"Yes, like strippers. Think tattooed, pierced, ripped fishnet, roller derby, goth strippers."

"Holy shit, that sounds amazing. Yes, let's do that," she said.

I suspected it might be something up her alley. I had never taken a woman to Mynxx before, but I always made it a point to visit when I was in town. It used to be because the girls reminded me of Chloe, but the last two times I'd gone, I appreciated the burlesque and pinup style girls a lot more because of Shelby. The place was dark and charmingly grungy, with graffitied walls, black light, and bathrooms wallpapered in stickers like a proper punk club. The thing I liked best about it was it was queer-owned, and the dancers looked like they were actually having fun.

We took our time at dinner and rolled into Mynxx about 9:30 p.m. Of course Shelby looked amazing. A black, high waisted, body-hugging halter dress. Platform peep toes. A black fabric dahlia in her hair and her signature red lipstick. She'd encouraged me to watch her get ready again, after which she'd graciously allowed me to fuck her on the bathroom vanity. I only had to solemnly promise not to mess up her hair or makeup.

I led us to a table along the wall, a perfect place to see the stage, but where I could also have Shelby all to myself. I also wasn't sure how she'd feel about getting approached for a lap dance, and she most definitely would get asked instead of me. These women were smart.

We sat down just in time for the next dancer to take the stage. Muse's song "Madness" came blasting over the speakers. The waitress came over and took our drink order, scotch rocks for me, and a vodka tonic for her. The woman on the stage was dressed in a vinyl catsuit and as she peeled it off, she revealed full sleeves of tattoos and legs that were well on their way to complete coverage. I looked over at Shelby and she was mesmerized. Once the dancer took to her pole, Shelby leaned forward in her seat, following every movement and swaying along to the hypnotic beat. I congratulated myself for one of the best ideas I've ever had and looked forward to satisfying the itch I could tell Shelby was starting to get.

The next act was a pinup burlesque dancer I'd seen before. She was voluptuous, cheeky, and loved making the audience laugh. She even did the whole classic twirl the tassels on her pasties thing that always got a big reaction.

Several acts later, two women took the stage. Short pleated skirts, white and black striped thigh highs, white button-down shirts and student ties. Matching pigtail braids. This was a new one for me. They stood facing each other when the music came on, and as soon as the first couple of beats hit, I recognized the song. It was the "Cicada Mix" of Depeche Mode's "World in My Eyes."

I looked over at Shelby and we both smiled. She knew how much I was going to enjoy this. The two dancers stalked around the stage like cats, never tearing their eyes away from the other. They'd each reach out a hand then bring it back, as if they were forbidden to touch. It was scorchingly hot.

As the intro was coming to an end, I caught Shelby out of the corner of my eye. She was swaying in her chair with her eyes on me instead of the stage. She stood up, grabbed her chair and set it down in front of me. I sat up straight at rapt attention. I didn't know what she was up to, but whatever it was I was certain I was going to like it.

She began to lip sync the words.

Inching up the bottom of her dress all the way up to barely covering her private bits, she sat with her legs spread wide on the chair in front of me.

She put her hands on my thighs and began to move her body side to side.

Holy. Shit.

She raised up off her chair and while bent over, legs still spread, she ran her hands up and down my thighs. I had absolutely no interest in what was happening on the stage, and it was obvious the people around us were pretty damn captivated by what Shelby was doing as well.

She turned to face away from me, teasing my lap with the undulation of her ass. I raked my hands through my hair as my cock snapped to full attention.

She spun to face me once again, lifting her dress even higher, straddling me and coming to rest firmly on my lap. I tried to kiss her, but she angled her face away.

Fuck me. She was role playing again.

The edgy electronica filled my ears while Shelby dominated every single one of my other senses.

Then she began to grind. I didn't know how far she was going to take this, and I didn't care. *If I'm meant to come in my jeans right here in this club, so be it.* I was certain it was par for the course in a place like Mynxx.

Her grinding became more frenzied, and I grabbed onto her hips holding on for dear life. I was on the verge, so fucking close, when without warning, she stopped.

Fuck.

My balls seized in protest and my mouth dropped open.

She brought her mouth to my ear. Breathing heavily, she asked, "Bathroom or car?"

"Jesus Christ, woman. You're going to be the death of me," I panted.

She grinned and bit on her fingernail. "Bathroom or car?"

"Car."

Shelby grabbed her purse and my hand, dragging me through the club. A few tables from ours I caught the eyes of an older woman, a college professor type with short silver hair, peering at me over her glasses. Just as I began feeling self-conscious at what I'd assumed was her disapproval, she winked and held out a hand for me to subtly high five as we passed. Damn, how I love it when people surprise me.

The bouncer asked if we needed a hand stamp to get back in, Shelby shot a mischievous look at me and cackled as she blew past him. We made our way to the car, mercifully parked in a dark corner of the lot. Not that I cared too much, but a visit from a cop might have killed the mood.

"Front seat or back?" she asked.

"Front. Passenger side. I just want to continue the ride." Then I had an idea.

I started the car. I pulled out my phone and attached the auxiliary cord from inside the console. I searched my iTunes and pressed play and the same Depeche Mode song playing in the club filled the SUV. I started undoing my pants while

Shelby busied herself taking off her underwear outside the car, holding onto the side for balance.

"Shit," I said.

"What's wrong?"

"I don't have a condom. I left them at the hotel."

"It's okay." She smiled and twirled her panties around her finger. "I have an IUD. And I'm not sleeping with anybody else."

This was just getting better and better. Core memory bank material for sure. But the way she looked at me, it was clear she needed me to confirm the same. "Me neither."

Shelby ran her hands over her body and swayed to the music. "I think I have a natural talent for this. Hey, that reminds me. Where's my tip?" She laughed, holding out a hand.

"Baby, you're getting way more than just the tip." I pointed to my crotch for emphasis. "Get that sexy ass up here and finish this lap dance. Right. Fucking. Now."

Shelby's expression changed so fast I nearly got whiplash.

Her mouth dropped open at first, but then she pressed her lips into a hard line. She balled her fists, her eyes turning steely and hard.

"What's wrong?"

She didn't answer. She just stood there staring with this beautiful fury. I knew I was supposed to try and fix it, but I was once again caught off guard and all tangled up in her sudden twist of emotion. I was incapable of forming a coherent sentence.

"Shelby?"

She threw her underwear in my face and stormed off. I quickly zipped and loosely buckled while scrambling out of the car to chase after her.

She walked quickly with determined steps, but it was

obvious she didn't have the slightest idea where she should be heading in a city so unfamiliar to her. She paused and tried to get a sense of her surroundings. By then I'd caught up to her and I reached out to grab her arm.

"Don't you dare fucking touch me!" She yanked away.

I recoiled at the venom. Something I had done had triggered her, and while I knew it wasn't entirely to do with me, I was still the target of her vitriol, and it stung like hell.

I began searching my hero data bank for the appropriate script for this scenario.

"What the fuck just happened?" I'd considered pleading, apologizing without knowing what I'd done, but something told me to spar with her a little, to hold my ground. Maybe I'd be able to coax out something meaningful.

"I don't want to be told what to do. Ordered. Commanded." As the words were coming out of her mouth, there was softness creeping in around the edges.

"Okay, but there's no way I could have known that. I can't read your mind."

She was still fuming, chest heaving. I watched her as she was rolling over something in her head. She inhaled, opened her mouth, then quickly shut it again.

"Shelby," I kept my voice soft and measured. "I know that you get triggered sometimes. Maybe if you talked to me about things that have happened to you... I just want you to know you could. You could talk to me."

"Why would I want to do that?" she challenged, all hard-edged again.

Ouch. "Okay, fair enough. But then it's unfair to lash out at me when I'm essentially flying blind here."

"How about just don't act like a raging asshole, and we should be fine."

"Hey, maybe I got carried away in the heat of the moment,

but I certainly wasn't being an asshole. And in my experience, women have responded well to me talking like that."

"Well, you can't just assume it works for everyone," she said.

"You're right. But you refuse to tell me what doesn't work for you. You won't tell me what not to do." I scrubbed my face with my hand as I considered something. "What if you told me what *to* do, instead?"

"What?"

"Why don't we try you telling me what to do. Ordering me. Commanding me, as you put it."

She rolled her eyes and scoffed.

"Think about it. You've had the reins since the start, and you seem pretty comfortable with that. And with teasing. Just try ratcheting it up a few more notches."

She looked down and shook her head, silently arguing with me.

"I'm serious." I got down on my knees in front of her. "Here I am. Once again at your service."

Her eyebrows raised a little in curiosity.

"I will do anything you say." I took her hand gently. "And... and don't be afraid to hurt me."

"Get up, Jake."

I quickly did as I was told and stood with my hands clasped behind my back as I awaited further instruction.

"I can't do this," Shelby said.

"Well, then dare me."

"What?'

"If you can't order me, dare me," I said.

She cocked her head, looking at me with derision. "Dare you. As in 'dare you to do it?'"

Yes, the irony. I smiled and nodded.

"I don't know...here? On the street?"

The street was quiet, but not private. I looked to my left and saw a dark alleyway with two side by side loading docks. The perfect place to duck into. "How about over there? Or we could always take this back to the hotel..."

Shelby was already walking toward the alley. I had to keep from stepping on her heels as I followed closely, eagerly behind her.

She stood with her back up against the brick wall in between the loading docks. I got close, but not close enough to be aggressive. I gently brushed her hair from her face and stroked her cheek with the back of my fingers. "What do you dare me to do, Shelby?"

"I dare you to get back on your knees."

I did as I was told.

"I dare you to touch me," she whispered as she began tenderly petting my hair.

I put my hands on her hips and looked up at her. "Tell me where."

She lifted her dress, spreading her legs wide enough to give me access. "Here."

I placed my hand flat against her pubic bone. "Tell me how."

She swallowed hard and began to squirm a little with excitement. "Thumb on my clit and two fingers inside."

Lightening coursed through my veins as she began to find her voice. My fingers moved into position, and I groaned as I discovered her soaked. In no time at all, she was grinding against my hand. Her fingers massaged my scalp, and as her pleasure increased, so did her pressure. She grabbed a fistful of my hair and yanked my head back. Hard.

I gasped at the exquisite pain as my cock strained violently against my jeans.

Shelby swung a leg over my shoulder. "Now, bury your face in my pussy and don't come up for air until I tell you to."

Halle-fucking-lujah.

I eagerly obeyed and soon she was bucking and writhing in spectacular orgasm. Once her shuddering had stopped, she pulled my head back to look up at her, a wicked smile curling the corners of her lips. She wiped my mouth roughly with her thumb, pulling down my bottom lip and forcing it inside. As I licked and sucked on her thumb like the good boy that I was, she held my lower jaw in a vise grip. My imagination sparked at all the intense sensations she could offer between her strong massage therapist's hands and her knowledge of the human body. How easily she'd find the perfect pressure point and fell me in an instant with the very thumb I held in my mouth.

I couldn't take my eyes off her, just staring in wondrous awe. Shelby in her pain was vulnerable, soft and so achingly beautiful. But Shelby in her power was a raw, magnificent force of nature. A fucking *Goddess*.

"Fuck me, Jake. Hard. Like you're trying to bust through this goddamn wall."

AFTERWARDS WE STUMBLED BACK TO THE CAR ALL SEX DRUNK AND giggly. I was grateful to find no one had noticed it unlocked. And still running.

"Oops," I said.

"Oh my God, what if the car had been stolen? Can you imagine?" Shelby laughed.

"Hmm, let's see. If my rental car had been stolen because I left it running when the woman who had given me a spontaneous lap dance in public had a meltdown and took off, so I ran after her and then had the hottest sex of my entire fucking life in an alley..." I inhaled vigorously. "That would have pushed this night over the edge into complete implausibility.

"I'm already going to have a hard time believing it actually happened in the first place."

CHAPTER
SIXTEEN
JAKE

We'd only been awake for a few minutes, basking in the morning sunlight streaming through the hotel room window. Shelby was on her back staring up at the ceiling.

"Tell me what it is about pain," she said.

"What?"

She rolled over onto her stomach and met my eyes. "I want to know how you find pleasure in pain."

"Oh...well, I'm sure some people would be eager to dissect that, assuming it's some way of compensating for affection I never got as a child...blah, blah, blah. But for me it's pretty superficial. It's all about the sensory experience. Or at least it had been until last night."

"What do you mean?" she asked.

"Well, I'd only been with one partner where I'd explored that part of my sexuality. And it was mostly...experimental. It was like 'let's try this,' and 'let's try that.' Obviously, there was a significant element of control, but it was never about full domination or full submission. But last night, an entirely different component clicked with me." I reached over and cupped Shelby's cheek. "I loved being dominated by you. The pain was a gift. Like I would gladly beg on my hands and knees for any scrap of physical touch from you. Any way you'd serve it, it would be perfect, and I would lap it up and beg for more."

Shelby blushed and pressed her face into the pillow. She was still unsure about exploring this side of herself, but I vowed then and there to move mountains to help her own it.

"So, the woman you experimented with, she would ask you... you communicated?"

"Oh, absolutely. Communication and implicit trust are the most important things in a relationship like that. I had safe words. We stuck with the basics. If I was okay but didn't want her to ramp it up, or to make sure she continued to check in with me, it'd be yellow. Red was obviously a hard stop. Chloe was also very conscientious about aftercare." I didn't feel the need to go deeper into detail about the aftercare falling off when Chloe and I spiraled into murkier territory.

Shelby was quiet, turning something over and over in her head while flicking at her index finger with her thumbnail. "Aftercare," she said softly. It wasn't a question as much as a wistful observation.

"Yes. It's a huge part of this kind of relationship. Physical aftercare involves things you might expect like ice, massage, sometimes even antibiotic ointment. But the emotional after-care is even more important. Praise, gentle affection, cuddling. If not for that, the relationship could be horribly unbalanced. I could see how it could have completely worn me down otherwise."

Shelby looked down at her hands and took a deep breath, her exhale ragged and loaded. "I bet I'd be good at aftercare," she said quietly.

I leaned over and pressed my lips to her forehead. "I know you would be."

. . .

EARLY IN THE AFTERNOON AFTER I'D PARKED THE SUV IN AN uncomfortably tight spot in a pay lot, I offered my hand to Shelby as we walked. I'd been tightlipped about what the plan was for today.

We rounded the corner and I slowed to a stop when we got to a zebra striped storefront with a pink neon sign in the window advertising the shop's specialty.

Shelby looked at me with wide eyes. "Oh my God. Are you about to get your first tattoo?"

I smiled. "Yup."

She clapped her hands and jumped up and down in giddy approval, and I couldn't help but laugh. Part of her kaleidoscope included this jubilance bubbling out of her like fountain soda fizz. It was infectious as hell.

As we walked in we met Mike, the artist I'd been messaging back and forth with for a few weeks. I'd been thinking about getting a tattoo for years but could never seem to pull the trigger. Spending time with Shelby and her beautiful inked body had finally inspired me, and I was so grateful to have her with me when I got my tattoo cherry popped..

Shelby put her lips close to my ear. "So, are you going to get turned on a little by this?" She pulled her head away and smiled, teasingly poking my side.

I laughed. "I doubt it. It's all about context. Like, I don't get a hard-on at the dentist. Now, if you were naked and had the tattoo gun in your hand, that'd be a different story." I grabbed her by the waist and kissed her cheek.

Shelby giggled and laid her head on my shoulder as we walked through the shop.

Mike led us to his private cubicle and wheeled in an extra

stool for Shelby. I took off my shirt and Mike pulled out the stencil and positioned it on my left side.

"Ribs for your first time? Damn, that's hardcore." Shelby said.

"Shit. Now you tell me."

"Mike should have told you." She laughed. "No, you'll be fine."

I was starting to get a little nervous. "So, what? You just get used to the needle after a while, right?"

Mike and Shelby looked at each other and laughed some more. I shrugged, guessing I would be finding out soon enough.

I knew I wanted a Depeche Mode inspired tattoo, so I settled on an image of the rose on the front of the Violator album with lyrics from my favorite song. Although after last night, "World in My Eyes" had risen in the ranks enough to tie it.

"Halo" was my savior anthem. My theme song. I interpret it as a man telling his lover he sees her; he sees her guilt, her shame, and her pain and implores her to lay it all at his feet. In return, he will give her misery the company it craves and offers to soothe her with his sex. And finally, when it all comes crashing down, even as doomed as they are, it will have all been worth it.

Looking at the lyrics I knew by heart facing me backwards in the mirror, I felt a ripple of guilt in my gut. For the first time I considered that I wouldn't be able to handle it if it all ended in disaster with Shelby.

Mike had me lie on my right side on the table while he set up his station. He put on his gloves with a snap and loaded his needle into the machine. For as advanced as most technology was, tattoo guns still looked so old school—almost a steampunk aesthetic.

"We'll start with the rose, okay? Here we go." Mike said.

The low-pitched buzz started, and I braced myself. Shelby was sitting close and offered her hand for when the needle hit. I held my breath, but thankfully it was much more irritating than it was painful. "That's not so bad. I can handle this."

Shelby gave me an encouraging smile. "You'll do great. I'm so excited for you."

An hour and a half in I fully understood what Mike and Shelby were laughing about when I'd foolishly asked if you get used to the needle.

You don't.

In fact, it gets worse.

Just when you think he's done with one spot, he swings back around and hits the raw flesh again and again. You want to crawl out of your skin. I found myself conjuring all kinds of creative thoughts about the needle wielding demon.

In my imagination I had Mike naked and strung up by his ankles. My loud, maniacal laughter echoing through the room as I repeatedly poked at his dick with a white-hot spike.

Shelby was working so hard to try and distract me. She'd animatedly engage with Mike about her artists and tattoo experiences and asked to hear his stories. She'd tell me how much I was going to love it when it was done, and how much I'd want to get another one.

I highly doubted that.

Beads of sweat started to form on my forehead. I felt cold and clammy, and subtle waves of nausea began to creep in. I started some box breathing to try and control it. *Inhale for one, two, three, four. Hold one, two, three, four. Exhale one, two...*

Shelby squeezed my hand. "Hey, where's your restroom?" she asked Mike.

"Around the corner to the right."

She bent down to look me in the eye and put her hand on my cheek. "I'll be right back, okay?"

"Mmhmm." I managed a weak smile before she turned to walk away.

"She's gone. You can scream now if you want to," Mike offered.

I shook my head. It was better if I didn't open my mouth at all.

"Do you need a break?" Mike asked.

I shook my head again. A break meant I'd be here longer. Enduring this longer. No thanks. The minutes already dragged. *Where is Shelby?*

After what seemed like a lifetime, she came back in making a beeline toward me with two cans of orange soda. "Good thing there's a pharmacy next door. Mike, let him have a minute." She helped me sit up and cracked open one of the cans. "Here, drink this. It will help."

After the first few sips of the cold sweet fizz that transported me to childhood summer, I started to feel better. I had a wave of embarrassment realizing that Shelby had been fully aware I was about to pass out, but I rationalized that it had been her own experiences that taught her what to do, and now we just had one more thing in common. She held the other cold can to the back of my neck. *Yes, Shelby, you'd be good at aftercare. Brilliant, in fact.*

When the torture was finally done, Mike cautioned me to stand up slowly and go check out my new tattoo in the mirror. It looked badass. The lyrics were in black in a cool gothic font, the rose itself red and intermixed with negative space. It was perfect.

"Fuck, that's hot." Shelby stood behind me running her hands over my back as we both looked in the mirror. Something clicked in my brain, like the shutter of a camera.

Mike walked over with a sheet of cellophane. "We'll put this wrap on for now, then in an hour or so, you'll take it off and wash it with soap and water." He looked at Shelby. "Can you give him a rundown of everything he needs to do?"

"Absolutely," she said.

When he was done wrapping me, I shook his hand and gave him a generous tip. "This is my apology for all the names I called you and how badly I wanted to bash your head in during that whole thing."

He laughed. "It's all good, man. Everyone hates me when they're on the table. They all love me when they see the finished product, though." He leaned in closer and said, "And you're gonna love me *a lot* later when she shows you what she thinks of this ink."

An hour later we were back at the hotel getting ready to go to dinner. I casually took off my T-shirt the same way I do every single day and I was shocked by a ripping sensation on my side. Shelby noticed my wincing as she walked into the bathroom.

"Yeah, that's going to be tender for a while. You don't realize how much you move your ribs doing normal things. Just wait until you forget and roll onto your side in the middle of the night."

"Oof, yeah. Not looking forward to that."

"Here, let me help you." She pulled at the edges of the tape with quick movements. It reminded me of when she showed me how to wax.

She peeled away the cellophane and inspected the tattoo. "God, this line work is incredible. You found a really good guy."

"Yeah, Portland is like the tattoo capital of the US. I knew I wanted to get it done here." I swallowed hard. "How bad is this going to hurt?"

"Nothing is as bad as the needle. But I'll be gentle. Promise."

Shelby washed her hands. She brought some of the warm water to dampen my left side, then lathered her hands and began to gently wash my sore, sensitive skin.

As I watched her in the mirror, I considered her having worked so hard to both encourage me and distract me. Her touching my face, making jokes. Knowing exactly when it was all going to shit and how she had so quickly and instinctively come to my rescue.

And now, tending to my aftercare.

She was so inextricably woven into this experience I may as well have been tattooed with a picture of her face.

I thought of the question Shelby asked me on the day we met—if my love for Depeche Mode had to do with a girl. The answer was still yes, but the girl was no longer Chloe.

"How old were you when you got your first tattoo?" I asked Shelby after the waiter had taken our order. We were keeping it casual—Mexican food and margaritas.

"I wanted one so badly, I got my first one when I was eighteen."

"Which one?"

"Oh, you can't see it anymore," she laughed. "It was so bad."

"What, was it like dolphins frolicking or hearts and rainbows?" I knew it wasn't a regretful tramp stamp. The only tattoos on her back were a peacock surrounding her right shoulder blade and an anchor with yellow roses on the back of her neck.

"No. God. It's still kind of embarrassing though. I was obsessed with Twin Peaks. Obsessed. I got a little owl framed by the owl petroglyph on my left hip."

I thought of the pinup girl cradled in the crescent moon piece that lives there now. Poor little owl buried underneath. "So, you got over your obsession with Twin Peaks and covered it up?"

"It wasn't that. It was so *bad.* Terrible line work and he went too deep, and it got all blown out and blurry. I didn't know enough to ask to see his portfolio, and this was before the internet. He was not a good tattoo artist, and I was so disappointed. I waited a long time to cover it up though, and when I met Ari, he teased me about it all the time."

Ah, an opportunity to get in. "Did he have any tattoos?"

"He did. Half sleeves when we met. A few on his chest. It was all well and good for a chef, but before that he was in school for finance to get into business with his dad. The tattoos had never gone over well with his parents. And once the wheels were in motion for him to go to culinary school, he got his neck done. There was no going back to suits and ties after that."

Bad boy chef with tattoos; I could see the appeal for her. After she had told me his name, of course I couldn't help myself—I looked him up online. I knew full well that he was well inked.

There were one or two pictures where Chef Aristotle Ristow was smiling, but in most of them, he was serious and brooding. Butcher knives held in crossed arms, daring to be fucked with. He smoldered with an intensity that intimidated me a little, and to be honest, kind of made my skin crawl. My curiosity was bubbling over. "How did you meet?"

"You know what? I'm done talking about him now." She was curt.

"Of course. I'm sorry. It's just that you never do, and I want you to know that you could. Talk to me about him, that is. I don't mind."

"Well, I mind." Shelby busied herself straightening her knife and fork at her place setting. Nervously looking around at everyone but me.

"I'm sorry. I didn't mean to upset you."

"I'm here with you. That means I just want to be here," she pointed down at her seat, representing both the restaurant and the present moment. "I don't want to talk about my husband, my son, my past. This is supposed to be fun. And right now, I'm not having fun."

Fun? Is that all this is for her? I was surprised at how much that stung. What I was doing here was not exactly pure and noble, but I was in way beyond fun.

I put my hands up in a subtle surrender, "Okay, got it."

Out of the corner of my eye I saw two women walking cautiously toward our table. *Crap.*

"Hi, I'm sorry to bother you, but you're Jake Ford."

No shit, Sherlock. "Yes, hi. How are you?" She was in her forties and had a warm smile. I was immediately grateful I hadn't snapped at her. She turned her attention to Shelby.

"And... you. You're the woman from the episode. The waxing lady."

Shelby smiled kindly and nodded.

"My husband and I *loved* that episode," the woman gushed. "We both said how cute you guys were together and we wondered if there was something there. And now you're actually *together?*" She clasped her hands together excitedly.

One look at Shelby's fallen face told me everything I needed to know. She was terrified of this getting out—she hadn't told anyone about us. It was likely Kendra was still the only one who knew. Maybe Darius. But certainly not her family. I wanted to explain to her that I was nowhere near famous enough that any of this would make it to the internet or the tabloids, that our secret would be safe. But here on the precarious ledge where we were already losing our footing, I knew it'd be useless.

"Oh, no we're just friends," I told the woman. Then I shot a look straight at Shelby and said, "We're just having fun." It was petty bullshit, but I was rubbed a little raw.

Shelby heaved a sigh and looked down at her hands.

"Oh." The woman looked disappointed, but it was no match for the hollow ache that seemed to be blooming in my chest. "Sorry to bother you, have a good night," she said.

Shelby and I both stayed quiet, barely looking at each other, neither of us knowing what to do or say next.

I broke the silence. "I'm gonna run to the restroom. I'll be right back."

I stared at myself in the mirror and thought about what I could say or do to put this evening back on track. Shelby was leaving the next day and I needed to salvage what little time we had left. I could sort through the maelstrom of emotion I was experiencing after she'd gone back home.

I'd decided it'd be best to apologize again and try to appeal to her with affection.

I made my way back to the table and I stopped dead in my tracks about ten feet away from Shelby. I was on her periphery but could still see most of her face. Her eyes were glassy, and she was staring straight ahead. I followed her gaze to an older couple with what looked to be their adult son sitting at a table a few feet away. They were all laughing, and the dad was squeezing the son's shoulder while the mom looked on in adoration.

This was a mirror image of her family in the not-so-distant future. Only on her side, one of them was gone.

I was certain I was finally witnessing her grief.

I couldn't get her to admit it or talk to me about it, but here I had stumbled upon it. I felt a pang of guilt at spying on her in such a private moment, but I couldn't tear myself away. As the tears began to run down her face, I was more mesmerized than ever.

I felt compelled to stand there and stare through this window because I wasn't sure she'd ever let me in.

After I'd dropped Shelby off at the airport, I headed back to my mom's. I'd pushed back my flight another day; I needed some time somewhere safe and familiar to decompress.

She still lived in the house we grew up in, and as soon as I opened the door, I could smell the *arepas*, my ultimate comfort food. I guessed that she had heard the angst in my voice when I'd asked to stay one more night.

I nearly stepped on the orange tabby that had wound its way between my legs as soon as I walked in. I picked up the loaf of a cat and nuzzled my face in his fur. "Hi, Kenny."

"Is that you, *Cariño*?" I heard my mother call loudly from the kitchen.

"It's me, *Mamá*." Trevor and I had grown up with our father speaking to us in English and our mother speaking to us in Spanish. I'd had someone comment once that my Spanish had a hint of an Australian accent as they'd likely fused together in those early developmental years.

As I walked in the kitchen, she dropped the spatula she was holding and rushed to gather me in her arms. I could hide a lot from my mother. She certainly didn't know about my predilection for unhealthy heroism, or really anything about my relationships, but she always seemed to know when I was lost or when I was hurting, like only a mother could.

"Where's Don?" I asked her. My mother had found love

again over twenty years ago with a widower from church. She hadn't been interested in remarrying and I often jokingly gave her a hard time about "shacking up" with her boyfriend. He was good for her and good to her, and he'd won me over easily.

"I told him to go spend time with his friends today. I feel like you need to talk."

She gestured for me to sit at the table. She filled a plate, placed it in front of me and petted my hair just like she had when I was a little boy. The simple gesture nearly leveled me. I'd never been so grateful to be home.

She sat across from me, her elbow on the table and a hand on her cheek, wordlessly inviting me to unburden myself in any way that I needed to. I took a deep breath and told her about Shelby. I didn't get into anything about my motivations, and I spared her most of the details of our intimate moments, but as I was winding through our brief history, realization was hitting me square between the eyes. My mother saw it too.

"Oh my, *Cariño*." She offered a smile of maternal compassion with just a hint of mischief in her eyes. "It sounds like you're in love."

CHAPTER
SEVENTEEN

May 2013

I was reeling for days after coming home from Portland. I vacillated between experiencing raucous butterflies when I'd remember my unnaturally bold and spontaneous turn as an exotic dancer or my dalliance with dominance in that alley, and waves of embarrassment and shame when I thought about my irrational outbursts and how awkward things got on our last night together.

Not to mention my personal little pity party at the restaurant when Jake stepped away. I just could not seem to tear my eyes away from the blissful trio at the next table. "Happily ever after family" was never to have been my future regardless of Ari's life or death.

Jake and I had managed to quietly recover that last night, watching a movie in the hotel room and talking about everything and nothing at the same time. By the time he'd dropped me off at the airport the next afternoon, I felt like we'd gotten back on track, me leaving him with a kiss that seemed to scramble his brain beyond recognition.

"Hey, I meant to ask, how was your convention?" Brody asked as he rinsed his breakfast plate and put it in the dishwasher. I was happy he'd so easily made himself at home here too, despite Marion's original, irrational concern.

"What?"

"The esthetics convention? In Portland?"

"Oh, yeah...sorry. It was pretty good. I found a new makeup line I think we should carry at the salon." I hated lying to him, but I had no choice.

"That's great. I'm so glad you're getting to do these things now. You never used to."

"I know. Dad... Dad didn't like the idea of me traveling alone."

"Traveling alone, or traveling period?" Brody arched an eyebrow at me.

Damn, so very little got past this kid. A few times I'd gone to educational events in Chicago, but always with coworkers. Even then, Ari would be blowing up my phone demanding to know where I was and what I was doing. I'd always found it perplexing that he seemed to have all the time in the world to obsess over me when I was gone, but he couldn't be bothered to respond or to check in with me in our regular day to day.

"Okey dokey, Mom. I'm heading out."

"Aww, I feel like you just got here. I'll miss you." I reached my arms out wide and drew him in, having to stand on my tiptoes to reach him properly. I smiled as his stubble scratched my cheek.

"Me too. Hey, let's go out to dinner next Saturday."

"I'd love that. My treat."

"Uh, that's a given." Brody smiled, such sparkle in his green eyes. They were just like his father's, but at once the complete opposite. My heart melted like it always does, affirming his existence had been worth all of it.

How easily I could say that now, since the "all of it" was less and less of a shadow looming over my every day.

I HAD BEEN FEELING INSPIRED TO START MAKING CHERRIE BOMBSHELL content again, and I was excited to show Darius my latest video before I uploaded it.

"Damn, girl. You getting some good dick on the regular is making these videos extra hot. It's like you know someone is getting off watching these."

It was truer than he knew. When I'd watched it back, I'd also noticed the knowing little smirk on my face from time to time.

Part of me wanted to dish everything to Darius, knowing how much he would adore it, both for his love for juicy gossip and his love for me. But I didn't want to talk about Jake to him or anyone. It was all I could do to keep glossing things over for Kendra; she wanted *details*. But I found I'd preferred to keep things separate. There was my son, my friends, my family, my house and my job here, and there was Jake over there. This was working for me. And when things ran their course with Jake, as they inevitably would, I would be in a good place right here at home. Maybe even in a good enough place to consider a real relationship.

The next morning while doing some video edits on the sunporch, I glanced up to see a delivery man walking up to the front door with a good size box. I searched my brain thinking of something I'd ordered but was coming up short. We made eye contact through the window, and he set the box on the porch with a nod of acknowledgement.

It was tall and somewhat awkward. I didn't even bother to

look for a return address or sender before grabbing a wine key to open it. I carefully pulled apart the paper that whatever it was had been wrapped in, and gasped when I discovered the wood vase I had been obsessing over at the vintage store in Portland. There was a note taped to the side.

> Shelby,
> I noticed you eyeing this up at the store and I wanted you to have it even if it didn't fit in your suitcase.
> Our time together can be whatever you want or need it to be. Like I said, however you serve it, it will be perfect.
> Jake

I WAS MORE THAN A LITTLE BLINDSIDED BY THE THOUGHTFUL gesture.

"Thank you for the vase. You really didn't need to do that," I told Jake on the phone minutes later.

"I know I didn't, but I wanted to. You seemed so happy in that store. And getting you the vase was way easier than trying to send you a sofa."

I giggled. I'd have been perfectly content to move in there.

Jake started to laugh, and I heard someone else's exhale into the phone. A sharp pang of jealousy hit me out of nowhere when I realized he wasn't alone.

"Lunchbox, knock it off!"

Lunchbox? Oh my God. It's a dog. "Lunchbox?"

"Yes, Lunchbox. Technically he belongs to my upstairs tenants, but most of the time I leave my back door open, and he likes to just go back and forth. See who has time for pets and treats."

"Aw, that's adorable. What kind of dog?"

"He's a golden retriever. A big, huge love bug."

Waves of warm tingles radiated through me as I thought of Jake loving up on this ball of fur. Such a wholesome picture. Quite the opposite of how I usually imagined him.

"Do you have any pets?" Jake asked.

"No, not since I was a kid. I had this black cat named Shadow who hated everyone except me. He died just before I graduated high school.

"Aww, that must have been hard. Why haven't you had any since?"

"Ari was allergic so we couldn't have anything with fur. Brody had a bearded dragon for a while. But I have been thinking about getting a pet now that I'm on my own."

"You should. I like the idea of something to keep you company when I'm not around."

"Hmm, maybe. Hey, how's the tattoo? Are you shedding little black bits of skin everywhere yet?"

"Holy shit, yes! It's everywhere. The things that no one tells you. I'm being very diligent about my aftercare though."

Maybe I could no longer take it, but I was becoming increasingly intrigued by the thought of dishing it out. "Mmm. That's my good boy," I said, the words dripping with more innuendo than I'd originally intended.

I heard a sharp inhale followed by a low groan. "Fuuuck, Shelby."

"What?"

"How have you got me so conditioned already? As soon as you said that, I got hard."

I sank deep into the couch and smiled with delicious satisfaction.

. . .

Two weeks later I was finishing up my workday. I grabbed my bags and headed out past the front desk and past Darius.

"Hey, Shelby. Hold on a sec." He looked up at the clock. "I... I need your help with something."

"Okay, sure." I put my things down and walked behind the desk. "What's up?"

He looked around the desk, shuffled some papers, and looked over at the coffee bar, all the while fidgeting at around a six on the Darius scale.

I put my hand on his arm, becoming concerned. "Hey. What's going on?"

He took a deep breath and smiled as he looked out the front door. Walking up to the salon was a young woman carrying what looked to be a cardboard pet carrier.

He walked out from behind the desk to greet her as she walked in. "Hi Darius," she said, "Today's the day! Are you excited?" She put the carrier on the floor.

I stood watching this play out while lost in utter confusion. Darius getting a pet and having it delivered to the salon made no sense whatsoever. He and Randall had a beautiful saltwater fish tank at home. Aesthetically pleasing, contained pets whose environment they could completely control. There was no way he'd be cool with something that pooped, peed, chewed, scratched, shed, or even ate outside of a tank.

Just then, I heard the faintest, most heart melting little mew. Darius smiled and crouched down to open the carrier, pulling down on the drawbridge-like front. He traced a finger back and forth on the floor in front of it to try and coax out its occupant. One little paw gingerly made its way out before it finally gained the confidence to fully emerge.

It was the tiniest, fluffiest black kitten I'd ever seen. She stood frozen with her huge amber eyes wide, fur sticking out in every direction, and her tail pointing straight up in the air.

Darius scooped her up and held her to his face. "Oh, thank you so much for bringing her here, Chelsea. I wanted the staff to meet her before we brought her home."

"My pleasure!" Chelsea chirped. "Well, it looks like you're all set. Enjoy your new family member."

"We will, absolutely."

As soon as Chelsea was out the door, Darius grinned at me with the little black bundle still snuggled against his chest.

"What is happening here, Darius?" I quickly became aware of my heartbeat.

Still smiling, he raised the kitten up in front of his face and cooed at her, "Are you ready to meet your new mommy, little one?" He handed her to me.

I took her in my arms as the thud of realization nearly knocked me over. I held her to my face and she began to purr, melting my heart instantly.

"She's a gift from Jake." Darius said.

"I know." I closed my eyes to fight the tears that were threatening. "I know."

After I recovered from my emotional glitch, I pulled out my phone and handed it to Darius. "Take our picture."

I think I will call her Minx. <3

I SENT THE PICTURE AND TEXT TO JAKE. ONCE I WAS DONE, I redirected all my attention back to the little kitten.

"Be careful, Shelby."

"I've got her, Dar. I'm not going to drop her." I said, snuggling Minx closer to my cheek.

"No. I mean be careful with Jake."

"What?"

"Don't you dare be reckless with that poor man's heart." Darius cautioned, his face filled with gentle concern.

"I don't know what you're talking about. Jake and I are just having fun." My brain snagged a little on the phrase, remembering Jake's snarky tone at the restaurant. "It's nothing serious."

"Do you have any idea of what he went through to gift you an adorable baby kitten from thousands of miles away? He called all the local rescues, looking specifically for a black one. He reached out to me for help because they wanted to do an interview and home visit. It was a whole thing. And, by the way, if anyone comes asking, this girl belongs to Randall and me.

"Oh." I was nearly speechless. "I guess I have to thank you, too. I'm sorry this caused you so much trouble."

"No, no trouble at all. We were happy to do it. But you need to realize that this man is as smitten with you as you are with this baby right here. No two ways about it."

My phone dinged.

LOL that's perfect. Omg she's so sweet.

This makes me so happy to see. <3

ON MY WAY HOME I STOPPED BY DARIUS AND RANDALL'S TO PICK UP all the things Jake had sent or that they had generously picked up at his request. Food, bowls, litter box, litter, tons of toys, and a retro atomic style cat tree so adorable I'd squealed with glee.

As much as I was touched beyond words that Jake had done all of this, a sick and heavy feeling was growing in my stomach. I could feel the edges of a dark déjà vu creeping in and unsettling me to my core. As I sat on my couch and watched my new kitten tentatively explore her new home, the murky memory fully bloomed.

WHEN ARI AND I FIRST GOT TOGETHER, HE BOUGHT ME THINGS. I'D get in his car, and he'd have a little box on the seat waiting for me. Earrings, a bracelet, a necklace, each time the sparkle quotient increased exponentially. When I'd meet him at his house, often there'd be a larger box containing a designer handbag, perfume set, or even a pair of shoes. All of it flashy and expensive, and none of it resembling anything I would have picked out for myself. Though I was always touched by the gestures so deeply—no one had ever given me that kind of attention before.

When I'd talked about it in therapy, Kelly had called it love bombing. The gifts combined with constant, possessive attention were often the number one tactic in the narcissist's playbook in pursuit of the object of their obsession. She pointed out how the gifts had dwindled when we moved in together and stopped altogether after we got married. Ari had gotten what he'd been after—me, the hapless prey caught in his sticky web.

I sickened at the thought of Jake now being the love bombardier. First the airline tickets, then the vase and now... now little Minx. My heart rate started to increase, and prickles of sweat began to form on the back of my neck. I put my head between my knees, trying to push the thoughts aside and just breathe.

I lifted my head when I heard two little chirping sounds.

Minx.

I watched her clumsily ambling closer and closer, her eyes meeting mine. When she opened her mouth for another barely audible mew, I picked her up and held her to my chest, the soft vibration of her purrs slowing my heart rate. Opening and shifting my perception.

I smiled as the darkness began to dissipate.

Jake wasn't trying to love bomb or *acquire* me. The gifts weren't flashy, and they weren't overly expensive. The things he had done for me were well within the normal range for someone—granted, an extremely thoughtful someone—who liked another person, and wanted to see them happy.

It wasn't a cunning strategy in the game of possession I'd mistaken as loving attention.

I now had things I appreciated and treasured because of the quiet attention Jake had actually paid. He had listened. He had noticed. He had actually *seen* me.

Darius's cautioning words were still rattling around in my head, however. *"Don't you dare be reckless with that poor man's heart."*

CHAPTER

EIGHTEEN

SHELBY

Late May 2013

11:00 P.M. AND I WAS JUST ABOUT TO GO TO SLEEP WHEN I SAW MY
phone light up. It was Jake.

"Hey." I answered with a reflexive smile.

"Hey. I'm sorry to call so late, were you sleeping?" he asked.

"Just about to be, but it's okay. Are you driving?"

"I am. I'm on my way to Sebastopol to meet the crew. We
are doing fire recovery starting tomorrow."

"Oh, that sounds heavy," I said.

"Yeah, but then I get to go right home. It always helps after
heavy shoots to be able to decompress there. I pushed myself a
little too hard today—over nine hours on the road and I've still
got one more to go." He sounded like he was dragging, his
voice gravely and at least a full octave lower than usual. I
found myself genuinely worried for him.

"I'm happy to help," I said.

"I appreciate that. Tell me about your day."

My day. Where would I even start? And I would most definitely be bending the rules of my "here" and "there" delineation I had with Jake.

"Well, Lyric and I went to a VFW event today. Do you remember Lyric? The tall receptionist with the long black hair? You met her last year when we filmed."

"Oh yeah, I remember her. She's kind of hard to forget."

I gave him the benefit of the doubt that it was her height or her motorcycle Morticia Adams vibe that he meant and not anything else. "It was an event for World War Two vets, like a meet and greet and photo op. They really get a kick out of seeing the pinup girls or 'nose art' as they like to call us. I had done a few of these, but it was Lyric's first time. She really got into her pinup character, and she even gave herself a name. Mimi Montrose."

"Cute. I like that."

"Things started out well enough. I was talking to this one guy, Bob, who was telling me about his plane getting shot down over Italy—he said it in two syllables, like It-ly—and spending time in a POW camp. Out of nowhere, I heard Lyric scream, 'What the fuck?'"

It had all happened so fast. I sprinted over to her and found the old man in the path of her wrath shouting as loud as she was.

"What kind of outfit is this? I thought there was just gonna be girls here, but you got one of these here... these here ladyboys? Maybe it's the kind of thing the boys who did tours in 'Nam like, but not me!"

I stood gaping at him. I wish I could say I was shocked by his tirade, but I wasn't. This reaction was, unfortunately, par for the course as I had quickly put together what had happened.

"He groped her." Jake was pretty sharp on the uptake, too.

"Yes. And believe it or not it got worse. The organizer sees the kerfuffle and comes over to us, trying to get everyone to calm down. Lyric is making her case that this guy assaulted her and meanwhile he's bemoaning the fact that she didn't have the parts he was expecting when he did. Guess whose side he took?"

"The vet's."

"Yup. He started talking some bullshit about 'misrepresentation' and our contract. We had signed something very informal, basically indicating our compensation, that was it. Nowhere did it specify what was to be in your pants. I pointed out that by that time we had been there an hour and a half with absolutely no problem whatsoever, and it wasn't until this guy crossed a line that anyone even knew. Or cared."

"Misrepresentation. That's interesting." Jake said.

I stiffened. I thought maybe Jake was about to take the organizer's side. I was pretty sure Ari would have.

"That's like saying a woman who colors her hair is misrepresenting herself. It'd be ridiculous and has no bearing on anything in a context like this," Jake said.

I was relieved, also touched by his consideration. "You know, most of the time these guys are fine. Some so sweet you want to put them in your pocket and take them home as your little souvenir grandpa. But there are a few...talk about misrepresentation. People think they are these great war heroes who can do no wrong, but hey, guess what? Sometimes they also happen to be lecherous fucks who think they can get away with this shit because they're pushing ninety and everyone thinks it's cute."

"Is she going to press charges?" Jake asked.

"She hasn't decided. We did get the guy's name, so she can think about it. It's not that she's ashamed of who she is, she's out and an outspoken advocate for her community. But it still can be mortifying to have to go through that, particularly when you can predict pretty accurately how it's going to end up."

We talked until Jake got close to his hotel.

"Thanks for staying up with me. I would have had to pull over if it weren't for you."

"My pleasure."

"Hey...we have a break in our schedule coming up and I'll be home for a while. What would you say about coming to San Francisco? To my house?"

I leaned into the phone. I did find myself missing his company in more ways than one. I missed his hands, his mouth, the string of breathy expletives he'd spout when he was about to come, yes, but also missing the dimples on either side of his low back that I loved to dip my fingers into. Missing how he'd hold his hand to his solar plexus as he laughed at something I said. Missing the way his body as the big spoon felt against mine, at once like a blanket and a balm.

And I was curious to explore our new dynamic a little more, too.

But going to his house seemed too real. We'd stayed in hotels up until now. Impersonal. Neutral. No one having home court advantage. This was venturing into more intimate territory, and I wasn't sure I was ready for that. I had an idea to try and keep things on a level playing field.

"If I say yes, you have to do something for me."

"Anything. You should know that by now."

I smiled and felt my cheeks flush. "When are you back home?"

"Friday night."

"Okay, Saturday night, I want you to call me and tell me a bedtime story."

"What?" he asked.

"Yes, a bedtime story. And it needs to be sexy."

"Ohhh, we are gonna go there, are we?" he mused. I could imagine the wicked grin on his face.

"Maybe..."

"Well then, you have yourself a deal," he said.

I went downstairs to grab a glass of water. I tiptoed quietly through the living room so as not to wake Lyric. We left the event early for obvious reasons and decided that multiple drinks were necessary—also for obvious reasons. Many, many vodka cranberries later, Lyric was wasted, and I made her spend the night at my house. I'd intended for her to sleep in the guest room, but she made herself very comfortable on my couch instead.

"Shelby?" Lyric mumbled.

"Shit, I'm sorry. I didn't mean to wake you."

"No, I was awake." She sat up on the couch, the room dimly lit with a light I'd left on for her in the kitchen. "I never thanked you for today."

I walked over and sat down beside her. "Oh, baby, I didn't do anything. I wish I could have done more."

She lowered her head, looking down at her hands as she absentmindedly picked at her long fingernails, immaculately painted with intricate designs—another enviable talent of hers. I hadn't seen her looking this vulnerable since the day she'd first walked into Aspire.

"You know, I am out here every day trying my best to represent as a proud Latina trans woman. I own it, I celebrate it." She took a deep breath, and I could see her fighting the tears. "I hate to say it, but today? Today I walked into that event hoping and praying I would pass."

"Oh God, Lyric."

"Yeah, I felt the vibe right away. I knew something like that was going to happen. I shouldn't have been there."

"I should have known, too. I'm so sorry. I should have been sensitive to the fact that it could have been unsafe for you. I mean, there are a lot of other events I wouldn't feel good about having you at." I hated to admit it, but it was true.

"I can see how you could think these guys might have been harmless, that maybe I wouldn't have to worry about being beaten bloody 'cause they're old, but they are still pervs. I saw you get your ass patted, pinched, or grabbed at least half a dozen times."

I lowered my eyes.

"Shelby, how can you be so protective of me, of the staff, doing those role-playing things to help keep us safe, meanwhile you just let things slide when they happen to you?" she challenged.

It was an excellent question. Leave it to Lyric to be bold enough to call me out.

"It's something I'm working on. I have a people pleasing problem. Mostly, a 'men pleasing' problem. It has to do with Ari."

Lyric looked in my eyes with sympathetic understanding. She was quiet, waiting for me to say more.

"It helps me to be protective of all of you, so you don't have to go through the same things that I did. But I need to remind myself that I deserve that protection and those boundaries, too."

She grabbed my hand. "Yes. You do." She laid her head back on the couch and sighed. "You know, I've thought a lot about whether to have the surgery. Days like today make me question again. Like, I think to myself, 'Sure I would still have been violated, but it would have been less *complicated.*' I mean, how fucked up is that? But you know what? Ultimately it comes down to this—I like dick. I like men who like dick. I like gay bars because I feel safer and more at home in queer spaces. I don't wanna be out there trying to hook up in straight bars and having to defend my existence as is. If they can't handle my dick, they sure as hell wouldn't deserve my pussy. Straight men are trash."

I laughed. "God, I love you. I love your fierceness. I love that you don't need to fit in anyone's box and I'm just so fucking proud of you, Lyric, I could cry."

She stood up and put her hands on her hips moving her head across her shoulders in cadence with her words, "*Mírame*! I'm a muthafuckin' unicorn!"

"Damn right! Your horn's just in a different place." I winked.

She howled and collapsed on the couch next to me. "Ahhh...fuck," she said as her laugher faded. "Bitch, I love you so much." She turned to face me. "Shelby, you know I think of you like a mom, right?"

It was a punch straight to my heart in the best possible way. I put my arms around her and said, "I'd be more than honored to hold that place in your life, baby girl, but we'd need to talk about you calling me bitch as a term of endearment."

She laughed. "Hey, you know how I said straight men are trash? There is one exception."

"Oh yeah? Who's that?"

"Brody. I'm sorry, but that boy is as sweet as honey and fine as hell."

I paused. "Hmmm."

"What?"

"Well, Brody hasn't come out as straight yet."

Lyric straightened up so fast it made me jump. "What?!"

"He has brought both girls and boys home. Never announcing anyone specifically as someone he was involved with, but I could spot those puppy dog eyes and chemistry sparks from a mile away. And he's had it with both."

"Well, well, well." She smiled.

"But now you told me I'm like your mom. Which would make you and Brody like a Greg and Marcia Brady situation."

"Who?"

"Greg and Marcia Brady? Like the Brady Bunch?"

"Ohhhh, yeah. I saw that movie! 'Marcia! Marcia! Marcia!'" Lyric laughed as she impersonated whiny Jan.

"Fuck you. Stop reminding me I'm old," I chided.

We wound ourselves back down and decided it was time to get some sleep. Just as I walked toward the stairs, I turned back to Lyric.

"Hey, just so you know I told Jake what happened today. I hope you don't mind."

"It's fine. Why would I mind you talking about it to the guy you're dating? Who, by the way, sounds like another example of a pretty decent straight man."

"We're not dating. We're fucking." I waved off a flash of a distant memory. *Why would I have said it like that?*

"You know Shelby, I'd be all about the slut life for you, but I—"

"What? You don't think I can handle it?"

"Darius told me what Jake did." She pointed to Minx curled up on the chair across from the couch. "With this kitten. I think you can handle it just fine. You need to make sure he can."

That's the second person within weeks who seemed overly concerned with Jake's heart in my hands.

CHAPTER
NINETEEN
JAKE

Saturday morning, I walked out toward my car with my load a little lighter after my latest emergency therapy session. As soon as I got back from Portland, I emailed Dr. McCallum to see how many extra hours we'd be able to fit in whenever I'd be home. I needed help. Lots of help.

I was finally being honest with myself, admitting that I was in love with Shelby. I needed to figure out how to draw out and separate those feelings that were now all messy and enmeshed with my fucked-up savior complex. But I did know that my love for her was now greater than my need to save her.

And it was high time to focus on my own redemption.

I was ready to be honest with Dr. McCallum and come clean about Shelby's history. I'd admitted I'd been tempted by the fact that she'd lost her husband and how I'd been more than willing to undo all the hard work I'd done up until that point. To her credit, she had simply looked at me expressionlessly and said, "I see." I suspect it took reliance on every ounce of her professionalism and restraint not to stand on her chair, point at me and shout, "Ha! I knew it!" I was extremely grateful for that.

I'd also shared my new suspicions that Ari had been abusive to Shelby in some capacity, but these new revelations had not triggered my hero complex as much as they triggered a seething anger toward a ghost. How could someone having been given the precious gift of Shelby's heart, her love and her trust, how could he have squandered it like that? Betrayed it? How had it been possible for him to knowingly hurt her? I admit I had been mesmerized by her tears, but only because I'd not been the one to cause them.

There were skeins and skeins of yarn here to unravel. And yes, I had begun using Shelby's metaphors.

Having her come to San Francisco was Dr. McCallum's idea. It would feel safer for me, and more meaningful for her, hopefully indicating that I was serious about trying to move forward and have a real relationship if we could get the footing solid. She said I had to be ready for the possibility of Shelby getting angry and not wanting to stay, so I'd tentatively held a room at a hotel and Brenda booked a flight for the next day, just in case. I would never force her to stay with me if she couldn't handle what I was telling her.

But first, before we got into all of that, I had to make up a bedtime story.

As I was working on it throughout the day I'd typed and deleted so many drafts because nothing was feeling right. It had started out dirty, downright filthy, and while it succeeded in turning me on, I had my doubts it would do the same for Shelby. She didn't seem to appreciate much explicit language. At least not yet. I'd come to hope that if we made it past all of this and she took full agency of her power, maybe someday all sorts of vulgarity would drip from that gorgeous mouth as she'd have me whimpering for mercy. But this was not to be the story I told her.

I reworded and tweaked and finessed until it was time to call her.

"Hello there," she purred into the phone.

"Hello yourself. Are you all comfy and cozy in your bed, ready for your bedtime story?"

"Yes. Hang on," she said. I heard rustling and a tiny meow. My phone pinged and I saw a text from her come through. It was a picture of her in bed with little Minx, soft light from the lamp beside her bed illuminating her freshly scrubbed and moisturized skin. I ached with affection.

I sighed into the phone. "God. You are so beautiful. I wish I was there next to you."

"Mmm. Me too."

"Okay, here we go." I took a deep breath. After this, no amount of laundering would be enough to get the stain of my heart off my sleeve.

"Once upon a time, in the prosperous kingdom of Vesuria, there lived a beautiful princess named Iliza. Vesuria sat nestled at the bottom of Mount Eptou, giving the kingdom, as well as the six others that surrounded it, the awesome responsibility of protecting the secret that lay near the mountain's summit.

Iliza's father, King Gohran, had promised her hand to Prince Ossian of Zoya, another of the Seven Kingdoms. The wedding was to take place in less than two weeks. She knew it was her obligation to marry for the good of the kingdom and their union would further fortify protection for the mountain. Ossian was charming and rakishly handsome, and Iliza was the envy of all the women of the surrounding lands. She should have been over the moon.

But she wasn't. She felt sick.

All she could think about every day, all day, was Balthazar, the captain of the guard ten years her senior. One day, when she'd been a young girl of thirteen playing a game of chase with her brothers, she'd carelessly crashed into this solid wall of man. She'd put up her hands to press herself away from him. Feeling all heat and muscle. Smelling all musk and sweat. It awakened feelings inside her that she'd never known. Balthazar had simply grabbed Iliza by the shoulders and effortlessly lifted her up and moved her out of his way with a grumpy huff, continuing about his business. Since that day, thoughts of him consumed her and whenever he was near her, she felt things in secret places she could hardly admit to herself.

Balthazar could not be bothered with children. The day she'd crashed into him, this child, this spindly mass of arms and legs and hair was most definitely a bother. He'd been tasked then to head a long campaign to keep the threat of invading warriors at bay, only to return five years later to see Iliza was no longer a child. Where there had been straight lines and spindles, there were now soft curves. Where there had been wild, tangled hair, there were now shiny waves of crimson that cascaded down her back. Pillowy lips and bright azure eyes. She was still a bother, make no mistake, but now for an entirely different reason.

Princess Iliza longed for Balthazar to notice her. And sometimes she swore he did. Their eyes would meet across the courtyard and hold a gaze so intense she thought she might faint. Her wedding was fast approaching, and she would be moved to Zoya, never to see Balthazar again. She was often bereft and inconsolable, not able to tell anyone the reason why.

Then, inspiration struck.

It seemed the fates were on her side as The Great Wishing would be upon them in just two days' time.

The secret that lay at the summit of Mount Eptou, the secret that the Seven Kingdoms were bound to protect was The Wishing Lake. Once a year, under a full moon, the residents of these kingdoms would make the sacred pilgrimage up the mountain. It was said that if you made a wish on a stone and threw it into the lake, your wish would come true. And it was well more than folklore. The Kingdoms were prosperous, babies all born healthy and well, marriages all blessed, and the sick were healed. Neighboring kingdoms were allowed to make an earnest appeal to the Seven to be able to make the journey as an outsider. But always, great care was taken to keep the pilgrimage manageable and protected.

Iliza decided she had to make her way to the Wishing Lake and be freed of her obligation, wishing to finally be in the arms of Balthazar. She summoned her handmaiden, Greta, and together they hatched a plan. She told her father she wanted to make the journey to Zoya before the wedding to ease her mind of the unknown. She'd seen the common spaces of the castle, but she wanted a say in how things would be set up in her private chambers, and she wanted everything to be in place as soon as the wedding was over. Her father agreed, but insisted she be escorted by two guards. This would make things complicated, but not impossible.

The journey was two days long. They made camp the first night, conveniently near to where the pilgrimage was to make its way up the mountain. After the guards had made dinner over the fire, one took out a satchel of mead. Greta shamelessly snatched the satchel, drained it, and began to flirt with the guards. Iliza feigned ill and went to her tent to retire for the evening. There she waited while Greta executed her part of the plan. Iliza couldn't help but watch Greta enchant the amorous guards with her wiles. She stood mesmerized as Greta, breasts bared, and legs spread wantonly, took one guard in her hand

and the other into her mouth. Iliza had never seen a naked man before and while she was barely able to tear her eyes away, she was more determined than ever in her quest to make Balthazar hers.

In the distance she could see the lantern trail of the pilgrimage. She lit her own lantern once she knew she wouldn't be seen by the distracted guards and hurried to join the group. She hid her face under her the hood of her cloak and kept her distance, not wanting to be recognized.

Once the pilgrimage reached the area surrounding the lake, the search began in earnest for the perfect stone. Each person was to look for a stone that spoke to them, one that called out to them and felt right settled into their hand. Once you'd found your stone, you'd make your wish. If your wish was to have money, you'd put the stone in your pocket. If your wish was to be healed, you'd place the stone near the wound or source of your pain. If your wish was a healthy baby, you'd hold the stone to your belly. If you were hungry, or if your village was suffering famine, you'd put the stone in your mouth, and so on.

The Lake was not for making wishes that would cause harm to others, and people who made wishes such as these would soon suffer their own terrible fates. These lessons were hard learned and well known, but still, people driven by hate or greed would continue to take the risk, and ultimately pay the price.

Iliza's need was clear to her, yet she'd never heard of someone making such a wish. She had to get creative. She searched and searched until finally she came upon the perfect stone. Oblong. Smooth. Reasonably long and thick. She picked it up and went to find somewhere to hide. While everyone else was surrounding the lake making their wishes, Iliza could not be seen. She found a secluded area behind some bushes and knelt on the ground. She wiped the stone on her dress and held it to her lips, closing her eyes and imagining Balthazar standing naked before her. She timidly touched her tongue to the stone and began wishing that someday she might do the same to him. She lifted her dress and slid it back and forth across her neediest place, imagining the broad shadow and weight of Balthazar's body above her as he patiently took her virginity. Before long, Iliza found herself moving the stone in and out of her soaked sex, frantically working her way to climax, biting her lip to keep from crying out. Once her convulsions had ceased, and tears began to spill out of her eyes, she got up and joined the others at the edge of the lake. She closed her eyes and made one final plea before casting the stone into the cerulean water.

When she returned from the journey to Zoya exhausted from having to push Prince Ossian and his wandering hands away from her, she went in search of Balthazar. She stalked the outside of the guards' quarters in the courtyard and waited patiently until finally she saw him. And he was headed right toward her.

'My lady.' He bowed.

She curtseyed her greeting in return, her heart pounding in her chest.

'Might I have a word with you in private?' Balthazar asked her. 'I wish to discuss the transfer of your care to your new guard in Zoya.'

'Of course, Balthazar,' she said. She was thrilled and terrified at the thought of being alone with him. Just then, Greta came rushing toward them.

'I've been asked by your father to summon you, M'lady. There is news.'

Iliza was saddened to leave Balthazar just as it seemed her wish was to come true, but she did as she was told.

'My daughter,' King Gohran said, 'I have news of great

sadness. Just after you left Zoya, Prince Ossian was thrown from his horse and has been killed.'

Iliza crumpled. It was not grief she was feeling but guilt. She had not intended to cause harm to anyone to make her wish come true.

What she did not know was that Ossian had also joined the pilgrimage anonymously. His own malicious wish had been for his father to die, not only to take the throne, but also to form an alliance with a large warring faction soon descending on the Seven Kingdoms to overtake Mount Eptou. Wishing to cause harm to others, Ossian had met his own terrible fate instead.

Days later, Iliza once again found herself outside the court-yard and watching enraptured as Balthazar approached her. 'My lady,' he bowed once more. 'Shall we continue our conversation?'

'Have you not heard?' Iliza asked incredulously. 'Prince Ossian has died. There will be no wedding.'

'Oh yes. That is quite tragic,' Balthazar said, with no hint of sadness in his eyes. In fact, to Iliza, it looked more like amuse-ment. 'But there will certainly be a funeral, and planning for your safety will need to be arranged.'

'I suppose you are right.' Iliza had never been asked for her opinion in these matters, but she did not dare question it if it was to mean she'd finally be alone with Balthazar.

He tenderly placed a hand on the small of her back, the simple gesture nearly leveling her as he'd not touched her since the day she'd crashed into him years before. He led her confidently to his quarters ignoring the gaze of curious onlookers in the courtyard.

Once Iliza had crossed the threshold of Balthazar's private quarters, she was barely able to breathe. She heard the door close behind her, his footsteps slowly approaching until he was close enough for her to feel the heat radiating off his body.

"My lady,' he said. She'd heard the phrase hundreds of times by hundreds of people but never, ever in a way that made her knees threaten to buckle beneath her. A way that made her insides twist and coils of heat and ache ricochet throughout the lowest part of her belly.

Balthazar grabbed her arm and spun her around to face him. She gasped at the suddenness and roughness of the act, but instantly his hands were tenderly caressing her face.

'My lady. Iliza. I think of you every hour of every day. I dream about you every night. I can't tell you how long I've waited for this.' He looked deep into her eyes with all the need he couldn't express with words.

She put her hands on his chest. Remembering so long ago when this very chest had awakened those feelings in her.

'Tell me. Have you been with a man before?' Balthazar asked.

She shook her head.

'Then I will try to be as gentle as I can. I can't promise I will succeed because I've wanted this for so long. Imagined this for so long. But I will try,' he said.

Iliza couldn't speak, and even if she could, she wouldn't have known what to say. This was a moment that transcended words. She only wanted to touch and to be touched. To ravage and be ravaged. To have the only thing that escaped her mouth to be moans and screams of pleasure intermixed with the name of the man responsible for it.

Balthazar fisted Iliza's hair firmly, tilting her head as he claimed her mouth. His tongue breaching her lips and exploring, finding her so warm and inviting, and so, so eager. He trembled with desire, desperately fighting the urge to take her as roughly and as possessively as he had done in his imagination a hundred times before. But he did not want to scare her. He did not want to hurt her. He did not want to do anything to ruin this moment. She pulled away from the kiss and walked toward the bed. Still turned away from him, she slowly began to undress. He was thrilled beyond measure that she wanted this as much as he did. He pressed himself up against her back, his lips tasting every inch of skin as she bared it.

She freed herself of her clothes and turned back to face Balthazar. The way he looked at her was frightening. Lusty and driven, like a man possessed. But it also exhilarated her, sparking and igniting her entire body from the inside out. He began to undress himself and Iliza didn't blink. She didn't want to miss a second of watching his fingers move deftly over his clothing as his eyes stayed fixed on her. Unveiling muscle after muscle, plane after plane of solid man. Once he was naked and she'd finally been able to wrestle her eyes away from the curious and compelling divining rod between his legs, they landed on his mouth just as he licked his lips. She clenched her thighs together as her sex wept with need."

A LAUGH BURST THROUGH THE DAM OF CLOSED LIPS ESCALATING INTO A full cackle.

"Aw, come on! That's not fair—you laughing at me." I whined.

"I'm sorry, but 'her sex wept with need?' I can't." Shelby laughed harder. "I can't."

"You know, I did *research*! I read a bunch of smutty excerpts and found all the euphemisms I could because I didn't think you'd like for me to say 'cock' and 'pussy.' I worked hard on this!" I wasn't mad. I'd rolled my eyes more than a few times as I'd been writing. "And you're messing up the hottest scene! God. You're insufferable."

"I'm sorry. I am." Still laughing. "Now, 'divining rod'? That is a new one. I like it."

"Okay, how about you just listen to the damn story and try not to judge my word choices?" I'd hoped she could feel me smiling. The excerpts I read were often equal parts hot and awkward, as was writing this scene. I've got to give the Bodice Ripper Brigade a lot of credit when they can strike the balance well.

"I can do that," Shelby said. "But as long as we are taking a break, I'm gonna pee quick."

I grinned to myself.

A break in the middle of the sex scene was pretty on brand for us.

CHAPTER
TWENTY

JAKE

"Okay. All good to start back up." Shelby said, a little out of breath.

I was touched that she'd hurried for my ego's sake. After she'd kind of shit all over it, that is.

"We left off with clenching and weeping," she giggled.

"Shut up." I laughed. I cleared my throat and continued, "Balthazar swept Iliza into his arms and laid her gently on the bed. He pressed his lips to hers before teasing them open with his tongue, her hands raking through his hair, nails dragging across his back, arching her body upwards to get closer to him. He licked and nibbled his way down her neck and the front of her chest before pulling his head back to once again admire and worship the most beautiful breasts he'd ever laid eyes on. The breasts that defied all gravity and made him shift and readjust his trousers whenever Iliza would wear her ball gowns with the tight bodices. And now they were finally his to play with. He cupped one in his hand and swirled his tongue around the sensitive peak of her taut, pink nipple. She inhaled sharply and arched her back, further pressing her body into his mouth. She was so perfect, so responsive.

Iliza moaned with pleasure as Balthazar continued his oral assault. He made his way down her body, and she shuddered when she felt him pause at the apex of her thighs. He reverently whispered her name into her most sacred place before swiping his tongue across her wet and swollen flesh. She wriggled and writhed as he teased and tasted every bit of her with his greedy mouth until she could no longer contain her ecstasy. She screwed her eyes shut and screamed his name as she unraveled beneath him.

Balthazar propped himself up to look deeply into Iliza's eyes. Pride washed over him as the flush on her face, her neck, and her chest let him know just how much pleasure he had given her. She had completely melted under his touch. But he was nowhere near finished with her.

Just as Balthazar was about to gently instruct Iliza on how to handle a man's erection, her delicate fingers had already wrapped around his. He watched with wide eyes as she moved her mouth toward it like it was a vessel containing the elixir of the gods. She locked her eyes with his as she teased his tip with her tongue. If she had truly never been with a man before and this was just sheer instinct, he said a silent prayer of thanks to have been blessed with a goddess such as this. Iliza took Balthazar fully into her mouth and worked his length with her hand at the same time.

Knowing he was on the verge, in one sudden and fluid motion, he grabbed Iliza by the waist and twisted her around to lie beneath him. She spread her legs wide and stared in wonder as he positioned himself at her entrance. 'Oh, my sweet Iliza,' he said, 'I've waited for this moment for so long.'

He slowly guided himself inside her, watching her face contort with pain. He was careful, so careful, but every inch of her felt like pure heaven and he was hardly able to contain himself. She whimpered and clawed at his shoulders, but as he began his tempered and measured movements, Iliza's facial expression softened. Her whimpers turned to soft moans, and she wrapped her legs tighter and tighter around his waist, meeting his every thrust with her hips. Balthazar could no longer hold himself back. He let her inner muscles grip him tightly as he thrusted unabashed until finally spilling inside her. He pressed a kiss to her lips and smiled as contentment and peace he'd never known settled over him.

For several months, the lovers snuck off to various places to continue their secret affair. Balthazar convinced the king to allow him to instruct Iliza on how to better handle herself on a horse lest she suffer the same fate as Prince Ossian. The king had agreed and their options for seclusion became limitless.

After nearly a year had passed, it was clear the king had been arranging for Iliza's marriage once again, and before long she was betrothed to Prince Elden of Gyllian. Gyllian was what was known as a border kingdom. Located just outside the Seven, the inhabitants were allowed the privilege of the pilgrimage in exchange for helping to protect Mount Eptou.

Iliza was heartsick at the thought of leaving Balthazar.

One night, soon after the engagement had been announced, the bells in the courtyard began their furious ringing.

This meant only one thing. The kingdom was under attack.

The villagers began to scatter, frantically seeking shelter as the front gate seemed to be under the assault of a battering ram. Fiery projectiles began raining down inside the courtyard and against the castle walls. Iliza raced through the halls desperate to find her mother and father, all the while consumed with worry for Balthazar knowing his place was at the front of the battle.

She passed by a window and heard a scream, a voice she recognized. She looked down and saw Greta crying out in the courtyard, trapped beneath a large wooden beam. Iliza ran down to her as fast as she could.

Once Iliza had reached Greta, she yelled out for someone to help her. A passing guard grabbed her by the arm. 'Princess, you must get to safety at once!' He shouted.

'I cannot leave my handmaiden!' Iliza urged.

Just then, a crack louder than thunder echoed through the courtyard.

The gate had been breached.

Warring soldiers wielding swords came rushing in, and Iliza crouched over Greta to protect her. She looked up to see her father standing side by side with Balthazar, both armed with swords and ready for the onslaught.

Iliza bent over Greta trying desperately to wish the violence away. She felt so helpless and vulnerable and terrified that something would happen to Balthazar.

In a flash, the violent grip of one of the warriors crushed her arm, dragging her across the ground and laying her at the boot of the menacing war lord, Gregor. Gregor yanked Iliza to her feet, holding her in front of him as he faced her father.

'This looks to be someone important to you, King. What say I spare her if you surrender?' Gregor growled.

King Gohran tried to bluff to protect his daughter, but the panic on his face was evident. He bowed his head and whispered, 'I cannot surrender. There is too much at stake.'

Gregor held Iliza's petrified body in front of him. Just before he could cross her throat with his blade, he lurched violently forward as the tip of a sword burst through his chest barely missing Iliza's body. Eyes wide, Gregor dropped to his knees before falling dead.

Behind him stood Balthazar enraged, blood dripping off the end of his weapon.

Iliza collapsed onto the ground. Balthazar lifted her to him gently with one arm, careful not to surrender to his overwhelming relief and betray their secret. He released Greta from the beam and demanded the king get the women safely inside the castle.

With Gregor dead, the warriors lost their vigor just as soldiers from neighboring kingdoms had come to lend assistance. The battle ended just as the sun rose.

The next day, the king approached Balthazar. 'I come to you with more shame than I have ever felt. More shame than a man can bear. I made the vow to protect the mountain at all costs, but I never thought I would have to choose between it and my daughter. I had been willing to sacrifice her life, but I never would have forgiven myself for having done so. You not only saved her life, but mine as well. Please. Please name your price. To show my undying gratitude, I will give you anything you want.'

'There is only one thing I want more than anything in this world,' Balthazar said.

King Gohran replied, 'Anything my son. Whatever you ask for is yours.'

THAT EVENING, THE KING SUMMONED ILIZA TO HIS CHAMBERS. Her breath caught in her throat as she saw Balthazar standing there.

'Iliza,' her father said, 'I don't know if you can ever find it in your heart to forgive me for the choice I made that nearly cost you your life. If not for Balthazar, neither of us would be standing here. I have offered him anything of his choosing from my kingdom in gratitude. He has chosen... your hand. Would you have him?'

She stared in wonder at her father as tears sprang to her eyes. She ran to Balthazar and leapt into his waiting arms. 'Yes!' she cried.

He kissed her tenderly, 'I love you with everything I am, Iliza. I am yours forever.'

Throughout the previous year, Balthazar had not only lusted after Iliza, but he had fallen madly and deeply in love with her. He knew it would only be a matter of time before she was to be married and would leave the kingdom. On the night of the last Great Wishing, just one week before the invasion, Balthazar had made his way up the mountain with the pilgrimage. He began his search for the perfect stone. And there, with the full moon casting its light in affirmation, was the one. The one that spoke to him. The one that felt right and true in the palm of his hand.

He stood at the edge of the lake and whispered his fervent wish over and over as he held the stone tightly to his heart.

The End."

SHELBY WAS QUIET. TOO QUIET. THE THOUGHT OF HER HAVING FALLEN asleep as I laid my soul bare in a bedtime story was horrifying. But more horrifying was the thought that maybe she was quietly trying to formulate the right words in order to break my heart.

Finally, she spoke. "Oh, wow," her words barely above a whisper, "I...I didn't expect...Jake, that was incredible. Did you make that whole thing up yourself?"

"Not exactly. Most of the Wishing Lake stuff was from an actual story my grandmother told me when I was little."

"That's so sweet. But... do you feel guilty for sexing it up?" Shelby giggled.

"Nope. She would have loved it. She was a feisty lady. I owe practically every dirty joke I know to her."

"Now I love it even more," she said.

"I'm so happy you liked it."

I planned to leave it at that and not say any more. Let it all germinate. Then, when she came to visit, I would confirm every suspicion that had bloomed in that beautiful brain of hers.

CHAPTER
TWENTY-ONE
SHELBY

June 2013

THAT WAS *UNEXPECTED.*

I'd asked for a sexy bedtime story and instead got this epic romantic fairy tale. Jake didn't specify which parts were in the original story versus what he had made up—apart from the sexy bits—and I found myself preferring to assume everything else, Iliza, Balthazar, all of it, had been taken from his grandmother's sweet tale.

Never mind that so many things sounded more than a little familiar and had me holding my breath as he'd told me the story.

I'D TOLD JAKE I WANTED TO PAY FOR MY AIRFARE TO SAN FRANCISCO and that I would make my own way to his house from the airport. While I'd accepted his thoughtful gifts throughout those weeks, I wanted to draw a few lines and maintain some control. I was grateful he hadn't argued at all.

Because I'd been concerned about saving myself some money, the cheaper option meant I was in for a full and exhausting day of travel. By the time I was in the cab on my way to Jake's house, I was practically falling asleep. I did want to enjoy the scenery though, since it was the first time I'd ever been to a city where the drive from the airport was immediately interesting. The sloped streets looked even more strange and Seussian than I'd imagined. I guessed that women here were very particular when and where they choose to wear heels. I'd best be careful, I thought, or I'd end up on my ass, or worse, twisting an ankle into a pretzel.

We drove through a neighborhood the cab driver called The Mission. He'd been giving me a guided tour the whole way for which I was grateful, because it kept me engaged and awake. He pulled over and stopped the car. "That's it. On the right."

It was a fairly large but narrow, white, three-story house with a wrought iron fence and gate in the front. There were at least ten steep steps up to the front door, and a half turret off to one side. Very "Full House" classic San Francisco.

Jake had asked me to text when I arrived and not ten seconds later, he emerged from the house, coming down the stairs and jogging through the front gate. A giant smile lighting up his whole face. I paid the driver as Jake pulled my carry on out of the trunk.

"I'm so glad you're here," he said as he pulled me in for a kiss. My curiosity at seeing inside of this beautiful house was thankfully overriding my nervousness.

"Is this all yours?" I asked as we walked up the steps.

"I own the place but it's a duplex. I rent the upper two floors to Kyle and Gina, Lunchbox's parents."

"Oh, Lunchbox! Will I get to meet him?'

"No, unfortunately, they all went camping. I guess you'll just have to come back another time."

I nodded but plans like that seemed a little too overwhelming to consider.

As I walked in, I instantly fell in love. The house was not unlike the old duplexes on the East Side of Milwaukee with their high ceilings, crown moldings, and built in cabinetry, but even more grand. Yet, at the same time, not at all stuffy. The ceilings had to be at least fourteen feet high, with tall windows to match. Old wood floors that creaked in all the places you'd expect. Where we'd entered in the living room a huge fireplace was lit and welcoming, surrounded by what looked to be the original mantle-piece and more of the classic molding.

The lighting was all perfect. Nothing overhead or harsh, all lamps and ambient light. I inhaled the soft smell of leather from the couch as soon as I got near it. It wasn't black leather with cup holders and reclining sections like I had been used to, but a soft, light brown. Worn, but not shabby, with soft curves and a line of tufting buttons along the top and in front of the arms, it looked like it would be very at home in a library.

"You like the couch?"

"Huh?" I looked down to see my hand running across the buttery leather. "I do. It's lovely."

Jake gently twisted a stray strand of my hair around his finger. "You seem exhausted. Would you like to lie down for a little while?"

"Oh, no I'm okay," I lied. I wanted nothing more than to collapse on this beautiful couch in front of the fire and pass out.

"No really, I'm just prepping dinner and it's going to be awhile. I've got no major plans for us tonight." He grinned and added, "At least none that involve leaving the house."

"Are you sure you don't mind? I mean, I just got here."

"Honestly, nothing would make me happier right now than to have you all cozy on my couch. You're here, and that's all that matters."

I was so grateful I nearly cried. I sat on the couch, practically sighing at the generous give it had. Jake knelt on the floor and began unlacing my Chucks, gently taking one off, then the other. He pulled a white cable knit blanket off a nearby chair and repositioned a throw pillow for my head to land on.

He continued kneeling next to me, stroking my hair and within seconds, I was asleep.

An undeterminable time later something lovely invaded my senses and told me it was time to wake up. The most captivating smell that I couldn't quite place was coming from somewhere else in the house. Dinner. I looked around for my phone to see what time it was and noticed it was dark outside. *How long had I been asleep?*

I looked to my right and there on the end table was my phone. On a charger. *Had I done that?* I was so tired when I'd arrived, I couldn't remember.

I stumbled through the house to find Jake. And a bathroom.

I passed by a butler's pantry with gorgeous lit shelving. I turned and saw open set of double pocket doors and there he was working away in the kitchen. He was facing away from me and had yet to notice I was there. He was wearing an apron over his soft grey Henley and faded jeans. Barefoot. It was all I could do to keep myself from swooning.

"Hi," I said.

He turned in a flash. "Oh, hi! You're up!"

"Mmhmm," I rubbed my face. "Can I use your..."

"Oh, of course."

Jake led me around the corner to a small powder room and gave me a kiss on the cheek.

I was having a hard time getting my bearings. I don't know what I had expected to find coming here, but none of it was this. This house, Jake's house, was so comfortable. Welcoming. I was so sensitive to spaces, and there I felt completely settled. Which, in turn, unsettled me completely.

I wandered back toward the dining room. He had set a beautiful table with an eclectic grouping of well used candles on a tray, sisal placemats, and mismatching yet complimentary dishes and flatware. I smiled thinking of Marion having a fit at the sight of it. I, however, was completely charmed.

"Dinner will be ready in fifteen minutes. Would you like a tour?"

"I'd love that."

"How about a glass of wine?" Jake asked.

"Yes, please.'

He handed me a glass of red. "It's a nice zin. Californian, of course," he winked.

I took a sip and smiled. It was the most delicious wine I'd ever tasted.

I could never tell him, but while Ari had a fantastic palate for food, I never appreciated his taste in wine. He'd proclaim the wine to be excellent based on the name, the price, the exclusivity, all over actual taste. I, on the other hand, preferred wines that spoke to me no matter the pedigree. This one whispered sweet nothings in my ear.

"Damn." I whispered.

"Sexy, right?"

I'd never heard a wine described as sexy before, but it sure was.

The house was a bit of a maze, and it was going to take me awhile to figure out the configuration. I liked that about it, though. Unpredictable. Like the architect had a sense of humor and whimsy. Jake took me back up though the living room to the large bedroom in the front of the house. Another set of double pocket doors. A king bed with fluffy yet crisp white bedding. Tasteful Oriental rugs, minimal furniture, lovely art decorating the walls. A few healthy plants on the wide windowsills that curved within the turret, and stacks and stacks of books. I smiled, reminded of my own mini garden libraries at home. Off the bedroom was a larger bathroom with walk in shower, a clawfoot tub and what looked to be a newer, larger vanity than what had been there originally.

"How long have you lived here?" I asked.

"Ten years. I was grateful it was pretty turn-key, I didn't have a lot of time to spend on renovations."

"It's wonderful. It feels so comfortable."

"I love it. Coming home here is one of the best feelings in the world," Jake said wistfully.

He led me back through the dining room and showed me another full bath and the second bedroom he had made into an office. Beyond that was a room that seemed to have been converted from a porch. On one side there was a bicycle, a few toolboxes, a cooler, and other things one might find in a garage. On the other, a futon.

"Kind of a catch all and guest room at this point," he explained.

We went out the door from there to the backyard. On the large deck was a six-person hot tub. The lid was off, and he'd turned some outdoor lighting on.

"I thought maybe we could hang out here later."

My first thought was panic that I hadn't brought a swim-suit. But as I glanced around at the tall wooden fencing and large greenery surrounding the yard protecting it from neighboring eyes, I knew it might not be necessary to have one. I smiled. "Hmm. That would be nice."

"One more room." He led me back into the house and I

couldn't help thinking that if I wandered around in the middle of the night, I would most likely get lost.

"Ohhhhh," I said as my eyes widened.

"Yeah, that's the reaction this room usually gets."

The library. Floor to ceiling bookshelves along one whole wall. With a goddamn library ladder. I'd never actually seen one in someone's home.

And there, in the center of the room, a beautiful antique baby grand piano. Original wood. Not cold white. Not gaudy black lacquer.

"It's a 1927 Steinway. I know, it's gorgeous. But…it's not mine."

I looked at him, curious.

"It belongs to my friend Doug. They sold the house after the divorce, and he had to move to a smaller place. He couldn't bear putting it in storage, so I offered to hang on to it for him. He's keeping it for his son, Wyatt."

"Does it get used at all?" Honestly, I would love to have this in my house just to have. It was so beautiful. Although an instrument like that—it would be a shame if it didn't get played.

"Wyatt is at Berkeley, so when I'm not home, he does come and play. He's so talented, I'm glad he gets a chance to use this." Jake moved around to sit at the piano.

"He told me once that playing piano for a girl is the ultimate 'panty dropper.'" He looked up at me. "What do you think about that?"

"I'd like to think I'm at the age I could spot some ploy at 'panty dropping' from a million miles away," I told him. "But I could see someone young being affected, sure."

Jake looked down at the keys in front of him, then lifted his eyes to mine. "You know, I think someone sharing their art with the masses or even with a group of people is wonderful and brave, and we as humans are all the better for it. It's what makes the world magical and interesting. But sharing your art with one person, for one person...it's different. It's almost sacred. Painting or drawing someone's portrait, playing or singing for one person, even making someone a special meal, it all comes with a certain responsibility and shouldn't be done recklessly."

I nodded. I was feeling fuzzy and overwhelmed and I wasn't even halfway into my glass of wine.

Jake put his hands on the keys and began to play. "I've been fooling around a little and taught myself a few things by ear. It's kind of fun."

He began a rhythm with his right hand for a few bars, then started the melody with his left. It was impressive for a beginner. I recognized the song, but for the life of me I couldn't place it.

"What song is that?"

"It's... it's nothing. Come on. Dinner's ready."

Jake had refused my offer to help with getting dinner on the table. I sat down and waited until he walked in and placed my plate in front of me.

"Oh, this looks amazing." And it did.

"It's just a John Dory with a lemon cream sauce, wild mushroom and asparagus risotto, and a frisée and fennel salad." Jake waved it off so casually. As if he'd plopped a frozen pizza in front of me and called it a day.

"Just? I think you may be forgetting that I know what went into making this." I sat and stared at the plate as he went to sit down. I thought about what he had said about sharing your art with one person, how powerfully intimate that was. A cloying sensation poked at me.

Ari made food for me all the time when we were first together, but it was in that reckless way that Jake pointed out. It was part of Ari's love bombing. I'd venture a guess that it may have been successful at "panty dropping" as well, if my panties hadn't already been incinerated the very first time he kissed me.

In later years when he made me food, it was because he was trying a new recipe which was an always a risky game. I had to be careful to say I liked it, but not gush. Point out something specific that I noticed, otherwise he'd think I was just placating him. But I could never, ever tell him it wasn't good or suggest ways to change it in any way. It was exhausting.

Once again, Jake was proving himself to be someone else entirely from what I'd been used to. I warmed at the thought of him planning a menu and taking the time to shop for the ingredients. Even going to a specialty fish market, or even the wharf itself, because John Dory would not likely be at your corner grocery store.

And not only dinner but caring for me with the simplest gestures. Taking off my shoes and settling me down for a nap. Putting my phone on a charger. No one had ever tended to me in that way. I was in uncharted territory, and I didn't have a single clue as to how to process any of it.

I gingerly took a bite of my food, my stomach cautioning me to take it slow. I never had much of an appetite on long days of travel, but I suspected something else altogether was stirring in my gut.

"Oh my God. It's delicious, Jake. Thank you."

He smiled. "Oh!" He held up a finger. "One more thing." Setting his napkin on the table as he got up, he pulled his phone out of his pocket and walked over to a speaker set up on the credenza.

Music.

And not just any music. Otis Redding. Sam Cooke. Chris Isaak. Lyle Lovett. Haunting troubadours and tender soul singers. Songs laced with love and longing. *Had I told him that I liked this?* As we ate, I found myself unreasonably irritated that he would remember. And if I hadn't told him, I was unreasonably irritated that we would have this too in common.

I managed to make my way through most of my dinner, taking it slow and sipping water along the way. I felt so claggy still, like I was wading through molasses.

Jake pushed his plate forward and got up. I was vaguely aware of the start of a different song, and his movements seemed to be choreographed to it. He walked over to me and held out his hand.

"Dance with me."

I sat dumbfounded. Frozen. It'd been forever since I'd danced with anyone anywhere but at someone's wedding. Had it been since my own?

I took his hand and stood up. It took a second for my legs to steady. He led me to the open space to the side of the table, weaving an arm around my waist and holding my hand in his.

It was then that I recognized the song. I knew it was Van Morrison, but I'd only heard "Tupelo Honey" a handful of times.

We swayed back and forth to the music. That was about as much as I was able to manage. I rested my head against his chest to feel his breath combining with the melody and the beautiful, poignant lyrics I couldn't ignore. I could feel myself beginning to tremble.

Just then, Jake pulled away from me slightly and gently put his hand under my chin to lift my face to his. His eyes spoke volumes of sonnets to mine as he held my hand to his chest to feel his heartbeat's message as well.

He tilted his face toward mine and placed the sweetest, most tender kiss on my lips.

The whole evening had been leading up to this moment, and somehow, the simplest gesture of affection hit me like a blitz attack.

Jake was throwing down the gauntlet and daring me not to fall in love.

The room began to spin and collapse into me from all sides. Van Morrison's voice slipped farther and farther away as the ringing in my ears got louder and louder. I could feel the darkness coming and I consoled myself with the knowledge that Jake would without a doubt catch me as I fell.

I SLOWLY BECAME AWARE OF MY SURROUNDINGS AND FOUND MYSELF once again on the magic leather couch. Jake was sitting beside me holding a cold washcloth to my forehead.

"Hi," he said.

"What happened?" It was all a blur.

"You fainted."

I was starting to remember the sense of overwhelm I had been feeling. Jake's house. The wine. The dinner. The dance.

The kiss.

I might have blamed my passing out on a long day of travel and a significant time change, but a pull toward something else entirely was becoming undeniable.

I was starting to have real feelings for Jake. And it scared the shit out of me.

It was just supposed to have been fun. A distraction and an escape. But being enveloped within these walls, feeling such warm, loving care from the moment I walked through the door made it crystal clear that some part of me longed for more.

I'd only been in love once before, but it was all fused with and tangled up in my trauma bond. I had no clue when and where the love ended and the addiction to the drug that was Aristotle Ristow began.

He'd taken my love and twisted it into something unrecognizable. And since he'd been incapable of loving me the way I'd wanted him to, I'd just given up. Something in me had withered.

He'd taken my desire, performed the Devil's alchemy, and threw it back in my face as shame.

And cruelest of all, he'd taken my trust and hid it away in his dragon's hoard, never to be seen again. It wasn't that Jake hadn't earned it, because of course he had. But I couldn't bring myself to trust him because I couldn't remember how.

Therapy was helping, but I was still wading through the mire and the muck trying to get to the other side.

Jake helped me undress and get into his bed. He undressed and climbed in next to me and the way he just held me without words, without any expectation, reminded me of our first night together. He was just there. Solid. Strong. Dependable. Holding space for me in a way that no one ever had. Even without knowing all my secrets. No question.

I took deep measured breaths as I tried desperately not to cry.

• • •

"Hey, good morning" Jake said as he woke. "Wait, what are you doing?" Jake asked.

I was gathering my things from the bedroom and pulling on my pants. "I've got to go. I've got to get to the airport. Brody texted me in the middle of the night and I didn't see it until this morning. He was in a car accident."

Jake leapt out of bed. "Oh my God. Is he okay?"

"I just got off the phone with him. He's okay, but I just need to get home. I need to be with him."

"Of course! Here, let me call Brenda and have her check the flights." He grabbed his phone. "I'll drive you to the airport."

"No, no you don't have to...I already have a car coming," I said.

"Oh. Are you sure? I just want to make sure you're okay." He looked so helpless. "What can I do?"

"Nothing. I'll be fine. I've got to get home."

Jake stood in front of me and tenderly tucked a strand of hair behind my ear. *Please stop that,* I silently begged.

"Let me get you some coffee and something to take with you to eat. I worry about you after last night."

Last night.

I felt that familiar twinge in my stomach. You know the one. The one that physiologically and painfully reminds of something you forgot. Making it difficult when you *want* to forget. So, instead, you ball it up as tightly as you can and tuck it away.

My ride arrived and Jake walked me out through the front gate. He gave me one last hug, one more hit of his pure and solid essence before opening the car door for me.

"Please call me when you get home. I want to know you're home safe and that Brody's okay."

"I will." Again, that unreasonable irritation was scratching at me.

Later that afternoon, once I was home, my phone pinged. Like I knew it would.

> Everything okay? How's Brody?

> Everything is fine. I made it home safe, and Brody is okay. A little sore but okay.

Scratchy feelings again. Jake being so concerned about my son. The line between my 'here' and my 'there' was officially blurred. He was invading, bleeding in.

And I had yet to discover how much that was true.

CHAPTER
TWENTY-TWO

SHELBY

"So, I take it this is an unplanned pregnancy?" Dr. Bronner asked.

What could have possibly tipped you off? I looked at my ashen complexion in the mirror across from me in the clinic room. *The fact that I look like I've seen a ghost or the fact that my breakfast is now in your waste basket?* I snarked in my head. She wasn't my regular OB/GYN, but I had no choice but to see the associate. My regular doctor, Dr. Lindsay was spending a month in New Zealand with his wife.

I had fainted at work the day before. Luckily it was in the break room and not in front of a client. I had dragged myself into work the last few days unable to shake off this nagging exhaustion. Randall sent me home and I called for the appointment. Today I woke up with some cramping on my right side.

"But I have an IUD, this isn't supposed to happen."

"No birth control is one hundred percent with the exception of sterilization. We do worry with an IUD though. I want to do an exam."

She had me lie down and I grimaced. "What's wrong?" She asked.

"Oh, it's nothing. Just some shoulder pain...I've had a lot of stress lately."

"Are you having any other pain?"

"A little," I told her. "Some cramping this morning."

"Hmm."

She had me put my feet up in the stirrups and lubricated her gloved fingers to do a pelvic exam. "I am going to feel your uterus now. When did you have your last period?"

I winced as another sharper cramp gripped me. "I don't really get periods with this last IUD. But I guess I had unprotected sex around six weeks ago. I wonder if you'd be able to give me a referral..."

"You want to terminate. No problem, I'll give you a list of options before you leave." She put two fingers inside and I felt the pinch as she hit my cervix. "I'm not feeling your IUD threads. It has definitely either migrated or it fell out at some point." She pressed her fingers in above my pubic bone, and I flinched with another cramp. "I don't want to lie to you, Shelby. This does not feel right to me, and we need to do a pelvic ultrasound right away. I think we might have an ectopic pregnancy here."

She was still poking and prodding when she pressed on the source of my cramping. A pain ripped through me like she'd stabbed me with a broad sword. I screamed and rolled up like a pill bug, vaguely aware that my foot had connected solidly with some part of Dr. Bronner's head.

"Oh, dear... Shelby, I am going to need to try and relax and stay calm. You are bleeding. A lot. I am afraid that you might have a rupture."

"A rupture? Of what?" I growled through gritted teeth as I clutched my stomach. I could feel wetness in between my legs like the most intense period I'd ever had. I began to whimper and rock my body back and forth trying to wish it all away.

"Likely your fallopian tube. I know it sounds strange, but it explains your shoulder pain. The nerves are all connected. Hang on just a second, okay, I'll be right back."

Dr. Bronner stuck her head out of the door. "Jane, can you come here a minute?" A pause. "Call for an ambulance and then call over to Froedtert and tell them we've got a possible ruptured ectopic pregnancy patient on the way."

"What?" I started to shake.

"Yes, Shelby. You're going to need to have surgery. And if this bleeding continues, maybe even a transfusion."

I was grateful for her calm, measured tone even if I hated all the horrifying things she was saying.

Surgery.

A transfusion.

Shit.

"Who can we call?" she asked.

I panicked knowing I never changed my first emergency contact after Ari died. And I was quite certain my mother was my second. My mother. *No, no, no. No one can know about this.*

"My phone…" I was starting to panic. I was also starting to feel dizzy. *No, no you can't pass out now.* "I need to call my friend, Kendra. She's the only one who can know. No one else can know about this pregnancy. Please."

Dr. Bronner fished my phone out of my purse and handed it to me. I was fading fast. I opened it, clicked on 'favorites' in my phone app. Everything was blurry.

Then everything was dark.

I woke up some time later in a hospital bed. I was groggy and my abdomen was sore. Bits and pieces of the afternoon were starting to come back to me. A gurney. An ambulance. Bright lights and people in masks with kind eyes and calm voices.

There was a Styrofoam cup with a straw on the table positioned near my bed. Grateful it was within my reach without having to strain, I gingerly grabbed it and took a sip.

"Hiiiii." I heard a gentle cooing voice.

I turned to see Kendra sitting on the chair on the other side of the room. As soon as my brain registered her presence, the floodgates opened. I knew I was okay. That everything was okay. And soon I would be able to unburden myself with everything I'd been feeling over the last few weeks to my most loyal friend in the whole world.

"You gave us quite a scare, lady," she said. "Surgery went well, but you needed a few liters of blood."

"Us?" A little panic.

"Yes, your parents are outside. Brody is on his way. I didn't want to worry him too much, so I called him after you were out of surgery."

"But what do they...do they know?" More panic.

"As far as anyone else is concerned, you had a ruptured ovarian cyst. I made sure the doctors were not to speak to anyone but me. I'm the only one who knows about the pregnancy."

She held my hand as round two of the emotional tsunami was unleashed. I knew she would know what to do. In that moment I doubted that anyone on earth was as blessed as I was to have a best friend like Kendra.

Two days later as I was waiting to be released from the hospital, Kendra asked the question I'd been expecting.

"Are you going to tell Jake?"

I had been thinking about this nonstop. When you are trapped in a hospital bed with nothing to do, no one to talk to, bored with reading choices, and annoyed by TV, all you can do is think.

"Yes."

I was going to have to tell him about the pregnancy and what happened as a result. I was going to have to tell him a lot of things.

And then I was going to have to tell Jake Ford goodbye.

CHAPTER
TWENTY-THREE

JAKE

July 2013

"Hey, can we set up a time to brainstorm the shooting schedule for next year with what we've got so far?" Rita asked as she peeked her head into my office. "I want to plan our family spring break and summer trips ASAP,"

"What? Oh...sure. That's great." I was only half paying attention.

She walked all the way in and stood in front of my desk. "What's going on? You've been more distracted than usual. And grumpy. I don't know how to deal with grumpy Jake. It's such a foreign concept."

"Agh, I don't know. Nothing. Everything." I ran my hands through my hair and leaned back in my chair.

"I would say we could talk about it tonight, but everyone will be there, and it will be too crazy. Why don't you tell me what's going on now?" She sat down in the chair across from me.

"It's Shelby. She's been so distant ever since she left my house. We've texted a little and talked a few times, but she's been...different. I don't know. Guarded."

Rita sighed, leaned back in her chair and crossed her legs. "Well, if I'm being honest with you, I think she got rattled. If I was over two thousand miles away and one of my kids got into a car accident, I'd freak out. That mom guilt is like nothing else."

Rita had three kids—a seventeen-year-old daughter, and fifteen-year-old twin sons. I hadn't really thought about asking her questions about Shelby and motherhood because Brody was so much older. "But Brody is almost twenty-one. And it was just a fender bender. He's fine."

"I get that you think because he's an adult, it would make it less traumatic, but I can tell you, those maternal feelings don't change. I feel just as protective, if not more so, of my kids now than when they were small. It's less about bumps and bruises these days and more about life altering decisions and poor choices with long term consequences."

"I guess."

"Plus, I think you need to consider that fender bender or not, a car accident itself could have been a huge trigger for her. After all, that's how she lost her husband."

I hadn't thought about that. "Wow. I bet you're right."

"I mean, think about it. How would your mom feel if you had even the slightest heart scare?"

That punched me right in the gut and I immediately felt like shit. I hadn't said anything regrettable or pushed too hard, but here I'd just been feeling sorry for myself when Shelby was likely going through an emotional crisis.

"Just give her some time and some space. Let her know that you're here if she needs to talk."

Why would she start now? I thought, right back to feeling sorry for myself.

"District at five. You better be there." Rita poked her finger at me as she stood up. "This is a big deal."

"I know. I'll be there."

It was a big deal.

It's not every day your show gets nominated for an Emmy.

A FEW DAYS LATER SHELBY CALLED, AND OUT OF THE BLUE SHE ASKED me to come visit her in Wisconsin. Not only was this what I'd been wanting for weeks, but it had always been me making the plans, me orchestrating our time together. For her to finally initiate something, especially having me come to her home, I was over the moon.

And I would finally be able to talk to her. To tell her everything.

I called and booked a hotel room downtown Milwaukee for that first night, just in case. Confessing my love once again included confessing my ulterior motives that started this whole thing and I was more unsure than ever as to how that would go over.

I pulled up to her house in the late afternoon on a gorgeous sunny day. I was so excited to see her, but a sense of apprehension was clouding everything. I felt nervous and restless as I got out of my rental car and walked up to the house. I climbed to the top of the steps and peeked in the window. She had her enclosed porch set up with a retro couch with lots of throw pillows, a small coffee table, a few stacks of books, plants, and a vinyl record player. I smiled, picturing her spending time out there often with a cup of tea or a glass of wine, her legs tucked up underneath her, and a black cat curled up on her lap.

I reached my hand up to knock on the door when I saw Darius walking toward me from inside the house.

"Hey man!" he said as he opened the door and gave me a hug. "Nice to see you."

"Hey! You, too." I was a little taken aback. "What are you doing here?" Then I heard more voices coming from inside.

"Shelby thought it'd be fun to have a little party while you're here. Come on."

Darius began to lead me through the house. It was a 1920s bungalow, so charming and warm, with gorgeous wood molding and intricate built-ins. And as I expected, much of it was filled with mid-century modern pieces and decor. I could see and feel Shelby in every inch of the space.

I saw the vase I'd sent her proudly on display on an end table and it made me smile. Then, I immediately thought to look around for Minx. As if I'd willed her to appear, the beautiful, black ball of fluff strolled in and brushed up against my leg. I picked her up and she started to purr. "Just like your mommy," I cooed at her.

The smell hit me as soon as we entered the kitchen. Something smoked and something sweet. It smelled like summer and my mouth started to water.

"Hi!" Shelby said as I walked into the kitchen. She was surrounded by Randall, Kendra and someone I assumed was Kendra's husband. I made my way through the crowd and hugged Shelby tightly, trying to hide my disappointment that I didn't have her all to myself. She let me go and Kendra immediately thrust a glass of champagne at me. They all held up their own glasses. I smiled when I realized they'd heard the news.

"An Emmy! Jake, that's so fantastic!" Kendra gushed.

"Just the nomination so far. We'll see how it goes. But we

couldn't have done it without Shelby." I held up my glass to toast her, too.

She waved it off dismissively, but she knew better than to argue with me. The show would not have been the same without her.

We ate dinner out on Shelby's back patio, the sun hanging low in those magical summer evening hours when everything just feels right with the world. Gary had smoked the ribs at home and brought them to finish on Shelby's grill along with some fresh sweet corn. Kendra had brought homemade corn-bread and Darius and Randall made a southwest style quinoa salad. It had been a long time since I enjoyed hospitality like this, and I was no longer annoyed that Shelby and I weren't alone. I indulged myself in imagining many, many more nights like this in the warm company of her friends. Her friends that could become my friends.

Kendra and Shelby disappeared back into the house emerging minutes later with Shelby carrying some plates, forks and a pie server. Kendra came bearing the most beauti-fully intricate lattice crust pie I'd ever seen. Two red cherries with stems topped with a green leaf all made from dough sat artfully on top of the lattice. I nearly cringed when Kendra cut into the work of art, and I regretted I hadn't taken a picture.

The smell wafting from my forkful of the warm cherry pie they'd served me mercilessly teased my nose just before I put it in my mouth. The crust was buttery, flaky perfection. An explo-sion of sweetness and tartness made my salivary glands spasm in the best way, and I am fairly certain I moaned in a manner that could only be described as pornographic. I startled everyone when I slammed my hand on the table.

"Holy shit, Kendra. This is the best thing I've ever eaten in my entire life!"

Kendra smiled like the Cheshire Cat, shaking her head as

she pointed at Shelby. Shelby looked down and smiled bashfully. I should have known—the cherries on the top of the pie matched the tattoo on the inside of her wrist.

"You made this?" I didn't want it to sound like it was something I couldn't believe, but I couldn't believe it. This seemed like one of those things you couldn't possibly *not* know about a person. Like sleeping with Adele for seven months and having no idea she could sing.

I'd only explored Shelby's surface, that was all she had been willing to show me so far. And me waiting, desperately wanting to know all her secret pain. But there was so much more magic in her depths than I'd ever realized, and I couldn't wait to dive in headfirst. I couldn't wait to hear all of Kendra's stories about Shelby, middle school sleepovers, crushes and heartbreaks, embarrassments and triumphs. I would listen enraptured as Darius shared all of Shelby's clients' testimonials gushing over her magic hands and tender care. And I couldn't wait to meet Brody and watch the mother in Shelby beam over her son—the love of her life.

"What is all going on here? This is not just any cherry pie," I said.

Shelby's little moment of self-consciousness was beginning to fade. She sat up straight and said, "The crust is flavored with vanilla bean, and there is a little cola syrup in with the fresh cherries."

"Vanilla cherry coke pie. Damn," I said in wonder as I took another bite.

"Shelby is the best baker ever. It's a wonder we don't all weigh four hundred pounds." Darius said, chuckling.

"Did you learn as a kid from your mom? Or your grandmother?" I asked, already eyeing my second piece.

"Nope. Self-taught. Pretty much right after Brody was born." She looked down and took a breath, then raised her head with a look of conviction I'd not seen on her face before. "I couldn't do anything right in the kitchen as far as Ari was concerned. He was hardly ever home for dinner, so I cooked for Brody and me. But when he would get home and heat up leftovers, or if he was home and didn't want to cook, he was always so critical of everything. Everything I did would be scrutinized and analyzed or just condescendingly dismissed. It wore me down. Over the years I just became numb to it.

"But Ari couldn't bake. It wasn't a skill that he was able to master, he was too heavy handed. So, I decided to learn how. He thought it was 'adorable' when I made cookies, cakes, pies. I could see it bothered him a little when I would successfully make proper puff pastry or fancier things like créme caramel and perfectly executed macarons. But when I tried savory things or made bread, that was encroaching too close to his territory, his insecurity, and he'd rip me apart again. So, I just stuck to sweet."

"And how much bread have you made this last year, babes?" Kendra asked with a wink.

"So much. So, so much bread." Shelby smiled with satisfaction.

I sat in shock processing the conversation that told me so much more about Shelby's relationship with her husband and about his narcissism than she'd ever shared with me, but it was clear that she felt safe and comfortable in this company— bolstered by her friends. I also knew there was much more— more darkness that wouldn't be shared quite so casually.

As we all helped to clear the table, I walked past the hall where Darius and Shelby were having a conversation. A conversation I wasn't meant to be hearing.

"I don't think this is a good idea. Why can't you just take a beat? See how things go?" Darius said.

"I have to do this. He has to know, Darius."

"I get that he has to know, but…"

I walked away quickly before I heard more. They were talking about me. If it was good, I didn't want to spoil it. If it was bad, I didn't want to know.

I had a thought. It was a reach, but it was what my brain had put together with the puzzle pieces I overheard.

Maybe, just maybe, Shelby wanted more. Maybe she was unhappy with our arrangement of every other month meetups. Maybe she was ready for something more serious, and she was unsure whether I felt the same.

I'd been here before. If it wasn't me ending things because I'd lost interest after I'd "fixed" them, women I'd been involved with would inevitably become fed up with my obsession with my work and my reluctance to commit. They'd wanted more, and I was always unwilling or unable to give it to them.

But not now. Not anymore. When Shelby asked for more, I would give her everything. We'd make the distance work somehow. I wanted to share my life with her.

And I wanted her to be my date to the Emmys.

A little after nine, it was clear everyone was getting ready to leave. I was happy it was still so early, and I would have time with Shelby. Time to talk.

I got a little knot in my stomach. I needed to tell her so much, but decided I would let her go first.

I sat waiting in the living room as Shelby went around and turned off most of the lights in the house. She emerged from the kitchen with two small rocks glasses each with one cube of ice, and a bottle of Knoppogue Castle Irish whiskey. She put the glasses on the table and poured two fingers into my glass and hers. If I wasn't already head over heels, this would have tipped me over the edge.

Shelby handed me my drink and sat down beside me. I moved my glass toward hers to clink a silent toast before we each took a sip. She smiled softly, but it looked pained. Like someone about to deliver bad news.

The silence became a black hole that immediately sucked all the hope from my heart.

I took another large sip of my drink, set it down, put my hands on my knees and braced myself. The conversation was not going to go at all the way I'd hoped.

Bolstered by her friends. They had been there for a reason.

CHAPTER
TWENTY-FOUR

JAKE

"Jake," she said, "Some things...some things have happened. There are things I need to tell you and I don't even know where to begin."

A few short months ago I would have been riveted, thrilled to be on the cusp of her confession, a window to her pain. But now, with a gut feeling it was to be the end of us, I didn't want to hear it.

She set her drink on the table and ran her hands up and down her legs. She looked up at the ceiling and took a deep inhale. She didn't look at me as she began to speak, focusing instead on her hands and the way her fingers wrapped around her thumb.

"I met Ari when I was nineteen. He was everything I thought I wanted. The way I grew up, with parents who were so strict, so...hands off, Ari was like the sun. He drew me in with his confidence and swagger, and he was so attentive, affectionate, and passionate. Four months after we started dating, I got pregnant. I didn't want a baby then, I was in college, I wanted a career. I wanted to wait and see how things

275

went with Ari. But this baby, the only grandchild...Ari used him as leverage to get his parents to invest in him, in culinary school and in a restaurant. They planned and paid for a huge wedding and bought us a house. It was like I had gotten on a train and wasn't able to get off. And it was the wrong train. To a terrible place.

"Ari's confidence and swagger were the shiny surface hiding his narcissism. He was a difficult person to deal with most of the time. He would twist everything little into something big and he had an awful temper. His attentiveness and passion turned into a possessiveness that scared me. He was very controlling. Especially...especially in the bedroom."

I couldn't speak. Somehow even though I'd guessed most of this, it was too horrible to imagine Shelby having lived through it. Again, my rage for someone I'd never met, someone I would never meet, boiled lava hot inside me. My spine stiffened and I clenched my jaw before realizing that Shelby didn't need me to react. She needed me to listen. I relaxed by my body the best I could, and I reached out and gently grabbed her hand. She let me.

"He took advantage of my need for his attention, and he used my sexuality as fuel for his sadistic games. He knew he had me backed into a corner—that I would do anything to please him, and he used that against me. He'd edge me to the brink over and over, not to enhance my pleasure, but his own —he got off on the control and the cruelty. He humiliated me. He degraded me. He...he hurt me. And because I was aroused, because I came, he assumed I liked it. So, it kept getting more intense. And he would push further and further. And while I know that there are people who have healthy, satisfying relationships like that, that's not what this was. When it was over, and I'd hide in the bathroom for hours and cry, he wouldn't care. There was no safe word, no soothing. No balance. No...aftercare."

It was then I understood every erratic moment Shelby ever had. Even the praise, even the "good girl" had been laced with dark intention and had not been praise at all.

She looked up at the ceiling again and sighed. My heart broke for her, but in a way I wasn't used to. For the first time in as long as I could remember, I saw someone's pain as their own and something completely separate from me. It was as if a force like a hundred mile an hour car crash pushed me into a universe separate from hers, and while I could see and hear and touch her, I would not be able to affect her.

It was a fucking breakthrough. And while Dr. McCallum would have been so proud, I was completely gutted.

"I know I've been a lot," she continued, "I'm so sorry for the way I treated you."

I grabbed her hand tighter. "Hey," I gently touched her chin to turn her face up toward mine. "Hey, it's okay. I understand. I can't begin to tell you how sorry I am that you went through all of that. You were traumatized. You have triggers. I get that." I turned my body further towards hers and sat up straight, trying to convey as much of the optimism I was feeling as I could. "We can work through this, Shelby. You can let me know when things get... tricky. We can take our time." I let myself believe for a minute that we'd be okay.

She shook her head, taking her hand away and with it, all the breath from my lungs.

She wasn't finished.

"There's more." She drained the last of her whiskey. "A few weeks ago, I was in the hospital. A ruptured ectopic pregnancy."

I sat there silent, blinking, trying to absorb what she had just said.

Hospital.

Pregnancy.

"Oh, Shelby. God. I'm so sorry. Why didn't you tell me? I could have…" I trailed off as she shook her head. There was nothing I could have done. I'd already done too much, apparently.

I could feel the prickles of threatening tears. For her. For me.

"I'm fine now. Everything is fine." She didn't seem quite convinced.

I stared at her in sheer awe. Here I had thought she was this damsel in distress and I, the clumsy, oblivious white knight, would come riding in and rescue her. But no. She was a warrior goddess slaying her own goddamn dragons this whole time. And then left to face the ultimate battle alone. After what she had just told me, of course a pregnancy would have been the ultimate trigger.

"It… it brought it all back. It all got churned up again." She became quiet, tightly pressing her lips together trying to hold back something desperate to get out. When she opened her mouth, the words came out with a gut-wrenching sob. "And they told me if I wouldn't have gone to the doctor when I did… if everything hadn't happened the way it had, I might have bled out. I might have died. And… and…," she was hardly able to get it out. "Brody. I would have left Brody. He would have lost both of his parents within a year."

Her body wracked with sobs as the tears fell fast and hard. I grabbed and held her close to my chest as she shook. This whole time, she hadn't cried until now.

Ari had betrayed her. He didn't deserve her tears.

I hadn't nestled into her heart in the way I had hoped. I hadn't earned them.

But Brody. Her tears were all for her son. He was her entire world and the thought of leaving him broke her. It didn't matter that the circumstances were accidental and not the result of her having done anything overtly reckless. She still felt responsible. She still felt the guilt, a weight far heavier than she was able to bear.

There was nothing I could do. Nothing. And it was killing me.

Anything I said in that moment, all my promises of how it would all be alright, any confession of my love and devotion, any amount of begging and pleading, it would all have been meaningless. Screaming into the fucking void.

"I can't do this anymore, Jake."

"What are you saying?" I knew, but I needed to hear the words. The words that would shatter my already broken heart into tiny shards and send me careening away from her orbit. Directionless. Helpless. Hopeless.

"It's over. It has to be over." She looked at me. There were no more tears. Her resolve was set.

How ironic. I finally no longer wanted her to need me. I desperately needed her to want me. And she didn't.

"I'm sorry about having you come all this way... for this. But I needed to tell you in person."

"No, I get it. It's okay." It wasn't okay. None of it was okay.

"You don't have to leave...it's late. You could...," as soon as the words came out and she read the look on my face, she knew I had to go. "Jake, I'm...I'm so sorry."

I felt the hint of an instinct to try and make her feel better, but I was empty. I had nothing more to give. I got up and walked toward my bag I'd left by the door without giving her another reassurance.

Shelby stood up and hugged her arms over her chest.

I bowed my head as I realized leaving her like this would have broken me, and I would have regretted it forever.

I put down my bag and walked back over to her. I put my hand gently on the back of her head and kissed her forehead, then pressed my own forehead to hers and closed my eyes. "Goodbye, Shelby," the two words ripping and burning their way through my soul leaving a trail of ash in their wake.

I MADE MY WAY TO THE DOWNTOWN HOTEL I HAD BEEN SO CERTAIN I wouldn't need. I drove in a fog, not wanting to pay attention to any landmarks or things that Shelby might have wanted to show me in the alternate ending. The ending where we'd have fallen asleep in each other's arms, all breathless and sweaty after round two of devouring each other. The one where we'd have gone down to the lakefront, or a museum, or a festival, or a baseball game the next day. The one where I'd have moved heaven and earth to have been back here as often as possible to spend time with the most amazing woman I'd ever known. The one that wouldn't have been an ending at all.

I passed a billboard plastered with a handsome, smiling, silver haired man advertising the ironically named Ristow Investment Group. I slammed the brakes on my brain before it could go down the rabbit hole of wondering if he was related to her.

I was beyond grateful that the hotel bar was still open. As I sipped on my scotch, I wondered how many glasses I would see the bottom of before I found enough anesthesia. I was wholly unprepared for how much this hurt.

Fundamentally, I understood why she had to let me go. But my heart could not hear and would not listen to any of my brain's logical explanations. It was wailing and screaming too loud, and in the days and weeks ahead, I would continue to drown out the logic with melodies and lyrics that affirmed and enabled my suffering.

I was beginning to feel the dulling of heartbreak's sharpest edges near the bottom of my third drink when I heard the words that made my skin crawl.

"Oh my God! Jake Ford! You're Jake Ford."

No, no, no. Not now. Please, not now.

She plopped herself down on the barstool next to me and angled her head in front of mine. I hadn't even turned to acknowledge her at all.

"Hi! Oh my God. I'm such a huge fan! I loved you on *Sault Ste. Marie.*"

I shifted my eyes to look at her. She was older than I was, probably six or seven years. She had most likely been a young mother watching soaps while her kids played outside. Now, she was too blond, too tan, and wearing so much perfume I could taste it when I made the mistake of breathing through my mouth.

"Hi." I nodded and forced a polite smile. I'd hoped that would be the extent of it.

"Hey, excuse me," she waved enthusiastically to the bartender. "I'll have what he's having!" She decided she was joining me.

Fuck.

She was already a little drunk. Which made her brave. I could see it. I could see her wheels turning like now was her chance and she was going to take it.

I was in no mood.

Normally, I am good natured with fans. Especially now when most of them want to talk about *Dare Me.* But sometimes the soap fans get a little...intense.

Shelby had been the exception, and of course I didn't mind one bit.

"Soooo...what are you doing in Milwaukee?" She crossed her legs toward me. As the bartender set her drink in front of her, she reached toward his bar caddy and pulled out a stir straw. She stuck it into her scotch and took a sip.

She made a face and coughed, and I had to seal my lips shut to keep from laughing. She was trying so hard.

"Oh, I don't like this." She waved the bartender down again." Can I get a margarita instead? Blended...," she second guessed herself as the bartender glared at her. "Oh, I guess on the rocks is fine." I rolled my eyes as he and I shared a smile.

"I'm in town scoping out some ideas for my new show." She needed to know nothing of the truth.

"Oh, I think I heard about that. Where you go around and do icky things that no one wants to do, right?"

"Something like that." I had no energy to engage her, so I just left her to her assumptions.

"I bet you look sexy when you're dirty," she said in the smokiest voice she could muster, wasting no time at all.

I shrugged. When you aren't flirting, what the hell do you say to something like that?

"'Cause you sure look sexy when you're clean."

Is that your best line, lady? Jesus. I racked my brain to try and figure out a way to get her to leave. I didn't want to be the first to walk away and have her try and follow me to my room.

"Ya know I used to fantasize about you when I'd watch you on TV. Mmm, Foster McBride was so sexy." She traced a finger on the bar, then walked two fingers toward my arm. "I might even be fantasizing about doing things with you right now." She stroked my arm up and down.

I stared at her hand touching me. It felt disgusting. I wanted no part of it. Of her. And I didn't care enough to try and spare her feelings. I was angry at her for intruding on my private pain.

"Well, reality is never as good as the fantasy, sweetheart." I growled as I snatched my arm away, the action and tone hopefully making it clear the 'sweetheart' was not a term of endearment.

"Oh, now I don't think that's true." She reached up and twirled a piece of my hair.

Jesus Christ. Stop.

I couldn't take it anymore. I snapped.

"Well, if you don't believe me, we could just go in the bathroom over there and I could disappoint your brains out." I spat.

She recoiled, stared at me for a second, and then grabbed her drink.

"Wow. You're an asshole." She stormed off.

"Ah, shit," I said.

The bartender put another drink in front of me. "You okay, man?"

"Yeah, just...she's probably going to go around blabbing about what an asshole Jake Ford is. Or tell people I wanted to fuck her in the bathroom."

"I wouldn't worry about the type of people she would tell," he said. "Doesn't seem like she runs with a crowd that would matter."

I still felt bad. She was a fan taking her shot, albeit way too aggressively, but I've had this happen before. I can usually be affable, letting them down gently so they have a good memory or story to tell.

She was just coming at me at the wrong fucking time and got caught in the crossfire.

CHAPTER
TWENTY-FIVE
SHELBY

September 2013

"Did you watch?" Kendra asked me on the phone.

The Emmys had aired the night before and I'd stayed far away from my television. "No. I couldn't. I really thought about it, but I couldn't."

"I understand why it'd be hard for you."

"Did you watch it?" I asked.

"We did. And I recorded it just in case..."

"How was it?" I asked. I wasn't sure how much of the details I really wanted to know.

"You know they won, right?"

I did. "Yes. I saw it online this morning." I didn't click on the article for fear of more pictures, but I was happy for them. For Jake.

"He brought his mom. It was so cute." Kendra said.

This little detail made me smile. I bet she beamed the

284

entire time, especially with everything they'd been through together.

"He thanked you by name."

"What?" I found that impossible to believe.

"It's true," Kendra said. "Granted, he thanked all the women in the episode by name, but he did it in reverse order of how they appeared on the show. So, your name was last. He paused, looked into the camera, and said, 'Shelby.' I don't know, maybe I was reading too much into it, but it seemed like a little message."

"You're definitely reading too much into it." Obviously, not having seen it I couldn't be sure, but I knew I would not be watching for a long time just in case she was right.

I hadn't let myself think about Jake too much over the last month and a half. Just wound it all into a neat little ball and tucked it away as usual.

The following Friday I was hosting a dinner party. My parents had been over to see the house, but not my in laws, and Andrea had let me know in no uncertain terms that Marion, in particular, was feeling slighted by my not having invited her. I needed to continue to make nice with them considering they were still so involved in Brody's life and kind enough to be paying his way through Marquette.

I'd invited my parents, David, Marion, and Andrea. I'd extended the invitation to Ari's oldest brother Dave and his wife Rebecca out of courtesy, but I knew it would be something they would likely pass on. They were always in attendance for major holidays and milestones, but they would always be the last to arrive and the first to leave. Whip smart introverted surgeons, they preferred to mostly avoid family social situations. I never faulted them for it, but Marion often chided them gently to their faces and not so gently behind their backs, placing the blame mostly on Rebecca.

"Oh! It's so...quaint!" Marion exclaimed as she walked in the house. I could tell she really wanted to say small. Or old. She kissed the air next to my cheek and patted me on the back so lightly I barely felt it.

David brought me in for a big hug. It had been a few months since I'd seen them. I didn't feel the need to reach out all that often since Brody had continued to work part time at the firm after his internship, maintaining his own connection to his grandparents.

It felt though, like David had missed me.

"David, did you lock the car? I'm not so sure about this neighborhood." Marion pinched.

I resisted the urge to rub my forehead in frustration. "The neighborhood is perfectly fine, Marion. Nothing to worry about at all."

"Still, I'd like to leave before it gets dark." Her eyes darted around outside through the window. I had conveniently forgotten how insufferable this woman could be. It'd been nice.

"That won't be happening, Mom. It will be dark in less than an hour," Andrea said.

"Oh! You have a cat!" Marion exclaimed as Minx came sauntering down from upstairs.

"Yes. Her name is Minx. I got her a few months ago."

"David, do you remember Fred?" Marion turned to me. "When the kids were small, we got the most darling little gray and white kitten. We let Dave name him and that's what he chose."

"Aw, did you have to rehome him then, when you found out Ari was allergic?" I asked.

"Oh no! We had that cat until Ari graduated from high school. He passed from old age. Ari wasn't allergic. What would make you think that?"

"Because he told me he was. That we couldn't have a cat, or any pet because he was."

"Oh, I'm sure that's not true." Marion dismissed me with a wave of her hand.

David said a warm hello to my parents and asked if he could help get everyone drinks. I walked through the dining room with glasses of white wine for Andrea and Marion and before I rounded the corner to where they were standing in the living room, I overheard their conversation.

"Why wouldn't she have kept the beautiful furniture she had? Now she's got all of this, all of these...used things. Second-hand things. I don't understand." Marion was trying to be discreet, but not doing a good job of it at all. "It's all so *dated.*"

"That's the point. Shelby loves this retro, vintage stuff. Always has." Andrea said.

"What's that supposed to mean?"

"It means that she probably would have wanted to decorate her other house like this all these years. She was just being nice."

"Well, I don't get it. Look at this table. It has scuff marks on it," Marion said.

"Jesus Christ, Mom. Let it go. None of this is a personal reflection on you. It's not like people in your circle are going around like 'Oh my God, did you hear? Marion's daughter in law got her coffee table from a *thrift store.*'"

I was grateful to Andrea at that moment. It made me wonder if she'd defended me like that more times than I would ever know. I cleared my throat to announce my presence and gave them their drinks with a smile. "Oh, and if you are going to put these on the coffee table, make sure to use a coaster. Thanks," I said. Andrea gave me a nod and a smirk as I turned to walk away.

. . .

"This is a lovely piece," my mother said as she stood in front of the art on top of my fireplace mantle after dinner. "I could do without the nudity, of course, but I do like it." It was a print I'd gotten framed of a nude, red haired woman against a teal background. She was removing a mask with a somber expression to reveal an identical expression on her own face underneath. I connected with it so deeply.

"It's fine, I suppose," interjected Marion. "I just really preferred the beautiful wedding picture above the mantle in your other house." She looked around. "You know, I don't see any pictures of Aristotle here at all."

I began nervously wringing my hands, my fingers finding their home settled firmly around my left thumb. I had a feeling this might have proved to be a point of contention with her. So much so, that I almost asked Kendra to bring one or two pictures over to put out. Just for today.

"I understand that since he is gone it must be so painful for you, Shelby. But we can't erase his memory. Don't you think Brody needs to see reminders of his father?"

"I get that, Marion...it's just that—"

Marion looked around again, this time with a much more determined look in her eyes. I knew right away what she was looking for and not seeing. "Where is the urn?"

"Um...I...uh..." I stammered. I could feel myself beginning to sweat.

"Shelby where are my son's remains?" she demanded.

"At the restaurant. In the basement." There. It was out there and there was no going back now.

Marion had a shocked expression on her face I knew would be seared in my memory forever. She was about to learn the truth. At least as much as what wouldn't kill her.

I unclenched my hands and stood up straight.

"Marion, to be honest, I needed to move on. Not just because Ari died. But because our marriage, our relationship... was difficult. He was not a good man." I knew that wouldn't be anywhere near a sufficient explanation, but I had to start somewhere. Ease them in.

"How dare you! How dare you say that about Aristotle! He was a wonderful man. A devoted husband and father. He sacrificed so much, he worked so hard to provide for you and Brody all these years. Doing everything he could to make that restaurant successful for the sake of his family!"

"Marion, stop," David interrupted. "There was no sacrifice of anything on Ari's part. We both know I put him through culinary school. Fine. I was happy to do it. I leased the space and my partners and I fronted him the money for the buildout and everything that goes into opening a restaurant. He had vision and he was so excited, I thought I was helping. All with the understanding that he would pay us back.

"Ari was a brilliant chef, and he could charm the pants off a snake," he continued. "That's what made The Scorpion so successful. But he was a terrible manager and didn't care about wasting money. He'd blow through overtime hours for his kitchen staff, working them until they dropped. He'd have an idea for a special feature, spend the money on all kinds of hard-to-get ingredients, then change his mind. All of it would go to waste. He came close to bankruptcy twice. Not to mention the other failed concepts, which I should have known better than to enable. He was my son and I loved him, but he made it very hard for me to like him." David was like a dam that had been stressed to the point of breaking for years.

Marion looked aghast at her husband speaking such blasphemy about her son. "He was passionate! I loved that about him. He was passionate about his food, and passionate about his family." She turned to me. "He loved you, Shelby. How can you deny that and just erase him like this? He brought little Brody to our house so often after he was born because you were having such a hard time as a young new mother. He wanted to give you a break and take care of you."

I took a deep breath. "Do you know why Ari brought Brody to your house so often? Because he couldn't stand that I was giving attention to anyone but him. He was jealous of his son. His own son! I would beg him not to take him away, but he wouldn't listen. I'd just sit there and cry until he got back from your house. And then when he got back, it was...worse." I glanced down at the floor, considering how much of the details to give. "And how he 'took care of me' as you put it? Ari was... intense. Physically. In ways that I would never want to explain to his mother or say in front of my parents."

"I know he had a bit of a temper, but I can't see him actually laying a hand on anyone." She didn't seem to understand what exactly I was implying.

"With what you would consider typical domestic violence, you're right. He would yell, slam doors, throw things, and he once punched a hole in the wall... but he never lashed out on me like that in the moment. He wasn't violent...I mean, he wouldn't hurt me," another breath, "outside of the bedroom."

It pained me to say it as I could see Marion trying to reconcile it all. Her precious baby boy being a sexual sadist.

"Marion, he was stepping out on Shelby, too." David said. My head snapped up to stare at him in wide eyed shock. I had no idea anyone knew. He turned to me. "I am a recognizable man, and Milwaukee is a big city, but it can feel like an awful lot like a small town. People had no trouble telling me what my son was up to."

"I just don't believe that. Any of it." Marion said softly. Her wall of denial would not be cracked this evening.

"Ari doesn't belong anywhere near the pedestal you put him on." David said to Marion. He turned to me. "Shelby, I'm sorry I didn't check in on you more throughout the years. I had no idea what was going on with the two of you. If I had known..." he trailed off, his emotions getting the better of him.

"David, none of this was your fault," I said. "And I'm working on believing that none of it was my fault either." I turned to Marion. "You have to understand that I have to move on without all the reminders of him, but I won't let Brody forget him. I never spoke badly about his father to him, although I can't honestly say Ari was a good father. Certainly not the father that Brody deserved." I looked down and then back up at David, my voice cracking. "You have been more of a father to him than Ari ever was. I'm so grateful for that." Tears filled his eyes, and he brought me in for a hug.

My poor, shocked parents were just sitting there trying to absorb all of this, not knowing what to do or say.

Marion threw up her hands. "I just can't believe any of this. And everyone is just ganging up on me. Ganging up on Aristotle, and he isn't even here to defend himself."

"That doesn't matter, Mom. Here you are defending him just like you've done his entire life," offered Andrea.

"I just...David, take me home. I can't be here anymore."

David gave my back a gentle rub and walked toward his wife. As he helped Marion with her coat, he locked eyes with me and for the first time I fully recognized his pain. His resignation. I knew at that moment that he and I had much more in common than I'd ever realized.

Ari. Marion.

I had the apple. David had the tree.

My parents also decided that the evening was coming to an end, and I began to walk them out. They were so visibly uncomfortable I could feel their wheels turning as they tried to wrap their heads around everything I had said. I suspected anything they would say to try and comfort me would be God-centric and vague. As per usual.

"Shelby, those were some hard things to hear," said my dad. I held my breath as I considered he might have something heartfelt to say about what his daughter had gone through.

"If only you and Aristotle had continued to go to church with us, it's likely none of this would have happened." Unfortunately, no secular empathy was to be had after all, instead, my father was right on cue with his brand of calm yet biting righteous indignation.

It was true that when we started dating, Ari and I went to church regularly with my parents, but it wasn't as cut and dried as they might have thought. "We only went to church with you because Ari wanted to get in your 'good graces' so to speak. He knew we'd be moving fast, and he wanted you not to fight it. Admit it. You felt better about us living together before we got married because we were still 'on the path.'"

What they never needed to know was that Ari had another ulterior motive. Yes, we'd dutifully go to church with my parents, but he'd always politely decline their invitation to brunch after, which was their tradition. Instead, Ari would take me back to their house and delight in defiling me literally six ways to Sunday in my childhood bedroom. Role playing the ruin of a good Christian girl. I became so conditioned to this ritual that with a just subtle stroke of his pinky along my thigh during the service, he'd have me in a state of desperate want. Fantasizing about him taking me right there on the pew, the echoes of my screams ricocheting through the nave.

My father continued, "I think it's a good time for you to come back to church on your own, then. A good opportunity for you to get back into God's grace."

My mother put her hand gently on my arm. I could see

tears filling the bottoms of her eyes as they met mine. Every great once in a while, I could see another version of her, a soul empathetic in her own right, not just an empty channel regurgitating the appropriate verses she'd memorized. Her lips parted, she inhaled, ready to speak. Then, as she was always apt to do before she did or said anything, she looked at my father.

"Yes," my mother said, redirecting and dutifully agreeing with her husband. "Renewing your relationship with the Lord, unburdening yourself through prayer."

Ah, yes. Good and baked in right from the start, I'd been primed and ready for a life of subservience. After all, I had learned from the best.

I smiled politely at her. "I unburden myself plenty with my therapist, Mom. And guess what? She talks back."

Since I'd been honest with everyone else that evening, I got brave and kept going. "You know, shame is a hell of a thing. Honestly, shame is just a hell. I'm finally working my way out of a darkness that has consumed me for over twenty years. I am finding my own version of a relationship with God, but it doesn't involve going back to church. You'll just have to trust that I'll find my way."

We hugged lightly, awkwardly like we always did, and they made their way out the door.

It was true. I was finding peace through my own version of spirituality—making my way to a light in the darkness.

And forgiveness was my compass.

It wasn't Ari that I needed to forgive. I'd accepted who he was and who he wasn't and that was enough.

Who it was that needed and deserved my forgiveness was that young, naive, terrified, nineteen-year-old girl in the bathroom staring at a positive pregnancy test on that cold December morning. I had been blaming her just as much, if not more, than Ari for everything that had happened. When Ari became thrilled at the prospect of using the pregnancy to get what he wanted, why couldn't she have been strong enough to say what she wanted instead? To stand up for herself. To not get on that fucking train in the first place. I'd been so angry at her, and I needed to let that go.

Find it in myself to forgive her.

Open my heart to love her.

It wasn't going to be God's grace that would save me. It was my own.

"GOD, SHEL. I'M SO SORRY...I WISH I'D HAVE KNOWN," ANDREA offered. She stayed after everyone had gone to make sure I was okay. "I always knew Ari was a dick, but God."

"He was your brother. What could I have told you?"

"I know. I get it. But you've always felt more like a sister to me than he felt like a brother. And my mom. Jesus. I can't get over how she acts sometimes. But I'm impressed as hell at the way you stood up to her," she said.

"It had been a long time coming, but I could never do it when Ari was alive."

"God, I wish Rebecca would. The way my mother treats her is abhorrent. Like she's defective. I mean it's not like it was her fault."

"Wait, what wasn't her fault?" I asked, not understanding at all what I was missing.

"That she couldn't have kids." She could immediately tell by the shocked look on my face that this was new information. "Oh God, I thought you knew."

I'd already been blessed with one revelation of a decades old lie tonight, what was one more? "I thought Dave and

Rebecca just didn't want kids. Too busy with their careers. That's what Ari had always said."

Andrea looked at me with wide eyes. "What? No. They tried for *years*. Long before you came along. She had at least two miscarriages that we knew about, but I suspected there were more. I think after a while, after the way my mother would find a way to blame her, she probably didn't want to tell us anymore." She sighed. "That's why they don't come to family things all that much. Because of my mom. And...because of you."

"What? Me? Why me?"

"Well, you can imagine. In the middle of their infertility struggles, here you come along getting accidentally pregnant, like boom. It was too hard for them to be around you and Brody."

"Oh God." I frantically searched my brain for anything unintentionally hurtful I may have said over the years not knowing all they had gone through.

"Ari told me Brody was going to be the grandchild they always wanted because no one else was going to have kids. God, why am I so surprised he manipulated me like that? He probably thought I'd be less likely to want to keep the baby if I knew the truth." I took a deep breath. "I was going to leave him, Andrea."

"What?"

"The week before he died. I was making plans to leave him." I hadn't told anyone this. Not even Kendra.

"Oh my God. The night you came to my house. I just thought you guys had a fight. You didn't really say much."

"I know. I just needed a place to go to get some space. To think. If I would have gone to Kendra's all hell would have broken loose."

"What happened?" she asked.

I wanted to tell her. Tell someone other than my therapist. But it was hard, especially since I couldn't get past the fact that it was her brother.

"That night, when he came home, I could tell that something was wrong. He was on edge, much more than usual. I found out later that his new investors had backed out. They'd started talking to people and decided he was too much of a risk. He was furious, pacing back and forth like an animal in a cage. He was unpredictable when he was like that, I never knew if he was just going to start venting or if he was going to try to decompress in...another way."

Andrea looked at me, blinked slowly and nodded. She was letting me know I could tell her anything.

I continued. "Sometimes he'd come at me. Consume me physically without words or just order me to do things. It was usually easier just to let it happen and when it was over, things would be better. This next part is a little...delicate. And personal."

"You can tell me, Shelby. It's okay."

"After I had Brody, anything...anal...was very uncomfortable. Sometimes excruciatingly painful. My doctor said I had internal hemorrhoids, and it would most likely be something I'd always struggle with. Every time Ari and I tried, we had to abandon it because it wasn't working for me. He didn't push the issue, and I was grateful." I looked up at the ceiling. "Looking back now, he was probably getting that itch scratched somewhere else."

Andrea nodded.

"That night he was erratic. Out of control. I just let it all happen hoping it would be over soon enough. He practically tore off my clothes and ordered me to lie face down on the bed."

It was a position I'd become familiar with as the ultimate

power play. Sometimes he'd hold my hands behind my back or up over my head and I was helpless to do anything.

"He started to fuck me. In this position, things would…slip out, need to be readjusted. He held my hands up over my head, so when it slipped, he readjusted. And it was in the…wrong place."

He'd thrusted. Ripped. Seared. Burned. I screamed. "No, Ari! Wait, stop! It hurts!"

He didn't stop. I kept crying, begging and begging him to stop. But he didn't stop. The sick son of a bitch continued cruelly wielding his chef's blade, delivering a pain sharper than any I could have imagined.

Tears spilled onto the bed as he ignored my pleas and continued, completely feral and consumed in his own pleasure.

I could only lie there helpless, whimpering and praying for it to be over.

Finally, he finished. Panting, he whispered in my ear, "You have been keeping this little treasure box from me for almost twenty years, baby. But not anymore," his words thick and dark, pressing a wax seal firmly onto this nightmare.

My skin crawled so violently I shuddered. He'd somehow managed to morph into an even more evil version of the Ari I'd come to know.

He went to the bathroom to clean up. I just lay there. Paralyzed. I tried sitting on the edge of the bed, but it was too painful. Ari came back from the bathroom, climbed under the covers, content to just drift off to sleep. I got up and started slowly and carefully making my way to the bathroom.

"When I turned on the bathroom light, I saw it. The blood. A trail from the bed. All over the sink. It looked like a goddamn murder scene." Tears fell. "Andrea, he knew, and he didn't care."

"Shelby...oh God, Shelby."

I nodded.

"He raped you."

I never gave myself permission to say the word to describe what happened, but yes. He did.

The spell had been broken. I knew there was no coming back from this. I finally saw Ari for the monster he was, and I was ready to be done.

"I came to your house because if I'd gone to Kendra's she would have demanded I tell her what happened. And then she might have gone to Ari, and she might have done something... regrettable. I needed someone safe, but also someone who wouldn't ask questions. Just somewhere to take a second to think things through."

"I'm glad I could be there for you, even if it was just to give you a safe place to land for a minute. I hope you know I would have helped you get out," Andrea said as she looked at me, her eyes filled with warmth and compassion.

"I know," I said. "I was also going to ask your dad for help."

"You know, if you'd have asked me if he would have before tonight, I would have said maybe. Maybe he would have been willing to help a little, mostly for Brody's sake. But now? After the way he stood up to my mom I know he would have bent over backwards and would have done anything he could. I never knew how he really felt about Ari."

I sighed, feeling a lightness and a sense of relief, no longer bound and burdened by all the secrets I'd been keeping all these years.

CHAPTER
TWENTY-SIX
SHELBY

Early October 2013

A week after the Night of Family Revelations, Brody came home for dinner. His roommate and her boyfriend were having a "crossroads conversation" and he wanted to give them some space. I made Pizza Margherita, and we shared a bottle of wine.

"Can I stay tonight? I'm getting a little tired and I don't think I want to drive. Plus, I don't want to walk in on them if it's still awkward. Or if they've made up." He laughed as he laid his head on my shoulder. We were snuggled up on the couch in the living room, and I was debating putting on a movie to bask in a little eighties' nostalgia.

"You don't ever have to ask. This is your home, too. Hey, do you want to watch 'An Officer and a Gentleman'? It's been a long time, and your impression is getting a little rusty."

He hunched his shoulders and squinted his eyes, poised

and ready to channel Zack Mayo before dissolving into chuckles. "Aw, I don't think I'm up for a movie. Another time, okay?"

He scooted forward on the couch getting ready to get up.

"Hey, can I ask you something really quick?" I asked.

"Sure." He sat back and readjusted his long legs to be able to face me.

"How would you feel if I changed my last name?"

He looked down, not sure quite how to react. "Wow. Hmm. Like, would you go back to Baker?"

"No, I don't really connect with that name either." Changing my name was something I'd been mulling over quite a bit lately, even though it seemed so drastic to me. "I...I just think I need to start over. Forge my own path."

I'd been preparing myself for a potentially difficult conversation with Brody. He would never know everything, but maybe it was time he knew more.

"You want to make sure I'm okay with you having a different last name than me."

"Yes. I assume you would keep Ristow, especially since you and Grandpa Riz are so close. And you'll be taking over the company from him someday," I winked. "If he ever retires, that is."

"I'd be taking over the company from Andrea someday, but yes." He smiled. "I would keep Ristow."

"Brody, I...I just want to make sure you are okay with being on this path. That you haven't felt pressured to go into finance, into the family business. Pressured by your dad, or by Grandpa," I said.

"I mean, it's been a thing for a long time. They brought up to me even before I hit high school. But I was always cool with it. Wow. It's so weird that you bring that up. Grandpa asked me the same thing last week."

"He did?" I was sure the shock on my face was less than subtle.

"Yeah, he wanted me to really think about the trajectory I was on and to make sure it was what *I* wanted, not something I was doing for anyone else. He told me how he felt like he had made a lot of mistakes with Dad when he was my age."

Ari had always made it seem as though not only were we to provide a long-awaited grandchild in exchange for him to get to chase his dream, but also that we had to sell our son's soul to his grandfather and encourage Brody to fill the shoes that Ari hadn't. But David had realized his mistakes, likely well before last week, and was able to develop a rich and meaningful relationship with his grandson. Which *also* happened to be blossoming into a mentorship.

Brody pinched his eyebrows. I always appreciated all the nuanced expressions of the empathy and emotion that he was so easily able to access. So unlike his father, despite resembling him so much. "Mom? Can I ask you something?"

"Of course."

"Are you changing your name because of Dad?" Brody was incredibly intelligent, just like all the Ristows. Which meant that not only had he excelled in academics, checking off AP class after AP class in high school and having been easily accepted to Marquette without the need of a legacy boost from David, but also that he knew far more about his parents' marriage than I ever let myself believe.

Part of his education and part of my parenting had been to teach Brody how to manipulate the Ari equation like I was able to. But unlike me, he would push against the algebra and challenge his father. Mostly when it came to defending me.

"Yes. It's because of Dad."

"Mom, I know he wasn't good to you." Brody moved his body to face forward, looking down at his lap. This was hard for him. "Even when I was little, I knew. When you would tell me everything was okay, I knew that it wasn't. I would follow you when you would go and hide, and I'd hear you crying."

It broke my heart to picture my sweet curly haired boy trailing me to my bedroom as I fought the tears until I was safely inside. I hated that much of his childhood had been spent in such worry and concern. I had tried so hard to keep him sheltered from our storm, but with a force as strong as Ari was, that was impossible.

"He wasn't a great dad. But he was an awful husband," Brody admitted.

I nodded. There was no use denying it. And Ari didn't deserve my defense.

"He...he dismissed you," he said softly.

My eyes filled with tears. Not because of how truly dismissive my husband had been, but because of how insightful my son had become. He saw something that had taken me so long to realize. To admit.

"It's such a shame," he continued. "He didn't appreciate you, or really even know you. I don't think he knew your favorite color or your favorite movie. He didn't get to see the person that I've always seen when it's just the two of us. How smart, how funny you are. I mean, you hardly ever laughed when he was around. He missed out on so much."

"He missed out on you, too, Brody. It's not an excuse, but he wasn't capable of loving us the way we should have been loved. The way we deserve to be loved." The words made my heart lurch sideways. There was something tugging on it that didn't seem to be about Ari or Brody.

"Maybe someday you'll find someone who doesn't dismiss you, Mom. Someone who will want to get to know you, really know you. Appreciate you. Someone who *will* love you the way you deserve."

With that, the image of a ball of yarn rolled out from a dark corner of my mind.

"I'm going to go up to bed. Are you going to be okay?" Brody asked.

As I wiped a few lingering tears so grateful for this gentle and wise soul of a son, I said, "I'll be just fine. I love you so much, Brods."

He hugged me then, in the special way he would when he knew I needed it most. He wrapped an arm around my back and put a hand gently behind my head, holding me to his chest. It was a gesture so tender, so protective. I smiled. *Someday, someone else will love him the way he deserves too, and in turn, he will hold them like this. Even if they are over six feet tall.*

Halfway up the stairs, Brody turned back to me. "Mom, you do deserve a happy ending. I would hate for you to think that happily ever after is something you can never have."

Something I can never have.

Brody had just tugged on the end of the wayward ball of yarn.

"Something I Can Never Have." The song that Jake was tinkering around with on the piano at his house. A Nine Inch Nails song for his "darker moments." Had his darker moments been about me? Had he known I would break his heart?

Just then Minx jumped up on my lap, and it all began to unravel.

For a long time, I managed to convince myself that Jake was a merely a distraction and an escape from the responsibilities of my real life. A long overdue, much needed, and well-deserved vacation for my nervous system.

Or even a pair of training wheels to learn how to be with someone who wasn't Ari.

Physically with Jake, I could never get close enough, desperate to meld with his body in every conceivable way. But emotionally, I'd held him at arms' length; when I wasn't actively pushing him away, that is. And he knew it.

In fact, he'd told me a bedtime story about it.

Since the night he left my house, the night I'd let him go, I'd been very careful not to let myself think about him. I hadn't watched the Emmys. I immediately pressed "next" if I heard a few recognizable synth beats of a Depeche Mode song on an eighties' playlist I was listening to. I avoided the Encounter Channel at all costs. Those were easy.

Having to give up making Cherrie Bombshell content was harder. Even the simple act of getting myself ready in the morning snagged sometimes, when I swear I'd catch his reflection behind me in the mirror.

At work, in the spaces where our story started, something would often haunt me without warning, and I'd have to stop and nurse a powerful wave of an emotion I couldn't define.

And he managed to infiltrate my dreams nearly every night.

Those mornings, in the moments between asleep and awake, I would allow myself to think about him. Whatever the dream had been I would allow it to continue to play out in my imagination or I'd roll through a memory like a scene from a favorite movie. How could I possibly have fully denied myself indulgence in the some of the best moments I'd had in the last twenty years? Then, after full consciousness took over, I would dutifully start my avoidance practices all over again.

• • •

In San Francisco, after I had fainted, after Jake had put me to bed and we'd both fallen asleep, I woke up thirsty in the middle of the night. I carefully got out of bed trying not to wake him, and I began my cautious navigation through his house. Thankfully, thoughtfully, he'd left a light on over the stove in the kitchen. I was able to easily find my way through the maze toward it, and I started looking through the cabinets for a glass. Standing in the kitchen in my bare feet wearing one of Jake's T-shirts, I started to wonder. I wondered what it would be like to wake up in the middle of the night here all the time. I started to wander around the house.

I walked slowly through each room, trying it all on to see how it would fit.

What would it be like to curl up on this magical couch with a cup of tea and a book on a rainy afternoon with a golden retriever houseguest snuggled up next to me? To sit next to Jake at the piano while he'd play me a new song he was learning. To set the table with the charming, mismatched dinnerware and light the candles while Jake was in the kitchen making food for me—sharing his art in that powerfully intimate way. Having Jake watch me bake and stumbling upon another one of his quirky and endearing kinks for us to explore.

Dancing in the dining room on a Tuesday night.

I walked back into the bedroom and climbed into the bed. Jake lay fast asleep on his side, the curtains open, bathing him and his new tattoo in soft moonlight. Shadows and hues of grays and blues danced along his peaceful silhouette as I traced my fingers along his body millimeters away from his skin. *Just for now. Just for tonight.* I allowed myself to wonder what it would be like to spend forever next to this man.

After Ari died and I'd been released from the prison of my life with him, I hadn't taken one step of freedom before immediately erecting another set of walls. For protection, I told myself. *A fortress.* And although within it, I'd done a good amount of healing, I was still alone. Still captive in a prison of my own design.

The reality of the next morning at Jake's house had chased the dream away in an instant. I reinforced the fortress walls that had been compromised, and I left.

But I didn't just leave.

I ran.

"HELLO?"

I shivered when I heard Jake's voice even though I was already trembling. Had he already deleted my number? Or was he just being cautious?

"Jake, it's me. Shelby."

"Heeeyy," he said, gently. "How are you? Everything okay?"

Warm, friendly, curious, concerned. I don't know why I would have expected anything else.

I was terrified. I'd so quickly pulled up his number from my "favorites" contacts and clicked on it before I fully knew what I was doing. Before I could talk myself out of it.

I began to verbally vomit into the phone. "Jake, I lied to you. At your house. I don't know why I did it, I guess I was scared...I...I got scared." Tears welled and began to fall. "Brody hadn't been in a car accident. I just...being in your house and you being so good to me. It was overwhelming. I had to leave."

Brody had, in fact, texted me that night, but it had nothing to do with a car accident. He was headed to a water park for the weekend and needed to know where his swim trunks were.

But that morning, in my panic, I'd fabricated what I'd

thought was a good and valid reason for sprinting back home. One that no one would question.

And I'd spent my entire travel day in tears.

"What? Oh." Jake seemed at a loss for words.

"I realized... I realized that I had feelings for you. Feelings I wasn't ready for. Or at least I didn't think I was. But I shouldn't have let you go."

"Shelby—"

"I hope it's not too late. Is it too late?"

"Shel—"

"I... I love you, Jake. I'm in love with you," I said, between breaths, my lungs struggling to keep up with my racing heart.

Silence. I was aware Jake had been trying to interject, but my words had been trapped and buried so long and they'd all been so desperate, tripping over themselves to get out.

"Shelby, I...I can't do this."

"What?" My stomach seized.

"I can't do this right now, I'm sorry. I'm so sorry," Jake said, sighing.

I opened my mouth in protest, but no words would come.

More silence.

He'd ended the call.

And with that, my heart blew apart.

A million pieces of shrapnel shattering and scattering in every direction. My chest, hollow and heaving, excruciating pain radiating from the blown out, gaping chasm to every inch of my bones, muscles and skin. My shoulders, burdened with the sudden, massive weight of a thousand regrets, twitched and ached and burned. The tears blinding and stinging as I convulsed and collapsed into wracking sobs on the floor.

Grief.

I didn't grieve the loss of my husband when he died, but

here I was grieving the loss of this love I could have had. A love that I couldn't or wouldn't see from behind my walls.

A love that could have stitched and mended all my last remaining torn and broken parts. Filled all the cold and empty spaces with warmth and tenderness. A love able to wind its light through me and illuminate every dark corner.

Jake's love. The love that I deserved.

I dragged my body up to my bedroom and before my heavy head hit the pillow, I texted Darius that I wouldn't be able to come to work the next day. And that he had been right about Jake.

I hadn't been careful with his heart at all, and I had annihilated any chance I'd had with him.

CHAPTER
TWENTY-SEVEN
SHELBY

The next forty-eight hours dragged with me trying to fill time with distraction and sleep. Kendra offered several times to come over, but I decided I needed to swim solo in my feelings and get through the worst of it on my own.

For years, when I was feeling sorry for myself and for my situation with Ari, it helped to play music that spoke to my angst, my sadness, my anger, or my melancholy. I'd light candles and journal or even take a stab at writing horrible poetry.

That night I finished watching *Mr. Holland's Opus,* ugly crying both happy tears for Richard Dreyfuss and sad and pitiful ones for me, and I headed toward the sunporch. I turned on the small lamp, lit a few candles, put on an Otis Redding record, and reached for my journal. Avoidance was no longer an option. Instead, I elected to fully immerse myself in memories and emotions. Some would consider that torture or self-sabotage, but since I'd only sought therapy after Ari died, I attributed my survival in an abusive marriage over the last twenty years to practices like these. A tether and a touchstone to keep me sane and connected to my own identity through all the gaslighting and manipulation. My little lighthouse in the storm.

This time it would be the way for me to navigate this heartbreak.

The only way to the other side is through.

I'd gotten through half a page of stream of consciousness journaling when my phone lit up. My breath caught in my throat.

It was Jake.

I slid my finger quickly across my phone to answer, trying to keep my mind from racing too far ahead. "Hello?" I still had his number saved, but I was being cautious.

"Hey. It's Jake."

It seemed so surreal to be here. Where we had to announce to one another who we were. I didn't know how to respond to him, and I was trying not to guess what he wanted or get my hopes up. I stayed silent.

"I'm on the road. I hope you don't mind that I called you, but I need a little help staying focused."

I tried to keep my voice steady. "Of course. Any time." I sighed and leaned further into the phone. *Any time. In any way. Forever.*

Jake was quiet for several seconds, and I had to resist the urge to fill the silence with nonsense.

Finally, he spoke. "Shelby, I'm so sorry about the other day. I... I just needed a minute. I wasn't in a good place to hear what you were telling me, and I needed a little time to figure some things out."

"Okay." I needed him to say more.

"You told me you lied to me. I wasn't mad that you lied.

Everything that you've said or done is understandable after all you've been through."

"Not really. I—"

"Shelby, please let me finish. You were brave enough to be honest with me and I...I haven't been honest with you."

My stomach dropped. I was trying and failing to keep my brain from imagining all kinds of things that Jake was about to tell me. Secrets that he was about to confess. But apart from having a wife and family stashed somewhere, I couldn't think of anything I wouldn't forgive.

"I was attracted to you, and I wanted to be with you because...well, because you were a mess."

"What?" Okay, maybe this was going to be trickier to forgive than I thought.

"I was attracted to you before we met, yes. And when we finally met, there were definite sparks. But when Kendra told me your husband had died, I couldn't resist you. Not because you were single. But because you were a widow."

For the life of me I could not wrap my head around what he was saying.

"Have you ever heard of a savior complex? Sometimes it's referred to as a hero or white knight complex."

"I've heard the terms, but I guess I never knew it was a real thing."

"It's most definitely a thing. And a more destructive thing than people realize. I've struggled with it ever since my brother died. Actually, even before he died. I thought his death and helping my mother through her grief was the catalyst, but I'd been assuming a caregiver role since my father left us. Since I was five years old.

"I'd always looked for broken people to fix. And if they wouldn't let me, or if I couldn't do it, I would move on. What's worse is when I *would* be able to help them, but once they didn't need me anymore, I would lose interest. I've never had a healthy romantic relationship. Ever."

"Oh." Still speechless.

"I had been struggling for years with finding the big 'why.' I finally realized it was me avoiding processing my own grief with my brother's death. If I was so busy and consumed with other people and their problems, I wouldn't have to deal with my own shit."

Oh, Jake. How was it that I was finding what he'd thought a fatal flaw so completely endearing? "That makes a lot of sense. And if you were already primed for it, like you said, in a care-giver role. It was a natural progression." I melted at the thought of Jake struggling with all this churning inside while maintaining his solid and strong outer shell. The shell he put on for me.

"And you want to know the worst part? The part I never told anyone, other than my therapist, was that my father—my horrible, selfish, asshole of a father—could not be bothered to come to his own son's funeral. When Trevor died, he—" Jake's voice broke as he tried to rein in his emotion, "The bastard sent a card."

"Oh, Jake. I'm so sorry."

"I just dove into rescuing everyone else so I wouldn't have to think about any of it. The relationship I'd been in when you and I met was the last straw—I treated her so unfairly. I got back into therapy after that, and I was doing well. That is, until I got Kendra's email about Ari's accident. I don't know if she ever told you I'd emailed you. I reached out to tell you when the show would air, and... and to let you know I was into you. Knowing you were married."

"She told me. The next day after our night together in Vegas, she told me everything," I said.

"At first the fact that I'd reached out to you before I'd known he was gone felt like progress, because for the most part, you were so confident and together. It wasn't like me to be so attracted to someone like that. But in hindsight, I could see the cracks. Over the years I've gotten very good at seeing someone's pain, even if they hide it well. The day we met I could see the little dips in your vibrancy, the hesitation, your calming practice of holding your thumb when you get nervous. Looking back at something as innocuous as you not wanting to use your own phone to take a picture of us together, I knew there was something casting a shadow over your life. Subconsciously I think I knew it had been an abusive relationship and I'd hit on a married woman to try and rescue her."

I swallowed hard. I didn't know whether to be offended that he was attracted to my messiness and pain or to marvel at the universe for creating someone who'd been able to see me so clearly.

And the irony of having gone from being at the merciless hands of an abusive narcissist into the arms of a man with a savior complex was not lost on me either.

"I was already so drawn to you in so many ways. When I heard that you were a widow, and I had no reason to believe you weren't a lost and broken grieving widow, I couldn't resist you. You were my fucking holy grail.

"The worst part was that I couldn't or wouldn't see to the end. To when ultimately, after I'd help you turn your light back on, I'd once again just ride off into the sunset. And I wouldn't have considered how badly I'd hurt you. I always convinced myself that I did more good than harm when more often than not, it was the other way around.

"But then something happened, Shelby. I couldn't save you. You wouldn't let me. You kept everything inside, and while it drove me crazy, wanting to know everything that was bubbling under your surface, you were quietly and effectively saving yourself. For the first time, I not only appreciated that, but I admired that. I was *attracted* to that. You clicked something back into place for me.

"I just have to believe that we were sent into each other's lives for a reason. You showed me that I'm able to see someone's pain as something separate from me and isn't my responsibility to fix. That I could admire strength and confidence and even be attracted to those qualities. And that I might be capable of having a healthy relationship someday. But I am still a major work in progress. I'm not good for anyone right now."

Jake's soft voice making his heart's confession was almost more than I could bear. The distance between the two of us was gut wrenching as it was, and he was trying to push me even further away. I desperately searched for the tiniest bit of ammunition to fight with. "Jake, you said maybe we were sent into each other's lives for a reason. Why do you think you were sent into my life?"

"I don't know. Maybe an escape? You always said we were just having fun. Or maybe a way to get the taste of Ari out of your mouth?"

"Is that all you think you were for me? Yes, I'll admit it's what I wanted to believe at first, too. Because it was too overwhelming to think about falling in love. Falling in love with Ari was like falling into a black hole. It turned me inside out and upside down, and I couldn't see myself going through it all again. Or having the first clue of how to do it right.

"But somehow, without knowing why, you gave me exactly what I needed. At every, single turn. From the very first day we met, and you asked me questions and cared about my answers. You laughed at things I said, but with me, not at me. You said,

'You should be so proud of yourself,' when no one had ever said that to me before.

"And then, you were gentle and tender, but you didn't treat me like I was breakable either. You offered this warm bubble to explore and push myself to see what I was capable of. You encouraged me to take back the control I'd lost, again without knowing why. How? How did you always know what I needed even before I did? I don't know if it was your savior complex that informed and guided you or not, but you know what? I don't care."

As I was talking, I realized I had managed to tiptoe outside of my fortress a few times within the last several months, finding a new safe place to visit. "Despite what you think, Jake, you were not just an escape. You were my refuge."

Silence.

I had no idea if what I'd said was enough.

"That's a lot to think about." Jake said, followed by a tortuous pause. "Hey, I'm coming up to where I need to be. I'm a little nervous though, because I didn't have Brenda arrange for my stay tonight."

"Well, you could always play the 'I'm Jake Ford' card at some hotel," I said as I recognized more irony. I'd always been so closed mouthed, now it was Jake's turn. And I didn't have the energy to push.

"It's cute that you think that I'm that famous. But honestly, I hope that might help me out here."

The thought of him hanging up and riding off into the sunset thrust me back into my feelings. The gaping chasm was aching again, and I could feel the tears. My nose started to run, and I sniffled.

"Before I go, I have one more confession." Jake said. "I've been working hard this year on my relationship with pain. Not the kink, not physical pain, but other people's emotional pain.

I am attracted to it. It used to scare me how much, sometimes it still does. It made me feel like I was sick and twisted because I tend to conflate it with being romantically attracted or even turned on. But Dr. McCallum helped me realize that it's compassion that drives that attraction. That it's someone's ability to easily access their emotions that attracts me, not the pain itself. It's their openness and vulnerability. Like appreciating a flower in bloom. Bearing witness to an opportunity for deep connection with another human."

I lay down on the couch, not caring about soaking it with my tears. Damn him for continuing to break my heart, torturing me with poetic therapy speak. I heard his car door shut through the phone. Our time was almost up, and the hollowness started to swallow me again.

"But you, Shelby, God. No one on the face of the earth is more beautiful than you when you cry. It makes my heart leap and weep, and it convinces me of the existence of a higher power. You, the most perfect flower in bloom that has ever existed.

"But that was when your tears were not for me. Now that I'm the one making you cry it makes me want to rip my heart out, it hurts so fucking much. Ahh...I hate this. I don't want to let you go, but I have to." His voice was soft, barely above a whisper. "I have to let you go."

"Don't, Jake. Please don't let me go." I couldn't control myself, softy sobbing into the phone. I wanted to hear him tell me more and more about everything he loved about me. Forever. I sighed deeply, desperately. "I wish Mt. Eptou and the Wishing Lake were real."

"What?" Jake breathed a soft chuckle and sighed. "And if they were, what would you wish for, Shelby?"

"I would wish that you were here."

. . .

TO THIS DAY THERE ARE THREE SOUNDS THAT I LOVE.

Number three is a baby's squeals turning into joyous, infectious rolling belly laughs.

Number two, the sound of rain on a roof mixed with low rumbles of thunder in the distance.

But number one, my absolute favorite above all others, is the sound a finger makes tapping on a window.

TAP. TAP. TAP.

My heart began pounding through my chest, it seemed to know what was happening well before my brain could fully process it and command my head to tilt upward and my eyes to lift to the window.

Jake.

With his forehead pressed to the window, his eyes full of longing and promise, his hand held up against the glass in a gesture of deep connection, there he was.

After achingly long seconds of feeling frozen in time, my limbs finally got their orders to get up and go to the door.

As opened it and started at him, I was finding it hard to form words and my shock was not letting me touch him. I feared if I reached out, he would evaporate into mist, and I'd realize it was just a dream. "What? What...what are you doing here?"

"I would have been here sooner, but I had to stop for snow tires in Colorado. Damn October blizzard."

I looked out the window toward the street and saw a beige Range Rover. It hit me like a cinder block. *That is not a rental car. It's Jake's car. He drove here from home.*

"But I thought you said... that you weren't good for anyone right now. I didn't think..."

"And I meant it. All of it. I just came to give you this back."

He opened his hand producing my black thong that I had left in his backpack in Vegas all those months ago. I looked up and he was smirking.

I somehow managed to arch an eyebrow at him. "Did you at least wash them?"

"Fuck no. That would have been a travesty."

I laughed, so grateful for a moment of levity.

He gently wiped the remnants of tears from under my eye with his thumb and I could hardly keep from collapsing to the floor. "So beautiful," he said as his smile faded. "Shelby, I am so sorry I had to get off the phone like that the other night. It wasn't my intention to hurt you, but my brain got so busy right away. Frantically making these plans as a favor to my heart."

"And mine," I said, my eyes swimming. "I hope you think my happy tears are beautiful too."

His deep brown eyes glistened with his own happiness. "Absolutely breathtaking." He held my face in his hands and once again spoke his silent sonnets before saying, "I know we will have a lot to work through. Individually and together. But I also know it will all be worth it. I love you, Shelby Ristow. With everything I am. I am yours forever."

I smiled as all my hollowness was filled to overflowing.

My Balthazar.

"I love you, too." I looked deeply into his eyes, spilling poetry of my own, trying to convey the multitude of emotions I'd never find the words to describe.

He kissed me then. A cataclysmic supernova of a kiss that contained all the attraction, all the spark, all the lust, and now bursting with all the raw and epic emotion of our love story's climax. A kiss like I'd only ever seen in movies or imagined in books. The kiss I'd never, ever had—the one that seals the happily ever after.

Jake broke away from my mouth to fall into me and hold

me as tightly as he could. I whispered into his neck, "It's McGrath."

Jake pulled away from me, his puzzled, bemused face tilting. "What?"

"My last name. I'm changing it to McGrath. It means child of grace."

EPILOGUE

JAKE

Some Time Later

THE NIGHT SHELBY CALLED ME, THE NIGHT SHE CONFESSED HER LOVE, as soon as she started speaking, I knew I had to get to her. I got off the phone so quickly, feeling terrible for leaving it the way I had, but there was much to do.

I immediately called Rita and told her I'd be leaving in the morning, and they'd have to reschedule shoots. It was a pain in the ass for her, but she knew how important this was for me.

I packed my bags and took a sleeping pill. I needed to make sure I could quiet my brain a little and get some rest. I had a long drive to prepare for.

I also wanted to wait to leave until after my doctor's office opened the next morning so I could talk to him about a urology referral.

I needed to schedule a vasectomy ASAP.

· · ·

OCTOBER 31, 2014

I SIGHED AS I PULLED INTO MY DRIVEWAY.

One more night alone before I got to see Shelby after two and a half weeks apart.

She was flying in the next day and then we'd be driving to Palm Springs to celebrate my birthday. I was excited to show her the mid-century modern design capitol of the US, and I was surprising her with a stay at an atomic ranch rental. I couldn't wait to see her reaction when she saw how authentically they'd decorated the place, complete with tiki bar and a backyard pool bedecked with Astroturf and pink flamingos.

Shelby left her job at Aspire in the beginning of the year, wanting to split her time more between her house and mine, and she didn't feel like it was fair to her clients to be gone so much. It broke her heart a little, but she redirected and set herself up as an independent educator for ethics and safety in the spa industry. She started traveling the country, going to various salons and spas to teach professionals better ways to set boundaries and protect themselves. Between that and the modeling gigs she still took here and there she was often traveling more than I was. Sometimes that meant coordinating hotel meetups in random cities and our adventurous rendezvous would continue. Still "having fun."

Over the last year, just as I predicted, we'd had some rough spots, but it all has been more than worth it. Shelby sometimes had a hard time opening up to me, or she'd be afraid of repercussions if she'd say what's on her mind. I still found myself being overly precious with her once in a while, but we were getting there.

She still struggled with getting triggered in bed too, and it sometimes seemed to come out of nowhere. Luckily in San Francisco there are all manner of progressive professionals to choose from, and we were fortunate enough to find Jolie, our brilliant somatic sex therapist. She's worked with Shelby one on one to help her find little pockets of trauma locked deep inside her body by combining purposeful movement with meditation. And we work together on ways to navigate anxiety and build on our foundation of trust. Shelby insists that whenever we want to nudge against the edges of our boundaries, we do it at my house. She said it's the place she feels the safest. And she told me it was where she first realized she loved me.

Shelby has excelled at her occasional role as a Domme as I predicted, too. Again, mostly at my house, but occasionally, spontaneously other places too. It is important for her to have my consent—something she was never offered with Ari. She'll ask, "Do you want to play?" before anything begins. My answer is always yes. Scratch that. My answer is always *fuck yes*.

She has gotten creative with our games because she can't abide by most of the things that had been done to her. She can't bring herself to humiliate or degrade me or call me names. She doesn't hit. She doesn't put her hands on my throat. It was gut wrenching to have to assume what she'd been through by learning what she wasn't comfortable with, until finally she was able to tell me, too. And I was grateful to have been able to just listen, offer an ear and a shoulder and not feel the need to take it all on as my own.

When she commands me, she's strict, but it's undercut with a kindness. Like a teacher you respect—but a gorgeous one with a filthy mouth.

She can be physically forceful but follows with tenderness.

An aggressive pull of my hair followed by gentle petting. Kisses planted on fresh bite marks. The sensory and emotional switchbacks melting both my brain and my heart.

Sex with her is always amazing, no matter what—she is like a master guitarist finely tuning and making the sweetest music with the instrument of my body. But when we play, she plugs me into an amp to tease out the distortion alongside the melodies.

ONE MORE DAY.

For my birthday, she'd been sending me sexy pictures all day long, making sure to have one on deck every time, I'd text her from a stop. It was the sweetest torture.

My phone dinged again.

Hey, have I told you Happy Birthday?

Only about 25 times today. <3. Just got home.

Another ding as another picture came through.

It was a closeup of her hand on her most sacred place, her middle finger disappearing inside.

JESUS FUCKING CHRIST. Are you trying to kill me?

If you stop stalling in the driveway, you could come in and find out.

My heart began to thrum in my chest.

I walked into the house and saw the lights on. She was a day early and already inside. I looked at my phone at the three dots as Shelby was typing another text.

I made my way through the house and stopped dead when I reached the doorway to the dining room. The scene I saw made my mouth drop open.

"Good evening, Mr. Ford. Right on time for your appointment," Shelby said with a grin.

She was wearing her Aspire T-shirt and a scandalously short skirt. She'd set up her portable massage table, and next to it was a utility cart with cloth strips, cotton pads, large tongue depressors, and a pair of tweezers.

And a pot of hot wax.

"I have you down for a Brazilian wax this evening, is that correct?"

Imagine being seven years old riding in the backseat of your parents' car thinking they are driving you to school just like any other day. But then they roll past the school and announce that you are going to the airport instead because they are surprising you with a trip to Disney World. You are beyond excited, but you've never been on a plane before so you also feel a little like you might throw up.

"Uh, yes?"

"I'll need a firmer confirmation than that, Mr. Ford."

The 'Mr. Ford' business was doing things to me I hadn't expected. "Yes, that is correct."

"Excellent. I'll need you to take off all your clothes and get on the table."

"All my clothes?" I asked with an eyebrow arched.

"Yes. We wouldn't want to get any wax on anything. This can get a little...sticky."

I started to unbutton my shirt with my trembling fingers, not taking my eyes off Shelby. She moved over to the cart and while staring at me with her molten eyes, she pressed a button on her phone.

"How You Like Me Now" by The Heavy started to play over the speaker. She grabbed a stick and began to stir the wax, drawing some of it up and letting it drip down back into the pot.

I froze. Not only Disney World, apparently. I was also heading to the North Pole. Maybe a stop in Narnia too.

Somehow, I managed to get my clothes off and stand in front of Shelby.

"Oh, good. You're aroused," she said casually. "It does make my job easier, and it will be more comfortable for you as well. I am going to do my best to make sure you remain aroused through the whole service. Is that alright, Mr. Ford?"

I swallowed what little saliva was left in my mouth and nodded. "Yes."

Before I got up onto the table, I blinked several times to make sure I was seeing correctly. Attached to all four legs of Shelby's table were Velcro restraints.

I lay down and she grabbed the padded cuff closest to my right wrist. She trained her eyes on mine and paused, our wordless request for consent. I nodded.

When she'd finished securing my wrists and ankles, she moved up to my head and stroked my hair. She crouched closer to me as she lifted my head to fit a silky blindfold over my eyes. Her hot breath in my ear, she cooed, "Remember your safe word, baby."

What happened next was a flurry and frenzy that I would be hard-pressed to be able describe in detail. I know that after The Heavy's song that thrust me back to remembering her audition video—the first time I'd ever laid eyes on Shelby

McGrath—the album "Playing the Angel" by Depeche Mode came on.

She touched my upper thigh to let me know she would be coming at me with the hot wax, mercifully easing me in. She laid an application across my skin on the outer edge of my pubic hair, and then pressed down the strip. She paused. Teased. Letting me stew in delicious anticipation.

The sharp sting of the rip pulling out deeply rooted hair stood me on edge enough, but then she grabbed the head of my cock and swirled her tongue up and down the underside of my shaft. I shuddered and arched up from the table. This was going to be beyond anything I'd ever experienced before.

"You have a remarkable cock, Mr. Ford." She traced a finger up and down my stomach before gripping me firmly again. "Mmm. So luscious. And you are so fucking hard. It's like waxing around a steel pole."

I convulsed against my restraints.

She continued this ballet of pain and pleasure across my entire body. Dancing between the hot wax on my scrotum and teeth on my nipple. Skillfully ripping off a strip full of hair, then tracing the same spot with her tongue. Plucking at a hair with tweezers, then, from out of nowhere would come an ice cube. She'd glide it across my lips, down my neck, all the way down to my balls, soothing tender areas she'd waxed.

I couldn't even venture a guess as to how long this went on. It had to have been at least forty-five minutes based on my vague awareness of the album that was playing.

I was in a state of constant tension, and I could feel my muscles starting to rebel. My nerves were a jangled mess, and I was beginning to unravel. Not being able to predict where she was going, what she was doing, winding me up tighter and tighter with all these brand-new sensations, I didn't know how much longer it would be before I snapped.

I heard the floor creak as she walked up toward the head of the table.

"Open your mouth," Shelby commanded.

I did as I was told.

She slid two of her fingers in, coated in her own sweet honey straight from the pot. I moaned as I sucked voraciously. Her voice velvet and deep, she said, "My God, Mr. Ford. You are making me so fucking wet. Do you like the way I taste?"

I nodded as I growled and groaned at the image of her playing with herself, dipping her fingers in and out while simultaneously playing me like Santana on acid.

I was slammed with my full body and soul's desperate need for connection with her, and this was all she was giving me. I practically sobbed as she pulled her fingers out of my mouth, and along with them, my safe word.

"Halo!" I could feel the hot tears streaming down my temples. "Halo!"

Shelby responded in seconds, abandoning everything she was doing to attend to me. She put her hand over my eyes as she removed my blindfold to help me gradually adjust to the light. She removed my restraints and kissed my wrists and ankles. She came up to my head and gently brushed the sweat soaked hair off my forehead, planting kisses on my salty skin.

"Tell me what you need," she said.

"It's just too much. I...I can't." I panted. "I need..."

"Do you need to come now, baby?"

I nodded feverishly. "Yes. Please, Shelby. Please."

Still peppering my forehead and cheeks with her kisses she said, "Oh, my sweet angel. You never, ever have to beg."

I started to attempt to get up, desperately needing to be with her. Inside of her.

She gently placed her hand on my chest, pressing me back onto the table. "No, no. You stay right there. There will be plenty of time for that later. Right now, I don't think you have the strength."

She was right. I assessed my physical state, and although I was still deeply aware of my nerves firing and my muscles twitching, it seemed as though my body had vibrated my bones into dust.

"Let me take care of you. But you will watch. This is how we stay connected."

We were so in sync, especially in moments like these, she always, always knew what I needed.

She put a pillow under my head to allow me a better view.

She reached toward the table and grabbed a bottle of lube. My eyes widened and my core clenched in anticipation.

Don't get me wrong, blow jobs are great, but Shelby's "handy" work was incomparable.

She lubed up my entire shaft and smoothed a little over my balls to remove the last of the wax residue. I had no idea if she'd managed to finish my Brazilian or not, but I didn't care.

She moved her talented hands up and down, around and over, with varying degrees of speed and pressure. All the pent-up energy of the last hour percolated and concentrated in the center of my body.

My breaths came in ragged pants. I gripped the edges of the table, my restless legs twitching uncontrollably.

All the while, Shelby made sure to look at me just as much, if not more than at what she was doing. She wore such a perfect expression of hot benevolence, my heart exploded with love for her.

She cupped one hand around my balls and began to undulate her fingers. My instinct was to close my eyes to keep them from popping out of my head as I began to brace myself for the most intense orgasm I'd ever had.

But I kept them open, and I watched as she squeezed a little more lube onto her finger.

Continuing to stroke me with her other hand, she pressed the finger briefly onto my perineum and pulsed.

She smiled, watching me as she slowly breeched my back door. The tight ring of muscle relaxed and welcomed her easily, as she had visited several times before. As soon as she applied the slightest pressure to my ripe prostate, I split apart.

Every cell in my body exploded out from my center with a shock wave I was certain shook the house off its foundation.

I arched my back so violently that to a casual observer it might have appeared as though I'd been electrocuted.

I heard a sound, and while I was aware it had come from within me, it in no way sounded human. And it was loud and concerning enough that Lunchbox offered a few good boy guard dog barks from upstairs.

I felt Shelby's tongue glide along my stomach and chest. My skin like lit up like a live wire, my entire being rocked with a violent spasm. I was still so on edge, but even in my fog, even with my eyes closed, I could clearly picture her licking every drop of spilled cum off my body. And it was an image hotter than sin.

I'd heard about this kind of experience with intense sensation play—where you transcend to another plane of existence entirely. I lost track of where I was, what day it was, even who I was. But there was still Shelby. She began rocking my body gently while compressing firmly on my legs, my hips and my arms, sensing the state of my nerves far too fragile for any light touch. She was my tether.

I could feel myself making my way back from my out of body experience and having a more than a little trouble with re-entry. I could not open my eyes. My heartbeat was still erratic. I erupted into chills.

Shelby, the reigning queen of aftercare, covered me with a blanket and brought a Gatorade with a bendy straw to my mouth.

After a few long, desperate pulls of the electrolytes my body was craving, I still couldn't open my eyes. "God says 'hi,'" I croaked, managing a weak smile.

Shelby laughed as she continued stroking my hair. Finally, I was able to open my eyes to look at the face of the love of my life. Her eyes widened and her face contorted into an "oh shit" expression. I tensed.

"What?" I asked.

"Oh my God. I think I broke you," she said, chuckling.

"What do you mean?"

"Your eyes. You look like I did after I had Brody. I pushed so hard I broke a bunch of blood vessels."

I smiled. That sounded about right.

AN HOUR LATER WE WERE SITTING ACROSS FROM EACH OTHER ON THE living room floor, and on the coffee table between us was the most beautiful cake I'd ever seen. Shelby had likely spent the afternoon in my kitchen making the small, flawless, chocolate mirror glaze work of art that once again, pained me to think about cutting into. Two candles, number shapes of a "5" and a "0" were flickering on top.

"Happy birthday, Jake. Make a wish," Shelby said sweetly.

I smiled as I considered her request. I was already, without a doubt, a blessed man. I had my health, a beautiful home (actually, two beautiful places to call home), a great job I loved, family, friends, and the love of the most incredible woman on the planet.

That didn't stop me from being greedy though, and I

thought of the thing I wanted more than anything in this world.

I closed my eyes and blew out the candles.

MAY 2015

I KNEW I WAS SUPPOSED TO BE WATCHING THE STAGE, BUT I COULDN'T tear my eyes off *her*. Every time I think Shelby couldn't possibly become more beautiful, that I couldn't possibly fall more deeply in love than I already am, she proves me wrong.

That day, I was utterly spellbound by her tears of pride.

After Brody's college graduation ceremony at a large downtown auditorium, we all filtered out to the crowded courtyard to meet up with him. Shelby never let go of my hand. It was as if she wanted to reassure me that I was not an outsider—that I belonged right by her side at such a momentous occasion.

BRODY DECIDED TO STAY AT MARQUETTE ONE MORE YEAR AND POUND out his MBA. Along with being crazy smart, I'd come to admire the kid's ability to balance his drive and ambition with staying down to earth and having one of the wittiest, driest senses of humor I'd ever come across. He and I have had some deep and amazing conversations, and I see so much of his mother in him when we do. Brody is an old soul, but I'm sure much of the maturity he shows has to do with everything he'd gone through having a father like Ari and witnessing the turmoil in his parents' marriage. I can't begin to imagine all the ways he helped Shelby through those terrible years, whether he knew it or not.

Talk about a hero.

Of all his qualities, the way he fiercely protects and unabashedly adores his mother is what I admire most.

His approval was very important to me when Shelby and I got serious. Luckily, all it took was seeing how happy she was and how much I truly respected and cherished her. Once, out of the blue, he gave me a pop quiz—a little test to see how well I knew her, asking me what her favorite song was. When I was able to blurt it out without hesitation, almost before he'd finished asking the question, he was sold.

We all posed for a few pictures with Brody. His grandfather's girlfriend, Linda, was hesitant to be included, but everyone encouraged her since she'd made David so happy over the past several months. He had asked his wife for a divorce a year and a half ago, and while I don't know all the details about what happened there, the family has seemed much lighter as a result. Andrea, Dave and his wife Rebecca, along with David and Linda, have all been regular fixtures in our lives.

Everyone's expression shifted when a slight, older woman approached us. She was wearing sunglasses and a constipated look on her face. Shelby was the first to acknowledge her.

"Marion! So glad you could make it."

Marion breezed past everyone, offering subtle hello gestures, and making a beeline for Brody. She whispered something to him, kissed his cheek, and handed him a card. Once she turned back toward us, Shelby tried again.

"Marion, this is Ja—"

Before she could get my name out of her mouth, Marion was gone. I felt no sense of loss at not having met this woman.

· · ·

IN THE AFTERNOON WE STOPPED BY TO CELEBRATE THE GRAND OPENING of Lyric's new beauty boutique, *Míra Míra*. Darius and Randall were impressed by her vision enough to invest in this little space in the Walker's Point neighborhood of Milwaukee, just south of downtown. There were shelves and shelves of makeup and skin care products along with a few makeup stations. Lyric called the style of the boutique "whimsical goth glam," and it fit her perfectly. Black walls with gold accents, pastel rainbows alongside framed black and white prints of butterflies and skulls, and a unique "anatomy of a unicorn" illustration that Shelby had commissioned for her.

She was shedding more than a few tears of pride for Lyric, her daughter-friend that day, too.

Later I noticed Brody and Lyric having a moment off to the side, both smiling and blushing a considerable amount. I couldn't help but grin as I noticed how much Brody's body language reminded me of myself the day I met Shelby.

AT THE END OF THE EVENING, JUST THE THREE OF US, SHELBY, BRODY, and I were left sitting in the back room at the Japanese restaurant near our house after Brody's graduation celebration dinner. Along with Shelby's parents and her in-laws, Kendra, Gary, Darius and Randall were all able to join us, too. I have been so grateful for all these amazing people that came into my life as a package deal.

Shelby grinned and shook her head as I finished my third Sake. It makes me feel all warm and fuzzy, and she loves how "adorably handsy" I get and how much I fawn all over her.

And I that night I couldn't stop staring at her.

I'd been considering broaching the subject of marriage with Shelby for some time, but I needed to take her temperature about it somehow before I'd ever propose. I worried so much about it triggering her. Lately though, it was all I'd been able to think about since I came across these traditional Celtic wedding vows that nearly made me cry with how perfect they were for us.

You cannot possess me for I belong to myself

   But while we both wish it, I give you that which is mine to give

   You cannot command me, for I am a free person

   But I shall serve you in those ways you require and the honeycomb will taste sweeter coming from my hand

   I pledge to you that yours will be the name I cry aloud in the night

   And the eyes into which I smile in the morning

   I pledge to you the first bite from my meat

   And the first drink from my cup

   I pledge to you my living and my dying, equally in your care

   And tell no strangers our grievances

   This is my vow to you

   This is a marriage of equals

"I'm so full. How did I get so full on just rice and fish?" Shelby patted her stomach—her "food baby" as she liked to call it after a big meal.

"Oh, just one more for me." Brody reached his chopsticks toward a few of the sushi rolls that were left.

"Which one is that again?" Shelby asked.

"Mmm," Brody put his hand up in front of his full, chewing mouth. "Godzilla roll, I think? Crab, eel, spicy mayo..."

"You mean *may-o-naise*?" Shelby asked with a smirk.

"Ha!" I laughed. Out of the corner of my eye I saw Brody open his mouth to say something, but my tipsy ass was already babbling. "That's funny. *May-o-naise*. That makes me think of *Officer and A Gentleman*. Did you see that movie? The guy's name is Zack Mayo, and the drill sergeant makes fun of him by calling him *May-o-naise*. The scene in the rain? Where he is all..." I scrunched up my face to do my best Richard Gere impression, "'I got nowhere else to go!'" I laughed at myself and shrugged my shoulders. Damn Sake.

Brody and Shelby stared at each other with saucer wide eyes before breaking into huge smiles that turned into giggles. They have always had so many inside jokes and seem to know what the other is thinking all the time. At that moment, they were both laughing at me.

I didn't mind.

"I'm sorry. I interrupted you, Brody," I said to him. "What were you gonna say?"

Brody just looked at me, still chuckling, and shook his head. "Nah, man. I'm good." He nodded and smiled at me. "I'm really good."

I laughed along with him, put my hand on his shoulder and gave it a squeeze. *Man, I love this kid.* It was honor to be sharing Shelby's heart with him.

I heard a small gasp and I looked at Shelby. Her eyes were glassy, her fingertips were held softly to her lips, and the very tip of her nose had the subtlest tinge of pink. I knew these were happy tears, but I asked anyway. "Everything okay?"

She smiled and nodded, keeping her thought to herself.

We walked out to the parking lot and as I watched Shelby hug and kiss Brody goodbye, I felt my heart swell. I became a volcano of emotion about to erupt and I decided I was ready to take a risk.

After Brody got in his car, Shelby and I started walking slowly down the sidewalk. I tried to feign a breezy casualness as I asked, "Hey. Do you ever think about getting remarried someday?"

She stopped cold while my own momentum carried me four or five steps ahead. I turned back to find her caught under a streetlight, frozen, with an unreadable expression on her face. Her arms were hanging at her sides, however, no thumb grasped tightly in her fist.

I may have successfully broached the subject after all, even if it had momentarily shocked her.

She stared at me blinking rapidly until finally, her expression softened into one I was more familiar with. "You know, there are about a million reasons why I would never want to get married again." She took slow, deliberate steps to close the distance between us, never tearing her eyes from mine. "And only one reason why I would."

For some reason my brain went right to pragmatic things like tax breaks and medical decisions. "Oh yeah? And what would that one reason be?" I asked.

She ran a hand through my hair and smiled, lighting up my whole soul like a neon sign.

"You," she said.

My heart began to jackhammer in my chest. I was not prepared. No meticulously planned elaborate gesture. No epic speech encompassing all the love and gratitude I had for her. No ring.

But it didn't matter.

I held her hands as I got down on the ground. On both knees. She grinned and teasingly yanked on my hair. No part of our story had been conventional, and this proposal would be no exception. I firmly grabbed onto her hips to more securely anchor myself in the moment as I looked up at her luminous face. My technicolor angel.

I took a deep breath to try and keep my voice steady. "Shelby Anne McGrath, will you marry me?"

Shelby knelt down on the ground with me and held my face in her hands, smiling as happy tears filled the bottom of her eyes. "Fuck yes," she said.

Afterword

Note To Readers

Thank you, thank you, thank you for choosing to pick up this book! It was written with the hope of creating "high vibe" fiction that might well serve someone who has gone through or is going through hard things like the themes in this story. I sincerely hope you have found some joy, some solace, inspiration, and a few other things to help you continue on your path of healing.

ACKNOWLEDGMENTS

I haven't a clue as to where to start, as I was beyond blessed to have had so many wickedly smart and generous people involved in this process. I guess I'll begin at the beginning.

Thank you to Emily and KristaLyn for creating (and accepting me into) the program that birthed my first draft. Words cannot describe how grateful I am for the tools you've given me that will last a lifetime. (Oops, that sounds like a limiting belief—HYDRATE!) And to my fellow Storytellers, Meg, Sarah, Gregory, Jaqui, Biz, Courtney, and Emory—you will most certainly never be Forgotten. A special shout out to Christie for turning me onto these lovely souls!

Thank you to the brave and generous women who shared their stories of what it's like living with narcissists. Especially for granting me permission to use the "constant/equation" analogy.

Thank you to my beta readers. As scary as it was to put my book baby in the hands of others for the very first time, you all gave me such thoughtful and helpful feedback. Tanya, I'll never forget you laughing out loud in a SPA when you got to "the slap." Nate, you grammar and structure genius, thank you for your notes, especially when it came to reminding me about Shelby's strength. Meg...oh Meg. Your special brand of beta brought me SO much joy when I needed it the absolute most. Thank you also to the betas who ghosted me—I'm not being passive aggressive when I say this. This was an important thing for me to go through, as my thin, fragile baby author skin was reinforced by several cell layers as a result.

Thank you, thank you to my sensitivity readers. Ashley, your feedback regarding Lyric and her journey was beyond invaluable. And Raphael, thank you, on behalf of Jake, his mom, and Lyric, too.

Nevvie Gane. My editor. Genius. Professional. Kind. Thorough. My brain is out of adjectives apparently since writing this book, but I can't begin to thank you for being so awesome. Even with completely opposite schedules (getting emails time stamped at 1:45 a.m.) I'll recommend you all day, every day.

To my cover team—my illustrator Heather Noethe, you brought "sexy cartoon" Shelby forth in a way I could never have imagined. I adore her so much, and she will forever be part of the "swag" connected to this book. (She may even be tattooed on me at some point, I haven't decided yet.)

To my cover designer Mickey Chan. I had a vision and you made it a reality. Thanks for putting up with my pickiness and delivering perfection.

To my photographer, Hyler Media. Such an eye you have, Chris, thank you so much.

And Alex Mariani, my cover model. It was a fun day at the office that's for sure. Thank you for bringing Jake('s arm) to life.

To my biggest, most unfailing, sexy cheerleader, my husband, Christian. Never once seeing my writing as folly, my goals as unachievable, my dreams as unattainable. Thank you for the mayonnaise and the inspiration behind Brody's hugs that I am blessed to receive every day. I love you beyond words and beyond measure. And to my not so little boys, Vaughn and Declan, thank you for your patience and for picking up the slack. I love you so much.

Lastly, to my nineteen-year-old self who kept the ember of this story alive and safe when I tried giving up on it eleven years ago. Knowing it was a story worth telling. Thank you.

About the Author

Stella Montrose is by day a massage therapist, esthetician, Reiki practitioner and meditation teacher. She has always loved to write—fantastical stories as a child, and angsty poetry as a teen and young adult. Currently, she has a professional blog that she faithfully neglects, choosing instead to get lost in writing romance, playing with characters like literary Barbie dolls. She is a member of exactly zero professional writing guilds, clubs, associations or groups.

Stella lives in Wisconsin with her husband, an angel baby chocolate lab, and a chaos goblin golden retriever. She enjoys reading, hiking, traveling and general merriment of all sorts.

www.ingramcontent.com/pod-product-compliance
Lightning Source LLC
Chambersburg PA
CBHW011139310726

48972CB00009B/2770